Going up

Camborne Hill

The Serpent Ring

A Novel

by

Selwyn Berryman-Morgan

Best regards
Selwyn Morgan

To my family and their children. May it shed light on our history and illuminate our future.

The Serpent Ring

From Minuet to Jig.
Conceived in the union of separate parts,
from affiliated passion, or single-minded rage,
came the firstborn babe, mewing and a spewing,
to commence its entropic dance, from a minuet to jig.
It trying to be different, yet condemned to be the same,
whether winning battles pyrrhic or losing at life's game.
Building spoil heaps of its triumphs, or grave- pits
for its fame, each fractal of existence spawned
a fractal once again, - from a minuet to jig.
Each spiral lost in the spiral whole, each
dance serene, until the final blow,
turns a minuet to...

1

The Carnival on the Green

Going down Camborne Hill, Almond had Spring in his step, even if winter's solstice was but three days past. He'd set out from Maggie's before the day's dawn and had seen the first bleach of red and gold dim the spangle of the night sky.

Almond had left the house in Beacon before the family had risen on this festive day, and before Jack returned off nightshift wanting his bed. The urge to return to Maggie's arms increased with each step he took, but still, he had made it back, close to home. He stopped on the hill for a moment and looked out over the village of Camborne. It was unusually calm. The houses were frost coated and the chimneys seeped the first wisps of smoke from the peat fires within. The bustle of the day had yet to begin, as the villagers took advantage of the day's rest. But from the surrounding countryside came the sound of the relentless grind of rock, and the belch of smoke and flame... From the tin mines, there was no relief.

Almond decided not to continue down the hill. If he turned up at home, wanting peace and quiet and a warm breakfast, there would have instead been questions to answer. Elizabeth, Almond's younger sister, would have been relentless in her interrogation:

'You mean you stayed overnight at her house...? What did her mother say...? Is she pretty, your Maggie...? Will she be your girlfriend now...? Does she have a sister as old as me...? Can I come with you next time?'

Almond cringed at the thought.

To his left, a hay barn offered a temporary sanctuary. He could stay there, catch some sleep and let the day unfold. Later in the day, there would be much more for his sister to do than worry about where he had been, and what he had done.

***

On the village green, the winter's sun shone on the Christmas Fair, the morning frost all but lost; except where shade had kept its rays from penetrating. Almond had watched the building of the fair from beneath the shade of a tree on the edge of the village common. The hours of sleep he had snatched in the barn had set him right and he was prepared for the day, but, for now, he was content to watch and wait for the festivities to begin.

***

'Morris Men', in their hobnail-boots, performed along the streets their spark inducing jig, whilst, in gentle comparison, the Maypole was circled by young girls who faultlessly remembered the choreography of their Harvest Festival dance. Stalls covered in bunting offered games such as 'Roll the Pig' or 'Splat the Rat'. For those who were uncertain of the future, and still had one to contemplate, there was a fortune teller reading palms, and a stall displayed trays of fancy cakes and fruit preserve. Next to it was a stall sporting a 'ducking-apple' barrel that tempted those who didn't mind being wet-through for the sake of a single, soft, autumn stored fruit; the stallholder having made sure the barrel was filled to the brim so it would spill water at every try.

Almond had wandered through the fair, uncertain what to do next, when from out of a ducking-apple barrel appeared a face, minus an apple, Almond knew well.

'Enid!?' he exclaimed.

Her long bronze-red hair was soaked through and clung to her frock. They knew each other from the chapel, and Enid had developed a crush on him. She had tried to speak to him when their parents were engaged in polite conversation about the merits of the sermon, but Almond was always too shy to answer in a way that encouraged her. Anyway, he hadn't been to chapel for a long while.

'Almond!' she spluttered, suddenly embarrassed at the indignity of the proceedings and her suspicion the crowd gathered around the stall was extracting its own pleasure from the event. She gathered her breath and tried to regain some composure by pulling at her frock; a vain attempt at making it hang in a respectable fashion. Almond made as if he hadn't noticed her embarrassment and replied,

'Yes... I've not seen you for an age.'

Almond couldn't help but notice Enid had matured, her clinging frock was testament to that. Enid was all too aware of how she had changed and had hoped Almond would notice, too, should they meet. But Almond's head was full of the delightful Maggie, and he was determined not to dwell on the young lady's blossoming, or comment on how attractive Enid looked. Again, he was lost for the words to continue and it was Enid, who spoke,

'Are you going to try and get an apple?' she asked, in the hope he might stay a while longer... maybe as a companion for the rest of the day? Yet again, she was to be disappointed.

'No, sorry Enid, I have to get along. But it was nice seeing you after all this time. Enjoy the fair.' He turned away.

'Goodbye, Almond.' After Almond was lost in the crowd, Enid continued to wave for a little while longer.

***

Almond hadn't decided what next to do, but he knew to spend time with any young lady other than Maggie would have been disloyal. In any case, Maggie was bound to arrive soon. In the meantime, he would wait for the pub to open and seek the company of men.

It was not meant to be a day for the righteous, even though Christmas was almost upon them. The endless supply of beer and cider ensured that by the end of the day's proceedings the villagers would, in one way or another, regret their excesses. Regrets such as the home truths told 'in drink', or the seasonal goodwill giving way to angry words in response to a personal slight, or the misunderstanding of a rebuke made in jest. And for young lovers, there would always be the recrimination felt after an awkward embrace, a hesitant kiss, or when emboldened by a willing response, the not knowing when to stop... All that was yet to come.

***

The pub on the village green was full. Miners sat in tight groups on benches set around the walls, or at tables nearer the fire. It was a miner's pub, there weren't areas set aside for women or the well-to-do, and, as a result, their likes were nowhere to be seen. The predominant drink was cider, locally produced from orchards in the surrounding countryside. It was cloudy and sweet and had an alcohol content far higher than the beer on offer.

Henry shouted to his son, James, who stood waiting for his round to be poured.

'Get another drink in James.'

Henry had spotted his youngest son, Almond, coming through the pub door; the boy would want a jar.

Bloody Almond, thought James, in a silent grumble, *saunters in, not having seen him since God knows when, but as soon as there's a drink on offer...* his thoughts became vocal, but inaudibly, thanks to the din around him.

'Bloody Almond.'

Henry waved Almond over.

'Come sit down lad', and turning to Evan on the bench beside him he said,

'Shift up Evan, make room for the boy.'

Almond sat close to his dad and Henry wrapped a welcoming arm around his shoulders.

'Where've you been son?'

Almond chose to tell some of the truth so as not to be caught out in an obvious lie.

'I spent last night round at Maggie's place,' and quickly added an explanation to make it clear to the others at the table,

'I was invited by her mum for tea... after I'd been round to the workshop to collect her oven door fixed by James.'

His father attempted to quickly gloss over Almond's story.

'That's good. It's just I was expecting you home last night, son.' Henry wasn't meaning to accuse but wanted to show he'd been concerned. Almond, in his anxiety, dug deeper into the hole he had created.

'As it was late, she let me stay rather than have me walk back.'

'It was nice of Maggie's Mum to let you do that.'

Evan's face melted into a knowing smile and spoke what the others were thinking.

'Going round for tea is one thing, boy, but staying the night sort of makes you... how would you say... a special guest?'

The men at the table let out a ribald laugh, the laugh reserved for misdemeanours of a sexual nature.

Evan was known in his youth for being 'a bit of a lad' and had a sage's insight into such matters. Henry was concerned for his son but didn't intervene. Almond, at sixteen, had grown into a man, and there would be many a wrong turn along the way, but Almond needed to negotiate each turn of fortune himself and emerge stronger and wiser for doing so. In any case, Henry knew Almond wouldn't have wanted his father to defend him.

As it was, Almond felt obliged to reply.

5

'Saved me a walk back to Camborne in the dark, and as Jack was on 'nights', doing maintenance, a bed was free... He said I could use it.' He quickly added,

'Maggie's mum changed the sheets for me.'

Almond winced. He knew he should have bitten his tongue. The nicety of 'clean sheets' was too much information, and Evan was not to be deterred.

'Aye, but did you stay tucked up warm in Jack's bed, or did you sleepwalk and do a bit of your own maintenance?' Those at the table erupted in laughter. Almond, still finding his feet in a man's world, flushed with embarrassment... and guilt. He knew *he* hadn't wandered from his room; it was Maggie who had done, but in either case, the result was the same. They had lain together.

'How could I?' protested Almond, 'Maggie was in bed with her two sisters;' which was only the truth in as far as it went.

Then across from another table, Melvyn said,

'Missed a real chance there lad, the whole family of daughters in one bed' It was as if the whole of the pub was in on the conversation. A cough from Henry attempted to bring an end to the 'men's talk.'

Maggie's was a household of women with a lone male lodger. It was known Jack was Maggie's great-uncle and he had lost his wife to 'Consumption' many years before. There were no children from his marriage and his moving in with his niece, Christiana, Maggie's mother, suited them both. They were content to let the 'Tongues' of the village wag. Those who knew the truth understood. Nevertheless, the family arrangement had been a topic of conversation for the men in the pub on other drink-fuelled nights and it was hoped, perhaps, Almond could provide the missing detail that would bring some reality to their lurid imaginings.

Melvyn continued the interrogation.

'Tell us then. What's 'appening with Jack and his harem?' Then Evan added to the pressure put on Almond by following up with a question that made it personal.

'More important, what's 'appening' with you and Maggie?'

Almond realised he had provided the grapeshot for his companions to pepper him with. There was no avoiding the questions. Inwardly, he groaned at his stupidity, but he managed to defuse the situation, at least for the time being, by laughing at the suggestions along with everyone else. He threw a wink at Evan. Almond knew the men could make of it what they wanted, but it left them wrong-footed, not sure if the wink confirmed his misdemeanour, or if it was his attempt to intrigue? Whilst the miners paused for thought, Almond added to the confusion,

'Something *may* have happened... or maybe not? Wouldn't you just love to know?'

Henry could see his son was growing into the man he'd hoped for and, at seventeen, he knew he'd handle himself just fine.

Henry was proud of Almond, and he couldn't deny he had a special affection for his youngest son, and they had formed a special bond.

***

Henry had four children, three sons and a daughter, Elizabeth, the youngest of all. Three other children hadn't survived to become adults. Miscarriages weren't discussed or recorded. Catherine, Henry's wife, had died, aged 36, some eight years before, during the birth of a stillborn child. She'd been a good wife and mother. On a meagre family income, she had managed to keep the home clean and tidy, the men well-fed and her infant daughter, Elizabeth, safe and cherished; and all this whilst working almost full-time at the mine, sorting the ore from rock. She would carry her babes in a woollen shawl wrapped tightly to her chest. Much of her adult life was spent pregnant, caring for a newborn, or both.

The eldest son, Charles, had left Cornwall with his family a year earlier, aged twenty-one, and he now worked in the foundries of the

South Wales valleys. He and his new wife were settled there and destined not to return. Then there was James, at twenty, a skilled man, who worked as a machinist in the mine's workshop. He had escaped the rigours of working at the rockface, unlike Almond, who, at the age of fourteen, had taken up his pick. Elizabeth, aged ten, had just started at the mine surface, small tasks, fetching, carrying, and being around as and when needed. She was Henry's dearest child.

With the death of the mother of the house, the men struggled to maintain it as before. Elizabeth would perform many of the chores, but now she was earning, contributing to the family, the chores had to be shared. There was a need for a wife and mother in the household, but there was to be no re-marriage for Henry. He was sure no woman could replace Catherine in his affection; anyway, even at the time of Catherine's death, who would have wanted to have taken on a family of four children and a man whose health was starting to deteriorate? There were tell-tale signs.

James and Almond got on well enough, but there was a rivalry between the brothers. James couldn't help but feel Almond was preferred by his father and Almond would play on his 'youngest son' status. The battles with parents to allow some freedom of action for the boys in the family had long been won by Charles and James, and Almond was not fettered by either an over-anxious mother or a dominant father. Henry had long tired of the continual need to discipline his children and now took pleasure from Almond's youthful antics.

And Almond was a handsome boy. As a child, he had straw blonde hair, lively blue eyes and a grin that would melt the hardest heart. His hair had now matured light brown, but his good looks remained, and he was blessed with a self-confidence that was unusual to find in men subjected to the hardship of work down the mine.

***

James returned with a tray of drink. He seemed restless and his mind was elsewhere. He said what he was thinking.

'I'll not stay after this jug. My boss is arriving on the green soon with a Christmas surprise for us all.' Henry inquired,

'Oh! And what might that be, Son.'

'Just something we in the workshop have been putting together, Dad.'

'That's the first I've heard of any surprises. Is it a King's secret?'

'Just something different for us all to wonder at.'

'We'll see what you get up to whilst we slog our guts out in the mine.' said Almond, half in jest.

James, not in the mood for sibling banter, was defensive.

'It's true, you work hard, but we keep the steam pumps working so that you don't drown in the briny from the Bristol Channel.'

'Tis true, but tightening a few nuts here and there can't be too hard, can it?' Almond was not going to let James off lightly as he knew he was saying what others often thought, and a diversion away from his own predicament was a welcome relief.

'We're working on new things all the time. If Trevithick gets his way, we'll soon have steam lifts to get you to the bottom of the shaft and back up again at the end of the day.'

'Why would the Masters bother, knowing we've got arms and legs and ropes to scramble down?' said Almond.

Of course, Almond knew what a boon a mechanised lift would be, especially to his father who found the effort needed to get to the workface exhausting. It would take several minutes for him to get his breath before taking up his pick. But it was Evan who was the first to state another reason why a lift might be installed.

'It's so we can spend an extra hour digging, that's why. It won't be to save our arms or our legs.' James again defended himself.

'Not just that. We lose men tumbling down the shaft. I don't need to tell you, Evan. You know how slippery it is. There has to be a safer way to get in and out of that hole.' The discussion was becoming heated, and as usual, Henry was there to calm things down.

'Enough talk of the mine. Leave it until we're there tomorrow. Let's drink to us all, and toast to our good luck at still being here to do so.' Henry always had a way to cool a hot temper. He was a good man to be around, above or below ground.

Good humour soon returned to the group as the men, who, as requested, reflected on their good fortune; a steady job, for the moment at least. James finished his drink and stood from the table.

'I'll go now. I've work to do this afternoon by way of entertaining you all. You may be a little more grateful after the show.'

'Have you a little tippy-toey dance prepared for us then, like the maypole lasses?' mocked Evan, not missing a chance to gain a laugh at his companion's expense.

'A performance it'll be, but you'll not see me with ribbons in my hair... nor bells on my boots.'

'Now that would be fun.'

'Whatever happens, it won't be as much fun as watching you trying to get home at the end of the day, Evan.' That was enough to redouble the laughter as everyone knew the truth of what was said, even Evan.

***

James would often drink in the pub and listen to workmates. They were older miners who worked and drank hard. Ribald stories were told of their lives before the mine, working the land from sun beamed dawn to midge ridden dusk. They would speak longingly of the sensory delights of the countryside from the blackberry to the columbine and would embroider tales of assignations amongst the meadows with young maids of a willing and eager nature. As peasant farm labourers, they had been poor, and their lives were at the mercy of the elements. There were cold winters, late springs, drought, flood, and famine, but in retrospect, living on the land seemed infinitely better than crouching, far from the light of day, in a cold and wet miner's stall.

Almost all the men assembled in the pub were comparatively short in stature, but had broad shoulders, muscular arms and strong backs. These were men who broke 'hard rock' in search of copper and tin deposits. The rock they mined was granite, not softer coal or brittle slate. To get to the mine face, the men would climb rope ladders to varying depths, where 'roads' ran for half a mile before the working face was reached; the miners would dig at rock that lay beneath the Atlantic Ocean.

The conditions in the mine were appalling. The minimal light was from candles, mounted on the leather helmets worn by the miners. The walls and floors of the tunnels were running wet from groundwater, and the heat at such depths meant men worked in boots and trousers; their upper bodies would accumulate scars from injuries sustained throughout their working life. The ore-bearing seams would be narrow, and so mining was carried out in cramped and miserable conditions. There wasn't the room for big men at the workface. Brute force was needed to excavate the required daily tonnage, using steel picks, mandrills, sledgehammers and shovels, and cooperation between the miners was essential, as lives depended on it.

The use of the mandrill and sledgehammer was the most dangerous operation. Two men would work, within each narrow stall. One would hold the inch diameter mandrill, ensuring the shaft was square with the workface, the other would strike at its end with the sledge, driving the hardened steel tip into the rock. To be holding the mandrill was to be at the mercy of your workmate who administered the blows. Trust between the two men was essential. The mandrill had to be held with a steady and firm grip, and the sledge was to be swung accurately and precisely, blow after blow in rhythmic succession. Accidents happened, and an injury to hands, arms, shoulders and, worst of all, the head, was common.

The hewn rock containing the ore would be shovelled away from the workface and then dragged in wagons by hauliers to the lift shaft.

11

Hauliers were often children. If young hauliers survived into adulthood, they would replace the miners at the face who were lost by attrition to accident or ill-health. The youths served their grim apprenticeship in the pitch-black tunnels and galleries of the mine, gaining strength and experience as each terror was overcome.

Every tragic death of a miner, haulier or labourer would be rationalised as a reprieve for those who remained. The longer a miner lived, the more he was able to cope, and his chances of surviving the next day would be that bit better. It had been that way for all the men in the pub this Christmas Eve. They had survived into adulthood and avoided being taken by the chance event of a rock fall, a careering wagon or the blow of a carelessly wielded hammer.

Silicosis was a major killer of the veteran hard-rock miner. Rock dust choked the throat and invaded the lungs. For those with 'the dust,' it often seemed like no amount of coughing would loosen the grit accumulated in their chest. The phlegm produced by the body gave some relief, once coughed up and spat out, but if you were in the grip of the dust, your days were numbered. Its effects were accumulative, and as Henry was forty-six, his days and nights were racked with bouts of coughing fits. His breath would wheeze from his throat and his speech would be punctuated by gasps for air. For Henry, the final nightmare had begun.

Mining was their life, and for almost all of them, it would be their death.

2

Trevithick Appears

On the road outside the pub, there was a commotion. A large cart pulled by six, silver grey, dray horses clanged, crashed and clip-clopped to a stop. Immediately, a large crowd of onlookers gathered around, being drawn by the grand sight of the company's horses wearing ceremonial bridles and harness. On the cart was loaded a contraption none of the crowd had seen before. It was certainly a big metal boiler, the fire basket and associated coal tender testified to that. But it seemed to have wheels? It was similar in design to the 'high-pressure boilers' used to power the pumps that emptied the mine of the water from the deep workings. The mine was notorious for using this experimental high-pressure design; its detractors claiming it to be too dangerous and likely to explode. For the doubters, the low-pressure boiler was preferred, even if it was less efficient and far less powerful. It was said those operating the traditional boiler would more likely see out the day and be in work the next!

The boiler on the green wasn't connected to pumps, as in the mine. It had the familiar cross beam with crank arms at each end, but they were connected to wheels at either end of an axle slung beneath. A pair of smaller wheels was attached to a second axle at the front of the contraption. it was clearly meant to move, but to where, and for what purpose?

Into the midst of the swelling crowd strode a young man well known to all. He seemed tall in comparison to those congregated on the green, and was a well-dressed gentleman in a black top hat, coat and trousers, with shoes of finely polished leather. His dark exterior hid the brilliance of the man beneath. Richard Trevithick was the twenty-five-year-old son of the Mine Captain, and he was the engineer who had designed the high-pressure boiler. For him, this was another opportunity to promote his boiler design, and an opportunity to demonstrate a novel application of his technology to a non-critical audience. If it failed to live up to expectations, his reputation amongst his fellow engineers would be safeguarded as they would be none the wiser; after all, this was a village fair, not a presentation to the London Institute. Foremost amongst his detractors was James Watt, the inventor of the 'Condensing' steam engine. His was an engine that drove pistons by air pressure, as steam *condensed* creating a vacuum in the piston. Trevithick had successfully introduced his high-pressure boilers to the Camborne mine and wanted to demonstrate the idea that the *expansion* of high-pressure steam into a piston could be successfully applied to the propulsion of a load. The load was to be the contraption itself, a trailing wagon and a few of the crowd as passengers... if anyone dared to come along?

The babble of excitement had reached the ears of those in the pub, and it was soon emptied of its patrons. They wanted to find out what was going on.

Almond, full of curiosity, was first out the door and he was glad to get some respite from the continuing teasing about his previous night's exploits. He made his way to the front of the crowd employing both a polite 'excuse me', and where an 'excuse me' wasn't enough, the brute force of a shove.

Some of the villagers, mainly the women and children, cheered and clapped. After all, stood before them was the son of the Captain, and the company had paid in great measure for today's festivities; the company had long before realised an occasional display of philanthropy worked wonders for the loyalty of the workforce and it also served as a sop to the owner's conscience. The experienced men on the green cheered less enthusiastically, for the next day they would be back in 'the pit' and this *'Gentleman'* before them, receiving acclaim, was part of the Management and he represented the mine and its horrors. Miners and their families had received company handouts before, but nothing about their day-to-day existence had ever changed. What once had been a feeling of gratitude for such small kindnesses had now been replaced with feelings of resentment and suspicion. But today, even the most cynical of disgruntled old men watched with fascination as the contraption was being unloaded.

It seemed no one was in charge, as the workmen at each corner, often at odds with each other, shouted conflicting instructions. Labourers tugged, heaved, cajoled and blasphemed at the engine.

'Come on you little sod, move an inch or two at least.'

'We got the bugger on Fred, what's stopping it rolling off?'

'It's you, you're the silly idiot. You must have left a wedge on your side.'

'My side's clear Tom. Oh no! It's the cart's floor that's buckled under the weight. Both of us need to be over here to bodge the wheel over.'

'Give us some slack on the ropes.'

'Are you sure? I'm afraid of it running away.'

'Just an inch or two.'

The boiler's wheels were inched on to wooden sleepers stretched to the road off the back of the wagon. They were to be used as ramps to lower the machine to the ground. The men at the front wedged the wheels, adjusting by fractions to allow the machine to descend, whilst others at the back, held ropes attached to the rear axle and took the weight at each downwards step.

The machine was the master, and it demanded care should be taken. The consequences of it crashing to the road, uncontrolled and in free fall were too serious to contemplate. If it should topple, the men would at best lose their jobs, or, worse still, those at the front could lose a leg beneath a wheel.

Finally, to the good-humoured cheers of the crowd and the theatrical bows of the labourers, the beast stood safe and still on the road. At last, it stood in equilibrium. A wag in the crowd shouted,

'It looks like the floundered whale that washed ashore on the beach yesterday.'

'The whale was prettier.' came a reply; both were grey-black in colour with surfaces that glistened with reflected sunlight. The difference was the beast set before them was soon to be brought back to life. It would have fire in its belly, hot, skin blistering, breath, and a single fiery nostril spouting flame and black smoke.

James and one other workshop fitter had stood close to Trevithick, and it was their moment to take over the next step of the proceedings. They began to busy themselves, feeding the boiler with water and priming the firebox with kindling from off the wagon. They arranged the sticks so that when the wood was lit, air flowed across it, drawn up through the stack. The flame from the fire was coaxed from being a yellow flicker to a throaty roar. With the fire well alight, coal was shovelled on top of the flame. Trevithick was active throughout the firing process, directing his stokers at each stage. In a little while, the responsibility for operating the machine would be his. For the machine was his. Each nut, each bolt, each rivet, he had designed and engineered to withstand the pressure now building up in the boiler. He strained to hear anything out of the ordinary. Every creak and groan and hiss of this 'devil' was noted and analysed. He not as much moved about his machine, he danced, easing pressure where necessary, turning water level taps, applying gear and bearing grease with licks of a broad brush, venting steam to the stack. All the while, he called for more coal. He was every inch the Professional Engineer and, as all could see, the Showman.

'It won't be long before we are underway!' he shouted to the crowd.

They cheered and pressed closer still.

'My machine is to carry goods and passengers,' he declared.

'We'll believe that when it happens,' someone responded, and another wag shouted,

'It's more likely to blow up in the trying.' The crowd eased back at the thought, paying the monster a little more respect.

'You boys! Come away from that boiler thing,' screamed an anxious mother. The boys ignored her.

Almond stood close by, in awe of the man and his machine. He knew James had a hand in making this contraption and Almond couldn't help but feel a grudging respect for both Trevithick and his brother. Not that he would admit it.

A half-hour passed, and more coal had been shovelled into the firebox to replace that which was exhausted and ashen; the used coal having lost much of its effective energy to the mass of the engine. But now the boiler was hot, the heat from the coal was being transferred efficiently to the water in the boiler. The engine was 'steaming'. When it was vented into the piston, the pressurised water within would convert to steam. The expanding steam was to be the source of the power, and it would provide drive from the piston to the crossbeam and then to the wheels.

Trevithick was content. The fire raged, the steam hissed, and the engine throbbed as if in anticipation of the job to be done. Now was the time to start the show! With a theatrical raising of his hat, and a wave to the gathered crowd, he commenced the performance of the first act. In a loud voice, in the manner of a fairground barker, he announced,

'This is my steam engine. As you see it has wheels, and I am going to take it for a ride. Who would like to come for a ride with me?'

James beckoned Almond who moved quickly to jump on the step of the footplate. From there he could see the flames from the hearth of the boiler. James continued to shovel coal into the fire's throat. Other young men found space to clamber onto the trailing coal tender.

The engine was soon to roll into history; an innovation that would both improve and blight the lives of the people of Camborne... and people of the world beyond.

3

The 'Puffing Devil'

James, from the footplate, turned to Almond and spoke to him so only they could hear.

'Be careful! If the boiler shows signs of breaking apart, or I abandon the footplate, you get well away, too.' Almond, excited at the prospect of the ride and full of youthful optimism, shouted back,

'I'll be alright, don't you worry.'

'You make sure to do what I say.'

Trevithick's engine-driver cracked open the valve that allowed steam to expand into one of the two pistons. Its vertical movement, via a piston rod, was transmitted to the crosshead beam above their heads. Almond, stationed on the fire-plate, watched the beam slide on two bright steel rods. At each end of the beam, connecting rods transmitted the motion to the wheels. A valve was actuated at the full extent of the piston's travel, and it allowed steam into the opposite end of the piston. The piston reversed its direction of travel, and the beam slid back to its original position, and exhausted its used steam from the initial stroke to the smokestack. One full rotation of the wheels had been achieved and the engine started to move. The process was repeated and the forward motion of the boiler on wheels continued. The crowd gasped. It was as if a wild beast had come to life and was about to pounce.

'Stay calm!' shouted Trevithick, 'We have it under control... You at the front there, make room!'

The crowd parted as requested, as no one was fool enough to stand in the machine's, way.

At first, the wheels kept contact with the road's cobbled surface, but, as more steam was applied to the piston, friction with the road was lost and the wheels spun out of control. Sparks from the wheel rims caught a group of onlookers by surprise.

'What in God's name?' shouted Edward Sugrue, as he leapt to one side, bowling over two children and their grandmother before crashing on top of them all.

'Sorry Mrs. Harvey,' spluttered Edward as he helped her up.

The two kids were already on their feet chasing after the monster, for it had gained a grip on the cobbles and had lurched forward in fits and starts.

Space had been left by the crowd at the front of the engine, but those at the sides stepped back. The movement caused collisions that rippled out to the back edge. Those spectators who were unsupported fell over.

It was then that a prospective passenger, Ted Turner, lost his hold on the tender and toppled backwards. The same two children were hit by another tumbling mass of an adult out of control. They got up, but they had been bashed by Ted's elbows, his knees, and his 'Sunday-best' boots. The children began to cry. No one cared, apart from their Gran, for everyone else ran after the machine as it trailed steam and black smoke.

In uneven bursts of speed, it screeched and chuffed its way towards Camborne Hill. Of Trevithick, James was later to observe,

'It was as if he was Moses parting the waves.'

Children described what they had seen as best they could.

'It was like a milkmaid jiggling her yolk up and down,' said an urchin, who could not have described it better.

'Yes, it's a milkmaid jiggling her buckets,' joked another.

'Though I've never seen a milkmaid that puffed as much black smoke,' he admitted,

'Nor one that had wheels, instead of legs.' said a third.'

Trevithick laughed a wild laugh, an uproar of a laugh. Almond watched and was amazed at the passion of the man as he waved his top hat at the crowd. Almond thought he had never heard such a laugh. Not even the laughter that echoed through the village when Evan was caught providing 'a helping hand' to Molly the barmaid; it didn't come close.

Trevithick shouted yet more commands.

'Move aside, we have no time to stop.' And to his driver,

'Gradual steam now... Keep the acceleration constant... Not too fast! Not yet.'

Fifty yards were covered before he turned back to the crowd and roared,

'It works. Glory be, it works!'

Christiana and her younger daughters, Imogene and Mary, arrived in the village square to be confronted by a strange machine puffing and steaming towards them with crowds in its wake. They made way for it. As it passed, they could see Almond was being carried along. The two sisters were startled by the sight and sound of the machine... and why should Almond be upon it? The girls waved and jumped up and down to draw Almond's attention. They shouted as hard as they could,

'Almond! Almond!' and although he shouted back, they couldn't hear what he said.

He was away in what seemed an instant.

'What a start to the fair,' said mother, as she hugged her daughters to her. She thought they would be unsettled by the noise and swell of the crowd, but Mary was having none of it. She wriggled free and weaved her way, ducking and dodging, through the mass of people who were going in the other direction, up the hill after the engine. Her thoughts were on the stalls and rides of the fair, not on some silly puffing machine. She had often been called 'a little devil' for her antics and high spirits and she liked it, and before running on to the fair she turned back and shook her fist at the receding engine and shouted what came into her head, 'Go away. You puffing devil.' She may have been the first to call it that; in any case, 'The Puffing Devil' is what it was to be called down the ages.

Almond had seen Christiana, amongst the crowd, with her daughters in tow. He looked hard but couldn't see Maggie. 'Hello, Christiana... Where's Maggie?' he shouted, but his words were lost in the commotion surrounding them. Christiana looked surprised and alarmed to see him aboard such a contraption. What a tale he would be able to tell them, and his Maggie, once he'd found her.

The engine began to climb the hill, and most of those following fell behind.

Camborne Hill was the main road leading up from the village and was fronted on either side by various small business premises: the baker's, the blacksmith's forge alongside it, an ironmonger's and Protheroe's the butcher with the knacker's yard to one side. Each seemed to jostle for dominance, one upon the other. The street smells alternated and intermingled. The aroma of freshly baked bread competed with the stench of the sulphurous smoke from the blacksmith's forge and the ever-present ammonia from rivulets and puddles of horse piss. Horse shit, softened by the piss and the previous day's winter's rain, spread out on the road as a slippery coating that in the sunlight reflected rainbow colours. The slimy horse droppings and the hill were the greatest tests of the ability of the engine to maintain a grip of the road. In the event, the engine coped well enough, and it continued its climb. The iron-rimmed wheels bit through to the cobbles and scoured an abrasive contact, occasionally slipping, but soon regaining purchase on the road beneath. The engine proved to have more than enough power to climb even the steepest part of the hill, and it soon reached the fields above the town. There the countryside flattened out and wound across the windswept moorland. The road followed the stunted hedgerows and low stone walls that offered some protection to the livestock kept on the land. The cheering crowds had been left behind, and two and a half miles ahead lay the village of Beacon. Beacon was Trevithick's destination... and it was the village where Maggie lived.

Even though Almond marvelled at the carriage that was propelled without horses, his thoughts turned to Maggie. The power of the piston's thrusts enflamed him, as did the heat given off from the boiler contributing to his nervous sweat. It all brought to his mind thoughts of the previous night. He longed to be with her again.

The control Trevithick had shown encouraged Almond to take control of his own life. The fumbling intimacies of the previous night ended with the shock of his premature release, and it was because he hadn't taken control. Maggie had seized control; and control of his manhood, so she could explore him without fear of penetration, and possible pregnancy. But she was ready for him, he was sure, and the strength of his need for her would overcome her caution. He knew what he wanted, and he was emboldened and energised by the extraordinary events of the day.

***

Ahead of them, a shepherd, Cedric Thompson, was in the process of moving his flock of a dozen sheep in search of fresh pasture. He could hear a commotion ahead of him. There were sounds he couldn't put an image to, not a cart - too loud, and not a carriage, at least no carriage he knew of - too clangy. Above the hedgerows, he saw snorts of black smoke and clouds of steam moving towards him. He didn't know what to make of it. All he knew was it was coming his way, straight at his sheep. There was nothing he could do about it; the sheep would have to look after themselves. They were already uneasy with the strange sounds of the steam engine, and as it turned the corner into their path, their otherwise obstinate nature was replaced by group panic. They turned and fled back along the road, knocking Cedric Thompson over, and they continued past the gate to their previous, grass shorn field. Some jumped walls, whilst others squeezed through hedgerows where they shouldn't have been able. Four kept going until they reached Beacon where they were gathered into the community pen; the villagers knowing they were

Cedric's sheep, and he would soon be following behind in a huff at their escape.

Cedric had got to his feet and cursed down the road at the machine and its passengers,

'What the devil? Bloody stupid thing to be riding on this road.'

He shook his fist at the top-hatted gentleman who was on board, waiting until he was sure he wouldn't be heard and pretending not to care if the traveller was gentry, he shouted with mock bravado,

'Come back here and I will beat you to within an inch of your life, you black-hatted bastard.'

Trevithick scoffed as he looked back at the mayhem he had caused and saw Cedric waving his fist.

'He looks a mite upset. Is it something we did?' He roared with laughter once again.

Twenty minutes later the engine steamed to the outskirts of Beacon Village where Trevithick called for the engine to stop. The nearby Inn would be a good place to take on water and re-steam. He would leave the process to his labourers. By way of celebration, he invited the rest of his passengers to join him in a jug or two; after all, the engine worked, and it was Christmas Eve.

'It will be an hour or so before we can get back, so we have time for some refreshment.'

Everyone, except the labourers and Almond, made for the Inn's guest room where they knew drink would be provided.

'Are you not joining us Almond?' James asked, sensing Almond had other things on his mind.

'You go on James, and I'll go and see if Maggie is still at home. I'll ask if she wants to ride back with us.' James replied,

'No doubt that will be alright with Mr. Trevithick, and some will be worse for wear from the drink and will want to stay.'

James watched as Almond hurried on into the village. He wouldn't have admitted to the feeling of jealousy that swept over him. James had avoided intimate relationships for the sake of the family. Being the eldest left at home, a mother who had died and a father whose health was failing, he took it upon himself to look after the family's needs rather than his own. In truth, it suited his nature, but the fact Almond was carefree caused James to begrudge the time he had lost where he could have looked for his own pleasure. He murmured,

'You'll learn soon enough that life gets tough, dear brother.'

Selwyn Berryman-Morgan

4

The Chores

In addition to her household chores, Maggie would work at the mine twelve hours a day, six days a week. She would separate the tin-bearing ore from the rock spoil, a physically demanding job but at least it was at the surface, not down the dreaded pit. The need for every member of the family to work was especially important. With no father in the house and two other girls as her only siblings, both younger than her, Maggie bore the greatest responsibility. Imogene was twelve, and she also worked full time at the mine, but at less arduous and poorly rewarded tasks. Mary was, at ten years of age, too young to work full time, and she earned money where possible performing the occasional task thought suitable for her age and strength. As with all the girls, Mary had become streetwise at an early age and was a handful. She had been spoiled by too much attention from her mother, who, after the death of her husband some two years previously, clung especially close to her. Their uncle, although he could get occasional work, was failing in health and could not perform any given task for an extended period. Often, he was overlooked when jobs were allocated.

Her mother Christiana, and Maggie's two sisters, had gone to the fair earlier in the day. The three-mile walk to Camborne was no bother as it was only a mile longer than their daily journey to the mine. Maggie was keen to join them as soon as she was able but had been left with the remainder of the daily chores. She had stripped to her blouse and skirt and whirled a three-pronged 'dolly' as fast as she could in a tub full of clothes set before the fire. The heat she generated washing the clothes meant she had no need for her winter coat and shawl. She added another pan of hot water from the range; it would be the final load for the day. The sweat dripped from her face and onto her exposed chest, the top three buttons of her blouse being undone. The thought of finishing and making her way to the fair and to Almond, had made her put in extra effort. A strand of her long hair worked loose from the ribbon used to tie it back and was hanging before her face. It was irritating, and she blew hard to remove it from in her gaze, but it persisted; it would have to remain that way until she'd finished.

Behind her, the door of the house swung open. It banged against the wooden settle beneath the window and the door latch clattered and the door knock rattled. The once excluded daylight flooded the room. Maggie was startled back into the present and abandoned her own workaday thoughts. She turned to see who had entered. It was Almond. The door rocked back on its hinges to rest at his broad shoulder.

Almond stood still. She knew it was Almond, although his face was shaded and her eyes were dazzled. The light from outside held her in sharp focus, and her face and bosom glistened with sweat.

'Almond! What on earth are you doing here?' she said, in a feigned scold.

'You're supposed to be at the Fair, and I was going to meet you there, once I...' She stopped speaking as she sensed an urgency to his presence. She knew it was not the time to squabble in playful banter.

But there was something about him, something unrecognizable. He was not the gentle, slightly insecure boy who had been in her arms the night before. His stance was upright, and she sensed he was tense, and his breath was heavy. He seemed taller and set firm. Yet he trembled?

Almond stood and gazed at Maggie, not saying a word. Maggie was stooped over her washtub, her hand providing shade to her eyes that blinked against the light. The wisp of light brown hair, still hanging over her face, shimmered in the reflected sunlight, her cleavage exposed, her modesty left unattended. Her quizzical look melted into a wry, lopsided, smile, the smile she kept for him.

She knew he loved her smile. Had she meant it as a welcome or as a provocation? She would, in retrospect, never be sure.

Almond took a step forward. He closed the door with an unintended slam, and moved across the room and stood in front of her. He became afraid to touch, afraid to let loose the passion that raged within him. Maggie sensed the need consuming him. She stood upright and raised her palm to his chest, partly as a reassuring gesture, but also as a plea to take pause. She needed to assess what was happening and respond to his needs as best she could. She had felt her own passions rising over the last few days and was undecided about when was the best time to give in to their mutual desires. Through his shirt, Maggie could feel his tremor, and her touch caused the tremor to swell into an involuntary shake that ran the length of his body. She smiled at him again, delighted he should respond to her in such a way. Almond saw her smile and was reassured he was welcome. He was emboldened in his determination to lay with her. Maggie understood, even though she had never before lost control, she knew what was wanted from her and it was his to take. The time had come. With her free hand, she loosened his front trouser buttons and felt for him, pulling him free from the constraint of his Sunday-best breeches. His hardness was as of the night before, when, beneath the blankets, they had intimately fondled each other until Almond had shuddered in his release. He had stifled a groan into a low growl to ensure the others in the house did not wake. She had not been ready to make love to him then, but she would not refuse him now. Maggie's arms encircled him and, without speaking, she kissed his parted lips. Almond drew her body to him and he hugged her as tight as he dare. Afraid he might hurt her, he relaxed his grip. He was aware of her slender body, her hardened nipples, and her maiden's hips. His passion flamed, and he lifted her from the ground, his hands beneath her skirt, cupping her buttocks and pulling her towards him, pressing her pubic mound against him. Her thighs parted slightly as she invited him as never before. She had made her decision. She pressed herself hard against him, disclosing her own desires; desires she had contained, but had now taken control. He lifted her off the floor and carried her to the oak dining table. Resting her down, he lay her out and pinned her arms above her head. She lay back in complete acceptance of his unspoken intent. With her skirt pushed back, he loosened her undergarments and pulled them away. He saw her for the first time. Her eagerness was displayed for him, and their union was made without the need to reassure. Stood between Maggie's thighs, Almond felt the powerful drive of his young body. It was as if each piston thrust of Trevithick's machine had been invested in him. He drove time and again, the imagined beat of each piston's pulse within his head and the power of the engine's furnace within his groin.

5

Cedric's Revenge?

The revelry in the Beacon village pub was in full flow. The mixture of the excitement of the trip on the steam carriage with the plentiful flow of free beer made for a rowdy gathering. The passengers from the engine had been drinking solidly for three-quarters of an hour when Cedric flung open the door. It bounced straight back at him off a table pushed too close to the entrance, knocking him back into the street. For an instant, he had been seen and a warning rang out.

'Look! Cedric's caught up with us and it seems he's 'ad a bad day.'

Cedric negotiated the door at the second attempt and made his way to the bar where stood Trevithick. Cedric was determined to have his say, no matter what. Even so, he was a little more respectful than he otherwise would have been, given the circumstances.

'Excuse me Sir, I would like a word in your shell-like.'

'Cedric, my fine fellow... for I am told 'tis you,' replied Trevithick, not wanting the shepherd to get into full flow.

Cedric paused in his efforts to remonstrate with the toff. *He knows my name*, he thought. *I'd better take care.* Then, in mock bravado, he continued to have his say.

'I don't know why I shouldn't knock your block off until it's just an inch away from Satan's door.'

'My dear fellow, what can be the matter?'

'You well knows! Because of that infernal machine of yours, my sheep are scattered all over Cornwall, and probably, by now, throwing themselves into Falmouth 'arbour.'

'I was about to say, Cedric, how sorry I was to have caused you, and your sheep, such alarm.' Delving into his coat pocket, Trevithick continued in his apology,

'I wonder if a sixpence would in some way compensate?' Nodding over to the beer counter he provided Cedric more solace,

'In fact, here's a shilling, seeing my visit here to your village has caused so much trouble.'

Cedric looked at the silver coin that had dropped into his hand and thought,

A shilling! A whole shilling! His anger turned to expressions of gratitude.

'Err...Well, thank you kindly, Sir... Well, I suppose it won't take me long to round the buggers up. They'd run off if you as good as fart at them would them sheep. Daft buggers they be... May I say what a fine machine you got there, Sir, went like the wind it did!' He raised his cap to Trevithick whilst edging his way to the counter and his favoured mind-numbing cider. To no one in particular, he said,

'It gave me such a fright it did. Very nearly bowled me over into Meredith's farmyard. I could have been covered in cow's shit, could I.' and from nowhere in particular, came a voice,

'It would have made a change from sheep's shit, Cedric.' They all laughed, including Cedric. By the time he left the pub, his sheep could have been in Dorset for all he cared.

6

Almond Takes His Leave?

'Steam is up, and we are to be on our way towards Camborne. Who wants to come back with me?' Trevithick bellowed, to surprisingly little response.

Much had been drunk by his outbound passengers and they were quite happy to continue doing the same. As much fun as his steam-driven machine was, the cider was better.

Almond and Maggie had that moment entered the pub.

'We'll come with you' said Almond, but from the rest in the pub, there was no reply, just the noise of their carousing.

The drinking in the pub had been continuous, and James had consumed much more than he would have had not the cider been free. He sat with John, who had been with them in the pub in Camborne and had come along for the ride. At first, James didn't see Almond and Maggie at the door. Maggie was hesitant, not entering the floor of the pub, not used to drinking houses, and uncomfortable in the presence of men in the state she found them. They were boisterous and blasphemous, and in one far corner, the atmosphere was tinged with an undercurrent of alcohol-fuelled aggression. Local lads, not in on the free drink, began to voice their objections with their own suggestions,

'Yes, it's about time you Camborne lot buggered off.'

John replied on behalf of the town's contingent.

'Worry not, we'll soon drink up. Nice it is, too, and we'll leave you lot up here to your own buggering.'

James caught sight of Almond and Maggie and spoke to his companions to calm their profane banter.

'Careful gentlemen, there's a young lady present.'

'Young lady? Tell her to come over 'ere, I've got a Christmas present I was keeping for my missus' said John.

'What you've got isn't worth unwrapping, it being all spotted and that,' said another, as neither were yet prepared to leave the banter for another time.

'Quiet lads.'

His companions had seen Almond and Maggie, but try as they might, they couldn't stop their pub banter.

'Sorry James, it is Almond's Maggie after all. Although it looks like he's been round for '*tea*' again.'

They laughed, including James, but he managed to calm the coarse laughter down to sniggering giggle. He looked back to the door and couldn't help noticing how beautiful Maggie was. He'd seen her in the mine over the years, growing from an annoying urchin to a useful young worker, and now, before him, was a young woman who would turn many a head with her fair complexion and flowing blond-brown hair. He could see why this grown-up Maggie had won Almond's heart.

The rivalry between the brothers gnawed at James' thoughts; *how can he get such a lovely girl, whilst I...? I don't know the first thing about getting one!*

James wasn't at ease with women, words would not flow. Many attempts at striking up a friendship, let alone a relationship, foundered, as his inner demons scuppered his advances and left him feeling awkward and inadequate. It wasn't he was unattractive; he just didn't have the easy smile and confidence to say what he really felt about his emotions. Almond had charm in bucket-loads.

'Damn him,' said James, under his breath, thinking how they were so different in their way with women.

Maggie has seen and heard enough,

'I'm not staying in here Almond, and I'm not sure that I want to ride that thing outside, either.'

'It'll be fine Maggie. I rode it here. Just remember to hang on tight. James is riding on it, too. He helped to build it he did.'

A young man of around twenty had come to stand next to Almond. He was drunk and had been amongst the group of discontented local lads. There was menace in his voice when he spoke.

'So, you be the lad coming to our village after our girls.'

'What's it got to do with you?'

'Oh... I'll show you what it's got to do with me, you little shit.'

Almond knew the lad was about to swing a punch, so he moved to shield Maggie and be in a better position to defend himself. The lad was ponderous in drink and his attempted blow sailed wide, as Almond swayed back and away. Regaining his balance, the assailant set himself up to try again, and that was when the fist of James connected to his chin. The young man lay on the floor, out of it, but James knew well enough there were other local lads who had hesitated, itching to join in, but were taking stock of their chances against the strength and resilience of mineworkers. James said,

'Come, Almond, it's time to go. We'll make room for Maggie on the engine.'

Trevithick was ushered out of the pub, although he wasn't above joining in a fistfight, if he could have found a safe place to keep his hat. Even in a fistfight, the rules of engagement were different for 'Toffs'.

The village thugs thought better of continuing the fight. It could be left until the odds favoured them, and on territory that would not get them excluded from their only local pub.

***

Almond and Maggie stood close together in the trailing cart, Almond enthusiastically telling Maggie of the journey from Camborne: the fire, the steam, the smoke and the speed. Maggie was anxious, but Almond held her tight and reassured her it would be alright. She felt the strength of his arms around her and she was sure it would be so. Whilst he was with her, everything would be alright.

The 'Devil' was well steamed up and the journey back to Camborne took less time than going out. Firstly, it was mostly downhill, and secondly, Trevithick, the driver and James were gaining confidence in the abilities of the engine, applying more coal to the firebox and more steam to the piston. The engine driver had soon learned that subtle adjustments when opening the throttle ensured a smooth movement forward from a standing start. With care, the spinning of the wheels, and showers of sparks as they spun on cobbles, could be avoided. The sudden jerk forward, that had threatened to jettison the passengers on the outward voyage, had been replaced with a smooth transition from rest to powered motion.

***

The remainder of the afternoon was a whirl of excitement for Maggie and Almond. On reaching Camborne, the fair bustled with activity, and time and time again, they played at the stalls, failing every time to 'catch the rat' or 'bowl the pig'. They joined in the dancing and sung along with the itinerant musicians. Almond listened intently to the tall tales of the storytellers, of adventures in lands afar. They both joined in with hoots of encouragement and loud applause at a story well told and poured scorn on the unbelievable... spotted horses with necks and legs as long as a 'knocker-upper's stick, indeed!

'What's left to do Almond?'

'Come, Maggie, Dad and James are in the pub, let's say hello before you go back with your mum.'

They made their way across the green, stopping along the way to speak to their relations and neighbours. A gossiper from the town inquired whether they were 'going out', wanting to be the first to spread the news. Maggie lied,

'No, we are just friends, Mrs. Harvey. I joined Almond on the way back from Beacon.' Pointing back to Trevithick's contraption, she proudly said,

'We rode that machine over there.'

'That's lovely.' said Ethel Harvey. Who half-turned and winked in a knowing way at her friend, Olive. With that, the young couple went their way.

Ethel whispered to Olive, 'She'll be calling me 'Auntie Ethel' before long and that nephew of mine will be producing more Rowes than I have pegs for the line. Lovely boy he is though, and they'll have lovely children... Did you ever see her father's brother, Tom? Now he was someone you could rest your bustle on.' They laughed a coarse laugh usually reserved for when the men were out of earshot, but on this festive day, there were few inhibitions.

At the door of the pub, again Maggie became uncertain,

'No, sorry Almond, I can't go in there, and I just saw your dad go by for home, so why would we?'

Much as Almond would have liked a glass or two, it would have to wait.

'Yes, you're right. It's just James and the boys in there. We'll go back and find your mum and your sisters so you can go back with them when they're ready.'

The sun was setting, and the day had been well spent. The fair was coming to an end, and it was time for Christiana and her family to make their way home, aided, as far as possible, by the short, midwinter twilight. Standing behind Trevithick's machine, Almond held Margaret in a warm embrace and kissed her as if he had not seen her for days. Their attempt to kiss unnoticed, failed, as a loud voice called out.

'Come along Margaret, it's time we were home.' Maggie untwined herself and walked away. Over her shoulder she mouthed,

'I love you,' then blew Almond a kiss of farewell and smiled her special, crooked, smile, for him to remember and come calling again. Of that, both she and Almond were certain.

The day was not yet over for Almond. The pub on the green was still plying its trade: refreshment for the thirsty, company for the lonely, and an excuse for drunken oblivion, if need be. With Maggie out of harm's way, the thought of one more hour spent with his brother and his friends in the pub didn't seem so bad, and the sound of comradely laughter drew him through the door. He wanted to retell the experience of riding Trevithick's machine and to ask what part James had played in its manufacture. James was at the bar with other workmates, laughing and joking around. Evan was sat in his usual place and had been joined by his other pals who worked alongside him. He was worse for wear after drinking for most of the day, and when he saw Almond enter, he called out to him,

'You weren't blown up then, by that weird steam cart?' It was the best he could come up with at short notice, but it still provoked laughter from those at the table. Then, feigning insult, he continued,

'Though I see your lovely Maggie has decided not to join us.'

Almond hesitated. He wasn't sure if he wanted to join in another round of banter about his activities and intentions concerning Maggie, but he smiled back. It was about time he got used to it. Evan took the chance to relent from his piss-taking.

'Don't mind us, lad. Come over here and sit yourself down.'

Almond, still not an accomplished drinker, and already intoxicated by the events of the day, found the alcohol to have more of an effect than usual. His resolve, not to drink too much, ebbed with each round, and each tall tale told. Tales he'd heard before, but Evan had a way of telling stories that left Almond wanting more.

The pub was full of locals who he knew well, and people from further afield who had been drawn by the thrill of the fair. The outside folk would have money enough, earned as itinerant workers or being employed by the King, as a soldier, on leave, or sailors ashore for the day. The pub was awash, not just by the drink, but with different accents and tongues. It wasn't unusual. Camborne being close to many small harbours had an itinerant population that existed alongside its mining folk. Ore from the mine was shipped to all corners of the world from its local docks, and no matter where the visitor hailed from, their need for a beer or a jug of cider was universal. The British Navy had its fleet tied up in Portsmouth and the British Tar was often seen in the streets of the town. Sailors, on shore leave, would stop at the pub before travelling on to their destination. Their family and friends wouldn't have seen them in a long time, years, perhaps. Such was the life of a sailor.

Sailors were great storytellers, and Almond would often listen to them when, after several pints, they had loosened their tongue. They talked of faraway places and battles won in the name of the King. They were hard and tough men, coarsened by the rigours and discipline of life in the navy. Almond felt an affinity with them, as his own working conditions were equally as hard, and life expectancy just as short. But this evening, Almond was content to keep the company of his own friends and workmates.

Evan was totally out of it and lay across the bench that had been left empty by others with more sense; the prospect of the next day's shift in the mine, with its heat, noise and ever-present dangers, had brought their drinking to a halt. Drunk though he was, Evan was famous for making it into work, no matter what, and he would be at his stall the next day, shifting his quota as fast as the next man. How he did it was a mystery to all who knew him. Almond decided he would leave him there, as the landlord would chuck him out into the street when he closed down.

Almond was unsteady as he got to his feet, already regretting the excesses of the day. There was still time to sleep off much of the effects of the drink, and tomorrow would be manageable. James had long departed. Almond slipped out of the door, leaving the determined drinkers to their eventual oblivion.

The night was clear and cold. A half-moon lit the village green and the road back home. The night air, crisp and clean, chilled his lungs, and the drink warmed his belly. He felt the joy of being alive on such a day he'd had.

He was not used to the effects of the combination of fresh air and alcohol, although he'd been warned often enough of how cider would creep up on you and steal your legs, and soon his ability to walk in a straight line and stay upright at the same time was put severely to the test. To steady himself, he stopped and leaned against the stone wall of his aunt Ethel's cottage. He tried to get his scrambled thoughts together. If he could, he was sure he'd be able to make it home. For the moment, the village swam around him, and the walls of the houses stepped out to block his way.

'Bastard walls! Stay still.' he cried.

He heard a voice from behind him.

'Having trouble there lad.'

Before Almond could come to his senses and assess the intentions of his new companion, strong arms clamped him and supported his weight. He became aware of other men either side of him. Uneasy with the uninvited assistance, he protested,

'I'm alright. I'm just fine thanks,' and half-turned to confront his new companion and helpmates. Before he was able to identify who it was offering such kindness on a cold winter's night, a blow to the head brought an end to his day and a set new course to his life.

***

Trevithick had been assured by his driver that his engine was secure and properly maintained. In that knowledge, he had retired to his family home, with its well-lit fire and comfortable bed. The cook and housemaids would make sure he was well-fed and rested. The next day he would be prepared for the adventure his invention would afford him.

Meanwhile, Trevithick's 'Puffing Devil' stood on the village green, as if brooding: its steam bled off, its energy dissipated and given back to the elements. The crowds had long since departed to their homes with their memories of the fair and of the comical steam engine.

Stabled adjacent to the green were the horses that had brought the 'Devil' to the village. Their day had long ended, but for sure, a new task would be presented to them in the morning. It would be a job that required their speed, power and endurance; tasks that for thousands of years had been theirs to perform. But today, on the green stood a new workhorse, the likes of which would one day consign the horse to industrial, agricultural, and military history.

***

The 'Puffing Devil' was to have a short life. Three days later, whilst Trevithick was not on board, the engine driver and fireman decided to stop at a tavern; after all, how long would one drink take? Some hours later, and much the worse for wear, they returned to a burnt-out engine. The water in the boiler had steamed away. No one had thought to dampen the fire.

'I left that to you, Sid. I went to get the beers in.'

'You never said, Jack, and I was talking to Mr. Travis 'bout his cows, they being scared an'all. You just left me to him. He was right pissed off.'

'Them cows would be bloody scared now the thing's going up in flames.'

'It's a good job then that old man Travis has already took 'em 'ome.'

'So, Travis has had the last laugh, I suppose?'

'More than I can say for 'his nibs', Trevithick, when he hears about what's 'appened here.'

The momentous significance of the short steam-powered trip to Beacon village and back was lost on most of the villagers. The steam engine was just one of novelties of the day; spectacular, but pointless. Two village wags were in agreement.

'Why build such a monster, fill it with water, and light a fire in its belly, when you could walk there and back twice over whilst it got itself hot under the collar?'

'If them there horses had been used to pull the wagon, it would have reached Exeter in time for lunch.'

'And would be on its way back in time for tea.'

'Aye, and it would have only cost two bags of oats.'

'Then there's all that smoke in your face. Wouldn't have fancied that all the way to Exeter... though, come to think of it, my horse's farts are quite a bit worse.'

How they laughed. The absurdity of the whole affair wasn't lost on them.

Handed down the years is a folk song written at the time. In an oft-embellished, bawdy, and good-humoured way, it expressed the thoughts of at least one onlooker:

Goin' up Camborne Hill, coming down,
goin' up Camborne Hill, coming down.
The horses stood still, the wheels went around,
goin' up Camborne Hill coming down.
He heaved in the coal, in the steam (the steam)
He heaved in the coal, in the steam.
He heaved in the coal, the steam hit the beam,
goin up Camborne Hill coming down...
The song ends,
...the horses stood still, the wheels went around,
goin' up Camborne Hill, coming down.

7

Times Change

Christiana Harris had to walk the three miles to the Rowe family home. It was late February and the winter's snow had eased. The road to Camborne was just clear enough, but the rutted snow was frozen hard and treacherous. She took each step carefully for fear of slipping and turning an ankle, or worse. Christiana wouldn't have ventured so far on such a day, but her business was urgent, and her family's situation precarious.

Over the previous few months, employment at the mines had dropped off. For her family, it was more of a problem than for most in the village. Since the death of her husband, from a fall of rock, she had managed to support her family and maintain the home, but now the family's combined income would not sustain the household. For Christiana, the scarcity of work was because of her age and continuing frailty, but for her middle daughter, Imogene, it was because she had injured an arm as rock poured from a careering wagon. Christiana had thanked God, as it could have been a lot worse. The responsibility lay with the mine, but none was accepted; no recompense or consideration of the family's plight was given. Her daughter would mend in time, but there was a slow downturn in the mine, and Christiana knew that soon there would be little work for any of them. She had seen it before; it was hard, but they had survived. Even so, there were yet other reasons why she stumbled on the road to Camborne and worried for the future. The dark cloud above her head had lowered and gave support to the gloom of the day, it, in turn, deepened the gloom she felt in her heart.

It was mid-morning, on a Sunday, and she was alone on the hill. Today, she would not go to church, where she could sing hymns of joy to lift her spirits and take comfort in the sense of community offered by her supportive congregation.

But this was not the day to forsake the Lord. Welling up from her simple belief, her voice quietly began to make a reality of the words and tunes that rolled in her head. Christiana's hymn grew with each note, each breath, and each step, and the sound of her voice rang out clear. It resounded from the stone walls that lined her way, fortifying her resolve, renewing her determination. Although there was no one to hear, except her God, she was sure He was at hand and listening.

Christiana and her family had been believers since the new Wesleyan Chapel came to the village. Now she understood the word of God. In clear English, spoken by men who lived amongst them, she had been told about His message of hope and deliverance. These were messages that made some sense of, and reason for, the hardships she faced. The hymns she sang were joyful and full of optimism. They flew in the face of the brutality of everyday life in a mining village. For such a kind, diligent and devout member of God's flock, there must surely have been time for him to help speed her way? But as often happened to those who believed, he chose not to offer an almighty hand, and instead perpetuated the mystery of his ways. It was not for Christiana to understand, it was enough that she believed.

With the cloud, there blew the stirrings of a cold moist breeze, not as cold as the frozen stillness that had accompanied her thus far. A herald of change was upon her. The day darkened still further. The first few flakes of snow were disturbed by her misty breath, the light breeze still unable to compete with her choral exhalation.

At first, she didn't notice the subtle change in the air that surrounded her, but a sense of foreboding slipped through the barrier of the song she sang and wrestled to possess her. She started a new hymn, a hymn that always gave her strength at times of hardship, a hymn Christiana had called upon many times before; the lowering sky had prompted her.

'Lo, he comes with clouds descending, once for favoured sinners slain.'

'Thousand, thousand saints attending, swell the triumph of his train.'

She paused to gain a new breath, and continued, yet stronger, yet louder...

'Hallelujah, Hallelujah...', she paused.

Christiana looked up at the sky. The flat, dark clouds had changed to a menacing, billowing, burgeoning mass of a storm. Rolling and tumbling, it bore down on her, increasing in spite and vindictiveness. A swirl of snow blurred her vision and drew a white curtain across her way. She stood erect, and faced full-on the inevitable blast, knowing it would try to frustrate her. She drew her loosened shawl over her head and then tied each end tightly around her chest. Before her next step, and with full voice, she continued her song;

'Hallelujah! God appears on earth to reign.'

Then, at the top of her voice, divested of tunefulness, and with an unaccustomed irreverence, she waved her fist at the sky and shouted...

'Hallelujah! God appears on earth to reign!'

She strode on... There were still two miles to go.

***

Henry stoked the embers and added more wood to the fire to keep the room warm and the cast iron cooking range hot. His family sat at the table for the day's main meal. Being Sunday, extra effort had been made to vary the bland monotony of the continually replenished 'stew'. In the stew's favour, it was always available, and always plentiful. The different shift patterns of the family members meant those 'off shift' needed to replace what they had eaten.

The ritual of the making of the stew had been more difficult to maintain since Almond had left; Henry and James' shifts would often coincide and Elizabeth, would always be out at the mine during the day.

45

The men would sometimes arrive home and bicker about who should have done what to the stew before they left home, and what was to do now the pot was empty. But on this Sunday, they had all joined in to make it special. Fresh bread was baked in the cast iron oven set within the range. Pork from the butcher added flavour and nutrient. The last of the stored apples had been cooked alongside the bread and it filled the room with a yeasty, apple cider smell.

The fire was the focal point of the home and served the space that was both the kitchen and living room. All other rooms in the house were where the family slept. Here, by the fire, was where they lived, and here, too, was found the wooden table and chairs. Outside family mealtimes, the table was pushed to the window, but it now occupied centre stage. There were wooden settles on either side of the fire, and they could be set at an angle to make the best of the fire's heat. On the far wall, away from the front door, was a storage cupboard and dresser that held the more treasured possessions. Displayed on its shelf was the crockery that was used only on 'high days' or times of celebration; even with his wife gone, Henry had his own ideas about housekeeping. The room was as clean and tidy as men living together could make it, but the extra touch of a woman's hand was missing. Henry tried his best, and Elizabeth tried to help, but James was always slovenly in his habits.

The room was filled with as much happiness as could be mustered. James was laying the table with plates, bowls and spoons. Henry sat on the settle with Elizabeth, who had wanted to be close. Henry was the first to speak.

'We will have to get to the table for our dinner soon, my little love.'

'Oh... I'm happy here for a little bit longer.'

'How has work been for you? Are you as happy as your Dad would hope?'

'Yes, I am, sort of... the ladies are kind to me and help me when I do things wrong, Daddy...but'.

'But what, my precious?'

Elizabeth fell silent. The protection given to her by the cuddles from her dad had been interrupted by her moment of reflection.

Elizabeth remained still. It was not so much working in the mine that troubled her. It was more she hadn't come to terms with the unease in her head that gnawed and intruded at times when she should have been content. It would send shivers through her, and jolt her out of the joy of being young. How could she put her thoughts into words? It was a hard question her dad had asked, and it was all because of her unguarded word...'but.'

'Well, I am sometimes sad Daddy... I am sometimes.'

Henry held Elizabeth in his arms, her head resting on his shoulder, her soft brown hair spilling across him. His eyes were fixed on the flames, half focused, half shut not really wanting to find out more... not today at least.

Henry suppressed a cough welling in his chest, willing the urge to do so to subside, to leave them this moment of love and tenderness, unblemished by the realities of life and its living... its dying. His cough, he knew, was the harbinger of the fate so many before him had faced. How could he leave the family when he was needed so much?

He clung to his daughter with the strength he clung to life. She was now his purpose, an unspoken promise to Catherine that her children would be kindly cared for; as would be the grandchildren, those already arrived, and those who were yet to come.

A minute or two passed. Nothing was needed to be said unless Elizabeth needed to say it. It was then that her spoken, 'but', she had let slip, again spurred her on. It rummaged amongst the deep-rooted thoughts she had left unspoken... until now.

'Do you think he will come back, Daddy?'

Henry knew the question all too well; after all, it was very often his own.

Yes, Henry already knew the question, he'd just not wanted it to be asked, for fear the answer would fall like a tossed coin, 'heads' for Yes, 'tails' for No.' He had many times spun the coin in his head but had caught it before it fell and gripped it tight in his fist, its omen locked from sight.

For the sake of his Elizabeth, he tossed and caught the coin again, but this time he opened his hand to reveal it... it was *'heads'*.

'Of course he'll come back. You know he loved you as much as I do, don't you'?

'I know he did, Daddy.'

'Well then, something must have happened that stopped him saying goodbye.'

'Something bad?'

'Yes, something bad, but not so bad that he won't, one morning, come through that door, as if he'd been to London to see the King.'

Elizabeth turned her head and looked up to meet his eyes, wanting to believe. And believe she did, but joked none-the-less,

'London for the day! How silly. You're a silly Daddy.' They both laughed.

As if in confirmation, there was an urgent knock at that same door. James got up from the table,

'Now who can that be out in this weather...?

Christiana! Come in. Why on earth are you out on such a night? You look frozen.'

Henry rose from his place by the fire and greeted his guest. His embrace of his neighbour was warm and welcoming, but he was surprised to find Christiana was cold and wet, and too exhausted to engage in the warmth of the greeting. She tried to speak, but the effort was too much.

Her head fell forward on Henry's shoulder, but at last, she felt safe...*just a minute or two*, she thought, *and I will be right.*

'Come sit here by the fire... here, with Lizzy.'

Henry took Christiana's hand and noticed its rigid fingers and swollen, arthritic joints, but most of all he felt it's coldness. He wanted to hold her close, to give her some of his warmth he had gained from the fire and some warmth from his heart; for whose heart would not have gone out to her? Instead, he spoke to Elizabeth.

'Lizzy, get your mother's shawl, it's in the dresser ... and a towel.' He sat Christiana gently on the settle, her head rested on the side panel; it protected her from the fire's fiercest heat. She tried to thank Henry, but her breath was short, the words wouldn't form.

'Stay quiet Christiana, there's time enough to talk,' said Henry. 'First, we'll get you warm and fed.'

She wanted to protest that she shouldn't eat, as food was hard to come by for everyone, and such kindness should be reserved for those with a greater need.

Henry knew differently. Christiana was too cold, too fragile, too near to that last breath he had seen his wife take, his beloved Catherine. He held Christiana's hands in order to anchor her to this world, to hold her firm this side of the grave's edge and resist Death's beguiling whisper...

This life's not all there is. Come stay awhile with me... come stay.'

Henry had been sure he had heard Death's voice when he last looked into the eyes of his wife. Her gaze had not spoken of goodbye, but of resignation. Her story had been told, and it was enough.

'No...!' cried Henry, disturbing the quiet surrounding them. He had begun to say, before stopping himself,

'No, *this must not happen again*,' but he came to his senses and focused on the crisis at hand. He started over.

'No... you must stay... and you will share our food.'

Henry removed her soaken shawl. She was wet beneath. There were no adult women present to remove her woollen top, so he turned to Elizabeth, who was standing next to him holding her mother's shawl.

'Lizzy, I need you to help Christiana get her woollen off. We can then wrap her in the shawl.' Turning to Christiana, he said,

'We'll soon have you warm and dry.'

Lizzy pulled at Christiana's top, attempting to draw it over her head, but Christiana was unable to move away from the back of the settle. For Elizabeth to accomplish her task, Henry took Christiana in his arms and held her weight; adjusting his gaze to preserve Christiana's modesty.

'Pass me the shawl, Lizzie...' He wrapped Christiana tight, the long shawl doubly encircling her. He laid her back on the settle.

The shawl, earthen brown, course spun and lanolin rich, brought a flood of memories back to Henry. It was the same shawl that had wrapped his children in a tight embrace, when as babes they suckled their mother's breast. Catherine would stand at the doorstep wearing it, waiting on his return, as did other mothers waiting for their men. They would gossip, even as the older children tugged at their mother's shawl to gain attention. The street would be abuzz, with the anticipating of the arrival of the men off shift. On arrival, he would lift a child on his shoulders, it being as grubby as he. The kisses he gave, the smiles he would get.

The shawl had remained hidden for so many years. It now had a renewed purpose, restored to its place at the centre of the home.

Elizabeth had brought a towel and had begun to dry Christiana's hair, and she continued to administer to Christiana, a pillow for her head, the removal of her shoes. She wiped her feet dry and helped her put on dry stockings she had brought from her own drawer; they fitted, as Christiana stood no taller than Elizabeth. Henry brought a bowl of the stew, and she accepted it, all thoughts of her being unworthy of this kindness dispelled by the genuine warmth of the welcome she had received. The family drew chairs to the fire and sat around it to eat their meal, to eat it with Christiana. In time, after the bowls had been collected by Elizabeth, and Christiana had colour back to her face, Henry asked,

'Christiana, what brings you out on such a dreadful night? You should be tucked up warm with your girls.'

She hesitated to answer, but her courage grew...

'It's our Maggie, Henry.'

'Yes... Is she still as unhappy... what with Almond going missing?'

'She is... it has been two months since he left...' Christiana hesitated... 'and now I am sure Maggie is pregnant.'

'And what is this of our concern?'

'She tells me it is Almond who is the father, Henry... Of course, it must be Almond, Henry.'

Henry could not disagree.

***

Later that night, father and son talked of their problems.

'What shall we do Dad?' asked James

'We will have to find a way, son. They're family now.'

'Almond! What was he thinking of, running off and leaving us with his problems?'

'It's nothing new, lad, and there's many a wedding has been brought about by a dalliance.'

'But there's no bloody groom to be wed and now there's no work for us able-bodied to feed the babe. That mountain of copper in Wales will keep our mines uncompetitive.'

Henry jumped at the chance to take some of the blame from his youngest son.

'Even if Almond were here, there's trouble in store. Christiana and her girls will be laid off soon enough and their Jack is a lot older than I am. He'll not work for long.'

'He can hardly lift a shovel, but I'm told he still gets the odd job above ground. It's all he's good for, what with his chest as bad as it is... I can't think how they survived this long.' James sat mulling over the problem before continuing,

'It's difficult to see a way to help... unless, that is, we take them in?'

'I was thinking the same thing myself, James. Now with Jack only working the odd day, you could take on nights if you wanted to. Then, we could have enough room here. This house has held more people in the past, when Charles, Sarah and their children lived with us. We coped then, and we could do it again.'

Christiana slept on the settle. The shawl had changed its purpose and it had become her blanket. Elizabeth sat close by. She assumed her duty was to care for Christiana. Caring would always be in her nature. Henry looked at them both, and warmth flowed over him, not from the flames of the fire, but from the thought Elizabeth could develop a fondness for Christiana and come to treat her as she would her mother; a relationship he knew Elizabeth longed for. Could it now be possible?

Henry continued, with a word of caution for James.

'We can take them in, but our charity might be seen in the village as something else. Would that matter to you?'

'I don't think it will matter to anyone, except for those hymn singing followers of Jesus, and you don't see many of them in the pub, or down the pit. Why would it worry us?'

'It would matter to Christiana. I still can't see how it would work. She wouldn't agree to it.'

'But what would be left for them to do, Dad?'

'What, indeed! We shall let her sleep, and tomorrow we shall talk it through.'

'Her girls are back in Beacon. She will want to get back to them.'

'She will, James, but she is not going back out on a night like this. She'll stay here. Her children are safe, for the time being, as will be our grandchild.'

As the warmth of the room drove the chill from Christiana's body, her dreams had resolved themselves from panic-ridden chases to a state of calm, then oblivion, as exhaustion overwhelmed her.

***

It was several hours later when Christiana awoke. She was, for a moment, content. She knew her message had been delivered and her problems had been shared, but, almost immediately, the unfamiliarity of her surroundings tugged her back into the panic of the afternoon before. The sequence of events played out in her head and she remembered she was in the home of the Rowe family. Her panic eased, and she was once more content. Next to her was Elizabeth, asleep on a mattress comprising of blankets and some straw that had been gathered in the Autumn for use in the chicken coop. Dawn was two hours away, but father and son were already awake and heating porridge on the resurrected fire.

'Christiana, you are awake.' Said Henry.

Christiana turned to Henry and replied,

'Yes, I'm awake, and grateful for your help, Henry.' Henry spoke quietly,

'We aren't able to stay with you, as we are both on 'day shift' and we'll be off to the mine soon. 'Elizabeth will stay at home so she can go back with you to Beacon. She can come on to the mine later. I will explain to the gaffer what's happening.'

'Henry, I didn't mean to stay the night. I meant to get back home.'

'You were going nowhere on a night the like of which we've just had. You were in no condition to do so. You had to stay. Tongues may wag, but they will not be the tongues of those we care about.'

'My friends and my chapel congregation will support me, but I will not be able to tell the truth, not yet.'

'We'll be able to in time. I will come around to your place tonight, with James, and we will talk about what can be done about Maggie and Almond. You know we will try to do what's best. We are family now, and we must take responsibility. For the moment, come sit at the table and join us in some breakfast.'

***

James and Henry made their way to Christiana's house at the end of their day's work. Henry knocked on the door, and Christiana was there to open it, expecting them to call.

She let them in. Maggie brewed tea, whilst the others sat at the table. Henry opened the conversation.

'Elizabeth told me you were much better this morning, Christiana, and that she enjoyed your walk back to Beacon. You made quite an impression on her, you did. It was "Christiana said this, Christiana said that".'

'She's a lovely girl, your Elizabeth. She's got a kind heart, just like her mother had, and held my hand all the way.' She continued,

'I'm sorry for being such a burden last night. It's just I didn't know what to do. Today, things are clearer in my head, and I am sure we will find a way. In the end, it's just one more mouth to feed. There've been harder times.'

'Be that as it may, Christiana, you know we are here to speak about what we can do together to support Maggie and the baby. With Almond gone, we don't know where, we feel we need to take on the responsibility on his behalf.'

Maggie had sat quietly in the corner of the room as her mother and the Rowes talked about her future. She felt ashamed that she and Almond had brought about the family crisis now unfolding. If only Almond had not gone, all would be well. She suddenly broke her silence.

'Where has he gone? Does anyone know?'

James, spoke up.

'All we can think is that he was press-ganged. He was seen to leave the pub. Soon after, three strangers left behind him. We have been asking at the dock in Padstow, and there was a coastal frigate that left on the following morning's tide.'

'But that can't be,' protested Christiana, the Navy has stopped doing that to our men.'

'Not at all, it seems. There were a couple of lads in Padstow who also went missing over Christmas.'

'Does that mean Almond isn't coming back?' asked Maggie.

'It means that if he does come back it will be at His Majesties pleasure. Depending on where his ship sails it could be a year or two before he sets foot again on these shores.'

Maggie raised her shawl to her face and sobbed. She grieved for her lost love and her lost innocence. The thought of bearing and bringing up a child on her own, with no husband, terrified her. She had seen the destitution of the young women in the village when their husbands had died in the mines and were left with young children. The charitable workhouse could soon be her only recourse and the fate of her child would be unknown.

Henry spoke. It was time to set out the course of action to take if Almond remained lost to them.

'We have a suggestion to make. For now, Christiana, you and the girls should stay here. The work that comes your way from the mine may still be sufficient to make ends meet and there may be some other work in the village. For the moment, we all have work and Elizabeth is of an age where she can take on more if it comes to it. Between us, we can maintain two separate households, but if work dries up, we might need to become one family under one roof.'

Christiana was having none of it.

'We couldn't live in one house, Henry. We are not very closely related, and every grown-up member of it is unmarried. The talk in the village would be too much to bear.'

'But what about when the child comes along, are you going to let the shame lie with Maggie, or are you thinking to claim the infant as your own? Please excuse me when I say you are a little too old for people to believe that. Either way, shame will visit you.' Christiana remained silent. Henry continued,

'As soon as it becomes clear to one and all that Maggie is expecting, why not let our two families be seen to share the responsibility of the child? In any case, perhaps Almond will return in the meantime and the situation will resolve itself.'

'Let's pray for that. The thought of a child of my daughters with no father to claim it as his own fills me with dread. As for living under the same roof, well, that cannot be. The sight of a widow and widower, a young man and a pregnant girl living in the same house, would set the tongues wagging. I couldn't face the whisperings at my chapel. No, I cannot allow it.'

The finality of Christiana's words struck home. Henry knew to insist on an agreement that covered all eventualities would set Christiana against the whole proposal.

'So be it, Christiana. Our homes will remain separate, but we will not see you or the children starve, nor will we see you thrown out of this home to be dependent on the workhouse. We will pool our resources. I know that the Rowes will be the major contributors, but as far as we are concerned, you are family now. The child will be our flesh and blood after all.'

Christiana looked at Henry as he stood waiting for her reply. She had known him from childhood, and they were related through his wife, who was her second cousin; their maiden names had both been 'Berryman'. Was this, in part, why he was determined to ensure her family's wellbeing? No, she knew there was more to him than that. He was a good man, known for his devotion to his immediate family, a man who had provided for them, emotionally and financially. He was, for his sins, no chapel goer, as he had left the pleas for God's help in the prayerful hands of his wife, but neither did he piss his wages against the pub wall. *Yes, a good man*, she thought. Christiana sat quietly for a moment, and then said,

'Because of my responsibility to my family, it's a proposal I cannot refuse. I thank you for it, and I accept.'

Maggie sat wrapped in her shawl, silently listening to her mother, Mister Rowe and the uncomfortably awkward James, discussing her welfare as if she were not there. Her guilt consumed her. There was no joy in her heart that she was to be a mother. She had longed for Almond's company. The escape from the drudgery of life in a mining village, that his passion for her had provided, had been a blessing, but she accepted her selfish behaviour was the reason for her family's straitened circumstances. Her dark thoughts blocked out the continuing discussion going on around her of the plans for the future, how best to cope. Why should she believe there was happiness to be had when her family were to suffer? The brief moment of bliss with Almond was a delusion; the misery of their existence in Camborne was the reality. The canker growing inside her was evidence of that. And soon it would be plain to see, her belly fattened by the growth of the Devil's spawn.

Selwyn Berryman-Morgan

8

Sea Mist

The sea was hushed. A cloak of mist bore down, smothering the tide's attempt to wash away the spring's storm cast weed and the carelessly discarded waste from the mines. The vaporous damp seeped into her clothes right through to her skin, then to her bone and into her mind. It dampened her hope, it extinguished her spirit. Maggie's despair had penetrated deep, and had disturbed the slumber of the child inside her. There was no comfort for it in its mother's nurturing embrace, as she had given up any care of it, and she grieved only for her loss and her abandonment. She thought of her lover?

Standing at the cliff's edge, she murmured his name and longed for him.

'Almond, my dearest love, where are you? Where are you?'

The mist cleared for a moment and she gazed at the rocks below her. The sandstone of the cliff was slow to erode, and was a bastion against the sea; it was not the slate or mudstone often to be found on these shores, that would quickly crumble and bear witness to the passage of time. For Maggie's short lifetime, the sea and shore had been in timeless conflict, the waves punch drunk, whilst the cliff stood firm. To her young eyes, the coastline was constant, ever-present, a place to be, a place to trust... a place to stay? It beckoned her with thoughts of summers past. How she'd run with her sisters to the cliff edge... bar one step. They laughed in the face of the elements, the sun, the wind and rain; and possible destruction, should they venture too far. The danger of their game, the confrontation of risk, and their triumph over it, affirmed the blessing that was life. If only she could relive those days? If only she could go back to laugh and run free again?

Her despair returned with a tempest's roar, to suck away her happy, childhood memories, like the kindling's smoke from a chimney stack. The chill she felt in her stomach gave witness to the fact she was not prepared to nourish the child within. She made her decision. It must be cast aside before it had the chance to trap her in its spell of helpless dependence. Dependence on the succour she would have to provide. The child had invaded her, she had not wanted it. Why should this have happened? It was only for a brief moment she had sought joy in the exploration of flesh. Her sin of wanting happiness had spawned a burgeoning baby, a bloated belly, a bastard.

She spoke to heaven as if it awaited her answer.

'It won't live, if I don't.'

Just a small step, she thought... then, as if to reinforce the thought, she spoke it...

'Just one small step.'

She shifted her weight over the toes of her shoes. Her topple forward, at first imperceptible, had begun. Gravity tugged at her shawl, pulling it away from her, and gravity would soon have her totally in its grasp. There would be no longer a need for decisions to be made, no shame to be borne, no child to carry as a burden of guilt.

Yet, the horizon remained in view? There was not as she expected, the blur of a tumbled world, a merged vision of sea and sky and rock, and the last imprinted vision of a released soul. Her fall had been restrained. Amongst the confusion of thoughts that rang in her head, a voice intruded.

'Maggie, is that you?'

He had seen her teetering at the edge and had moved quickly to place a gentle hand on her shoulder. The shoulder of the young woman he had been seeking.

His voice was not a shout. It didn't compete with her thoughts or demand her attention; but yet, it soothed. Her head turned. She hadn't meant to turn her head. As she did so, her forward motion resumed and accelerated. She was falling over the edge... *as it is meant to be*, she thought. He held her wrist with his free hand. Maggie lurched outwards, but remained anchored to the cliff edge by the intruder's hold upon her. She spun around, her free arm flying out over the void, but he pulled her back and held her safe.

'Maggie, what are you doing child? Come hold on to me.'

For Maggie, the tug back into his strong embrace was a tug back to life. Maggie clung tight; the morbid spell of her suicide pact with her demons had been broken.

Somehow, the reassurance she felt from his embrace seemed as natural as if it were Almond holding her close. Was it Almond? Maggie looked up to see James' face looking down at her. It was a face full of concern for her. It was the caring expression Almond would have had for her, given time, and his acceptance of his responsibility. But here was his brother offering support? For the first time, she was glad James was there. In that moment, too, James realised Maggie was no longer a child, but was a young woman who needed help... his help. Her embrace stirred emotions in him he had fought to contain.

'Your mother told me where to find you. Come, let me take you home.'

Their first step away from the cliff edge was their first step in their life of love and companionship.

Selwyn Berryman-Morgan

9

Pastures Green?

Imported tin and copper had depressed the price of Cornish ore, and this was making work difficult to find in Camborne, even for the youngest and fittest of skilled miners.

James was still in work, but Henry had been laid off, his ability to hew and shift large amounts of rock had been compromised by his failing health. Elizabeth still found work, being willing and eager to take on all that was asked of her. She was quick to learn, and she was able to move between all the tasks required at the mine's surface. Her physical strength ensured few ground level tasks were beyond her.

'I'll do that Gov.' was often her willing response to requests for volunteers for the most onerous tasks. Her enthusiasm would often be answered by,

'On you go lass, and when you've finished come back to see me. I'll find something else for you to do.'

For Christiana, Maggie and Imogene, work had been intermittent. Maggie had hidden her pregnancy from the prying eyes of neighbours and she didn't let it affect her ability to work; nor should it. Pregnancy was a condition that was almost continual for many women. Consecutive pregnancies were commonplace. The curse of multiple pregnancies would often only terminate with the death or serious injury of a husband or, perhaps, the loss of fecundity of a wife due to complications from a previous birth. When carrying a child, the foetus would run the same risks as the mother and the physical stress of the continued workload would be borne by them both.

The tipping point for the family came when Jack developed pneumonia and died within the week. Pneumonia was often a death sentence, as a miner's immune system was depressed by exposure over the years to radioactive radon gas found in the granite rock they hew. Aged fifty; he was buried alongside his wife, having outlived many of his contemporaries.

***

James strode into the house, and before his father could speak, he said,

'I've been thinking, Dad. We have no choice. We have to act on the invitation sent to us by Charles to move to the South Wales Ironworks. There's work there and we would be near to him and the support his family would offer.

'What's sure, James, is that there is not enough work here for us all.'

'I imagine Christiana and her girls will soon get thrown out of their house. Their position is all but lost now Jack has gone... and our position has become harder as you are in no fit state to go back into the mine. You know that Dad.'

Henry was reluctant to concede what he knew to be true, but said,

'How can we all move as a family unit? I don't see a way to do that? And when we get there how can we be sure that work is as available as Charles says it is?'

James knew Henry was losing hope, as his health and self-confidence seeped away; along with the strength in his limbs. His lack of breath was now debilitating. The long journey to the South Wales iron foundries might be too much for him to maintain a positive spirit for those who trusted in him. It may now be beyond him, and James knew it.

The offer of help to obtain work and lodgings had been sent from Henry's eldest son, Charles. He was sure the boom in the iron industry would continue. But Henry knew it didn't mean they would be sure to get work. In the time took to plan the journey and travel to South Wales, employment in the ironworks could dry up. He could be leading his family, and Christiana and her girls, from frying pan to fire. Henry was broken. The spectre of his life ending at a time of his family's greatest need haunted him. What had it all been about, the struggle they had all been through to survive? His toil in the mines had kept the people he loved safe; his wife, for whom he still longed, and his beautiful, brave, children; including the three they had lost, two stillborn, and one to cholera. Now, all his effort and devotion had come to nothing.

James spoke.

'There's further cause for hope that a move to Merthyr will turn out well.'

Henry broke free from his morbid thoughts and made an effort to show some enthusiasm for the plan James was proposing. '

'And what might that be, son?'

'Charles tells me that Trevithick now works at the foundries, he must have seen the way things are here in the mines, I suppose, and moved on. Anyway, he has asked to know if I decide to leave and join with Charles. I can only think he has work for me.'

'What about me? What am I to do?

'There are no pits for miners to work in, but I'm told coal is hewn from the sides of the valley. We have to follow the work, Dad.'

'You have your metalworking skills, James, and those Trevithick will want, but there are miners aplenty to do the grafting they need.'

'The foundries are growing by the day, and I hear that the iron ore seams come to the surface in the sides of the valleys, too, as well as the coal. There's plenty of work, and some of it will suit you. They'll have a need for labour, and it has to be easier than walking a mile underground to break the granite only to haul it a mile back and half a mile out. Then there are the foundries to work in, too.'

'An easier day's work would certainly help with my chest the way it is,' said Henry, but he couldn't help himself returning to his pessimism

'Of course, I would need to stop wheezing when I asked the gaffer for a job to do.' Henry hadn't meant to joke but they both saw the funny side of it, and they laughed together until Henry had a fit of coughing.

James knew his father's working days were numbered, but to do nothing in the face of their downturn in fortune was to commit them all to being destitute.

James looked at his father, whose head rested on the side of the settle. There was a vacant look in his eyes where once a fire of determination had roared. It was then James knew the family leadership that had always been provided by his father had been passed over to him; the final decision would need to be his.

'Father, I am resolved that we make the journey to Wales. The journey will be hard for us all, especially you, as the dust on your chest will make walking difficult. Maggie will find it hard, too. She is heavily pregnant, but to do nothing will condemn us all to poverty.'

'And how will you swing that with the Harris's'

'So that we may travel as a family unit, I have decided that I will marry Maggie.'

'Marry Maggie!'

Think Dad. If I do, then, Christiana will have no objections in joining us. She would be within her rights to live in the home of her 'in-law's'. Her chapel and its congregation would bless the arrangement... and they can go to hell if they don't.'

Henry weighed the implication of James' proposal...

'Has Maggie agreed to this?'

'She's an intelligent girl, and she will see the sense in it.' James had not spoken about what happened at the cliff edge. He continued,

'Believe me, Dad, she is desperate at the moment and she can't see any future for her and her child. It is our duty to take responsibility. I'm twenty-four and it is time I took a wife. Maggie is a good girl, from a good family. We are related, but not so close we couldn't wed. Together, working in Wales, the family has a future. There is no longer a life for us here.'

Henry had seen James' attitude to Maggie change, but he was still surprised at his son's announcement, and he was cautious for his son's sake.

'Have you spoken to her about how she feels about you... about Almond?'

'Not yet Dad, but I feel I need to look out for her.

'But what of Almond, what will he think? Have you thought about what he might think?'

'Almond is not here to tell us what he thinks, so we have to think for him.'

Henry sat quietly, and James let him be. For now, he had said enough. Minutes passed. Then Henry stirred and sat upright. He, too, had decided.

'So be it son. Make it happen and I will be at your side.'

Henry had finally been relieved of his responsibility as head of the family, and it would soon have four new members, with another on the way. Henry was happy James had lifted from him the worry he had carried alone. His role had been passed on to the next generation. Henry was both relieved, that his constant burden had come to an end, and saddened that the passage of time had rendered him incapable of shouldering it. Now, *he* was the burden. His eyes dimmed. The remnant glimmer of light that shone from them was the fire's glow reflected by a tear.

James stood by the same fire, and it gave him the energy to gather his thoughts.

***

James called out as he opened the door and peered into the front room. He had knocked but there had been no answer.

'Christiana... Maggie... are you home? I've brought some potatoes and a piece of mutton for you.'

Maggie was upstairs folding the linen. She heard him. *What did he want?* Should she answer? Did she want to answer? She feigned a pleasant response, when, truly, she wanted to be left to her shame. She had again been passed over for work, the gaffer glancing at her belly. He hadn't knowingly winked at her, but he may as well have.

'Come in James, you're back early from your shift.'

She continued, without waiting for his response, afraid of what he was to say.

'There was no work for me today, or for mum. She's still at the mine, hoping to be given something to do. I've been left with the chores.'

He had not spoken to her about their meeting at the cliff edge, but she knew their relationship had changed. He was still awkward with her, and she with him, but there was no denying they were close. They had shared the depths of her despair and he had not told of it.

'I knew you weren't in work, that's why I came around. Although, I had thought your mum would be here, too.'

James had entered a house that was becoming familiar to him. He had spent much time there in recent weeks, as he juggled with their joint incomes. Maggie appeared at the foot of the stairs. He thought she looked pleased to see him, a response he had noticed more often as time went by. But was he imagining that? He had decided to be more forward in his approach to her and now was the time to be courageous. Even so, he wavered in speaking directly about his intentions; but he sorely wanted the conversation to be different this time. He wanted it to be intimate; it would need courage in bucket-loads.

'Maggie, you look even more beautiful when you are doing the chores.' Maggie was taken off guard.

'So I've been told,' replied Maggie, her voice tinged with a coolness she hoped James would understand, but then she immediately regretted saying it. James had never asked about her and Almond, and she had avoided mentioning him in his presence, and yet her reply had hinted at the relationship. Now it was as if she had been disrespectful twice over, James having taken responsibility for her and her family.

James sensed Maggie's discomfort and guessed at the reason. Their relationship, if it was to grow, would need to overcome the legacy left by his brother's leaving and his fathering of Maggie's child. Maggie was trying to move on, he knew that, and now was the time to get her agreement about what was best to do.

'Maggie, we need to talk and now is a good time, before your mum gets back.' He launched into what he had to say without waiting for Maggie's response; he didn't want to be diverted from his task.

'Dad's plan to support the two families is coming apart.' He continued by stating what she already knew, as if she were a child to be told.

'You know work at the mine has slackened off and there is precious little at the other mines. Work has always come and gone as old mines close and new seams are found.'

'Yes, I know all this James. I live with it every day.' James ploughed on. He had prepared his speech and he wasn't going to be put off.

'But all the tin and copper coming in from elsewhere is making ours less profitable.' James sensed he was avoiding the point of the conversation and he could tell she was losing patience. He was still not quite ready to grasp the nettle, and so he shifted the blame for him having to speak about the obvious.

'Anyway, that was according to the gaffer today.'

'We know all this James.' Maggie repeated. 'There must be something else that you want to talk to me about?'

'Yes, of course, there is....'

Maggie moved to him and held him at the waist so she could look directly at him. She needed to know what had really brought him here, and why he was so concerned.

James put his arm around her shoulders and drew her to him. Maggie didn't resist. She was in need of any comfort he could provide her. James spoke quietly, whilst continuing to hold her close.

'Well... the gaffer... he laid off another six miners at the end of our shift, and one of them was Dad. He's laid off, permanently. They won't risk him at the mine.'

Maggie remained silent. She needed to weigh the implications of the news. Her head was full of all sorts of worry, the loss of Almond, the lack of work, the baby, and now the loss of 'family' income. James continued,

'There's not much work to do for a man of his age, even if he were fit.'

Maggie had her own news to tell, and it was not good.

'Mum was told yesterday that she was only wanted two days next week, and Imogene has worked less hours this week. We have seen it coming.' She paused before continuing.

'And James... I was going to tell you. I wanted to work less on the hard jobs... for the baby's sake. That would mean less money for us as well. But I won't do that now, not if I can help it.'

'There's no need for that.' He drew her closer. 'I am happy the babe is dearer to you than it was.'

'I am resigned, James, and as each day passes, well... you know.'

'Of course, and you should take lighter work, if you can get it. You've done your bit Maggie, and you've hidden your pregnancy from the "gossips" in the street, but you won't be able to do so for much longer. It is not just the baby, the problems affect us all and we need to deal with it together, as one family.'

It was as then Maggie realised their relationship was at a crossroads. She asked,

'So, what do you and your dad think we should do?'

'We, Dad and me, agree we will have to move to find work.'

'Would we come with you?'

'Yes, if you all agree.'

'But you know my mother wouldn't agree to move in with a family who were not related.'

James couldn't help himself but divulge his intention. Hesitantly, he asked,

'But what if you and I were married...? Your mother could have no objection then.'

Maggie was surprised by the suggestion and stepped from James' embrace.

'Married to you, James? But I bear Almond's child?'

'If you don't marry me, and if Almond doesn't return, the child will be yours alone.'

Maggie didn't want to face the prospect of Almond not returning, and her heart ached. She resisted accepting the reality with which she was confronted.

'But Almond will return.... won't he?'

James spoke with a confidence he was now becoming accustomed to. His assumed role as head of the joint household stripped away his self-conscious awkwardness. It allowed him to speak the truth about their predicament and about his personal feelings.

'It has been six months since he left, and we have had no word of him. If, as we suspect, the Navy have him, then it may be years until he returns. We have to deal with you and your child's needs without him, but on his behalf. I need you to be mature beyond your years and think about my proposal. You must know my feelings for you have grown, not just because of our shared responsibility, but because... because, Maggie, you have touched my heart.'

'James, you are a lovely, kind man, but I cannot truthfully say I love you. When Almond returns, what then? The die will be cast and we both could end up hating you.'

'It is a chance we must take for the sake of the family. Our present needs outweigh what is yet to come. Almond's future has already been

71

harmed and his life will have changed forever. It may never again involve us. Why not let you and me build a good life away from the bad that now surrounds us. Love sometimes takes the longer road.'

Maggie moved closer and once again wrapped her arms around his waist, laying her head on his chest. James was a man she could trust and with whom she felt comfortable, and yes, perhaps, there were the beginnings of a love for him. It was not the passion she felt for Almond, she doubted it could ever be, but she was reassured in his presence. Was that not a part of being in love, maybe the greater part? She needed time to think.

'James, we will need to speak to my mother about this, I need her guidance as well as yours. I cannot agree now.'

'I will stay until she arrives. Come sit, we can talk more, and I will make some tea... Yes, I have brought some tea as a treat. We should get at least a dozen cups out of it.'

***

'So, you are willing to enter into marriage with James, Maggie?'

'I believe I am, mother.'

'I've no doubt you'll be a caring husband James, but will you both be happy?' she asked bluntly, and continued,

'Will you, Maggie, be able to live without the father of your baby in your life?

Maggie, gained strength from James being at her side. Her resolve had hardened beyond what James had dreamt was possible.

'If we marry, then the child will be James'. If it's a boy, he, too will be called James. If Almond returns, he will hear the truth we wish to tell him. You see how my mind is made up...? And you mother? What are your feelings about our families joining and moving to Wales?

Christiana remained silent for a moment, and then she said,'

'I am at a loss to see another way.' Then she continued.

'Henry and James are men who I respect. They are good men and will do us no harm. My daughters will have a guiding hand and support from them, as much as they do from me. That's something I would welcome. It hasn't been easy bringing you girls up alone.'

'But what about your life here.' Asked Maggie.

'I shall miss my friends and the chapel, but no doubt there'll be chapels in Wales, and along with them, new friends.' Maggie had something to say about that.

'I'll not miss the chapel's gossip or their sanctimonious ways. Good riddance, I say.'

'You shouldn't speak about them in that way. They have shown us kindnesses over the years since your father passed. I couldn't have survived without the chapel and the help it gave.'

'Well, if there is a God, perhaps he'll smile on us now.'

'There is, Maggie, and he'll not forget us in our time of need.' James spoke up.

'So, we are agreed Christiana.... mother?'

'I agree, James... You'll forgive me. It will seem strange for me to say 'son' when I have spent my life with only daughters to look after. I will, in time... I've not done too bad a job have I, Maggie?'

'No mother, you have been all we could have wished for. And now your children...' Maggie paused, and ran her hand over the bulge in her abdomen. She continued, 'and grandchildren... are set to make a life for themselves.'

Maggie had regained the calm self-belief she had shown before her world had been turned upside down. Christiana looked from her daughter to her prospective son-in-law and said,

'Then, my son, show us the way.'

Selwyn Berryman-Morgan

10

Towards the Flame

James was true to his word. He spoke to his new family.

'The boat carrying ore to Swansea will leave from Portreath on Wednesday's high tide. That will be at five o'clock in the morning. We know no one there who can put us all up, so we have no choice other than to get there overnight. Arnold will take us in his cart. He needs to be at the market the following morning. He wouldn't take any money for it, but asked that we help load his cart. He worked with Jack, years ago, and he said it was his way of saying 'thank you' for his kindness.'

'Oh, that's good, James. We can take more with us on a cart, if we don't have to pay.'

'We can, Elizabeth, but we might not be able to find anyone to cart us to where Charles lives when we get to the other side. It's thirty miles from Swansea. We may have to walk, so we must have only our essential possessions packed for such a journey. We'll have to try to sell the rest'

'I'll help you pack Elizabeth, said Christiana. We can look at the clothes we have and take the best. We are the same size, so we'll have lots of choice. It will fun to share, and soon we will make more.

'Thank you, Christiana. I'd like to do that. I'll try to take my sewing box'

The young girls huddled together. Their heads were filled with the excitement of the new adventure, and the fear of the unknown. There were times when their loss of home, close relations and friends dampened their spirits, but they knew there was no alternative. It was in their power to make the best of it, and their optimism, often a companion of youth, sustained them.

At the table, James and Henry continued the planning of the journey

'There are only two days before we go James. Have we thought of everything?'

'I have sent word we are coming, but as yet I haven't heard from Charles.'

'We still have to go.'

'We do, Dad. We can't wait for a reply. Maggie is too far gone for us to lose time. At least we are leaving now, in the summer months. I would hate to do this in the winter. It would be too hard a journey for us once the cold rains set in.'

'For sure it would, and it will still be hard if we can't cart our stuff on the other side of the channel.'

'It's our tools that will be the weight. We will have to take them. We have no choice. I know tools aren't supplied by the Iron Masters and we won't have the money to buy more.'

'But at least we will have a roof over our head.'

'If Charles is right in what he says, there should be a miner's cottage waiting, digging for coal would be much easier than the granite, and much easier on your chest, Dad.'

'It is going to bloody well have to be, what with the state of my lungs.'

***

Arnold's cart had been loaded with ore by eight in the evening. The newly amalgamated family, along with their possessions, filled less than the remaining third of it. The essentials for life in their new home town, was all that was to be taken: tools, pots, pans, two chairs and spare boots. Clothing was to be carried in bags they could carry on their backs. Elizabeth hid her mother's locket in her stockings, stuffed in the bottom of her bag. Except for her mother's shawl, it was the only personal memento of her life in Camborne, and it would remain with her for the rest of her life.

Tram rails took ore and coal to and from the northern Cornish ports, but there was still some horse and ox-cart traffic. Arnold was making a living distributing coal as he travelled from Portreath, and, sometimes, he still had a small load of ore to take there

'It's time we set off,' Arnold announced. 'We've five miles to cover by midnight. The boat will have docked and unloaded its coal, and we need to be on time to help the boatman load my ore. No doubt, it'll pay for your passage over, though a shilling for the boatman's kindness wouldn't go amiss.'

The family took their place in the back of the cart, amongst the remnants of the coal from his last trip to the coast. The rest of the cart was full of copper ore; it was too small a load to pay for a tram to transport it. Arnold was to drive his ox and cart along a track used for over a century to transport ore for shipment over to Swansea. There, the locally dug coal powered the furnaces to smelt the ore. The trade of coal and metal ores sustained both of the regional economies.

Elizabeth looked back to the village she had grown up in, the memories of times when, even during the hardships, they found moments of happiness. Her tears were genuine and heartfelt, her life not yet tainted by the weight of the demands of the mine and its owners. Maggie sat across from her, holding her hand and also thinking of the past. She was leaving behind a bitter-sweet memory, the love she had for Almond. She looked back in vain hope that, as if by a miracle, he would at the last moment appear, smiling his smile and telling his tales of adventure. She imagined he would claim her, and their child, as his own... She shook her head and tried to dismiss the thought, as she and James were now 'man and wife'.

Elizabeth was the first to speak and break the spell in which the village and its memories held them.

'We will be alright won't we, Maggie.' Maggie was slow to respond, her thoughts still ensnared by the past, its joys and its misery. She turned to meet Elizabeth's gaze and looked into the face of a frightened child. It was then her responsibilities to her family, and to her own unborn child, began to wash the past away.

'We'll be fine, Elizabeth. We have a new life ahead of us to enjoy, and enjoy it we will, you and me.'... Theirs was to be a special friendship.'

When Maggie again looked back, the folds in the land hid Camborne from sight and she knew she would never see the village again. Her life was now to be with her husband James, and their child, his child, and their children yet to come. As the eldest girl, she needed to provide guidance and support to the younger members of the family. Her sisters, Imogene and Mary still squabbled over the distribution of the chores, and their rivalry for their mother's attention still caused an occasional upset. She would need to take on some of the responsibility to help keep them in order

For the united family, their backs were set against the life they had left, a life that had only brought them poverty and ill health. Maybe, life over the channel, the waters of which shone back, calm and welcoming, would offer them the opportunity to prosper.

***

The sun had begun to rise on the eastern horizon as they travelled the hill into Portreath, and sky glowed with the red of the day's beginning, and it mingled with the dark blue of what remained of the night. North, across the channel, James saw their future. The sky was also red, but from the furnaces, and he thought,

Is that red the warmth of the welcome, or is it the reflection of the fires of Hell? He had chosen their new path, and he was responsible for what they were to find at the journey's end.

***

Bernard Sampson, the Captain of the vessel, took James to one side.

'Right the ore's loaded. Now get yourselves on board. You are to stack your possessions at the stern, and I want you to stay for the entire trip. I'll not need you to help again until we tie up in Swansea. I'll not have you wandering along the sides of the boat. If you were to fall in, it's likely I'll not be able to swing this tub round in time to find you again, especially with it being dark for the first part of the journey.'

'We'll stay put, Captain Sampson.'

'You'd better had. Your family did well shovelling the loose ore into bags and loading them onto the boat. They're a hard-working lot. Though it wasn't easy for your father to keep up. Is he well enough for this journey?'

'You know how it is in the mines right now. It may improve, and I know it always has in the past, but our family situation is urgent. My dad knows the risks and he's willing to take them.'

'I'm told it's a difficult road to Merthyr from Swansea. I can't help thinking you would have done better getting to Cardiff and catching a canal boat up the valley.'

'Not so much traffic goes to Cardiff from here and we found we had little choice. We will have to deal with what we find in South Wales. We're grateful you were able to let us work our passage. Although not asked for, we have a shilling we hope you will accept.'

'No need. You have worked hard and there's more for you to do on the other side. You'll earn your ferry crossing I can assure you. For now, the breeze is up and it'll fill our sail. We can see Swansea's glow in the sky. We'll be there soon enough. Get some sleep if you can.'

When they were halfway across the channel, the sun began to rise and fill the sky. Swansea town and its metalworks were still lit up. Swansea was known around the World as 'Copperopolis', such was the mass of its output. The spread of industrial buildings was unlike anything Henry had ever seen before.

'What are we going to son?'

'I'm not sure, Dad. We must make it work though... for all our sakes.'

'I know James. It's just a tiredness has come over me... I'm sure it must be the fear of the unknown, but I am not the man I was.'

'You are what you have always been... our father. If it's time for us to take your load we will do it.' James turned and nodded towards the sleeping girls. 'Look at them. Haven't you always had a loving family? Even now, it grows. Even now, we need you to remain a part of it... We are your family.'

Swansea bay churned with the movement of imported ore and the exported ingots of precious copper and tin.

***

'Tie her up at the bow, James... That's right. Now get to the stern, and I'll throw you the rope.' Turning to the assembled family members, Captain Sampson continued. 'Don't try to jump ashore until I tell you that you can do so. Then I'll need you to help unload.'

James was already looking to find a possible means of transport onwards. There were carts, right enough, but they looked purpose-built for dock work, and tramways seemed only to supply to the mouths of the metalworks.

It took most of the day to unload the boat of its ore and load it again with coal, even with the help of labourers employed to do the work. Captain Sampson was happy, as he was able to turn around and get away sooner than other boats plying the trade. Getting back to Portreath before them would be to his advantage.

The Rowe family stood at the dockside and watched the boat cast off and begin its return to Cornwall. They watched until it was lost to sight, having tacked to the West beyond the harbour wall. The family members turned to James. None spoke. They waited for him to tell them what to do.

11

The Road to Follow?

Jenkins, the owner of an available cart, tried to be helpful.

'With what you have to carry, you won't get to Merthyr for at least three or four days. I can take you to Neath today. I've got very little to take back with me. Tomorrow you can get a canal barge to Glynneath, then a cart to Hirwaun, perhaps. You might need to walk the rest of the way to Merthyr.'

'Is the way clear to see?'

'There's a track from Hirwaun down into Merthyr and there may be carts that'll take you all the way. Of course, you could get around the coast to Cardiff.'

Mr. Jenkins was the second person of the day to suggest to James that the Cardiff route may be best. He thought he would ask again.

'If we wanted to get to Cardiff, how would we do that?'

'To walk to Cardiff from here is a long way, 'tis true. You wouldn't want to do that unless you've lots of time to spare, but one of the coastal barges can take you. It'll be expensive, though. You'll be taking up space they may want for the stuff they take out from here, but if they had space, it would save your feet. There's a new canal that takes you from the Cardiff basin right to Merthyr. You could walk the towpath, or ask a friendly bargeman to take you north.'

'How much would it be?'

'A couple of shillings would do the trick on a coastal boat. After that, I don't know what a canal bargeman would charge. Either way, Neath or Cardiff, you'd have to pay the ferryman.'

'Is there a difference in the cost between the routes, or are they much the same?

'My cart, the Neath canal and then another cart would be a lot cheaper and more direct, but you may need to do more walking as It's six miles from the Glynneath basin, where the canal ends, to your next stop, Hirwaun. Then it's the same again over the top to Merthyr. Although, who in their right minds would want to go there. It's a...?' James interrupted; he didn't want to hear any negative comment about Merthyr.

'We'll come with you in your cart and trust to luck we'll find other transport when we need it. Would sixpence be enough to carry seven of us and our tools?

'Ninepence would seem more like it. Penny each, and tuppence for the tools.'

'Ninepence it is. I'll bring the rest of the family. Will you leave soon?'

'Within the next hour.'

'We'll be here when you're ready to go.'

***

It was hard to sleep on a cart when travelling the rutted track to the small town of Neath. The way was scoured by the constant to-and-fro of raw materials and finished ingots of pig iron, and recent rain had turned the disturbed ground beneath to wheel-clinging mud. Progress was in fits and starts, the men aboard having to help to heave the cart out of the mire where the going was difficult. Even so, as the ox-powered cart jiggled and jostled its way, Elizabeth and Mary were able to snatch a few moments of rest. They lay either side of Christiana, on the bench that ran inside the front of the cart, directly behind Wilfred Jenkins, the cart driver. There was little sleep to be had, as Wilfred shouted encouragement to the ox at every opportunity. The language he used showed no regard for the presence of women and children.

'Get on there, you bastard; get on, or I'll whip your arse.'

The men in the family were still racked with doubt. What was their future to hold? For Henry, the shame of their circumstances weighed heavily upon him. He felt he was responsible for the predicament in which the family now found itself. In a quiet moment, he confided to his new companion.

'I don't know how it has come to this Christiana? Had I been harder working, had I made more provision for the day when the work became scarce. Had I not worked at the face, would better health now be worth more than the extra penny a day I got hewing the granite?'

The contradictions were hard to resolve. James, too, thought long and hard about the responsibility he felt for them being in such a sorry state. Could he have found another way to stay in Camborne, was there going to be an upturn in the work available in the weeks ahead? Had he been too impulsive, taking them to a new place of work, a new way of life? But most of all, he wondered if he was up to the job of maintaining the family unit?

As it turned out, the women were more resolute than the men. Imogene, now fourteen years of age, looked forward to the new adventure. She had some fear of what was ahead, but having worked at the mine she was sure she would cope with whatever came her way. Christiana had contented herself with her newly formed family group. Her son-in-law was proving to be a compassionate man, who she knew would be kind to her and her daughters, and would be strong enough in character to lead them to a better life. The two youngest children at her side needed her to be a constant source of love and parental guidance, and the men would need her to make the home for them all. She was happy to wait and see, and to carry on doing what she knew best, being a mother Maggie was also firm in her belief of her husband. In a quiet moment, when all around them were settled, he had confided in her,

'I am still not sure what to do for the best, Maggie.'

'You have been strong for us all, James. We know what our troubles are and you have spoken to us all about what we may do about it. You listened to what we had to say. Whatever you decide will be the best choice, I am sure.'

'It is your faith in me that keeps me going, my love.'

It was those repeated utterances of 'my love' that won her to him. It wasn't thrown away as if it were a 'good morning'. It had a warmth and sincerity that was not often heard from other men who worked the mines of Camborne. She reflected that for all of Almond's good looks and uncomplicated joy for life, he had never shown her any depth of feeling, or any hint that he wanted to be responsible. She knew that James, the man she had married, would be at her side until death parted them. She would accept the baby inside her as his, and, if lucky enough, bear and raise more of their children over the years to come.

12

The Arrival and the Departure

The first part of the journey took up most of the day, and they arrived at the Neath Basin at seven in the evening.

'I'll drop you here. Give me a minute and I'll see if I can speak to one of the bargemen for you.'

Wilfred jumped from the cart and headed to the furthest barge to have loaded its cargo. It was to navigate up through the nineteen locks to Glynneath the next day.

The canal ran along the length of the Valley floor, always near the river and crossing it at the Ynysbwllog aqueduct, some eight miles distant, then to continue on to the foothills of the Brecon Beacons. From there, they would need to take the tram track to Hirwaun and on over the hill to Merthyr. The final stretch would be the hardest part of the journey.

'This is Idwal. He has little English but is happy to take you all with him tomorrow. You can help at the locks and he will be glad of that, and I'm sure he would be glad of a penny or two for each person he takes. I'll wish you good luck and I'll be on my way.'

At dawn the following day, the family were sat in a huddle at the front of the barge. They had rested overnight as best they could, and were happy that the next 12 miles would be more comfortable and tranquil than the journey on the cart. The rest had allowed them to gain strength before they attempted the journey over the hilltops to Merthyr.

They had travelled two miles, the slow, calm progress of the canal barge a blessing after the jostle of the cart; although a slight drizzle of rain had set in. They arrived at the hamlet of Tonna, where they encountered the first of the locks on their journey. Henry and James were at the lock gates helping Idwal navigate through to the next level.

The lock keeper barked his instructions; it was clear to him that neither James nor Henry had any experience of how locks operated.

'You have to wind the sluice gate handle clockwise until it comes to a stop… Clockwise, I said.'

'Sorry, Mister,' said James, having got disorientated by the new experience.

'Now wait for the water to rise until it meets the up-slope water level. Then you push open the gate.'

'Yes, Sir.'

'I'll open this side. You two stay over there.'

Idwal stood tending his barge horse, amused at the goings-on. He and the lock keeper exchanged words in Welsh, and they were obviously not complimentary of the efforts that were being made by the two Englishmen.

The barge was through the last of the locks, and the family were happy to be soon travelling through the countryside at the gentle pace that was dictated by the speed the horse was content to plod.

It was then the contractions Maggie had felt over the last twelve hours, but had kept to herself, became frequent and severe.

'Mother, I think the baby is coming... I think it's coming!' The sudden break of her water gave instant confirmation.

'Oh, dear God, not now,' cried Christiana. 'Come, lay here, I know what to do.'

Over the years, Christiana had attended to the pregnant daughters of close family and neighbours. Childbirth was a moment of crisis shared by the women of the village, and it was when young mothers and their babies were most at risk. The experience of the older women was the best hope the mother and her unborn child would have to survive the birth.

Everyone was alerted to the situation Maggie had found herself, but it was the women in the family who congregated around her. The men finished their task before hurrying back to Maggie. Idwal urged the horse to pull the barge clear of the locks. Idwal understood what was happening and brought the barge to a stop. He shouted in his own language,

'Iesu Mawr,'

A blasphemy Christiana had admonished Welsh members of her own congregation for using, but for now, she cared not.

There was little time available before the barge needed to move along, as other barges were waiting to come up the canal, and so Idwal tried to help. He brought sacking to lay beneath Maggie, and basins he used to carry water for the horse. He knew water would be needed; he had eight children of his own. Then he returned to his task, ensuring the continued progress of the barge; no matter what was happening, he still needed to get on with his job and keep the traffic on the canal moving.

Christiana took control.

'Elizabeth and Mary, take the basins and run back and fill them from the stream we just passed. Not the canal, mind. It was where the horse took water. Be quick. Imogene, go in my bag and fetch my cotton dress. I can tear it into pieces.'

'Not your cotton dress, Mum?'

'There's no better use for it. We can wash Maggie and the child when it comes... We can find fresh water as we go along'.

'What is it I can do?' asked James.

'You can stay out of the way, and so can Henry. Best not have you around getting us all upset. This is work for us women.' James hesitated, but Christiana was determined to see the men out of the way. She said,

'Go on, be off. We are used to cleaning up after the trouble men have caused us.'

It was always the moments during the suffering of childbirth when women became intolerant of the unfairness of their burden. What use were men at such times and who was it who had caused the pregnancy in the first place? Even though the father of the child wasn't present, it didn't stop Christiana from letting the men around know how women's lives were blighted on a regular basis. James and Henry had no argument, given the problems caused by Almond's dalliance and his subsequent disappearance. They were content to stand back and leave the women to it.

But soon it was discovered not all was well. Christiana turned to James

'The baby's around the wrong way, James.'

'How do you know it's the wrong way round?'

'It's easy to see, one of its feet has come out from Maggie.'

'What does that mean, Christiana?'

'The baby's not meant to be born that way.'

'Are they in danger, Maggie and the child?'

Henry spoke up. He couldn't help himself.

'Our last babe came that way. That's why Catherine...

'It's not the same, Henry, not yet.'

'So, what can be done?'

'I've been with the midwife, Gwen Pritchard, many times when I helped at births in the village. I've seen this before.'

'And will it be alright?' asked James.

'It sometimes is, but it depends.'

'Depends on what?'

'I'll not give you false hope, James. This is Margaret's first child. She's not used to having babies and her hips are tight.'

'What does that mean?'

'It means there might not...' Christiana paused to regain her composure. 'It means there might not be enough room for me to find the baby's other leg to pull it free.'

'You have to reach inside her?'

'I'll have to. I've seen Gwen do it. If she can do it, so can I. It may be the only way to save my daughter and her child.'

'May God be with you, Christiana,' said Henry, asking for divine assistance for the first time since the moments before the death of his wife.

'He's always with me... but there may be others of his flock more deserving,' hoping humility was the best way to gain His attention.

On the cart, Elisabeth held Maggie's hand, but she could not take her eyes from the tiny foot that protruded from Maggie. It was her cousin trying it's best to make its way into the world. And what world would it come into? She felt desperate for it, her mother, her family... herself.

Christiana came to join them. All her children were in attendance, but waiting for their mother to take control and make everything right. She looked down at her hands. They were small, but her fingers were rigid and swollen with arthritis. *Can I do this?* she thought, before uttering to herself,

'I must.'

She did what she had seen Gwen Pritchard do, and plunged her hands into the cold water Mary had brought. Gwen's words were ringing in her head.

'You must always wash your hands almost until they are raw before going near the mother. Best keep the filth of the world away from the unborn child as long as you can.'

Christiana, washed as if to clean away the sins that had brought them to this pass. Maggie lay expectant, her face grey with the sudden onrush of pain, sweat pouring from her face. Christiana spoke directly to Maggie.

'I need to place a hand inside you. Lay still and do not push at the baby until I say.'

Christiana found room to pass one hand into Maggie, searching for the child's other leg. Could she find it, and would it be free of its cord? If it was, could she get the leg out without injuring the child or its mother?

Maggie couldn't help but cry out a high-pitched scream for fear of what was happening.

'Elizabeth, keep a tight hold of Maggie's arm. Imogene, you do the same with the other.'

Christiana searched with her fingertips along the child's leg, finding a way into the womb and feeling the baby's form. She found the other foot waiting to break free; she was sure of it. She hooked one finger around its ankle and pulled gently. She feared there was not enough space for the leg to make its way out, her own fingers being in the way. If she could get its foot out of the womb, she could pull on it and be sure to get the foot alongside the other.

The child's leg was moving forward... bit by bit, at each tug Christiana gave it.

It broke through. The baby had decided enough was enough, and it had kicked its leg out.

Christiana felt for the cord. As far as she could tell, it was not wrapped between the legs of the child. She could only hope the cord was not around the baby's neck. Now was her opportunity to help with the birth.

'Maggie, I want you to help push this baby out. When you need to push, I will tug on the child's legs. I'll not pull hard, I'll just help you.' Christiana knew there might come a time when she would need to pull hard; the child might not survive a prolonged birth as the child needed to be out. It was the best chance for both the mother and child.

Over the next hour, Maggie pushed as her contractions climaxed and her mother gently pulled on the babe to assist. There was no other way.

Christiana began to fret about the time it was taking for the child to arrive, when all at once, the combined efforts of all three people involved delivered the baby into the world. The baby dangled by its feet in the hands of its grandmother, its cord free from entanglement, still connected to its mother. It was a girl.

***

Eight hours later, they were at the canal basin in Glynneath, the newborn baby in the arms of its mother. Idwal had asked around the workers at the basin and had secured an onwards passage for the next day; an oxcart again, but it would mean Maggie would not have to walk with her child. James bade farewell to Idwal, his gratitude to the bargeman was plain to see. James' firm handshake and embrace overcame the barrier the different languages put in their way.

The oxcart was an expense they could have done without, but James would do no else. Maggie had insisted she would be alright with an overnight rest, and the oxcart wasn't needed, but James would have none of it,

'You will ride the cart, Maggie. We have our child to think about, too.'

The cart rocked and bumped its way along the track to the foot of the hillside. From there, it would twist its way up to Hirwaun; a village sat like a saddle at the top of the mountain between the two river valleys, the Neath and the Taff.

Light rain had taken the place of the fine drizzle of the previous day. The mother and baby lay on the back of the cart. They had little protection. The women did what they could to shield them from the worst of the weather, hoping the rain wouldn't turn heavy and persistent. The men walked behind, helping to heave the cart from a collapsed rut or an exposed rock. The needs of the young mother and her newborn were foremost in the mind of James and he hoped at the next village along the way he would find shelter. He'd inquired of the waggoner,

'Is there a place near that we can stop for the night?'

'There's a church with its hamlet ahead, a mile or two. You would be best to stop there. They may help you,' he nodded to the mother and baby, 'what with the difficult situation you find yourself.'

Henry was struggling and he needed some time to rest. James hadn't paid attention to his father; such were the events of the day and their haste to reach permanent shelter in Merthyr.

'James, I feel the day has got to me... It's my chest. I can't get enough breath in... Could we find somewhere to stop before too long? I need to rest for a while?'

'We'll stop soon, Dad. Just a mile or two. Are you right until then?'

'Yes, I'll be good until then...'

It was three steps, if that, when Henry sank to his knees and fell forward.

He had spoken his last words.

13

A Place to Rest

St Caradoc's was a church built by the local landowner for his family and the workers of his land. It wasn't open to the general public. A message sent from the villagers to their master had brought the landowner to its gate. He was anxious, as work on the estate had been disrupted, and he needed to know why, and when would his labourers get back to work. He asked,

'What's the trouble here?'

James spoke; the blow of his father's death being put to one side so he could deal with the difficult situation the family was in.

'We have a death in the family, Sir. We are not from these parts and have no congregation to turn to in order to give our father a proper burial.'

'You arrive here in the expectation that my church, my private church and its graveyard, can provide you with such facility?'

'In these difficult circumstances, we can only hope for good fortune and the kindness of others. We have had the fortune to find your church and we hoped we may lay our father here to rest. It is a fitting place'.

'Kept that way by the money I provide and the labours of my estate workers. Why should we take in a stranger and allow him to rest here for eternity?'

James looked around at the small church and neat graveyard. It sat in a steep-sided valley. The trees that had once covered the valley's slopes were long gone, having been used as fuel or building material for the industry that had sprung up along its length. Even in its denuded, polluted state, it had retained some of its beauty, but grey/black mounds of spoil were creeping up its sides like exposed ribs of a vast decomposing beast. James spoke.

'My father was a good man,' then, looking around him, said, 'and this is a good place. You have done good works, sir, it is plain to see, and I don't expect you to offer assistance to the undeserving. But this man... this man...' James was unable to finish his plea for help. His emotions got the better of him.

The gentleman landowner would have usually dismissed the vagrants without further discussion, but he'd looked into the faces of the huddled group of women travellers stood behind the man who spoke for them. One was with a newborn child. As callous as his decision-making could be in his effort to preserve and promote the wealth he'd amassed, he was not without some compassion. Nevertheless, he spoke of his misgivings.

'Those who are undeserving do not stay within my employ, or remain on my estate, and this grave would be permanent, unless I pay for its removal.' He hesitated. James sensed his decision was imminent but had not yet been made. James spoke up.

'I would show my willingness to take responsibility by digging the grave myself and making good the grave surroundings. We are of modest means, but we can pay you something for the plot now... a shilling... and commit to a quarterly rent. For the rent, you would need to take my word.'

The women of the village had congregated around the wagon with the body of Henry laid out on it for all to see, and Elizabeth was weeping at his side. It was not the wail of desperation she'd cried out when her father had fallen and was found to be dead, but a repeated sob of disbelief that he had left her. Christiana held Elizabeth tightly to her, in the hope she could restrain Elizabeth's heave of despair and bring her some comfort. Maggie stood with her sisters; her child tightly wrapped to her body by the use of her mother-in-law's precious shawl. Henry had brought it to her after she had given birth and had said,

'Here you are my love. This shawl has wrapped all my children. It's now for you to use.'

The village folk had listened to what James had to say and could see their master was undecided. They turned to him, and some moved forward a step, being careful not to displease him by their impertinence, but hoping the swell of sympathy would be taken into account. His decision was final and would not be questioned by his workforce, but he was also a shrewd businessman. He knew an act of benevolence, no matter how small, was cherished by those who were not used to receiving it. This small mercy would be weighed by the villagers against the rigours of his employment, and it could pay him a dividend when he asked them to do more. Even so, to show weakness in the face of a rabble could mean he'd be left vulnerable to them trying to influence him again, and the next time it could sorely disadvantage him. He needed to steer his way carefully using wisdom as his rudder.

'You say you can pay something for the plot, but I suspect it will not be enough. And as for quarterly rent? I know you will be gone in the morning never to be seen again.' He paused, as if in thought, but his mind was made up. Tell me, what can you pay today? A shilling will not be enough.'

James had very little money left after their journey and what would now be another day's rental of the oxcart and its driver. To pay more would leave them without any resource to establish themselves in their new home. He looked back to the cart, to his father, the person he would turn to when times were hard. There next to him, as if it were his final gift, lay his bag of tools.

'I have his tools. We have no need for them now. They are in used condition, but it was honest work.'

They were not worth much, but in the minds of the village people around him they would have been precious to the man who owned them and those left behind who could still earn their living with them.

'Bring them for me to see,'

The tools were laid before him.

'I see from these implements you are miners.' He considered what was in front of him. We have no use for a mandrill, but, along with your shilling, your chisels, hammers and spade, it will do.' He picked up the spade and thrust it at James.

'Go dig his grave. The churchwarden will show you where. He will take the other tools and the spade once you have finished. You can keep the mandrill. He may be able to provide you with a shroud to contain your father. It is for you to negotiate.

'I thank you, Sir.

'You will be delayed several hours digging the grave. You and your family are welcome to stay in the church overnight, but in the morning, I expect you to be on your way.'

***

The family laid Henry to rest.

***

James looked down onto the mass of ironworks as they belched their rage against the eastern hills. The buildings spread south along the valley floor; the valley's course having been determined over thousands of years by the ancient river. The once pristine valley was now blackened by this industrial outrage.

The journey over the hillside to the Taff valley had been made easier for the use of the cart. Dafydd, the young driver had not expected the drama of the previous day or the delay to his planned arrival in Merthyr, but he was content with the extra money he had earned, and it would be a story to tell. He spoke to James as if he couldn't have worked it out for himself,

'That's Merthyr, that is… Nearest place to Hades you'll find in this land'

James didn't answer, for there welled inside him a feeling of despair, the likes of which he had never experienced before. What had he done to bring his family to such a place? The raucous clamour and crash of the foundries, the smelting, the red-hot pouring of iron, the mechanical fettling and physical labour, gave out a mass groan.

Dafydd was right. The full-throated shout of orders and warnings from foundry men sounded as though they came from the gates of hell, where men struggled to get out against the tide of others wanting to get in. James and his family added to the press of those who needed the work.

James tried hard to rationalise the situation.

How bad could it be? Hadn't Charles told them it would be alright and there would be a welcome? But how such a place could offer a welcome, James could not begin to imagine.

They made their way down the hill, taking time to stop and regain their strength.

Christiana was the first to speak, even though her strength was at its lowest ebb. She, as always, found the resolve to summon up her reserves of energy to make things right.

'Our chapel preacher told us of the trials we sinners would have to face.' She spoke his words as if they were her own.

'With God beside us, even the devil can be defeated. If we have faith, we will be triumphant.' She clasped her hands and offered a short prayer, then she spoke in the knowledge and conviction that God was on their side.

'Come, children, James will lead the way. Let's hold hands on these final steps to our new home. Our heaven will be what we make of it.'

James thought,

If only I could have faith in a God who is content to allow his servants to suffer in the way we have... 'and as surely as we will suffer in the years to come,' he muttered under his breath.

If God did exist, James would not forgive Him for the hurt He had caused and James was sure that from Christiana's god there would be no respite. If the family were to prosper, it would be from his efforts and the efforts of the people for whom he was now responsible... Yet, James could not deny Christiana's words had brought the family together as they walked the road into the town, and he blessed her for the faith she had shown.

James looked back to Maggie sat in the cart. She had remained strong in her newfound role of mother, with her newborn child, Catherine, their 'Kate', in her arms. She set her gaze straight ahead, to the town destined to be her home for the rest of her days.

14

The Welcome

Charles' home was south of the town, a row of miner's cottages linked in a single terrace. It was almost like the row of houses they had left in Camborne, except it was built of sandstone, not granite. This isolated row was a better quality of housing than those blackened hovels surrounding the foundries. The skilled miner was afforded more consideration than the labourer at the furnace. The coal they dug outcropped on either side of the valley, and it was adjacent to the terrace.

The coal was easily accessible, and was excavated from 'drift-mines' that followed the dip of the black seams into the hillside. Steam-driven winches pulled the coal-laden trams along rails to the surface, where they ran by gravity, down to a spur of a purpose-built canal. The coal, transferred onto barges, fed the furnaces of the ironworks.

Dafydd spoke up.

'This will be the houses you're looking for Mister. If you all get off here, I'll turn the cart and be on my way.'

Dafydd was right. They had arrived.

James knew it was where Charles and his family lived. He made his way to the eighth house along the row and he knocked on the door. A young child answered. She cracked the door open an inch, and her eye peered out; these were unexpected visitors. She asked straight away.

'Hello, who are you?'

'We are looking for Mr. Rowe. Is he in?'

In the over-informative way children often speak, especially the girls, the child replied,

'He's at work and so is the rest of 'em.'

'Is there another grown up in the house?'

'My Dad is in bed from doing his shift. My mam won't be back yet, nor Mr. and Mrs. Rowe. They're still at the foundry, they are.'

'Oh? And how many are in your family?

'I'm not sure... I'm the littlest. I'm cooking tea I am. I can cook tea... My mam showed me how.'

'And what would your name be?'

'Beryl, Beryl's my name.'

'That's a lovely name, Beryl... Beryl, can you ask your dad if we could come in and wait for Mister Rowe to come back?'

'I wouldn't want to wake 'im. He's gone off to sleep in the back room. I'd get in trouble if I did that. You'll have to wait outside, Mister.'

'That's alright, Beryl. We can wait here.'

The rest of his family had gathered around the doorstep and had heard what was said. Once the door was closed, Maggie was the first to speak what they were all thinking.

'James! Another family lives with Charles and his brood? How many would it make us in the house... and there seems only to be two up and two down rooms, the same as in our houses in Camborne.'

'It's not much different to what many of us have to face back home. We'll cope, somehow. Although, I can't see us staying here... At least, not for long.'

'I know James... but the messages from Charles seemed to say it was better here. To live with another family must be hard, and remember, there's seven of us, what with the baby.'

'Charles said he had found us a place to stay.'

'But will we have to share?'

'We don't know what'll be offered to us. When we get jobs, we'll be better off and we'll be able to manage. For now, we have to wait for either Charles or Sarah to come home.'

Elizabeth and Mary were at the limits of their endurance. They held each other tight for comfort, and Mary began to cry.

'Why did we come to this awful place, Elizabeth?'

'Everything will be fine. We just need to find my brother Charles. I know he'll have a place for us.'

Imogene held Maggie and her baby close. She, too, was terrified. Their destination seemed to have been reached, but there on the doorstep of their sanctuary, they had been turned away. She sought reassurance from her sister.

'We will be alright, won't we Maggie?'

'It will be. We have got this far and we can't go back.'

The family set their bundles down against the front wall and sat amongst them. The day was late, and the sun had set behind the hill they had travelled down. The low cloud reflected the flame of the furnaces to the north. To the west, the sky was already black. More rain was to come.

In time, a gaggle of women and younger workers appeared at the end of the row. They were returning from sorting and loading coal, and they were blackened from the dust. It was on their clothes, their hair and their faces; only the white of their eyes confirmed they were human. There was a dozen or so of the wretched people. Upon seeing the huddled group of newcomers outside in the street, they hurried to ask who it was had arrived and what was their reason for being here. Henry and his family were expected, as word had spread along the terrace they were on their way, but no one was sure when they would arrive. As it was, there seemed to be only one man and a group of women. Were they the expected family? Gladys asked,

'Hello, my loves. Are you Charlie's family from Cornwall?'

'They must be. Who else could it be,' chimed Cissie?

Before anyone could answer, into the street came a smaller group of workers and from amongst them came the woman who knew the answer. She came running to the newcomers.

'James, you've come at last!' she cried.

'Sarah! Is that you?'

'Of course it is! And here's my lovely Elizabeth.'

Forgetting the filthy state of her clothing, she drew Elizabeth to her, and then, holding her at arm's length, she said

'What a beautiful young woman you have become. The last time I saw you were just seven years old.'

Elizabeth tried hard to see the person behind the black mask and try to relate it to the vision she had of her aunt from all those years ago. There was something familiar about her, but she was little more than a stranger.

Throwing her arms around James, Sarah cried,

'James, I am so glad you've come at last.' Seeing Maggie at his side, she asked,

'Is this your lovely new bride?' Maggie nodded enthusiastically. Sarah saw the bundle in her arms.

'And what's this? A new baby?'

'This is Catherine. She is a day old.'

'Catherine... after her grandmother. Isn't she lovely, too? And her grandfather must be proud.' Sarah looked around her.

'Where is he...? Where's Henry?'

Maggie lowered her head, not wanting to meet Sarah's gaze and have to answer. Sarah sensed the mood of the group change. They were hesitant to reply.

'Where's Henry?' she asked again. James spoke.

'I am sorry, Sarah. Henry died along the way.'

Sarah stood still, not speaking, trying to take in the bad news and control the emotions welling inside her. Sarah needed to confirm she had heard correctly.

'Henry is dead?'

'He died only yesterday.'

Sarah paused to think of the man and what he meant to them all.

'But we need him here...' she whispered, before remembering the tragedy of his life cut short.

'Did he see his new grandchild?'

'For an hour or two.'

'The child is a day old'

'Almost newborn.'

In disbelief, Sarah needed to ask again

'And Henry died yesterday?

James nodded in confirmation.

Sarah tried to remember a passage from the scriptures.

'Oh, James. "Our Lord giveth and our Lord taketh away." I've heard it said, but the like of this I've never witnessed.'

Sarah gathered her thoughts, knowing she would have to deal with the predicament they were in. There was no time for the tears beginning to trace their path in the dust on her face, instead, she gave out her instructions; Sarah was someone who would command, and someone who would be listened to.

'Almond, run tell your father, and ask him to come as soon as he can.' 'Yes, Mam.' The young lad ran back up the street.

'Gladys you get some food together and you can make us one of your stews. I've got bread in my house, and a piece of pork I've been saving. It's on the larder stone. Get it, too, and we'll all eat in your front room, Glad, as you've got the space. Cissie, you let everyone know who's arrived. Turning to Maggie,

'We'll get everyone round to meet you all, especially the new baby. For now, I have some tea, and the kettle will soon boil. We need to be quiet though, there's a man asleep inside.'

Indoors, James quietly introduced the new family members. The introductions were awkward. Sarah was used to being black with dust, but everyone else found it strange and disquieting. They had themselves been dirty before, from the dust of the tin mines, but this coal dust stuck to every part of Sarah, and she was a lady who they would have to take as their own. It was hard for them to warm to her in such a state, but Sarah busied herself and chatted as if she had known them forever. It was not long before the person shone through the grime.

In such a small room, there was not much space to spread out, and the small table had only four chairs. The settle by the fire was welcoming and Sarah beckoned Maggie and Christiana to sit.

'The '*ffwrrwm ishta*' is the best place for you. Come get yourself warm.'

The speaking of Welsh was discouraged in schools and workplaces, but after years of living in South Wales, Sarah had learned some of the language. Welsh words for common household objects had slipped into her vocabulary. Often, the Welsh word imbued a romance the English word lacked, and the mention of the ffwrrwm ishta would bring with it thoughts of the comfort of sitting at the hearth with its fire; a fire upon which the evening meal would have soon been cooking, if Gladys' stew hadn't been underway.

The rest of the family found space to sit at the table, or on the floor amongst their belongings. The quiet of the house was soon shattered. Gladys was in the larder and called out.

'Here's the bit of pork. Don't know where you got that...? And you've got some potatoes... I'll take them, too.' She entered the front room and continued in full voice,

'I'll call in down the street to get more. I'll soon have enough for us all to eat.'

Then she was off on her errand, knocking on each door in turn.

'Hilda, the Rowe's have arrived. I'm cooking something up for them. Have you got a cabbage?'

Then next door and into the backyard where clothes were being taken out to dry,

'There you are Mavis. Can I have two of your lovely leeks? The Rowes have come!'

'You can have one, Hilda. Dan's loves his leeks. He would rather count 'em than eat 'em, daft sod, and he's bound to give me grief.'

'One'll do, love.'

Hilda tried her luck.

'Have you got some carrot ready to harvest? Does he count his carrots?'

And so it went on, until every house had given something.

Back up the terrace, Sarah was in charge.

'We'll all stay here until Charlie gets home. He needs to know what's happened to you. Then, when we're ready, we'll go down to Gladys's and you can meet your new neighbours. There are more of you than expected so we'll need to find somewhere for you all to stay. We can't have you sleeping on the floor.'

Within the hour, Charles arrived back on the street. Sarah had been watching for him through the front window.

'James! Charles is back. You should speak to him outside.' Sarah was afraid the news about Henry would reawaken the grief felt by the family collected before her, and there had already been enough for them to bear.

'I'll go meet him.'

'I'll come.' said Elizabeth.

They went together, and James held her hand knowing she was now old enough to share the responsibility of telling the bad news.

From the window, Sarah saw them meet. Charles hugged his brother and pulled Elizabeth into the embrace. They stood embraced, not speaking, until they were sure they had wrung the last drop of joy from their reunion. James took Charles by the shoulder. He was about to speak of Henry... The story was told, and the three embraced again.

Down the road at Gladys's, there was a tap at the window. It was Dan with two more leeks.

Selwyn Berryman-Morgan

15

New Masters

Transportation of the ingots of pig iron from Merthyr to the coast had long been a problem for the Ironmasters. Horse or ox-drawn carts first performed the task, and they travelled along narrow, simply lain roadways, that clung to the sides of the steep valley. The going was slow and was often disrupted by the typically wet, South Wales weather, blown in on the prevailing westerly wind. A better way of transporting the iron was needed, and in 1770 the engineer Thomas Dadford began the navigation of the Glamorganshire Canal; it being commissioned by a consortium of Merthyr Ironmasters. The main contributor to the costs was Thomas Crawshay, the Iron Master of the Cyfarthfa ironworks. Its construction was completed in 1794. There were several ironworks in operation at the time, and all of the ironworks used the canal, but Crawshay controlled the traffic and prioritised the movement of his own goods. He also benefitted because the canal ran directly to his works. The other ironworks, being the other side of river, were disadvantaged. To get pig iron to the canal from the eastern ironworks a number of tramways had to be constructed. The tramways often ran side by side, as an agreement for the cooperative use of a single tramway proved hard to manage. All this gave Crawshay a commercial advantage. To overcome this, in 1802 the remaining iron masters finally agreed on a course of action, constructing a new tramway to transport their goods south, part of the way to the coast. It ran along the valley to a hamlet known as Navigation, some ten miles away, where there was a canal basin at which goods could be loaded onto waiting barges. In this way, they were able to reduce costs and remain competitive with Crawshay. This rail link was to be known as the Penydarren Tramway. The historical significance of this tramway was yet to be realised.

***

Crawshay was a renowned gambler. At a gathering of the mine owners at his home in Cyfarthfa house, a mansion unrivalled in the whole of South Wales, he was to lay down a challenge to Samuel Homfray, who was the Ironmaster of the Penydarren ironworks.

'So, your tramway has eased the jam of goods wanting to use the canal. An efficient use of the ample profits your tramway consortium has at its disposal.' exclaimed Crawshay.

The scarcely veiled jibe at the other ironmasters didn't go unnoticed as their difficulties were in large part the responsibility of Crawshay. Homfray was first to respond, and in return goaded Crawshay, hinting Crawshay's superior trading position might, after all, be under threat.

'The tramway has begun to pay us dividends, and as we make further efficiencies in the methods we use to load and transport our pig iron our investment will more than pay for itself.'

'And yet, you still need to use the canal from the Basin? We are both well aware there's a limit to what a horse can pull, and I fear you have reached that limit. One or two ton at the most, and having to stop every quarter mile to let an empty wagon back up the valley. No, you will still want to take advantage of the scheduled canal traffic from my works, and, of course, I will be happy to accommodate you... What are friends for?'

'It's true, there's a limit to the tonnage we can transport via the tramway at the moment, but I aim to mechanise the process.'

'How would you do it? You can't put wheels on a horse.'

'That's also true, but what if we replaced the horse with something steam-driven.'

'Samuel, the idea isn't new, but who would try it. Steam power is dangerous. I assume you would put the whole thing on wheels?' Homfray nodded in agreement.

'You would need to carry the boiler to generate the steam, plus the coal and water to feed it. All the time you would add to the weight. My God man! It would be the size of my foundry and then you would let it loose down a gradient. The last you would see of it would be at the bend in Quakers Yard as it fell into the river... Come now, it can't be done.'

'I think it can. I've purchased the rights to...' Crawshay interrupted, knowing where the conversation was leading.

'Oh, Trevithick's madcap invention. I've heard of it, and I've heard nothing good about it. It's one thing using his high-pressure boiler to power a hammer or to pump water from the Taff, a use I would champion, but to combine steam power with a contraption that moves on rails... I think not.'

'I've looked at his proposals. I've not as yet suggested to him that I'm considering the machines construction, but I am minded to do so.'

'I am prepared to wager it won't work. '

'On this venture, I am prepared to accept your wager. It will fill me with greater resolve.'

'Well, let me test your metal and your determination. Would you wager 500 guineas, or does your enthusiasm for such a hare-brained scheme not run to as much?'

'It does... Of course, we would need to agree the parameters within which we are to conduct the wager.'

Mr. Hill, the owner of the Dowlais Ironworks, sat across the table and was keen to calm the two men down.

'Gentlemen, please. The scale of the wager is too great, even for you Mr. Crawshay. Let's be reasonable. The project, if it should be undertaken, is ambitious, and has merit, no doubt, but is there a need for such high stakes?' Homfray was quick to respond.

'I am convinced it can succeed. If Mr. Crawshay would like to suggest the terms on which the wager would be conducted, I will be in a position to decide if they are reasonable.'

The terms of the 500 guineas wager were agreed. The steam engine would have to successfully transport 10 tons of iron the 10 miles to Navigation, and along with it, 70 passengers as observers.

Homfray needed to speak to his engineer, as his bravado might cost him dear.

***

The ironmaster and engineer met over dinner; Trevithick being invited to the home of Samuel Homfray.

'So, you told me it ran up the hill from Camborne and three miles beyond?'

'It did, with half a dozen men clinging to it. It also ran the return trip, and for several more days on trials.'

'What happened then?'

'The boiler was left to run dry with the fire alight, and the engine was destroyed'

'That was negligent. I wouldn't have expected my works engineer to have been so careless. Weren't you in attendance?'

'My work commitments at the mine meant I had to trust the engine to labourers who had been instructed in its operation. Unfortunately, the delights of a local pub were more important to them than their responsibility to me. They paid for it of course, by the loss of their jobs, but their lack of diligence meant I was unable to complete my trials.'

'Even so, it must have been an embarrassment to you? If you were to make another machine would it suffer the same fate?'

'I have designed a simple 'fail-safe' remedy for an over-heating boiler.'

'Do tell.'

'A lead plug close to the boiler's base will melt should its temperature get too high. The remaining water, for there is bound to be some, will then spill into the fire and extinguish it.'

'A simple solution, I think?'

110

'Yes, the simple solutions are always best. Other than the piston arrangement, my design has not drastically changed.'

'Mr. Trevithick, it's always a pleasure to invite you to my home for dinner, and, as usual, this after-dinner sojourn to the drawing room is where we speak of the matters I have in mind. So, if you will allow me, I'll get straight to the point.

'Mr. Homfray, it's always a pleasant way for us to discuss your requirements of me. You have my undivided attention,' Replied Trevithick with a small bow of his head in mock deference; Trevithick had his own status as an engineer of some renown.

Homfray smiled, and continued,

'Just so!'

'How may I be of service to you, Sir?'

'You'll be well aware that we still are paying too much for the transportation of pig iron along Crawshay's canal. From his point of view, he knows he can throttle my margins by adjusting those costs. Of course, I have kept the costs in check by using the tramway down to Navigation, but, as you know, there's a limit to the amounts that can be transported by horse-drawn trams. In consequence, I can't expand the business as I would wish to.'

Trevithick knew where this was leading and anticipated the proposal Homfray was about to make.

'You want me to replace the horse with an engine?'

'Yes, you are ahead of me. We should be able to transport greater quantities of goods at any given time, given the power an engine would generate. Do you think you can get one of your machines to run the ten miles on the tramway, drawing with it ten tons of pig iron and a given number of passengers? You would also need to make the return journey.'

'You are aware I've been looking at ways of developing my steam engine since my time in Camborne and you've kindly provided me with resources that enable me to do so. My design continues to improve, and

111

so has the efficiency of my high-pressure boilers, the power of your steam hammers testifies to that... I assume you will want me to now take it from the drawing board to a working example.

'That is indeed my plan.'

'I gladly accept the challenge. To keep the costs down, I'm sure I could convert one of our boilers to perform the task you ask of it. If you would allow it, we have sufficient stock.'

'You may, although I have a concern. We have the workshop with tools enough, but do we have the men with sufficient skills to make it?'

'With your help, and upon my recommendation, you provided accommodation to a skilled workshop man from Cornwall. He helped me build my first engine and knows how it was done. Your generosity in this respect will pay you dividends, I am sure.'

'As usual, my benevolence has its own reward.'

'The design will have to be on a larger scale, of course, and that brings along with it different issues to contend with. Measurements become more difficult and our tolerances need greater levels of precision, but I think we can deal with it.'

'Good! You understand, perhaps it would be only the one return journey I would ask it to make, and so I will have an eye on the costs. It must not be so robust that the production costs would be unbearable. I also fear that its running costs may be too great for it to continue in service for any length of time.'

'Then, Sir, I am surprised you would go to the trouble of asking me to build it?'

'Between you and me, Mr. Trevithick, I need Crawshay to know that we have an alternative to his blasted canal. I am keen to investigate the advantages your locomotive could offer, but a long-term beneficial effect on Crawshay's canal charges would be my main concern. I have to have a lever against his wretched canal.'

'I'd hope that my steam engine would prove itself to the extent that Crawshay will be asking us to transport his produce, rather than the other way round.'

'Well, there's a thought? We shall see! Tell me when you are ready, but be sure, Trevithick, I am not minded to continue with the venture if it proves too troublesome. My main purpose is on getting an agreement that Crawshay can live with that will be to my benefit.'

Homfray was unaware of the historic significance of this venture. If it were successful, it would be the first time the power of steam would be used to drive a locomotive along a rail. As it turned out, his vision was short term.

***

'So, Mr. Rees, what have you made of my drawings? Are you clear as to the method of construction?

'Yes, the drawings are perfectly clear.'

'And are you confident we have the ability to forge the components and machine them to the specified tolerances?

'The crankshafts can be forged easily enough and we've worked to fine tolerances before, but, in truth, these tolerances are more demanding.'

'But you can do it?'

'I believe so, and as you requested, I have placed Mr. Rowe in charge of the manufacture of the more precise parts. He's a skilled metalworker, and the fact he worked on your Camborne road engine has got to benefit us. I've shown him the new drawings and he is confident we can make it, but he's some questions to ask.'

'Yes, he is bound to want to know more. You know, not only did he help build my Camborne machine, he rode it, too. He knows how the engine should sound and how it will operate under steam. Come up with him to my office? We'll iron out the problems together.'

***

'You'll remember my road engine, Mr. Rowe. This is somewhat of the same design but scaled up. We'll use existing stock, as the boiler and flywheel are standard equipment. I want you to build the chassis strong enough to take the weight and to house the wheels and their axles. The crankshafts are to be drop-forged in the next two weeks. Then we have a month to machine them and assemble the locomotive.'

'I'm clear what you propose to do Mr. Trevithick, your drawings are detailed, but I am not sure if the tolerances you ask for are achievable, given the methods we use in the workshop. It's the increased distance between related bearings that will cause the problem.'

'Explain why that would be so.'

'I can use a steel button to measure against when fixing the coordinates, but even so, accurate positioning of the related boreholes over the distances we require will take some doing. Measurements would need to be very accurate.'

Trevithick was unconvinced.

'Why does that cause you problems?'

'If we totally rely on the measurement dials of our worktable, the backlash in the leadscrew is bound to introduce error. I reckon it could throw us out by as much as a sixty-fourth of an inch, if we don't adjust for it.'

Trevithick, who was stood at his desk, leaned forward, his palms flat on the drawings that lay upon it. For a moment he didn't speak. James knew he was in for a single-minded response, and his reservations would be made light of, but it was in a spirit of comradeship that Trevithick continued; or so James thought.

'I am sure you can do it, James. You were part of my blacksmith team that built and assembled my locomotive in Camborne. You were in a junior position, it is true, but you worked hard and diligently.' Then, Trevithick spoke with a scarcely veiled hint of menace.

'It was those characteristics that lead us to offer you the overman's position in my workshop, here, in Merthyr. I've put my faith in you. You will not fail me. I am sure of it.'

The veiled threat was not lost on James, and so he replied,

'We will be able to do it. I will find a way.'

'Yes, I am sure you will not let me down.'

James paused in order he might regain his composure, and then continued.

'I am told you have the date of the 21st of February for the first running of the engine, Sir?'

'Yes, that should be plenty of time to convert a boiler to run on rails.

'Yes, of course. But would it be too much to ask that I be allowed to travel with it again? Not with the dignitaries of course.'

'Not at all! I need you to come along. If anything goes wrong, you'd be the man to fix it. And why shouldn't the builder of the engine be involved?'

James was emboldened to continue.

'You'll remember my wife also travelled on the machine... on its return journey from Beacon.'

'Yes, now you mention it. She was, and still is, a lovely young lady. You are very lucky Mr. Rowe.'

'She has fond memories of the journey. Would she, and my daughter, be able to join me? I understand it may be too much to ask.'

'I don't see why not! And I'll invest in a new suit for you, and a new cap, too. Let's hope you won't have reason to take it off... should the boiler or engine fail.

'Thank you, Mr. Trevithick... In truth, sir, I have another personal reason why I wish to make the trip with you.'

'I'll not pry.'

'No, it doesn't need to remain a secret. You'll remember Almond, my brother who was lost to us.'

'Pressed, it was rumoured.'

'Pressed he was, but we have had word he's on his way back to make contact with us once again'

'Excellent! Although, does he know of his father?'

'We think he must, but we're not sure.'

'Still, it's very good news for you all.... but what has that to do with the run down to Navigation?'

'His ship is due to dock in Cardiff, and he can travel up to navigation on the day we are to make our run to Navigation. He'll follow the canal. There are enough barges making the trip and no doubt he'll ride with them.'

'He'll not travel onwards to Merthyr?'

'We believe his leave of duty is short. Getting down to Navigation would be an opportunity to meet him halfway, so to speak. Getting as far as Merthyr might well be beyond him. This way, he is bound to see some of his family in the space of time he has ashore.'

'I can see he'd like to meet his brother's new wife, and his niece, but wouldn't your older brother and your sister want to come along as well? I am not sure I can accommodate that many and leave room for those with business reasons to attend.'

'It would only be the three of us.'

'Then let it be. No doubt, too, there'd be a new dress for both the ladies in your party... supplied with my compliments, in the expectation we succeed in our task.

16

An Unwelcome Return

James and Maggie sat by the last embers of the fire, and whispered for fear of being overheard.

'Why would you think I'd want to see Almond again?'

'I wasn't sure you would, but I wanted you to have the choice. Getting you a ride on the engine meant you was excused work and you would be sure to meet him... should you want to.

'Why is it only now you're telling me?'

'I held back because I wasn't sure myself.'

'Sure of what'

'I wasn't sure I wanted you to face him... I expect he still has a fondness for you, and he must know we're now married. Evan would have been delighted to tell him... And of course, there's Kate.'

'And you want to take Kate with you.'

'If I tell him the truth of our marriage and of you having his child, he must be able to meet her.'

'Why must you tell him? Why must he meet her? Kate is our child, and has been from the day we married.'

'He'll know of a child. It was plain for all to see you were pregnant when we left. I think he'd have been told, and he'll want to know. I am almost sure of that. If he does, I can't lie.

'You did what you thought best for me and the child. One small lie won't undo the kindness you showed us then, or the love you have shown us since.'

'There are lies that don't matter, and then there are lies that will, one day, hurt.'

'Let this be a lie that's not meant to hurt.'

'But still… It's the lie that turns in on itself, and come back to remind of its telling that I fear.'

'But why must you take Kate? She bears no responsibility.'

'If he suspects the child to be his, he'll want to see her. I couldn't deny him.'

'And if he's not suspicious and you don't tell him, the lie remains the same as if you'd spoken it.'

'Then I'd tell him the truth?'

'For pity's sake James, don't do that!'

'For me to make peace with myself, I may have to.'

'I forbid it, James. You are my husband and the father of my children… including Kate. It is because of you that we've survived these last years. Where else could I have found a husband as true?'

'There can be no denying what happened.'

'I was no more than a child. It has nothing to with who I am now. Who we are now.'

'Then what are we to do, Maggie?'

'You can go, if you must…'

'And Kate? What about Kate?'

'If you insist, she can go, too… but,'

'You'll allow her to come, after what you've said.'

'Yes, I cannot deny he has the right to see her. But if he doesn't ask after her, you are to say nothing. We'll both find a way to live with the lie, and we won't let it come back to haunt us… I'll forget it happened, and you can be sure I'll not remind you.'

***

Saturday nights in the Brewers Inn was a raucous occasion. Good natured singsongs, led by the Welsh and Cornish. It would start with hymns, already well-rehearsed for the Chapel. Tenors were always a little too loud, with a tendency to go sharp when not under the control of the choirmaster, Jack Davies, who was fiercely teetotal, pious to boot, and never ventured into the pub. They would stand for the more rousing passages, and link arms for the singing of a top 'A sharp'. The basses, always out-sung, remained in their seats and echoed their voices into their beer mugs, content with the resonance of the lowest notes. The banter was rife, and young Hywel was the target of the humour.

'Hywel, who was that lass you were with last night?

'Overman's daughter I bet!' said Edward Richards.

'Hywel's been angling after a Stoker's job', said Royston, the furnaceman, who was always bawdy and good for a laugh; only for him to be out-done by a disembodied voice from the snug,

'He'll have to get a bigger poker than the one he's got'.

Hywel laughed as loud as anyone; it was nice to be noticed and included as a 'butty', but he thought it wise to keep his reply to himself.

James sat with Charles in a quieter corner.

'Finally, he makes the effort. It's been a couple of years since he turned up back at Camborne to find you gone. Why didn't he come to Merthyr sooner, this is where his family are?'

'He's still in the Navy, you know that Charles. I can only guess he's limited time onshore. To get here takes time he mayn't have.'

'He knows about you and Maggie.... and your children by her?'

'I can only suppose so. I got more word from Evan. He said that Almond showed up at the pub, bright as a button, wearing his Navy uniform and asking for us. He'd have been around the house and found us gone. I suppose those in the pub would have told him about our move, and of me and Maggie getting married.'

'And her with child. Evan would have laid it on thick.'

'Aye, no doubt, with nods and winks thrown in.'

'Almond's not going to be best pleased, James.'

'Be that as it may, what's done is done... Anyway, it turns out he's arriving on the same day Trevithick is to run his engine down the tramway to the basin. Trevithick's let me ride with it. So rather than walk, I've got us a ride.'

'Us? I'm not sure I'd want to go on that thing, James. It might explode.

'It'll be fine. You'll remember we rode his other machine in Camborne four years ago. It'll be the same thing only this time it will run on tram rails. Anyway, you're not included, you'll have to walk.'

'So, who else is going to go with you? I wouldn't have thought he'd be happy to see Maggie... nor you, for that matter.'

'I've spoken to Maggie, and it's true she doesn't want to see him. They were sweet in the past, but we've made our life here. Not knowing what happened to him, he can't have expected Maggie to wait until he turned up again... Our little one will come with me, too.'

'Henry? He's a bit too small to be shaken about on a wagon.'

'No, Kate.' We'll not mention young Henry to him.'

'Little Kate? So why would you take her... and wouldn't it be dangerous for her, too?' James avoided telling the true reason, and he made light of the risks involved,

'I want him to see we are a family. Elizabeth will come to look after her in Maggie's place. She doesn't want to miss out on the chance to meet her brother again. You know what she's like; she's a proud lass, and wants to show off how much she's grown. She'll have a new frock and mantle, courtesy of Trevithick himself... You'll try to come down to Navigation as well? You could take a barge down?'

Charles hesitated, then replied, 'No... We're strangers now, me and Almond, and I have my family to think of. He's survived, and so have we. But they'll need me to be at my place of work, earning a living. I don't have the luck, like you, to be invited wages paid. Wish him well from me. There may be another time, if in the future he decides to make his home here, as we have. Then I'll greet him as a brother should... Although, somehow I doubt he'll wash up here again.'

'That's true. He'll be his own man, having spent four years in the Navy. God knows how he'll have changed, but he's making an effort to get to us, so we'll soon find out. I want him to know that life goes on... That *we* go on.'

Selwyn Berryman-Morgan

17

The First Steam Train

Attached to the engine were 5 wagons containing the allotted load of iron, plus 70 passengers. There were notaries who were to observe the test run along the length of the track and testify to the ability of the locomotive to transport goods and people in accordance with the wager. Various dignitaries and Standards' Inspectors were amongst the passenger list, but there were also employees of the ironworks. Another employee who took part was Hopkin ap'Daniel, a furnace man. He had volunteered to take part, controlling the crowds. His family came along as well so they could witness the event. He was accompanied by his wife, Bronwen, and his children. Hopkin junior, aged 16, had not joined his father in the foundry but had gone to live and work on the canal barges with his uncle, Daniel ap'Daniel. Traditional Welsh families did not use surnames, but instead, their names used the Welsh conjunction, '*ap*', son of, or '*ferch*', daughter of. Young Hopkin was therefore known as Hopkin ap'Hopkin; it often being the tradition to name the firstborn boy after his father.

Bronwen had lost a series of children at childbirth, and to premature deaths, so there was a gap to the next two, Sian aged 7 and Bronwen aged 5. The young girls still attended the newly founded school in Penydarren and were learning to read and write, not in Welsh, their own language, but in English, as prescribed by the British Government. On this day, with there being dignitaries present, the family spoke in English, but mixed in with it were Welsh endearments.

'What do you think might happen, Sian?'

'I think they will let all the steam out, and it will fly like the wind, *Tad*.'

'*Da iawn!* You're a clever girl. It's all the teaching you get, *Cariad*.'

'Hopkin, *bach*, are you going to try to get a ride.'

'*Na Tad*! I'd fear it'd blow up.'

'*Tad!* Leave the boy alone. And I don't want my girls anywhere near that machine. I didn't want them to come today, anyway.'

'The kids will be alright and Hopkin will be off with his girlfriend. Anyhow, I need to get on, helping to get this crowd back.

'Hopkin *bach*, if you see your Lizzie, ask if she wants to come for tea on Sunday. It's time enough we met her,' shouted Bronwen, as her son receded into the crowd

Such was the interest in the outcome of the Ironmaster's wager and the novelty of the mechanical contraption, that all of the social classes were to be found crowding the head of the tramway. Hopkin senior was helped in his crowd control duties, as most spectators decided to stand well back as the engine was 'steamed up'.

***

The winter's day was cold and bright and hinted at the return of spring, with the sun higher in the sky than most would have remembered it being; the working day would have started and ended in the dark for the last three months. Trevithick's engine, newly manufactured, with minimal pressure testing and fresh from the workshops, stood on the tramway, fired up and steaming. A carnival atmosphere had built in the crowd gathered to see this '*new wonder of the industrial age*', as Trevithick had promoted it. In keeping with the significance of the occasion, many were in their Sunday best, winter clothes. Stalls provided hot food and drink, and bunting was flown across the tramway. Children ran excitedly along the rails in front of the engine, daring to come as near as they could before being shooed off by Tom Jenkins.

'Get away from the front there, you little beggars. Get away I said'

'What's it got to do with you Old Man Jenkins?' a rascal replied, knowing Dai Jenkins was a paid labourer for the day who would otherwise have been doing nothing, except waiting for the pub to open.

Side bets were placed on the outcome of the proceedings. Would the engine move at all? Would it get out of the ironworks yard? Would it fall apart? Would it explode!? Few, except Trevithick, Homfray, and James, had faith it would work, and would reach its destination ten miles away.

Four-year-old Kate stood at James' side, wide-eyed at the sight and sound of the steam locomotive. Holding her hand was Maggie, still unsure whether or not Kate should ride with James and Elizabeth. It would be a journey ending with Almond meeting his daughter. She had resolved it was the right thing to do, but to let go of Kate's hand was another matter.

'Keep her close James. Bring our daughter back safe and sound.'

'Our Lizzie, will hold her tight. She'll not let her go until we get down to Navigation.'

'You know she's fine with me, Maggie,' said Elizabeth, 'and my friend Hopkin is here, too. He can help us on to the wagon… If I ask him nice, he might come with us.'

'They'll not let me on, even if I'd want to come, Lizzy.'

James could see some sense in the idea.

'You could be my apprentice, you're scruffy enough.'

'Excuse me, Mr. Rowe, these are my Sunday best.'

'Only joking, Mister... er...?'

'Hopkin ap'Hopkin, Mr. Rowe. Hopkin was a good enough name for my dad so it's good enough for me.'

'Right you are lad! It's good enough for me, too. Mr. Hopkin-ap-Hopkin shall be my new apprentice. Although, for the sake of brevity, may I call you Hopkin?'

'Hopkin will be fine, and yes, thank you, Mr. Rowe, I will be glad to help, if only for the day.' Then Hopkin added, as if someone cared,

'I've got a barge to get to Cardiff with my Uncle. We start loading it this evening.'

He's got a spark in him, thought James. Not afraid to speak up for himself. He'd be a good lad for Elizabeth and she'd be good for any young man presently found in Merthyr. Hopkin was two years Elizabeth's senior. James thought him a nice lad but smiled at the awkwardness of Hopkin having a Christian name the same as his Surname.

Christiana Harris watched them from a raised platform set above the local crowd for use by local dignitaries. She could not bear to be party to the child's leaving. Christiana would not normally have thought herself worthy of such consideration, but the need to watch her grandchild be taken from her into circumstances out of her control gripped her with fear. The urge for her to be witness to the event overcame her disapproval. Her lowly status was of no matter, she pushed and shoved and begged indulgence, due to her age, to get to the front rail of the platform. No one seemed to care she was there. It wasn't the danger of the machine and the speed it may travel that was at the heart of her unease. No, it was the fear Almond, *the swine,* might have the right to the love the child had reserved for its family. Almond was no longer family as far as she was concerned. The hardships they had endured over the last four years were borne by those who now took pains to transport Kate to him. More than that, the special love that bonded the child to its grandmother could be broken, if Almond was to claim the child as his own... She had pleaded with Maggie,

'Why let him know? What is there to be gained?'

'James is determined Almond should know about Kate. No matter how I argued, I've not been able to stop him wanting to tell the truth of it.'

'We must try again... I will try to make him see sense. Make him see that it's of no help to anyone revealing the truth.'

'No, Mam. He is the head of the house, and I've decided to have faith in James' judgement.'

I'm not happy Almond's returned and I don't know what to do for the best.

'And if it turns out to be for the worst?'

'It won't! It mustn't.

***

'Come with me Kate, my love. We're going on that wagon pulled by the Puffing Devil.' The name given by Mary to the Camborne steam engine had stayed with the family, and was used by their friends left in Camborne where they still talked about it.

Kate, in response, held her hand out to Elizabeth.

That was when Maggie came face-to-face with the reality of her decision to let her daughter travel to Navigation.

Maggie fought the urge to turn and run back to her house with the child in her arms and leave James to his damned steam engine. It was then she finally made up her mind and there would be no turning back. She cried out,

'No'

'Maggie! We have agreed what we're going to do. Be strong.'

'We *will* do what we agreed, but I'm coming, too.'

James paused before speaking. He was trying to understand what would have changed her mind. Presently, he said,

'If you're sure and you wish to come?' Maggie nodded her head, not being able to repeat her words.

'In that case, Elizabeth, I'm sorry, you will have to stay behind?'

Elizabeth's heart sank. The chance to see her brother after all the years he had been away was slipping away from her. She knew it was right for Maggie to be with James and Kate, but she couldn't help defend her right as a sister.

'But Maggie had said she didn't want to go, and when will I have the chance to see him again?'

'There will be another chance, love. He won't be in the Navy forever.'

'Where will we all be in ten years?'

'We will be here, where else.'

127

'No! We agreed I would come with you. And Hopkin is coming, too. What about Hopkin?'

'I'm sorry, Elizabeth, I've made my decision. Hopkin can still come, I can use his help, and I've cleared it with Mr Trevithick, but there was only space allowed on the wagon for one other.

'But, but...'

Elizabeth could see there was no arguing with James. She turned and ran sobbing into the crowd, and was immediately lost from sight.

'I'll try to find her and see she's alright,' said Hopkin.

'Best leave her be, Hopkin. She'll see the sense in it. You're still welcome to come along with us. In fact, I would like it if you did.'

'I'm not sure Mr. Rowe.'

'You may not get a second chance to ride on a steam engine.'

'Well, if you think I'd be of use, I'd like to come.'

'The firemen have her ready and she's steaming. Trevithick won't wait for us, so let's go.'

***

James directed Maggie, Kate and Hopkin to their place on the first of the wagons, the wagon nearest to the steam engine.

'You can get on here. I can keep an eye on you, as I'll be riding on the engine with Mr. Trevithick.' James used his authority as part of the Company employees to get the already boarded passengers to make space.

'I can keep an eye on you. If there are problems, I can get back to sort them out. Maggie, make yourself comfortable at the front of the wagon. The trams with the pig iron are being attached now, so we will soon be off. Don't get moved away from the front. You stay here, too, Hopkin, but keep an eye on me. Should I need you I'll give you a wave.' James helped Maggie and Kate up onto the wagon and left them to join Trevithick on the footplate of the steam engine.

'There you are, Mr. Rowe. I have been waiting for you.'

128

'I am sorry, Mr. Trevithick, family matters. I know it shouldn't interfere.'

'I suppose it's a big day for all of us.'

'More than you know, Sir.'

The signal was given. All the wagons had been hitched and all the passengers were secure.

'Let us take up the load.'

The engine driver slowly opened the throttle to allow steam to the piston cylinders. The wait was over. Trevithick was to find out if, as he had predicted, the friction of the engine's wheels on the rail would hold sway over the weight of the train. Would the wheels roll on the track, or would they spin in a shower of sparks? The wheels turned slowly and the slack between the engine and the wagons was taken up in a series of jerks that had the occupants of the wagons gasp with surprise and the spectators cheer in ridicule of the predicament. It was the moment in the proceedings when the weight of the train of vehicles was pulled by the engine, and its wheels spun, generating sparks that shot backwards along the rails. The crowd groaned then roared with nervous laughter. Trevithick was calm in the face of such ridicule.

'Apply more steam, but gradually. She will bite.'

The throttle was opened up a notch and the wheels spun again, but then gained some purchase and imparted forward motion to the engine and hanging train of carriages. There was a slight downwards slope to the rail, imperceptible, but enough. Once the train was in motion, the gradient would help to maintain the forward momentum.

All I need to do now is keep it moving, thought Trevithick.

'Keep the same level of steam... let it do its job.'

The driver resisted the urge to apply more throttle, allowing the wheels to find purchase in between the spinning. Little by little, the train moved forward, much less than walking pace, but increasing its speed at each wheel spin. After the first minute, the engine's wheels gripped more than spun and the forward motion was smooth. The train was travelling close to the walking speed of a horse with a tram in tow. Trevithick's first aim had been achieved.

'Throttle back slightly and maintain our speed.'

The crowds followed, cheering the progress of the train of wagons and their contents. They soon passed the foundries that continued to belch their smoke, production continuing as it always had, day after day. In the canal close by, barges were still being loaded and unloaded, unaware of the significance the running of this engine was to have on their continued use as transporters of bulk materials.

The train carried on down the valley, leaving the town behind it but still being followed by the crowd that had started out with it on its journey. Trevithick was confident and encouraged by the performance of his engine.

'Gently apply more steam.'

The throttle was moved a notch to see the response. At first, there seemed to be no change but Trevithick noticed the urchins walking at the side of the engine started to add an occasional skip to their step, and then to continually skip, and then trot.

'Hold back the steam.'

The steam was throttled back, but the momentum of the train was maintained. It would require a fine balance between throttle, momentum and the friction of the rails to maintain speed and not let the train run away. The braking system had not yet been tested. Even with less steam applied to the pistons, the speed of the train increased slightly. Trevithick judged it to be safe, as the higher speed seemed to be suitable for the current gradient.

The number of followers on foot had reduced, as only the younger and fitter townsfolk could keep up the pace, and they would not keep up for long. They would need to stay back when the engine reached the tramway tunnel; the tunnel burrowed through an inconvenient rock spur of the hillside that ran to the river bank.

Trevithick kept an eye on the speed of the train asking for adjustment as he felt it was necessary, but James' eyes were drawn to the approaching tunnel. He had manufactured the engine to the precision the engineering drawings required of him, but the roof of the tunnel seemed low to the rails? It was more than enough for the trams but the engine's stack was designed to keep the smoke and smuts of the fire well above the driver and those who rode the footplate. Now, James wasn't sure if there was enough clearance for it? The more he looked the more he wasn't sure. Had anyone checked the height? Should he shout a warning? After a few moments more of indecision, he decided to call to Trevithick.

'Mr. Trevithick, we must stop! The tunnel, I think it's too low for us to enter.'

Trevithick looked up and instantly assessed the problem.

'Throttle off completely and apply the brake.'

James already had his hand on the brake handle, that, when pulled, applied a friction pad to the drive wheels. Trevithick joined him pulling at it as the brake didn't bite. When it did, the forward momentum of the wagons forced the engine to continue down the gradient, its wheel screeching against the rail and increasing the likelihood of derailment There was no alternative but to let go of the brake to gain a moment's control and then to reapply it. The train slowed in fits and starts as the tunnel came ever closer. It became obvious the stack was too high. It would not clear the tunnel's roof, and James wasn't sure if they would stop in time. Trevithick had given the commands as when to apply and release the brake, and, using his best judgement, they finally brought the engine stack to a stop one foot away from the tunnel. There was no chance for the party on the footplate to congratulate themselves as the wagons behind had the final word. Their unrestrained momentum carried them into the engine, driving it forward into the tunnel and jamming the top of its funnel hard against the tunnel roof. The four men on the footplate were thrown back against the rear plate and burning embers from the boiler hearth blasted out, showering their legs. Behind, in the wagons, the passengers were thrown forward.

Hopkin had seen it all unfolding, and he shouted,

'Maggie and Kate, come quickly and *cwtch* down in the corner.'

Maggie knew from the urgency of his voice she should do so without question. Hopkin stood over them, his legs apart and his arms braced against the front of the wagon. Upon impact, those standing toppled forward, one on the other, whilst the privileged, who had seats, slid forward into the seats in front of them. Those standing behind Hopkin fell against him. Some had hold of the side rail and were able to restrain their fall, whilst others completely lost their balance. The weight was almost too much for Hopkin to hold, but he was a strong lad, the loading of barges over the years had seen to that, and he held firm. The passengers righted themselves; the shocked cries of those with injuries, minor as they were, rang out.

'Emanuel, I've hurt my arm!'

'Is that blood on your face?'

'Are you alright, my love?'

Upon the footplate of the engine, the driver and stoker, whose leather aprons had saved them from the showered sparks, brushed down Mr. Trevithick before too much damage could be caused to his fine clothes. James looked after himself, although he burnt his hands in the process. Trevithick, seemingly unflustered, asked after him.

'Are you hurt badly?'

Although shocked by the sudden turn of events, James was encouraged by his employer's concern.

'I'm fine, sir. Small burns on my hands and on my legs where the embers burnt through. My trousers are old enough for me not to worry.' He was speaking to a receding Trevithick as his master was already assessing the damage and deciding what to do next. He shouted over his shoulder,

'You go along the carriages and tell everyone we'll soon be underway again, and apologise for the minor mishap. Then come back and join me here. We've got work to do.'

James went first to Maggie and Kate. 'Daddy, the train went bump and bumped me, too... here,' her news much more important to her than anything else. Kate pointed to her head. It seemed none the worse.

'Come here my lovely, let me kiss it better. There, you'll soon be on the mend. Are you alright Maggie?'

'Yes, thanks to young Hopkin here. He protected us... What happened?'

'Yes, we've had a little bump. It seems our measuring sticks weren't good enough and the train's top hat was a bit too big.'

His humour blended with the relief everyone felt knowing no one was badly hurt. Laughter sounded out down along the wagons. James announced,

'We'll soon be underway,' and he leant up and kissed Maggie, lingering a little longer than would have been thought acceptable in public, but this was a special occasion. He went back to the engine and Trevithick, who was surveying the damage and how to repair it.

'James, if we can break the rivets holding the main section of the funnel we can slide it down far enough for it to clear the roof. The trouble is the rivets that hold it are a quarter inch. They'll be a devil to cut through.'

'A big mandrill and a sledgehammer would do it in an instant.'

'Yes, I suppose it would, but we've not got a mandrill. We've got hammers and a cold chisel, but not big enough for this job.'

'I can soon get the right tools.' James announced, and continued,

'In the meantime, Sir, could the stoker use the chisels we have to cut away the edge of the rivets so we can get a purchase with the mandrill' James jumped off the engine and ran back to the wagons.

'Hopkin, you know where we live. Get back to the house. Around the back, in the coal shed, there's my dad's canvas tool bag. Bring it back here. Check to see it contains a mandrill... bring the sledgehammer as well. You'll find that there, too, against the wall. You'll be back here in half an hour if you're quick.' Hopkin set off.

Back at the engine, the Driver and stoker had used his chisel to fold over the edge of the first of the twelve rivets and was about to move on to the second.

'Once you've done the same on all the rivets you can try to shear one of them. We may as well try to get on with it.'

'I'll not be able to do that Mr. Rowe. This chisel's losing its edge just lifting the flange and we've no way to sharpen it. We'll need your mandrill.'

'It'll be here in half an hour,' said James.

Trevithick spoke,

'Even so, keep at it so our passengers know we're busy getting us back on our way again, otherwise they'll head off back to Merthyr and the taverns.'

Back up the track, Hopkin had remembered what he thought might be an eighteen-inch water pipe spanning the river a mile south of the town. He'd walked it before, as a childish 'dare'. It was a stupid thing to do, and nothing had changed, except the urgent need to get James his father's tool bag. James' house was also south of the town. If he walked the pipe he could shave a mile off his journey. It would be worth the risk.

The pipe was smaller in diameter than Hopkin remembered it. Looking at it now, it was more like fourteen inches, and its surface was flaked, deep with rust. He wasn't certain what he should do.

Should I risk it...?

'Well, there's no point hanging around,' he said to himself, as he stepped onto the pipe.

His first step confirmed that its corroded surface would crumble under his weight, but his foot seemed secure, it didn't slip off with the likelihood of it taking him with it.

I'll try one more step, he thought and moved forward. The pipe felt safe enough to commit to the crossing.

Concentrate, thought Hopkin, *one step in front of the other. The pipe is dry, and if I don't look down...* but the thought he shouldn't look down was the trigger for him to do just that. The Taff was in full winter's spate, and this high up in the valley the gradient meant it rushed in torrents. It would be another twenty miles before it would slow and meander to the coast.

He felt dizzy, and crouched low to the pipe to try to regain his balance. He stood straight again and focused on his next step. Twenty more and he would be across.

'What you doing Mister? Are you daft?'

Remnants of the hordes of kids who had chased after the engine stood watching him from the bank.

'Don't you worry about me, get back to school with you.' The same urchin replied,

'You'll fall off and wash up in Cardiff. My dad said not to go near the pipe. Archie Jones fell off it last year. Dead 'e is.'

'Bugger off and stop bothering me!'

'We'll just sit here and watch you fall off... You is going to fall off, you is going to fall off,' he began to chant. The others joined in.

Hopkin shouted over his shoulder.

'If you don't stop, I'll come back and box your ears,'

'You'd better keep going the way you is going... You is going to fall off, you is going to fall off;' they continued, knowing they were safe; even if this 'Mister' was to turn round they could run and be gone in a flash.

It took a couple minutes for him to reach the end of the pipe and he jumped onto the far bank. The young lads across the river cheered. Hopkin smiled and waved to them, before bowing theatrically, as if to acknowledge the applause.

'Well done mister.'

You little buggers, thought Hopkin, *I'll "Well done Mister" you, the next time I see your scruffy face.*

Hopkin continued at a trot. Mr. Rowe's house was few hundred yards ahead. He knew how to get around the back of the terrace and over the wall; he had occasionally been doing it for the last couple of months, meeting Elizabeth when they knew the house would be empty.

Fifteen minutes had passed since the accident and the passengers had become restless.

'This new-fangled engine is going nowhere. Stuck like a pig in a passage.'

'We may as well walk back. I've got a stew on the grate keeping warm. Better sooner than later.'

Trevithick broke out the beer and cordial; he had been keeping it for their arrival at Navigation.

'We won't be long before we are underway again, but until we are perhaps you would like a drink to wet down any food you have brought, and, if you haven't, we've some Welsh cakes for you, too.' The cakes were small and flat, made from a batter of plain flour and milk, and had been baked in quantity on a griddle that morning by Trevithick's cook. Sugar had been sprinkled over them. Everyone loved Welsh cakes, nearly as much as they liked the beer.

'How much longer is your lad going to be James? I'll soon run out of beer and cakes.'

James decided to come clean; he knew his "half an hour" was wishful thinking, and Hopkin had already been away twenty minutes.

'At best, another twenty minutes, Mr. Trevithick.'

'Let's hope it's not much longer than that.'

'We've got the rivets ready to take the mandrill. They will be off in no time. Perhaps, a further ten minutes, and we'll have the top of the funnel dropped by a foot.'

With that, a cheer rose from the wagons at the rear of the train. Back up the track, they could see Hopkin trotting towards them.

'It's Hopkin! He's coming back,' called Maggie. Back at the engine, James feared the worst.

'He shouldn't be back yet Mr. Trevithick.'

James ran up the line to meet him, and sure enough, there was Hopkin running in a slow trot, carrying Henry's tool bag hung from the sledgehammer he had over his shoulder.

'You must have flown, lad. You're a saint.'

'A saint? Not me Mister Rowe, although I did walk across water...'

James didn't know what he meant, but he let it go and turned their attention to the job at hand.

They stood on the footplate looking at the bent and misshapen funnel. James reached into the bag.

'Here's the mandrill I'll use. As you see, Mr. Trevithick its forged flat and ground to a chisel point.' James handed it to the fireman.

'Hold this whilst I wield the sledge. It won't take more than two blows a rivet.'

'I'm not sure I want you throwing that sledge where my hands might be in the way. What if you miss the end of the mandrill?'

'I know how to use a sledge.'

Trevithick stepped in.

'Never you mind. Give it to me and let's get on with it.' Trevithick stood holding the mandrill wedged against the first rivet.

'Strike away when you are ready.'

James held his breath before making the first blow. He was not sure if one blow would be enough to shear the steel pin. If it was, the residual force could mean the mandrill and sledge would carry through, perhaps striking Mr. Trevithick.

That wouldn't be a good result, he thought.

His first blow was careful, and it only cut through half of the rivet.

'It's mild steel. Same again will do it,' said Trevithick

James used the same technique for all the rivets. It took twenty-four blows to free the top section of the funnel from the lower stack, and it fell eighteen inches before lodging itself at the bend in the pipe. That was more than enough to create headroom for the train to run through the tunnel. Trevithick shouted back to the people in the wagons,

'Everything is repaired. As soon as we've steam up, we'll be on our way to Navigation.' Cheers rang out.

'Are we going now?' asked Kate.

'Yes, we are my love. Your dad's mended the engine.' Kate clapped her hands together.

'Clever Daddy!'

18

The Family Meet

Almond walked the canal towpath from the Cardiff Basin. He had cleared the docks, with its jumble of cranes engaged in either adding to mounds of coal, destined for the Merthyr furnaces, or unloading the hundreds of tons of 'Pig Iron' ingots waiting in barges. He had never seen the likes of it in any naval dock or any of the commercial docks along the coast of Cornwall; and he had thought those were big.

The countryside he travelled was pleasant enough.

Bargemen had words of encouragement for a sailor of the fleet. He was often called on.

'You back from fighting with Nelson at Trafalgar?

'Good luck to you son, and God bless! I'll raise a glass to you,' a particularly jolly boatman cried, and continued,

'Must be good to be on dry land for a while? You wouldn't catch me sailing any water that isn't flat,' he laughed.

'After five miles of walking, I think I have got my land legs, Sir. But, thank you for asking,' replied Almond.

The kids along the way, attracted by his uniform, rudimentary as it was, wanted to hear tales of life at sea and the adventures he would have had; questions they thought up for their own amusement rather than in the hope of getting a sensible answer.

'You've fought the Frenchies, 'ave you?

'Did you sink many ships?'

'Did you know the Admiral? Had he only got one leg?

In the spirit of the questions asked, Almond respond in kind.

'The Admiral's my best mate. He'd not only one leg but only one arm, and its hand had two fingers missing from it.'

'He must have been an 'andsome bloke,' laughed a scallywag.

'Yes, he was. Did you know he only had one ear and half a nose?' replied Almond.

The children's laughter helped to put a spring in his step.

His time ashore was short, and the eighteen miles he needed to travel, both ways, meant any friendly acquaintance made with a bargeman might afford him respite on the return journey; if he could persuade them to let him on board. But, for now, he needed to make all speed.

He had set off well before dawn. It was a cold February day, but there was no rain and the wind was light. Puddles at the side of the canal were frozen and the towpath was slippery. He needed to take care as he stepped out, at least until the sun was up and would melt the ice away.

The flat vale, north of Cardiff, spread out in front of him. The sun had risen, and had slanted light across the hedgerows; the farmland was set in its winter fallow. Some fields supported sheep, huddled in small clusters to keep out the chill of the night. It had been clear and cloudless, and the pink of the sun's rays reflected from the tops of the frost-tinged hedges. A river flowed in wide sweeps over the flat of the vale and was in full spate from the accumulated winter rains. From the elevated canal path, the river Taff could be seen in tree-lined sections, each section would bend out of sight, only for another section of river to appear further north, at another bend in its path. Although the river's tumble and swirl reflected the pale dawn light, its depths were black with the effluent of the industry hidden beyond the hills. They were already in sight and in full sunlight, capped with the remnants of light snow. Even as the light of the day grew intense, the deep black of the river stubbornly refused to accept the sun's gift, and brooded because of the filth it was asked to carry away. Ahead, in the distance, a gap in the hillside came into focus. It was like a cannon's sight worn into the rock by the flow of the river over countless centuries. Beyond the gap he knew would be his target, a meeting with his family, with James; Almond clenched his fist at the thought of his brother. He had questions he would ask Maggie: why she didn't wait for him, why did she fall into James' arms, why did she have his child? At the thought of her, the rage inside him turned to a melancholic longing. He thought how he would hug her to his chest... not as his lover, but as his sister-in-law.

***

Six months previously, Almond had arrived home in Camborne after more than three years at sea. The village nestled in the valley... smaller, perhaps, than he remembered it. It was mid-afternoon on a bright summer's day. He walked down Camborne hill to the village edge. He could see nothing had changed. The daily round of village life had its familiar plod of comings, goings, gatherings and gossip, whilst the toil underground lay hidden from the idyll above.

Where to go first? His family would be at work, as would Maggie's. He decided the best place would be the pub on the green; a beer to quench his thirst and perhaps a familiar face. There was bound to be someone he knew, someone who would clasp his hand in recognition and who would be happy at his return. And so it turned out... almost.

'Evan! My old friend.'

'Upon my soul, if it isn't young Almond... Come home at last!' he growled.

Almond ignored what was a cold response. He decided he'd continue as if he hadn't noticed.

'Back home after years away, I know. But it wasn't for the want of trying, Evan.'

'We guessed you'd been dragged off and thrown into one of 'is Majesty's ships, and by the look of your uniform, that's just what happened. What is it now... two or three years ago? You must have been around the World, and here you are back again.'

'Any land I touched was at least a hundred miles from here... Are you at work today, Evan?'

'I get work when I can, but there ain't much of that about nowadays, and what with my chest an' all.'

'Dad and James will be at work though, I suppose?'

'You've not been to the house then?'

'No, I thought I wouldn't find anyone there at this time of day.

'Well, at any rate, you're right about there not being anyone at home.'

From Evan's knowing look and obvious pleasure at toying with him, Almond sensed there was a side to the story he was not going to like.

'What do you mean, Evan?'

'Well...' Evan hesitated for effect... 'they're not there anymore.'

'But still in the village?'

Evan paused for effect.

'Stop playing games, Evan, tell me what's happened.' Almond knew a gradual telling of the truth would not take away the pain of knowing it.

'No, they've gone away.'

'Gone away? Where?'

'They've up-sticks and gone to Wales.

'Wales?'

They went and joined Charlie boy and his missus.'

Almond thought for a moment, and then he said, half to himself,

'We'd talked about it... and Maggie and her family had said they might one day have to leave.'

'Yes, Maggie... you were sweet on her, alright.'

'Well… what did that matter to you?'

Evan's good nature had, over the years, turned to bitterness at his turn of luck. He had become mean-spirited, and he would take a perverse satisfaction in bringing this young upstart down to his level of despair. Evan lay a hand on Almond's shoulder and spoke in as sympathetic a tone as he could muster; given the pleasure he had in telling the story.

'Truth is... and it pains me to say it... she went and married James, not so long after you left... a couple of months or so after... not long at all.'

Almond answered, again, almost to himself, 'Why would she do that?'

'Well, he was around her house sniffin' after you'd gone. Before you'd know it, they were up and married, and before they left it was clear she was pregnant, at least to the womenfolk it was... couldn't see it myself. He didn't waste much time taking over from where you left off... if you knows what I mean? No disrespect, like.'

Almond felt a rage swell within him, but he was used to controlling rage; he had been taught by experience in the Navy, showing rage, other than in battle, resulted in painful humiliation. He gathered his thoughts and inquired more of Evan,

'And the rest of the Maggie's family?'

'Oh, they've gone, too, with James, to Wales.'

'And Elizabeth, and my dad?'

Evan faltered in the telling his story and remained silent long enough for Almond to repeat the question.

'And the rest of my family? What of them?'

Evan had talked himself into a corner and he felt uncomfortable. His need to get revenge for the hurt in his own life had left him inconsiderate to the feelings of the people he had once held dear... the *person* he held most dear... Henry.

Had they not knelt together at the mine face and trusted each other. Trusted their companionship would get them back to the surface, alive and in one piece. As comrades, their union of purpose was greater than if they had knelt together in the chapel asking for God's assistance to live out the day; and unlike their God, their companion's assistance was more likely to make it happen. Now he had to tell of Henry's death, something about which he cared; in a world where little else did. Should he deny any knowledge of it? It would be the simplest way to avoid having to deal with his emotions. He thought,

I'll say they left, too, and I don't know what happened to them… but it would be denying Henry. Instead, he looked Almond straight in the eye, and for there to be no misunderstanding, he said,

'I'm told that Elizabeth is well, and lives with James and their young family, but... I'm sorry, Almond, your father is no longer with us. He died along the way.

Almond left the village to return to his ship. His thoughts were a mixture of grief at the news of his father, and rage at the thought both Maggie and James should forget about him so soon after his disappearance. He couldn't see any circumstance that would lead them to marriage unless, as Evan had implied, James forced his attention upon her, and made her pregnant. When Almond endured the harsh reality of life at sea, he had longed for home and to see Maggie and his family again, but now he vowed he would find them and they would answer to him.

***

The canal and its tradesmen had greeted the day. Almond asked,

'How far is it to Navigation?'

'You've a long way to go yet, over four hours, or five, maybe. Just follow the path, you can't go wrong. If you get tired a penny will get you a ride on a barge, but that will slow you up.'

The canal ran close to the river at Nantgarw, as the narrow gap in the hillside dictated the course the canal would take. The countryside changed from the flat of the farmlands to a steeply sided valley. It would continue for more than twenty miles to Merthyr Tydfil, the place where his family now worked and lived. But his destination was not as far. The proposed meeting was at Navigation, just fourteen miles further on. He would need his two days on shore to complete the round trip and it helped the canal ran almost straight, with the occasional lock for it to gain height. Alongside the canal, villages had grown; as the canal provided easy access along the length of the valley. Housing had sprung up along its path for the canal builders, and later, for lock keepers. And, in order to support them, maintenance crews joined the population. A supportive infrastructure had blossomed: boatyards, blacksmiths and farriers. Smallholders provided the food they needed.

***

The meeting had taken a long time to arrange. Once paid for their trouble, messages had been relayed by the canal workers of Wales, and the cart drivers of Cornwall. Daniel-ap-Daniel had been part of that chain. Their efforts had led to this moment.

It was almost two in the afternoon when he reached the canal basin at Navigation. It was at the eastern end of an aqueduct that spanned the river Taff, and was the canal junction with the tram road. Here the pig iron from the trams was unloaded onto the waiting barges.

Beyond the Basin, Almond could see the crowds milling around, and amongst the mass of people he could see the black of Trevithick's engine with its tell-tale stack. He knew what it was, but not why it was there...? And why were there crowds?

He looked for Maggie and James.

They must be here. This is where James said they would be, he thought.

Then he noticed Trevithick, unmistakable in his black suit and tall hat, and there, next to him, was James. There was no sign of Maggie.

Has she not come?

He strode along the towpath that edged the basin, trying not to run, trying to keep calm. What was he to say? It had gone through his mind a hundred times in a hundred different ways. Even now, he was not sure what words would come out of his mouth. He broke through the crowd by the engine and stood at the steps to the footplate. James was there and saw Almond. He jumped down to greet him.

'Almond, you've returned at last.' He took Almond in a brotherly embrace, but Almond didn't offer an embrace in return.

James guessed at the demons afflicting his brother; his torment at having been dragged from his family and having to endure life as a pressed seaman. Worse still, to find his Maggie *'with'* his brother.

'Come Almond, let's move away from here. We have a lot to talk about.'

'Where's Maggie?'

'She's just this moment left. We agreed to meet on the bank on the other side of the basin when I'd finished here. She's well, and in safe hands.'

They moved, leaving the crowd still applauding Trevithick; who responded to them like the showman he was, waving his hands clasped above his top hat.

'There's much to tell, Almond, but first, let me look at you... You're taller, but not by much. Your jaw has strengthened…It's clear, life in the Navy has seen you grow.'

James gripped him firmly by his shoulders and his gaze searched Almond's eyes;

'What was it like? Was it too bad to say?'

Almond was slow to respond and so James ploughed on, afraid of a pause in the conversation, wary of what Almond might say, now Maggie was his wife. What James went on to ask was somehow less difficult for him.

'Almond, I guess you've heard about Dad dying on his way here. We sent word to Camborne?'

Almond nodded in response, but he still didn't speak.

'He's a great loss to us all. Only now he's gone do we know how much we relied on him.'

It was if speaking of their father gave James strength. He grasped the nettle and spoke of what he knew was the cause of Almond's cold response.

'We both talked about it... you know, if Maggie and me should get wed.'

'Why did you?' snapped Almond. 'I think I know...' There was a shocked moment of silence between the brothers. It was broken by Almond.

'It was only a few months after I was taken that you wed, according to Evan, and he said you made her pregnant beforehand.'

Almond had set the terms of engagement. This was not going to be a joyful reunion.

Maggie, carrying Kate, broke through the crowd, Hopkin forcing a path for them. Almond saw the group scurrying towards him. His eyes focused on Maggie. She was no longer the young lass he imagined, the young lady for whom his heart longed, night after night... although she was still beautiful. He thought of those moments on the engine back to Camborne, and of the last smile she beamed before she left him. This was not the same Maggie. The anxious woman who approached him, carrying a child, whose very existence proved he had been cuckolded by his brother, had aged beyond the passage of time.

Hopkin, sensing this moment was best left to the privacy of the family, slipped back into the crowd.

Maggie stood before him, breathing heavily from her effort to intervene before too much could be said. She didn't know how she'd greet Almond. Different scenes had run through her mind: a warm embrace, words of love and remorse, words about the loss of the time they would have otherwise spent together... or would she face his wrath? She was not left to wonder a moment longer.

'So, this is James' child. You didn't miss my company for long, Maggie.'

She cared not about the rebuke. Maggie was relieved James hadn't told Almond the truth of it. She would tell her version of the truth as it applied to their reality, but before she could gather her thoughts, James spoke.

'It's not what you think, Almond...' Almond broke in and snarled,

'I know what it is, James... It's treachery!'

Almond stepped towards James and swung a clubbed fist with a hatred that had built since his meeting with Evan. James swayed away from the blow, such that it only brushed his face, but it was sufficient to knock him down. The blow that knocked him off his feet was the spoken word... 'Treachery'. And Almond wasn't finished,

'Get up, you bastard, Get up! Let's sort this out once and for all.'

'Almond, stop this!' Maggie cried, trying to hold him back with her free arm.

'Stay out of this, Maggie. I first have to settle this with James.'

He pushed her away and reached down to drag James from the ground. Before he could do so, arms encircled Almond's chest, restraining him. Almond let James go, turning to shake off whoever was trying to stop him taking revenge. He swung his elbow back hard and connected with the face of James' defender.

Elizabeth fell to the floor holding her face. Almond grabbed her by her shawl, not to inflict more damage but to throw her to one side.

'Almond! Please don't' cried Elizabeth...

Almond froze. He knew who this young woman was from her voice; he'd heard it echo in his memory through the years, and his violence towards her shocked him from his rage.

'Elizabeth...is it you?' She nodded, still holding her hands to her face, too scared to look at the man who stood above her.

Almond's rage subsided the instant he knew who it was.

'Lizzy, my love.' He lifted her to him and held her tight.

'Oh, I am so sorry, my Elizabeth.'

Elizabeth wept into his shoulder with the joy of knowing he had returned and was, after all this time, still the loving brother she had known in her childhood.

Almond's years of deprivation, both physical and mental, had convinced him he could never again enjoy emotions he'd once known; not even the love of family. Those emotions had been replaced with anger and resentment. Yet, here he stood, embraced in an act of reconciliation... Of reunion? *How could that be?*

James had regained his feet and stood with Maggie and Kate, protecting them from Almond's vengeance. Glancing over his shoulder, he saw it was Elizabeth who had arrived and she must have witnessed Almond striking him.

How did she get here? Did she climb on the back of a wagon...? She didn't need to see this.

Almond seemed to be calmed by his sister, but the blood streaming from her nose and her red, bruised eye told of Almond's blind rage. James knew better than to step between them. The family stood divided by intimate loyalties, each group seeking comfort in an embrace, hoping all would be well if blood-ties should win out and restore good sense.

James hoped they could now speak, man to man, in order to explain his actions and absolve Maggie of blame. But it was Elizabeth who was the first to speak. She needed to break the angry spell.

'Come, Almond. Come. Sit with me.' She pulled at his arm and he sat with her on the grass bank surrounding the basin.

'Tell me what happened, Almond. I want to know where you've been and what you've done.'

'Where do I start?' Then he hesitated and looked back at James, Maggie and Kate.

'Let me stay quiet with you for a moment, Lizzy. Let me gather my thoughts so I can talk with James and Maggie about what they did. My story can be told later.' They sat quietly for a while, neither speaking. Presently, Almond said,

'I'll go to them now.'

'I'll come, too. I know some of what happened but they'll need to tell you.' The two walked together, still holding hands, until they reached James' huddled group. James was the first to speak.

'I'll not fight with you, Almond'

'And I'll not fight either. I was wrong to strike you, James.'

'I understand why you did... but, Almond, when you disappeared, it was hard to know what to do for the best. We found Maggie was with child and I needed to take responsibility for...' Maggie broke in.

'That, he did... When you were gone, all of us fell on hard times. Our families joined together and I saw in James the man who would be my husband. It was then I fell pregnant with his child.'

'Maggie, please!'

'No, James. I must tell Almond what happened. It wasn't your doing that we got together... it was my choice... our choice.'

'Maggie, this isn't what we spoke of before...'

'But it's what happened!' Maggie continued to speak so James couldn't stop her, and instead, tell Almond the truth.

'What was I to do? You and me were young. Our time together was brief before you left me... We were destitute, Almond. James saved us all. She took Almond's hand.

'I was glad to marry him, and bear his child... Be glad for us.'

James was silent. He knew the decision had been made. Almond was not to be told he had fathered Kate. It was not a decision he was ever to be content with, but responsibility for the lie was to be shared and he'd act in accordance with it.

Almond felt the softness of her touch, the touch he'd longed for all those years. It was as he remembered. For a moment, it was as if his yearning was at last fulfilled. But he'd heard her words... she was *'glad to marry'* James. Almond knew he'd have to let her cleave to his brother. The warmth of her hand both taunted and seared him. He withdrew from her. Maggie let him go.

She had no more to say. Her mind was set on the future she had made, the mother she would be, with James as the father at her side. Having already borne him a child, young Henry, she would gladly bear him more. They had already spoken of calling their next son Almond.

James spoke;

'Almond, we come as family. Maggie and Elizabeth prayed for your safe return and their prayers have been answered.' Almond replied.

'It wasn't the homecoming I longed for during my years at sea, James.' With that, hardness returned to Almond's eyes.

'Apart from Lizzie, you're all strangers to me now. I will stay awhile with my sister, but you, James, and *your* family, can return to the crowd.'

'So be it. I hope there'll come a day you'll accept it all was for the best.'

Almond made no response to suggest time would heal the wound, and it was James who brought their meeting to a close.

'Let's go, Maggie. Goodbye Almond, I wish you luck.'

Maggie was quick to agree. She needed to get her words out before she couldn't help but speak of the feelings she still held for her lost lover.

'Yes... goodbye Almond, I wish you luck, too.' She silenced what was on the tip of her tongue... *I will always love you.*

Elizabeth remained in Almond's embrace. She whispered what Maggie couldn't say.

'We will always love you, even if you go away forever. You are our brother.'

Almond held her close. His thoughts were in turmoil, and he was lost in them.

After a while, he became aware of Elizabeth. Was she someone in whom he could confide?

'My years in the Navy have changed me, Lizzie. I wouldn't be good to be around now... I may never be good to be around.'

'You're still our Almond. Inside, you're still the boy we knew.'

'Aye, maybe, but coarsened by the lash... The King's Navy had to work hard to beat that young man out of me... I can see why it's right Maggie has found a life that doesn't have me in it.' His graciousness was short-lived.

'Yet it grieves me so.'

He thought, and would leave unspoken,

And it grieves me more that my brother has had the pleasure of her, the pleasure I thought was mine alone.'

'I know you, Almond. You will rid yourself of the navy and find love again.'

He looked down on his sister's face, still sweet, and, forgiving her bruises, without the blemish of worldly care. Her face was bright with the promise of the life ahead of her. He began to think about what her life might have in store. He surprised himself by asking...

'And what of you, my sweet Lizzie?'

She spoke of the family and their new life in Wales but was cautious not to tell too much. Instead, she told of her hopes.

'That boy that came with James and Maggie is Hopkin, and we're going to move away from this place... She gestured with a sweep of her hand at the spoils of industry that surrounded them... 'There must be more than this.' Alongside stretched loads of coal and pig iron passing in opposite directions. Above them, waste had been carelessly thrown into the landscape of the tree-robbed hills.

'Me and 'Hopkin are going to move away, as far away as we can. Not just to Cardiff, or Bristol. No, further than that. They need men and women in Australia we are told. Have you been there? Do you know how far it is?'

'No, I haven't, but I know it's a long way.' Then, not wanting to dampen her spirit, he added,

'But I know that if you try hard enough you can travel the World…
He pointed back at Trevithick's machine. Maybe that steam- engine you
came on will take you to Australia?'

'A steam-engine to take me to Australia? I'm surprised it got this
far… I didn't come on it, anyway. There was no room for me. I ran
along the canal and got here nearly as quick.'

'Ah, but Mr. Trevithick's engine would be a suitable carriage for a
prince and his young princess.'

Elizabeth laughed at the improbability of his suggestion and hugged
herself to him. She wasn't going to let him go too soon.

'Where have you been, Almond?'

Almond spoke with a maturity beyond his years.

'My job was to do the King's bidding. I've sailed the Caribbean seas
and chased Pirates. I've seen America, and winds have blown me to
Egypt.'

'How wonderful!'

'Yes! They are lands we have only have dreamt of, and they're all
so beautiful. Before the navy, I saw only wretched people, people like
me, who were the King's subjects.'

'But we must be loyal to our King.'

'You must get as far away from his reach as you can. Australia
sounds as though it will be far enough.' He had no idea what Australia
might be like, but it would do.

He smiled for the first time in a long while, not only because of the
encouragement he had tried to give his sister, but because those places
he talked about had awakened in him the joy to be found in a world
beyond the toe-end of England or the blackened crotch of South Wales.
He'd glimpsed how life could be. *Could Lizzie and Hopkin be part of
this new life, too?* He dwelt on the thought, and then spoke.

'You be sure to follow your dreams my sweet Lizzie. Whether you
walk, run, sail or get pulled along by a machine puffing smoke.'

They stayed, sat on the side of the hill. Lizzie told the tale of their journey away from Cornwall, of family loss and family gain. He spoke of the events at sea, and the battles he had fought in.

'Trafalgar! You fought with Nelson at Trafalgar? asked Elizabeth, in disbelief.

'I did, but I will not speak too much of it.

They both chose not to dwell on the hardships they had endured. Life was hard, no matter what, and to speak out loud of the hardship was to relive it. Their moment together was not to be spoiled...

***

Hopkin had come with what he hoped would be good news.

'They've unloaded the pig-iron, and they've attached the engine to the front of the trams. We are to go back now.'

'So?' replied Elizabeth.

'You can come back with us this time. Some of our passengers are worse for drink and can't face the trip,' he laughed.

'I want to stay with Almond until it's time for him to leave.'

'But I've asked Mr. Trevithick if you can come and he said you could.'

So Hopkin knew she was still unhappy with being left behind in the first place, Lizzy shook her head and said in a tone 'high and mighty'.

'I'll walk back along the canal, the way I came... though I had to run to get here in time.' She waited for the implied rebuke to sink in before continuing,

'I'll probably get back before you, anyway, and I seem to remember Mr. Trevithick's last 'Puffing Devil' blew up for the want of a drink of water.'

Hopkin was keen to make amends,

'Shall I walk with you? I don't have to go with them.'

'No! You can do what you said you'd do and help James and Mr. Trevithick.'

'Yes... I should do that.'

Hopkin was about to leave but hesitated. He could sense the meeting of the family members had not gone well and he'd heard the raised voices. Even so, he found the courage to speak up, and he introduced himself to Almond.

'Hello, Mr. Rowe. I'm Hopkin. Lizzie and me are good friends and she has told me lots about you.' Almond offered his hand and Hopkin shook it, man to man.

'Pleased to meet you, Hopkin. Lizzie has been telling me about you, and the plans you have.' Almond thought he may have spoken out of turn and made too much of Lizzie's story. He continued,

'Oh, I hope I haven't let slip something you told me in private, Lizzie?'

'No, it's good... Only, not a word about it to anyone else, because that's our secret.'

'Not another word, you can be sure.'

Hopkin bade his farewell.

'Goodbye then, Mister Rowe. I'll see you soon in Merthyr, Lizzie.'

Hopkin turned and left, eager to get back to the train of trams and the engine that pulled them.

***

Across the other side of the canal basin were the first passengers to have ridden on a steam-driven train. They had made history, although they were unaware of it at the time. The running of the first steam-powered train to carry passengers and freight on a railway was completed on February 21st, 1804. The principle of goods and passenger transportation by steam locomotion had been established.

Homfray had won his bet, but he failed to see the future of the steam locomotive. He didn't invest to improve Trevithick's design. His focus on short-term goals and increasing his profits, delayed the development of the steam engine for a quarter of a century. However, at an official function to validate the successful completion of the bet, Homfray changed the direction of the lives of a Rowe family member. It was Trevithick who introduced Hopkin to the ironmaster.

'Here is the young man I was telling you about Mr. Homfray.'

'How do you do, young man? I hear you were quite the hero Master Hopkin.'

'I ran as fast as I could, Sir.'

'You ran like the wind, I'm told, and without your effort, my venture would have been lost.' Homfray searched in his pocket and produced five coins.

'I would like you to accept five guineas as a reward, and as a mark of my gratitude. I hope you will put it to good use.'

Hopkin had never seen such an amount of real money, and he didn't know what to say or if he should accept it. Homfray encouraged him.

'Go on, take it, lad, it's what you deserve.'

The coins weren't 'Truck Tokens', paid out by Homfray's Company, that could only be spent in 'Company Shops', they were gold. The gold coins offered more than the monetary value. They offered an opportunity to improve Hopkin's life, and that of his Lizzy, in ways they had been dreaming of. Not believing his good fortune, Hopkin took the coins, and simply said.

'Thank you kindly, Sir. I was glad to be of service.'

19

The High Seas

The HMS Guerriere ran ahead of a sou'westerly blowing off the coast of Nova Scotia. Thankfully, the wallowing progress of the previous few days of unseasonable calm was over, for this dragooned, refitted, rearmed French brigand was a beast to sail in all but a steady wind. When it was captured by the British, its structure and armaments were increased, and a new forecastle and sixteen cannons were added. These additions were at the expense of the ship's seaworthiness. It was top-heavy, but its loveless marriage of old and new timbers was good enough to sustain its weight and to keep out the sea. And so, after the briefest of sea trials, the Admiralty allowed its deployment; times were pressing, as around the world, the King's Empire was threatened.

Almond Rowe had served his apprenticeship on various naval vessels, progressing from deck-boy to deckhand, then through stages to 'able seaman', at Trafalgar, and then, 'gunner' on the forecastle of the Guerriere. He'd seen the captain change several times, as the irksome duty of captaining such a bucket of a craft was rewarded by a promotion to a more prestigious command.

For Almond, there was no such dispensation, for his role was to endure the hardships of life aboard a vessel of the fleet, and, in part, Almond was grateful for it. He had endured the bullying, brutal nature of the command aboard ship, and as he learned the skills required of a sailor, where his value to the 'Senior Service' afforded him privilege and status.

It was at times of rest when Almond allowed himself to dwell on the past. His pronouncement at Navigation of his intended desertion of his family had been hollow. It was always the vision of Maggie that swam into the calamitous memory of the previous watch, with its brutal enforcement of seafaring duties: its gun drill, rigging maintenance and washing of decks. The tasks would be accompanied by the barked commands of the officers and their minions.

Without his summoning, Maggie would appear aboard the carousel of blaring, brutal images spinning in his head. Banishing all other thoughts he had, she would hold him, warm and welcoming. It would seem there was no thought of personal gain, no strategy for survival, no hidden contempt borne out of her personal predicament. She came because of her love for him, for the love of being with him.

Almond had many shallow encounters with women over the years, his young man's passion slaked by the proffered exchange of silver for a young woman's intimate caress. On each occasion, his thirst was quenched at an erotic, often exotic, well, but his continuing search for true devotion left him empty, dissatisfied and ashamed. But, in his hammock, between duties, he was content to be with Maggie again; even if it was in his dreams

***.

Almond was at his post on the top deck, manning his 32-pound carronade, when a shout from the nest announced the presence of a vessel on the weather beam. In these waters, the vessel would most likely be French or American. If luck was with them, it would be a merchant ship. If it was a 'man o' war' then the day could end badly for both crews, no matter who was victorious.

'Prepare your guns,' shouted Samuel Grant, the Master's Mate on the Forecastle, and then added for good measure,

'Be double-quick about it, you good for nothing bastards.' He felt it was his duty to chivvy the crews into action, even if it was obvious there was a dangerous foe bearing down upon them; Grant always held his subordinates in contempt.

Almond's well-drilled response meant that within 2 minutes, he and his gun crew had primed their carronade with powder, wadding and ball, but the thought of Samuel Grant's belligerence still sat uncomfortably with him. He glanced at Bernard, his assistant gunner who knelt across the other side of the gun carriage, and half-mouthed,

'We all know who is the bastard around here.'

Bernard's eyes narrowed and he mumbled, as if to himself,

'Maybe he'll get a ball up his arse and we'll thank God for its Jolly Roger.' The two men exchanged glances; there was laughter in their eyes; to grin would have drawn Samuel's attention.

Almond's gun would not issue the first shot of the engagement, as the carronade was short-barrelled and for use at close range. The bulk of the armament of thirty, '18-pounders' was on the gun decks below. Every man of each thirteen-man gun crew knew what to do. In the confined space between decks, the clamour when arming the guns was almost deafening. Skills perfected from years of duty ensured the guns soon emerged from their portals ready to angrily fume and spit within 3 minutes of receiving orders. As quickly as the noise had erupted, it ceased, and the anxious excitement amongst the men was replaced by a quiet stillness. The gun crews waited for the next instruction. The only sound to be heard was the frog-like croak of the old oak timbers as the ship rolled with the rise and fall of the ocean's swell.

The silence of the men below deck was in contrast to the frantic activity of those above. There were shouted course corrections as orders to steer to Larboard were issued and extra sail was set by sailors who clambered, spider-like, across the web of rigging. Marines assembled, running heavy booted to a muster station, lining up shoulder to shoulder, presenting arms to await instructions from their officer, Lieutenant Kent.

James Dacres, the Captain of the Guerriere, steered a course for engagement with the enemy vessel. Britain and America had been at war for a year, and although no major sea battles had been fought, the two sides had harried each other's naval movement in the North American waters. The Captain and crew of HSS Guerriere prepared to do their duty.

The first salvo of any engagement would be at some distance, in the hope of inflicting first blood, and the '18 pounders' would shout a deadly greeting to the opposing captain and crew.

The vessel on the horizon converged and showed no signs of turning to run from the King's battleship. It looked as if the fight would soon be engaged; rather than after a chase across open water. At least his crew would not have to endure action stations upon the decks, hour upon hour, day upon day. This action would be sharp and brutal.

Although the Guerriere was a pig to sail, it made up for it with the cannon power it possessed. What it lost in manoeuvrability was forgiven once her guns came to bear. Positioning her broadside on, early in the encounter, was Captain Dacres' priority, but the enemy vessel was not making it easy for the British Captain to gain the advantage. The American's tack to Larboard was perhaps its first attempt to flee from the British ship? Captain Dacres countered by steering to starboard, trying to gain some advantage from the prevailing wind. The Guerriere was flying ahead of the enemy ship, closing the gap. But the enemy's manoeuvre was a feint. It swung back in an aggressive approach. The Guerriere was disadvantaged, and Captain Dacres was now sure of his adversary's intention; but who was she?

As the vessels converged once again, it was clear the enemy craft was a Man-of-War. When it struck its colours, it was the 'Stars and Stripes' unfurled, waving defiance across to the representatives of the world's most powerful nation. On the Guerriere, the enemy's colours were seen, and they adorned a sleek, low profile battleship.

There came a shout from the crow's nest.

'She's an American.'

The word was conveyed to the Captain by the second in command, Robert Scott.

'Thank you, Mister Scott. Please tell our American sailors on board to step down from their duties.' Continuing, he said,

'Ask Lieutenant Kent to contain them below decks. The remaining men are to redouble their efforts.'

The order to the Americans to stand down was relayed throughout the decks and several men left their posts as armed marines escorted them away.

On the top deck, the American, Jeremiah, who was part of Almond's gun crew, bade his fellow gun crew good fortune.

'Stay safe my friends' had been his brief farewell.

'Move now,' shouted the marine, the aggression in his voice brought on by the impending battle and his need to return to his station on the top deck.

Jeremiah had been captive for the last 18 months after a naval confrontation off the Cayman Islands between an American 'Privateer' and the Guerriere. The Guerriere had the better of the engagement, and it resulted in Jeremiah's capture. He had to choose between imprisonment or agreeing to be pressed into the service of the King The choice was easy for him as he had lived his life in the open air, both on land and sea, and he was not about to be locked away. The pressing of American seamen into the Royal Navy had contributed to the hostility between the nations and the current declaration of war. He was sure to find other pressed men aboard

Jeremiah was a good sailor, even when in the service of the King, and Almond had learned to trust him. Now, with Jeremiah's compatriots about to attack, he would have to do without his fellow 'Cannonader' until the American vessel was repulsed.

Jeremiah was descended from the original European settlers of the Americas, and he was aware his family roots lay in the South West of England. To 'crew' with Almond was like meeting a lost cousin in unexpected circumstances. For his part, Almond regarded him as a fellow-traveller along the arduous path they had each been forced to take against their will...

Was he not a Cornishman in spirit? Jeremiah thought he was, but a Cornishman who had found a better place to live and a better nation to belong to.

For Almond, the stupidity of the war between the nations was suddenly clear to him. *Jeremiah a compatriot at heart? Wasn't he worthy of standing alongside rather than locking up?*

A less capable man was pressed to fill Jeremiah's place in the gun crew. A 'powder monkey', John, not much more than a boy, would need to help to haul the cannonade and load the 32lb ball. He passed Jeremiah on the top deck, and not realising the circumstances inquired of him,

'Where're you off Jeremiah?'

John was cuffed around the ear by a marine for his insolence.

***

The officers prepared for the engagement, concerning themselves with the tactics to be employed when trying to gain the advantage.

'What range do we have Mister Scott?'

'two miles captain.'

'Bring the ship to Starboard. We'll soon give her a full broadside and let her know what she's up against. That'll test his mettle. Prepare the guns, Mr Scott.'

It was time for Dacres to get inside the mind of the Captain of the American vessel.

The order rang throughout the decks. The gun portals opened and the cannons were drawn forward, their muzzles appearing like stubble on the face of the ship.

According to the given range, the gunners adjusted the height of their gun's barrel. At two miles, the gunners were confident some of the balls would hit their mark; years of such encounters had assured them of that.

On the quarter-deck, Captain Dacres awaited the moment when the American was most exposed, with his own ship on an even keel. The order to fire was given and its execution played its own rhythmic overture, as running down through the decks the incremental delay of firing resulted in an explosive arpeggio.

Almond, at his station and yet to engage the enemy with his gun, felt a surge of invincibility run through him as if the power of the cannon was channelled through him. His senses were aroused and mixed up. He was at once thrilled at the spectacle, proud of his ability to impose his will and yet, somehow ashamed. Was it the destructive consequences of the action he was involved in, or, perhaps, was it the discomfort of Jeremiah's detention weighing heavy? Were the shots falling on other Jeremiahs? Were there other Cornishmen pressed into the defence of America who would feel the weight of an 18 pounder that had been cast in Chatham?

Maggie forced her way into his thoughts, yet again. But, unusually, it was not the familiar memory of her, the moments of gentle caress and loving embrace. The battle ahead, and the frustration of the years spent apart from her had allowed his inner rage to well up and spill onto to her, contaminating the woman he once had loved with his seed of discontent. Maggie's hold on him had started to wane.

***

Captain Dacres looked through his telescope and viewed the near miss of his first broadside. He could see that some shot had found their mark, but seemed to bounce off the hull; he hadn't the luck to take down a sail. Still, the battle had been joined and his gunners would do better the next time. In a calm voice he commanded,

'Bring her hard to Starboard,' so allowing the range between the vessels to shorten and their paths to converge. He would soon bring her round again. Below decks, the gun crews primed and reloaded. The men stood by.

Young George, a London waif, had acquitted himself well during the first round of firing. There was no delay in bringing the gun to bear and ready to fire.

Jack the master gunner complimented the boy after the reload, for the lad had stepped up in place of an American and had shown willingness and common sense.

'Looked like a proper gunner there my boy. Supposin' we might keep you on, if you can keep your arms and legs out of 'arm's way.'

George had watched the 18 pounders recoil past him, and knew well enough to stand back. He would need to stay nimble. And George was never short of a quick-witted reply.

'Don't worry Jack, my bits will be well tucked in.'

'Best take care of your "John Thomas," you've got two each of your other bits,' was advice from along the deck.

George laughed nervously, and his laughter was joined by others. They all felt a need to relieve the tension of the imminent battle; laughter was always a foil against the threat of death or injury.

Jack gave George the evil eye

'Keep your jokes till we've sunk the bastard.'

The laughter stopped immediately. The Master Gunner was not to be crossed; as many a flogging would testify.

George thought his bravado when replying to Jack's encouragement might yet land him in hot water. The fact he was soon to face an enemy's broadside seemed a less intimidating prospect.

The British ship came round and sailed at 90 degrees to the course set by the American. After the first manoeuvre was completed, the Guerriere needed to sail on a convergent course. Captain Dacres' task was to time the course change so he could bring his guns to bear along the full length of the American.

'45 degrees to Starboard, Mr. Scott, then set full sail. With full sail, we can match his speed.'

Moments later, the turn was made and sailors in the rigging fully unfurled the mainsail. As the American ship showed no sign of giving way, the battle was about to be joined. The men amongst the sails hurriedly lowered themselves to the deck and took their station. Some had duties with the gun crews, whilst others took up arms ready to board if the ships became enmeshed.

The American bore down on the Larboard bow.

'Bring her round to Starboard now. Mister Scott. Give orders to fire when we have her broadside.'

The USS Constitution was big. Captain Dacres could not help but see the beauty of its lines and the quality of its construction. He looked back at his own ship. It was serviceable, but an inferior French creation. It was good enough amongst the minnows, but against this shark of an adversary, he knew his ship and its men would be hard-pressed. God, and good fortune, would need to be with them.

The Guerriere's turn to Starboard had been well-timed. The vessels would make a broadside pass. The relatively faster Constitution would make up the distance between them and then cannon would negotiate a conclusion to their high sea's diplomacy.

The Constitution ran straight and true, but the Guerriere, having completed her turn, wallowed to Larboard just as the ships met. Her guns were compromised as they pointed to the water between the ships and had no clear opportunity to fire. The ship needed to right itself... a few moments more would do it. But those few moments were filled with the boom of the opposing cannon and the subsequent crash of 32-pound ball. The Constitution had sailed by in a perfect position to dictate the terms and conditions of the negotiation.

On instruction, Almond had fired his cannonade but its trajectory was too low and its ball plunged into the ocean beyond the enemy ship. Then, in an instant, Almond's world disintegrated around him. Cannonball tore through the rail and decking, the percussive impacts, blasted men and equipment on the deck upwards and backwards, either to the Starboard rail or over its side. Wooden shards were hurled like spokes of a broken wheel, distributing the energy of the balls in an instant, across and throughout the ship, impaling and clubbing, acting as deadly pikemen to the main blow.

On the upper deck, the air around Almond's head was filled with sounds... The agony of impacted timbers, the crash of the guns of the opposing marines, and the zinging, ricocheting, spark spraying musket balls played a musical rendition ending in a drum roll of dull thuds. There followed a moment of stunned calm, as if all the noise in the world had been used up.

Almond, tucked against the rail, had seen the progression of the American ordinance puncture, penetrate and disfigure the ship and men alike. Harry had gone. He, and the debris created by a ball, had been blown away. It was as if a malevolent hurricane had gouged an amalgam of metal, wood and flesh, and had flung it across the ship to the sea beyond.

The silence was short-lived. The masts had been shattered and they broke in two. Each in turn, Mizzen, then Main, toppled; the sails spilling their wind as the masts twisted in an attempt to accommodate the conflicting forces of nature and find a new equilibrium.

Almond saw the white of the foresail as it fell towards him. The years of contempt he had for the ship welled up to defy the broken remnants of mast intent on his destruction. He screamed out what was likely to be his last profanity,

'Bastard French bucket of shi...' Falling sail and timbers struck him down.

The Guerriere righted itself and those still manning its guns replied in kind. Where George's station had once housed an 18 pounder there was a hole through the side of the ship. The cannon and its men had been blown back across the main deck. George was lifelessly entangled with Jack, who embraced him with his remaining arm; its hand resting on George's shoulder as if it was reassuring young George all would be well. The young lad lay as if comfortable. He was wide-eyed, staring through a newly created portal at the battle raging across the divide. But he couldn't observe the traded blows, nor cheer the thundering British cannon, nor groan at the retaliatory bark of the American guns. Perhaps, he and Jack were engaged in disciplinary matters with their God? George would have to pay for his loose tongue, no doubt, and Jack's still serviceable whip hand would be ready and willing to act in accordance with his Master's instructions. All who knew George would have hoped the new Master would have kinder intentions.

The Guerriere was crippled and it slowed in the water, whilst the Constitution was able to dominate a second and third round of broadsides. With the Mizzen and Mainmast toppled, the 'Fourth Rate' frigate of the British Fleet had no effective means to sail in its own defence. It lay dead in the water. Captain Dacres ordered the crew to strike the ship's colours.

What was certain was the surviving crew would soon have a new Command, and it was known American discipline would be less severe, more negotiable, than that rigidly observed in the Royal Navy.

Selwyn Berryman-Morgan

20

A New Beginning

The Constitution drew alongside the Guerriere, and its crew secured the stricken vessel with rope. American seamen poured over planking placed between the ships. They were to claim it as a prize, and it would be some retribution for the losses they had suffered. They had seen their own dead close -up, heard cries of pain and anguish felt for the loss of a comrade. They had feared 'Death' was soon to place a hand on their sleeve, to gently tug and whisper *'Enough. Come away.'*

They raged at the men on the Guerriere. Armed with truncheon, knives, pistols and cutlass, they were determined to find pockets of men who might resist capture, and on whom they could exact retribution.

Adam was one of the first to cross over, a short, bulldog of a man, with the physical strength to subdue any resistance from the British crew. He leapt aboard, running low and at full pace.

Orders were shouted.

'Move back...drop your weapons...raise your hands.'

Adam slid across the blood wet deck and toppled against a dislodged gun carriage. Raising himself, he was able to assess the threat the enemy posed. Before him lay what remained of a beaten crew, stunned into submission by the ferocity of the engagement. There was no further attempt to defend the ship, the striking of colours had been understood by all those British seamen left standing, and word had reached those below deck to lay down their arms, the fighting was over.

The top deck was a tangled mess of mast, timbers, sail, cannon and men. An orderly muster of those who were fit and able wasn't possible as there was insufficient clear deck for them to collect. Instead, there were small groups of sailors who had been gathered together by officers and midshipmen. Captain Dacres stood on the quarterdeck, where he had been throughout the engagement. Wounded in the leg from musket shot, he steadied himself against the rail overlooking the deck below. Over the clamour of the boarding party, he shouted,

'My men have surrendered and they know their orders are not to resist. Excessive force is not necessary.'

The senior member of the boarding party assessed what was before him, and, seeing no threat, he shouted back.

'Thank you, Captain. Please have your officers and men clear the deck so that you can muster here.'

He pointed to the area next to the boarding planks; the British seamen were to be taken prisoner.

It had been a beautiful day, other than a battle had been fought and men had died. Ordinarily, it was a day to be giving thanks for, a day when it was good to be alive, but now the air was thick with the stench of war: burnt gunpowder, the smouldering of timbers and, some would say, the smell of fear and relief.

The smoke of battle found new places to smother and choke; its noxious gasses contaminated the healthy and the wounded alike; sailors coughed it from their lungs and spat it out with the phlegm from their throat, and the steady sou'westerly used it to paint a broad stroke of pond-green across the bright blue of the summer sky.

Adam was assigned to a party to go below deck and look for men fit enough to stand muster. Those unable to walk would need to be carried off the ship to be attended to onboard the Constitution. Climbing down to the gun deck, Adam saw close-up the carnage a cannonball could inflict as it bludgeoned through the hull and into the deck's confined space. He was glad that his own ship was made of seasoned oak that resisted the full force of an eighteen-pound ball; there was good reason for the ship to be known as 'Old Ironsides'.

The dead were left where they lay, whilst the walking wounded were gathered together to be escorted above deck.

The boarding party found their countrymen on the lowest deck. Americans were expected to be on board, and, sure enough, the press-ganged sailors cheered in the knowledge that they would be at last set free. They shouted their affiliations.

'We're Americans... Compatriots!

'I am Elijah McIntosh, from Philadelphia...'

'I am Peter Erickson. I come from Boston...'

'Thanks be to God you came.'

Adam instructed the guarding British Marines,

'Lay down your arms! Your battle is over... Now, I said!'

The marines knew the ship was lost and they dropped their weapons to the floor. In any case, it had been a duty they were happy to be rid of.

Jeremiah stood against the bulkhead, not sure of his feelings about being freed from his enforced service to the British Monarch. It was true he was an American, but he knew that in the eyes of his liberators his allegiance to his country would have been tested; had he not acted on behalf of the British King? He feared it mattered little he was a pressed man. Fear of what changes were in store for him replaced the certainty of his duties whilst a seaman in the Royal Navy. His fears were justified.

Adam was suspicious of the men claiming to be American. They were now captives of the British, but had they not powdered the cannon and helped fill the sail of an enemy vessel? He would treat these men as harshly as he treated the British; at least until they were safely taken over to the Constitution where they would be able to explain themselves.

The American prisoners were escorted up through the ship. On the gun deck, the wreckage of the battle lay before him. Jeremiah thought, *don't look, face straight ahead.* But his resolve weakened, and as if by way of respect for his fallen comrades, he found the courage to take a final glance. He hoped the damage might be to the ship alone and there would be no horrors to haunt him. He was mistaken. His courage was not rewarded, and the pain he felt from that fleeting glance was greater than any physical injury he had suffered in his years at sea.

Shattered timbers had been moved to provide passageway along the deck, but either side of that the jumbled wreckage was a porridge of displaced cannon, scattered balls, wadding, splintered wood and red splashed slabs of fallen men. Most who lay there could not be recognised as they were in shadow, or disfigured, but sunlight lanced through the punctured hull and lit a face. It was the face of a 'powder monkey'. He knew it well. He was a young lad, a good lad; though he was 'simple' and had no brains, neither in life nor now his skull was cleaved in two. Further along, a uniform, once clean and smart, glinted gold braid as a reminder of the authority it once commanded; he knew of the man who would no longer gain warmth from the quality of its cloth.

The Lieutenant was regarded by his fellow officers as a hard man. A man who served his country with the traditional values expected of him. He never expected to be liked by his men, and he wasn't, but curiously, in death his excesses would be excused by the sailors he subjugated. The fact he died alongside his men would make him one of their own, and the seamen would later be heard to say, as if they believed it all along,

'That Lieutenant was a bastard... but not so much that he deserved to be cut down like that...'

'I was flogged on his orders a couple of times, but he was fair and treated us all the same...'

'He did that... We all got our fair share of "the Cat", God forgive him.'

Jeremiah could now see that few on the larboard portals could have survived the successive broadsides from the Constitution. A chill crept over him. His luck at being in the fortified lower deck dawned upon him. He had been out of harm's way. He felt sick knowing how Death had come close, only to look the other way and find souls that were easier to harvest.

Jeremiah thought he had no right to have survived; he should have been with his gun crew. He hung his head to remove his dead comrades from sight; and to hide his shame. Trying to escape the ghoulish tableau, he focused on the improvised gangway and stumbled his way to the stairs that led to the upper decks. As he lifted himself onto the first step, the joy of being alive began to lift his spirits and quicken his step. He raised his foot to the second rung, then, at an increased pace, the third. Each leaden-footed step took him away from the hell he had glimpsed and lessened the shame he had felt.

As they broke out into bright sunlight on the top deck, the American prisoners shielded their eyes. The masts were thrown down, and the shipshape order of the rigging had gone. The vessel looked more like a barge with cargo destined for the charnel house than a naval ship. What had once been a powerful frigate was now a floating pile of battle debris festooned with its dead. Bodies from the top deck were laid out where space had been cleared. At least twenty of the sailors and marines of the main deck had been killed. Those killed below deck would become part of the growing muster. It was as if the seamen were on parade.

'The dead, and those close to it, are they all here?' asked Captain Dacres

'All present ... but incorrect. Meaning no disrespect, Sir.' said a midshipman.

Jeremiah scanned the faces of those laid out before him. None were his gun crew. *They must be safe,* he thought. But then he glanced up to the forecastle. Where his cannon should have been, there were the remnants of the foresail and yard arm strewn against the rail. From beneath the pile poked an arm, the fingers of its hand pointing to some far-away place, as if it were somewhere the body longed to be. Jeremiah broke rank, not with a dash that may have ended with him being clubbed to death or filled full of pistol shot, but with a determined and confident stride. His eyes were fixed on the limb only he had seen. Adam, still his guard, was taken by surprise,

'Where are you going...? I said... Where are you going?'

Jeremiah strode on. He was not going to leave his close comrade unattended, if it was only to lay him alongside those lined up ready for their final journey. Adam ran to block his way and thrust him back with the flat side of his cutlass. Jeremiah was not to be moved. He raised his arm and pointed to the crumple of sail.

'There's a man there, maybe more than one. I've to get them out... I will get them out.' Both Adam and Jeremiah stood their ground.

'Back in line... Now!' Adam shouted, with a full-throated roar of menace.

There came a call from behind,

'Seaman, let the man go to his shipmate.'

It was Captain Dacres. He was stood by his fallen men. He'd watched as each was recovered and laid out before him, and now he could see there were more to be found. His voice was calm but determined. Adam heard him but chose to stand firm. He shouted,

'He may be American, but he's to get in line like the others!'

'Let him go I say.'

Years of obeying orders given to him by his superiors gave Adam cause to hesitate. He was not sure what to do. Wasn't this an enemy officer, one who he would have shot an hour before, given the chance? With his ship a pile of broken timber and tattered sail, what right did this defeated Captain have to command? Then came another voice,

'Let him be, seaman.'

It was his American Lieutenant. He saw the situation was getting heated and he wanted to keep the surrender of the ship as calm and orderly as possible. In any case, he decided it was time to show some compassion.

'Escort him to his shipmate and help get whoever is there back to this mustering point.'

The American officer and Dacres exchanged a glance and both gave a respectful nod. The agreement confirmed the order was honourable and, given the situation, expedient.

Adam stood back and growled,

'On you go sailor, but don't step so much as an inch out of line... or so help me God...'

Jeremiah pushed past him and half ran to the roll of sail. Adam followed in close order, and on reaching the sail, he kicked hard at the canvas where he thought the head of the man might be. There was no sound of a groan, or a pathetic plea for help.

'After all of your commotion, it looks as if we got a dead-un here. Unroll him seaman and be quick about it.' Adam couldn't resist mocking the fallen man.

'This must be the Britisher's lucky day. He might get a proper sailor's burial after all.'

Adam kicked again to vent his anger upon the corpse. He still seethed.

Jeremiah thought,

You bastard! One day I'll see to it you'll regret that kick.

Jeremiah pulled at the loose end of the sail. It came away easy at first, but the heavy sail had folded upon itself and the freed end refused to yield to him any further. Try as he might, Jeremiah could not get the sail to unravel. He adjusted his feet to gain more purchase and changed his hold to improve his grip. All the while, he cursed at the dead weight of the canvas. The mass of the sail pinned the loose flap, and it was too heavy to move away. He pulled with all the might a desperate man could bring to bear, but the sail remained stuck fast. Jeremiah knew the same weight bore down on his shipmates.

'They're dead... No one will 'ave survived under that. Leave it be sailor,' said Adam.

Jeremiah threw down the canvas flap.

'For pity's sake, help me pull this sail loose. We can't just leave them. Even if they are dead, we must give them the respect they deserve.'

The scene on deck had drawn the attention of an American work party engaged in recovering the valuable spoils of battle. They had stopped on hearing the exchange between the two adversaries... *two Americans*?

One of the men of the boarding party came and stood by Jeremiah.

'Let me help you, sailor.' He moved to add his weight to the task.

Others laid their weapons down so they could help. A time for reconciliation had been reached. There had been enough death, and now there was a chance to extend the helping hand, not the hand responsible for the neat row of corpses on the deck below. Adam stood fixed to the spot. His role was to guard his prisoner-of-war; he was not going to let his guard down.

Bastard British tars, he thought.

The canvas unravelled, and the expanse of sail was gathered, the excess being tipped over the side.

The men were uncovered, one by one: Bernard, the gunner who had pointed his way home, Ken, a midshipman, Lieutenant Smith, dead from a musket ball to the chest. They were laid out, one by one. Almond, and John, the powder monkey, had not yet been found and only the last folds of the sail were left against the rail with a fallen yardarm beneath. Anyone under the weight of timber would be dead. The last of the canvas was pulled aside to reveal Almond. The blow from the beam had glanced his head and shoulder, throwing him against the rail, away from the falling timber. His arm was twisted at an odd angle, dislocated at the shoulder Blood ran from a wound at the back of his head, seeping through what had already congealed in his hair. But blood ran. Was he still alive?

The yard arm was pulled clear, leaving Almond in a pocket of loose sail, and Jeremiah was able to pull him free

Adam hated the fact Jeremiah had been vindicated. A blow from his cutlass grip, for time-wasting, would now be uncalled for. He snarled at Jeremiah,

'Throw him on your shoulder sailor and get him off the ship. If he's lucky, our surgeon will get to him sometime during the middle of next week.'

Jeremiah easily lifted his shipmate, as Almond was a small man in comparison. He took one more look around. *No John,* he thought. *He must be safe... or is he over the side?*

More of the sail was cast overboard and the weight of it tipped the balance in favour of the sea. The screech of the shipboard canvas as it ran over the rail froze everyone in their task. The calm that had settled on the crews was broken and both captive and captor were instantly alert to danger. Those nearest the sail jumped clear for fear of being entangled and dragged off the ship. In not much more than a heartbeat the sail had gone, and with it went the hope the ship could yet harness the wind and be salvaged. There was a moment's pause. Then the Americans laughed and cheered. The loss of the sail became a symbol of their victory. In contrast, for the British it was confirmation of their defeat. They hung their heads in their sadness and their shame. A 'ragbag' American crew had defeated a ship from His Majesty's Fleet. They had been out-sailed and out-gunned.

***

The planks between the ships were narrow and swayed with the vessel's relative movement. It was time for Almond to be carried from the Guerriere.

With Almond's weight on his shoulder, it was difficult for Jeremiah to keep his balance, and if the plank moved too much, he would not be able to fall to his knees in order to cling on.

Concentrate now, or we'll be mashed to pulp, he thought.

He knew if they fell between the ships there would be no need for a rescue party. At each step he needed to regain his balance, as all the while, behind him, Adam prodded and cajoled.

'Get a move on you bastard before this tub sinks and takes us with it.'

They were walking the last of the boarding plank before reaching the Constitution and safety. An ocean swell ran beneath them, and the ships moved. They rolled apart and drifted lengthwise with respect to each other, lifting and twisting the plank. Jeremiah was in two minds, *should I try to walk the rest of the plank, or should I jump?*

He leapt to safety, spilling his human cargo across the deck of the Constitution. Almond's flailing arms and legs knocked men over as if they were skittles. Jeremiah got to his feet and then heard a cry from behind. Adam had toppled off the plank and clung with one arm to the outside of the rail. The ships began to roll back together as they settled into the trough of the swell. The top rails were to meet. Adam hung in between the ever-narrowing gap. The look of terror in his eyes hid any plea they may have made for help. Jeremiah moved, intending to thrust out a rescuing hand, and then he paused, his arm half extended. The thoughts of Adam's kick to the head of his fallen comrade, the mocking words of, *'he'll get a sailors' burial... they're dead, let it be'*, flooded back... *He's dead, let it be*, he thought, but somewhere inside his head, Jeremiah knew his sweet revenge would turn sour. The sailor's death would haunt him. As a matter of honour, he helped the man in peril... he offered his hand.

Adam swung his free arm for Jeremiah to catch. It still held a cutlass and for a moment, it seemed as if they were meeting in the heat of battle. Jeremiah swayed to let the blade pass and then caught Adam's trailing wrist. He pulled hard, and Adam climbed with the soles of his feet, gaining purchase on both ships. He thought he was clear, but the rails had come together and his trailing foot was trapped. His cry of agony rang above the surrounding chatter of surrender. Other seamen joined Jeremiah to pull Adam free, and in doing so broke his ankle and snapped its sinew but it was a better outcome than if Jeremiah had stayed his hand a second longer.

Whilst he was in surgery, American sailors ribbed Adam; whose bad temper had remained in force, making the ribbing more enjoyable for the sailors.

'It was just a bit of fun. Them there tubs were joshin' with you...'

'Must have riled 'em, fierce.'

'They thought they'd mosey on up and give you a nip, so that next time you'd show a little more respect.'

Sailors spoke of ships as if they had minds of their own. Theirs was a love-hate relationship with the vessels they manned, and, given the opportunity, a ship would bite back for all the trouble the sailors put it to. They always knew to be vigilant when onboard, and to judge the ship's temperament when under sail. The elements spoke using the ship as an interpreter.

Jeremiah could see Adam's injuries were relatively minor, although it was clear he would not walk for a month or two and, no doubt, it would never be completely right. He cared not.

That'll keep the bastard out of my way, he thought.

Jeremiah was led below by his new shipmates. He would be kept under guard until it was decided how he, and the other freed Americans, would be dealt with. Jeremiah was content knowing his comrade was safe and would be seen by the ship's physician. Almond now had a chance.

Captain Dacres was the last British seaman to leave the Guerriere, but only after he was sure those sailors left behind were beyond help. He was quickly followed by the American marines who had laid powder and set fires in the bowels of the ship. The ship was to be scuttled. Those dead, and those destined for oblivion were left where they lay; for even if the mortally wounded were carried over to the Constitution they would soon be dead. Their place was now with the ship and the ocean it had sailed. They were left to the fate many of them had foreseen, death upon the sea and burial within it.

Dacres stood on the Constitution, his duty to his ship now over. He was a prisoner of war. He clung to a midshipman for support. His own surgeon attended to the injury to his leg, stemming the flow of blood.

Dacres noticed a sailor sprawled out on the deck, unconscious and unattended. He motioned to his surgeon,

'Please, Mr. Jones, see to this sailor, his needs seem to be more urgent than mine.' The surgeon gave a last tug on the bandages he had applied and tied a knot securely.

'Yes, Captain.' He turned his attention to the sailor.

The restraining ropes between the ships were loosened and the boarding planks retrieved. Halyards were used against the sides of the Guerriere, and the ships inched apart. There was an urgency to move them away from each other, as the fires set on the British vessel would be taking hold and it would not take long for the flames to reach the powder magazine. Once away, the Constitution set its sail. The breeze was quick to fill each canvas, and as it did so, it culminated in a snap of rigging when the sail was restrained, the power of the wind harnessed for the use of the ship. The Constitution was alive, and at each set of sail, the battleship gained pace. Almost undamaged by the encounter her ability was undiminished. A course for home had been set and her Captain was free to leave the quarter deck. He now stood shoulder to shoulder with his adversary and was the first to speak.

'And who are you, Sir...?' Half turning to meet him, Dacres replied,

'James Dacres, Sir. Once Captain of HMS Guerriere. And you Sir?'

'Captain Hull, of this vessel, the USS Constitution.'

'Yes... We have met in passing on the high seas. In the spring of this year, I believe. Our flotilla laid chase to you in these very waters. You were too quick and agile, even for the best in our fleet.'

'I well remember the encounter, Sir.'

'You didn't at the time wait for us to be better acquainted.'

'Given your superiority in numbers, it was prudent of me to use our speed to my advantage. I knew there would be another day... and so it proved.'

'I, too had looked forward to meeting you again, but as you would expect, I foresaw a different outcome.'

'The ebb and flow of war, Captain.'

'Just so. But never the less, it was fine seamanship on your part. My regret is I didn't match it.'

'If you had, the parade of the dead would have outnumbered those chosen to inspect it.'

'Nevertheless, the consequences for my ship and its men are clear to see.' He gestured back to the Guerriere, flames now leaping from its portals.

'She was never a fine ship, but I made of it what I could.'

The gunpowder ignited and blew her apart.

***

John, the powder monkey, had survived and had dodged and dived from one opportunity to the next, keeping his head down avoiding confrontation, skulking amongst fallen timbers, fleetingly reappearing to ingratiate himself to his eventual captors, only to be cuffed aside as an annoyance; no matter what, he was sure to get his ears boxed.

He had the luck to latch on to an American lieutenant, who had once hailed from London. John held forth, never knowing when to stop.

'Can I do sumfin for you, Captain?' The Lieutenant ignored him, more concerned with events unfolding before him. John pressed on.

'From Southwark, me. Tis said my father was a sailor, too. Sailed with Nelson and lost his leg to a French cannonball... I'm a good worker me, I can even talk American.'

Rather than cuff him into line, the Lieutenant barked an order,

'Stand aside boy... behind me, here... and don't move.'

The Lieutenant kept an eye to ensure the lad transferred from the stricken ship, and later he sought John out.

'We need a boy to run for our surgeon.'

'I can do that, Captain.'

'Are you afraid of a bucket full of guts and what might look like your father's missing leg?'

'Not me, Captain. Worked in a knacker's yard in Fulham, I did. Shovelled cow's innards all day. You wouldn't believe the pong, 'specially if you left bits of it hanging about. You'd step on it and slip on your arse more often than not, come up smelling of...

'Enough, boy! Just find the surgery and say you've been sent to help.'

'On my way Captain, consider me gone.'

***

It was a painful awakening. Images were blurred by the throb in his head. Images of men engaged in acts of warfare... priming, loading, and firing. Then again, in re-occurring cycles, never-ending... priming, loading, firing, until the barrel of his gun melted away and he was conscious.

It was a blast of light too powerful to endure.

Clamp my eyes shut, he thought, *keep the World and its horrors out, just prime, load, fire, prime, load, fire.*

The imagined scene was a place of sanctuary from the pain trying to prise him awake.

He was on the gun deck. One by one, at each round of his gun's firing, the comrades at his side dissolved through the timbers until he was alone. He knew it was time to leave, as there was no one left to prime and load...

The world broke upon him. He found that he was alive. He was afraid. The truth of what was beyond the dutiful firing of his gun might be too much for him to bear. Yet, the World urged itself upon him.

Reality took hold and wrenched him from the safety of his perpetual dream.

Life was ephemeral. It danced in and out of focus, intangible, then oppressively omnipresent. He steadied his focus and looked around at his surroundings. He was aboard ship... not his ship. The beams from which the hammock hung were freshly cut.

His feet were bound. He tried to raise his hands to the throb in his head, but the pain from his shoulder became too much. He urged himself to think...

I'm injured to both head and shoulder... but I've been tended to... I am safe... but why I am bound...? I'm captive!

He saw John.

'John... Over here.'

From the shadows of the ship's ribs, John came to his side. '

'Almond, Sir! You are awake.'

'Where am I, boy?'

'On the American ship. The American that pasted us right proper. Our Captain and crew are in the hold. Some who is 'urt is here with you, in the surgery. That's so that Mr. Jones can keep an eye on you all. He's helping the Americans with those that's been bashed about a bit, like you. You've got a cracked skull you 'ave, according to Mr. Smith, and you've been asleep for two days and'

'Enough, boy...' Almond's head spun. He tried to make sense of the story John had told but could not arrange it in any order that made sense.

'Now start again and tell me *slowly,* what has happened and why I am here.'

***

The Constitution made port in Boston sooner than planned. The need to divest itself of its prisoners was urgent, as the ship didn't have sufficient provisions to remain at sea. A midshipman standing close to Captain Hull suggested,

'The news of our victory over a British frigate will make heroes of the ship and its crew, Captain.'

'Heroes...? Well at least for the time it takes us to fill our hold with cannonball and powder. Then we'll be back out on the next available tide and they'll expect us to do it all again or else return as villains.'

The crowds of townsfolk began to fill the dockside, and the unloading of British seamen told of its victory. They were eager to hear the story of the battle and to jeer at the prisoners as they spilled on to the quayside. Almond, still unsteady on his feet, was helped off the ship by Jeremiah, as was Adam, now unable to continue sailing until he recovered from his ankle injury. Jeremiah and the other pressed American sailors were to be interrogated by the town's militia before repatriation. Some of the freed American sailors choose to be enrolled aboard the *Constitution,* to make up for its losses and to continue seafaring. Also remaining on board was John, who now stood at the ship's rail, still talking, and wanting to see his compatriots one last time.

'Decided to stay I 'ave. They 'ave need for me 'ere and I want to try being American.'

Almond waved up to him and replied,

'You already look like a little Red Indian. Try not to get yourself scalped.'

John laughed at the idea, and, as Jeremiah had told in his stories of the Native Americans, he slapped his cupped hand to his mouth and whooped. Then, encouraged by the laughter from below, he raised an imaginary tomahawk to the sky and danced across the deck, rocking back and forth, whooping all the while, until someone on board cuffed him into line.

John was to prosper in his new homeland, where his cheeky optimism and willingness to work, afforded him a warm home, a large family, and a table upon which was laid food for them all; and enough for his friends, of which there were many.

Jeremiah and Adam stood together at the gates of the holding compound. Jeremiah had been assigned to take care of Adam and to provide physical support for him to reach his home. He was then to report to the port militia for them to assess his commitment to the Americas. Before leaving the dockside, he approached Almond and his naval escort. He wanted to be sure Almond was safe and cared for. Speaking to the officer in charge, and taking Almond by the wrist, he asked,

'Can I take this sailor to help me support your shipmate? He can come back to the militia with me after we get this man home.'

The officer saw the size of Adam and how he was unable to support his weight, even with the help of Jeremiah, and agreed on the understanding Jeremiah was to report back within the day; after all, he judged, this freed American sailor was not likely to abscond.

The three men set off, and Jeremiah said,

'We'll not go fast, Almond, not with the state of this lad's ankle. What's your name, sailor?

'Adam, Adam Berryman.'

'Berryman, did you say...? And this is Boston?' asked Almond.

'Yes, what's it to you?'

'Your father, was he a Thomas Berryman?'

Adam was slow to answer. He was assessing the situation that was beginning to unfold.

'No! But my grandfather was a Thomas. That means nothing?'

'His brother, was he called Abraham?'

'He was, I think? Although, I didn't know him. He stayed in England when Tom came here.' Adam was still suspicious and continued,

'Are you saying you know the family?'

'I think I am family, Adam. My mother was a Berryman, daughter of granddad Abe.'

Adam didn't reply; he wanted it to look as though he didn't care. He tried hard to dismiss the revelation. Why would it matter this Britisher was a distant relation? Adam's Grandfather had left the mines of Cornwall for good reason, and was proud to be an American he'd been told, as was Adam. The enmity that had built between the nations was greater than any blood tie could overcome. And yet, the thread of the past, the homeland, was still attached to his American family, and it tugged at him.

Adam lived with his family above a chandler's shop. The street was crowded. Steps to the side of the shop led up to the two rooms. There was the living room with the kitchen and fire where Adam's wife, Betsy, cooked and boiled water to launder clothes. The lone bedroom was beyond. The three men were greeted by Adam's two children, both boys, one of four years of age, the other, aged two. They rushed to hug Adam, who needed to fend them away from his injured foot whilst still making them sure he was glad to be back home with them all. Betsy came out from the bedroom to find out the reason for the commotion, and on seeing her husband, she also ran to hug him. The children demanded attention with their questions,

'Papa, where have you been? What have you done?'

'Have you brought something for us?'

Betsy held him close.

'You've been away too long my love. We've missed you so much.'

Adam was able to calm the children, only for Betsy to notice Adam's injured foot.

'Oh, my love, what have you done? How did it happen? Come sit by the fire and let me see.' Noticing the two men at the doorstep, she said,

'And who are these gentlemen you have brought with you?'

'Two men whose throat I would have slit up to a few days ago.'

'Adam, how could you say such a thing.'

'They're off a British Man-o-War.' Then pointing to Jeremiah, he continued,

'This hulk here is an American, so he says.'

'Good day to you Ma'am.' said Jeremiah.

'Well, seeing they brought you home, Adam, they'll be welcome in this house until I say otherwise. You couldn't have got here by yourself looking at the state of that foot.'

She turned her gaze to Almond. He was in worse shape, with his head bandaged and a bruise ran across his forehead and merged into two black eyes. A stitched cut ran down his cheek.

She asked of Adam, 'And who may this other one be?'

'This be a gentleman who goes by the name of Rowe. He tells me his mother was a Berryman.'

'From Cornwall?' asked Betsy

'From Camborne, no less.'

Betsy was Cornish-American, removed from Cornwall by two generations. Her parents, still living, talked of the land their grandparents had left, the mining communities and the friends and family that remained 'back home'.

'No! There has to be a family connection? On my mother's side, the Harvey's, they married into a Rowe family many years back, though there were a few Rowe families in the village. But we're not from Camborne, so I am not sure... but still?'

Here, on a foreign shore, Almond could see 'family', standing in front of him. He spoke without asking for permission. Somehow, he didn't feel as though he was a prisoner of war and was keen to confirm a connection.

'There were Harveys in my family, going back.'

'As far as I'm concerned, you're family. What's your name?'

'Almond Rowe, Ma'am.'

'Almond, sit at our table. And you, too, Mister...?'

'Jeremiah Haroldson, Ma'am.'

'A Norwegian family?'

'We are Swedish. On my father's side, for sure. On my mother's side, we go back to the first settlers of these shores. Maybe Dutch.'

'We have American royalty here for tea, Adam. You are welcome, Mr. Haroldson.'

Adam seemed content for it to be so. For all of his brutality as a fighting sailor, Adam Berryman was a family man.

***

Almond was processed as a prisoner-of-war by the local militia and detained until an agreement could be reached with the British naval authorities about what was to be done with them. In the meantime, like John, Almond asked to remain in America. For Almond, there was nothing, and no one, to go back for.

Jeremiah offered to sponsor him, firstly by providing room and lodge in his own home and then arranging for Almond to obtain work at the Shipwrights where Jeremiah himself worked. It was in the Swedish community Almond found himself a wife, Anna, a first cousin to Jeremiah, a sweet, caring girl. She spoke English and Swedish, both with an American accent, much to the dislike of her parents. To marry outside of the community was frowned upon, but the family took to Almond who tried hard to belong. He tried to learn their language, and it was Anna who was asked to be his tutor.

'*God Morgen Herr Rowe.* We will first start with numbers in Norwegian.'

'*God Morgen, froken Haroldson.* I would like first to say thank you for taking the time to help me.'

Anna was as matter-of-fact and efficient as she would always be, she replied 'You're welcome,' and continued,

'Now, if you are to work at the Shipwrights you must first recognise our words for numbers, starting from one to ten. Shall we begin?

As their relationship developed, Anna tried to speak with Almond of his life before she knew him. At quiet moments together, before the children were born, she would ask,

'Tell me, Almond, what was your old country like?'

It wasn't an unreasonable question. Her parents spoke of Sweden most days, not wanting to go back but to acknowledge the culture and principles their parents and country had given them: a love of family, their religion, a need to work hard and to respect others. It was all there, the makings of a good citizen anywhere in the world. But Almond spoke little of his days in Cornwall. It was a time he preferred to forget. His life started the day he set foot in Boston. He tried to answer her question without telling of himself.

'They were hard times, my love. Times I would prefer to forget. The mines, the ill health and disease, and the deaths of people before they should have been called. Why have me bring that to mind?

'But you must long for your family. I would?'

'No, they chose to live their life as they saw fit. I choose to do the same.'

'There must be times, though, when they come to mind and you wish you could speak once more or embrace one last time?'

'When I think of family, it is you and our family I think of. Your Swedish family, too. I think of the warmth and acceptance they showed me. But mostly, I think of you and your sweet face, your welcoming smile. As for an embrace, it's yours that will last me until the end of my days.'

Anna would try to take Almond with her to church. He went the once... the day they married. She would encourage him, but it had no effect.

'Please come with me, Al. What will God think of you not coming to worship him?'

'Your God will be good enough to include me in his thoughts if you ask him nicely.'

'But you must let God into your life.' replied Anna.

'My God left me years ago! I'll not see that God return. I'm happy you'll get salvation. And as long as you lead a good life, I'll get in to heaven hiding beneath your petticoat.'

His blasphemous ways didn't go unnoticed, at least not by Anna, and Almond took great pleasure in her playful attempt to chastise him.

His past life, and the family he left in Cornwall, became a distant memory. The hurt the memory carried with it was best forgotten. His new family in Massachusetts provided him with a joy for life, a joy lost to him for so many years. Anna and their three children, two girls Elizabeth and Anna, and a boy named Henry, filled his days.

21

Silver and Gold

Prospectors for gold were not the first to inhabit the mountainous region beyond America's Great Basin. For hundreds of years, the local tribe of American Indians, the Washoe, lived in the mountains and its plains to the east. They would live in harmony with the plants and animals to be found there, and offered prayers to the gods for the bounty to be had and the privilege of its use. They would hunt deer, antelope and rabbit, catch fish in Lake Tahoe and gather pine nuts from the forests. They had no need for silver or gold. If they had, it would have been fashioned and incorporated into their necklaces where it would have gleamed and jostled amongst bone and polished stone. But there never was such a gleam at night as they danced in the light of their fires. They were unaware of the 'white man's' wealth that lay beneath their feet.

It was the 'White Man' from the east who came in search of silver and gold, and in 1850, prospectors located the source of the Sierra Nevada deposits.

At first, they panned for it, and followed the streams to the ore bearing rock that outcropped on the hillsides; the ore would be hard to recover, as it needed to be mined.

By coincidence, a grey rock clung to the tools of the prospectors. It was found to be silver ore. In the early days, silver was the main creator of wealth, as, at the time, it was even more valuable than gold. If it were not for these rocks, there would have been no other reason for a settlement on the barren mountain slopes.

***

For the impoverished immigrants of the early-nineteenth century who travelled to America from Europe, the journey to California was long and dangerous. It would take six weeks or more to sail to the east coast of America from ports such as Plymouth on England's south coast. The seekers of fortune then joined wagon trains and continued their journey west. Delays would be inevitable as the wagon trains needed to be properly provisioned and safely escorted. It would take three months to travel across the central plains, deserts and mountains of North America to reach the mountains of the Sierra Nevada where the silver and gold-bearing rocks, known as the Comstock Lodes, were to be found. By 1869, the journey west riding the newly opened 'Transcontinental' Pacific Railroad would only take a few days.

***

John Rowe was an American, and he longed to take advantage of the opportunity the opening of the Pacific Railway offered him. Strong in the arm, and in the head, he announced,

'Father, I have something to tell you.'

Henry didn't inquire of him immediately; that was his way. He knew his son needed to say what was important to him.

'I hear they need men in Nevada to mine for gold and silver. I want to go and try my luck.' John waited for a response. He knew it would come, and he had to be patient. His father absorbed the news and then spoke,

'And what has brought this about?'

Henry wanted to know why his son was thinking of leaving his home and the security it offered. Had it been something the family had done to bring this about?

'There's little that'll keep me here, nothing that'll make me a fortune.'

Henry was shocked and saddened by the inferred slight.

'Is a fortune more important to you than your family life here? Think about what it gives you every day?'

'It's not the money so much. As I see it, I need to make my own way in life, and I want more from it than I have managed to find here in Boston.'

'Isn't it a good life?'

'I have neither right nor reason to complain, but I have to forge my own way now I've become a man. Boston is not the only place in the world. I could get on a boat and visit any country I choose, but I have chosen to travel in America.'

'You are only just eighteen, why would you risk going west...? There is still the threat of attack from Indians. You have your job at the chandlers. It was good enough for me and our fathers before us.'

'You've told me before how our fathers were miners in the old country. We were built for it, and there's more money to be had doing that than standing behind a counter.'

They remained silent for a moment whilst Henry took in the news. It was Henry who was first to speak. He had much he could say but chose to rely on his sense of duty and his work ethic for support. Those were part of his moral principles that been passed down over the years, from father to son.

'My grandfather was a miner, tis true, but he left that life behind. He chose what he thought was a better life, a better place to bring up his children. You bear his name because of that. You know your second name, Almond, was his name, too?'

'You have never called me Almond, and I have never answered to it.'

'That's true, John, and I cannot speak for him, but I know that when he came to this country, he didn't choose to be a miner. There would have been a reason for that.'

Once again, there was silence between them. To move on from the hurt he might have caused, John continued,

'Thousands are making the journey west. They tell me that if you hit a rich seam you can earn a hundred dollars in a day. How long would I need to be a miner?'

Henry couldn't help himself from angrily replying,

'We left the old country to get away from having to work in a hole in the ground.'

'It may not be for long.'

'Being strong and faithful to God allows us the strength to do more than live in the dark. If you want to do something different, you can plough the fields you pass on the way west, and there build your own home. Create your wealth that way, or any other way, but do it in the sun.'

'It's a chance for me, and I want to take it.'

'The whole idea sounds too good to be true, you may see it as a chance but what about the risk you will be taking?'

'I'm the right age to take the risk, Father'

Henry sighed, and spoke to his only son for one last time, giving him the freedom to decide but appealing to the remnants of loyalty to his family that John surely must still have.

'Then go, if we are not enough for you. No doubt, there will come a time when you will return and we will still be here. You will always be welcome.'

***

In the spring of 1869, when John was eighteen years old, he left his American family in Boston and boarded a train on the newly completed Transcontinental, Pacific Railway, going west.

From the train, the prairies seemed hostile and endless. Aboard, it was filled with those seeking a new life: veteran Confederate Army soldiers turned buffalo hunter, businessmen trading their wares, families, intent on making new lives for themselves, and seekers of fortune.

The train connected the nation, east to west, and divided it, north and south; its division heralding the demise of both the buffalo and the Native American tribes that had once roamed freely across the plains.

John arrived in Carson City, a bustling frontier town. It was on a spur line from Reno, a main station for those travelling west to California. Carson City was the destination of many folk, like John, who were attracted by the lure of the silver and gold to be found in the hills to the northwest. The bustle of the town reassured John. Whatever he did in these parts he was in touching distance of civilization, no matter it was an alien existence in comparison to the coastal town he had left behind.

The Main Street rattled with activity. Horse and mule carts carried goods to be traded in the town, either to the townsfolk or miners who came down from the hills. The arid, desert environment, ensured a light-brown coloured dust would billow from its traffic, coating surfaces, inside and out, and tumbleweed would clog alleyways and side entrances, their wind-blown progress halted by the town's obstruction. Beyond the town, cart tracks would be run by chaparral cocks, skittering to-and-fro, whilst above them, Bald Eagles circled in choreographed displays.

In support of this new economy, trading posts and stores had sprung up to sustain the population, and, soon after, saloons opened up to entertain them, redistributing their newly created wealth.

John had arrived in Carson City, intending to rest awhile and learn what he could before travelling onwards to his destination, the mining community of Virginia City. As it turned out, Carson City wasn't short of miners. They would be stopping over, as was John, or were out to enjoy spending the money they'd earned. He wanted to get information about the final leg in his journey and what to expect when he got there.

The saloons of the town were full of men who were lucky enough to have earned a fortune and enjoy themselves in the process. Those who had struck it rich in the mines had more than enough money, and so the price of drink in the saloons was high. All provisions came via the route

John had taken, and the charge for each drink reflected the effort made in bringing it to the thirsty townsfolk; the price of a drink was inflated once again by the eagerness the saloon's customers showed to consume it.

John stood at the bar. His face wasn't one recognised by the barman. Furthermore, he wasn't hooting and hollering as if he had entered with more than enough money in his pocket and wanting people to know it. The barman leant against the back shelf and looked straight through John as if he wasn't there. John motioned to the barman to get his attention but it had no effect. He was not the first, and certainly not the last, to ask out loud,

'What have you got to do to get a drink in this town?'

Standing next to John, and with his back half turned towards him, stood a hulk of a man, not tall, but broad-shouldered and thickset. The man spoke.

'You're new here, Mister?'

John shifted his stance slightly so as not to offer the threat a face-to-face reply might suggest; John knew to be cautious; he couldn't be sure where the conversation might lead. He was slow to respond. He needed to gauge the man and look to find any hint of menace.

Did this man want to gain from him in some way? His soft accent was reassuring and John knew he was Welsh. John recognised the rise and fall of it, not unlike the Cornish, but it had more of a song about it. The Welsh had always got on well enough with the Cornish community in Boston. In the distant past, the Welsh language was close enough to old Cornish for them to understand each other. In a town where he knew no one, this man would be worth a try.

'I got here today. I travelled from the East Coast.'

'Seeing that you've not come in your best suit, I suppose you're here to dig for gold?'

John looked around him and said,

'I am... but I don't see many in here dressed for church.'

The raucous groups of men in the saloon sat at tables with bottles of whiskey set in front of them. Keeping them company were ladies dressed in the low-cut finery of their profession; at least, keeping the company of those who could afford what was on offer. The ladies were not like any other John had seen before, and he could not help but admire them. But John had urgent matters to discuss, so his interest in the women would have to wait. He turned back to his companion and nodded in the direction of the tables.

'I see quite a few miners have got here before me, and from the way they're spending their money they've done alright.'

'So they have... for the time being. But you shouldn't be too eager to get swinging your pick.'

'What do you mean?'

'There's many more in the hills still swinging theirs, and all they've got in their pocket is the sparks that fly when they're a doing it.'

'But I'm told there's still silver to be mined, and it must be true otherwise these men wouldn't be here?'

'There is... That, and gold, too, which nowadays pays more.'

The Welshman paused but raised a finger to show there was more to be said. He leaned closer and spoke quietly, as if telling a secret he alone knew.

'But you never know when you are going to find it or how long it will keep giving. Men find a vein and think they're rich... then the vein stops giving... but they don't.'

'How so?'

'They just keep swinging their pick until their strength, or their breath, runs out.'

'It's worth the risk though. These men are proof of that.'

The Welshman leaned back and returned to full voice.

'There's a lot outside this saloon, the ones with sparks in their pocket, and it's them that'll tell you the opposite. As for whether it's worth it...? Well, it depends on how much you're prepared to invest, and I don't mean money... although you'll need enough of that!'

'Well, I have enough money.'

'I see you've no tools with you. Outside are they...? On a mule?'

'No, I thought I'd get them in Virginia City.'

'You'd best see if you can buy your tools from around here... from some of the miners who are on their way home east. There'll be some use left in them if you're lucky... give or take a new handle, or a new head... or both.

'I'd thought I'd buy new.'

'Prices here are sky-high, even for basic tools. The nearer you get to the mines, the higher the price'll be.'

'I'll think on,' said John. But the stranger wasn't finished.

'Then, when you get there, you'll need to find work.'

'I'm young and strong. I'll get work easy enough.'

'There's plenty of young miners already waiting and hoping for a new shaft to be sunk, and they're a hollering for work when a seam is found. You may well stand around for weeks.' John's companion looked him up and down, and continued,

'Are you American, or do I hear some Cornish in you?'

'Going back, a grandfather came from Cornwall. I must have some of the way he spoke in me. We sometimes use our old voice at home and some of the Cornish words.'

'And you look like a 'Cousin Jack'. You're the right size, short in the leg, broad at the shoulder. You might want to play that up, as there's plenty of Cornish and Welsh digging in the mines. You see, we know about digging in hard rock, so we get hired quicker than say, your French or Chinaman.' The stranger again looked John up and down, and said,

'Yes, you look as though you might be Cornish.'

'I can be as Cornish as Camborne when I want.'

'I don't know what or where Camborne is, but I'll take your word for it.' He called the barman,

'Set this man up a whisky, and another for me.'

It was as if the barman had been waiting for the Welshman to make an order, and the drinks were soon set on the bar. The stranger raised his glass to John and said,

'Here's to you making your fortune, Mister...?' He called for a reply with a slight tilt of his glass.

Thinking again of his roots, John surprised himself by the way he answered.

'John Rowe... John Almond Rowe.'

'That's a bit of a mouthful. What can I call you...?'

'You can call me Al.'

'Here's to you, Al. No doubt when you get back this way from Virginia City with your fortune made, I'll be gone.'

Selwyn Berryman-Morgan

22

The Mining Town

In the September of 1869, John Rowe stood for the first time on the boardwalk of Virginia City. He was amazed at the raw energy of the frontier town riding high on its wealth; it would soon become apparent to him the great capacity of its townsmen to drink, gamble and fornicate their riches away.

The town of Virginia City had flourished only because of the precious metals to be found in the hills surrounding it. The first miners dug shafts that followed 'tell-tale' seams exposed at the surface by erosion. They had been sunk on the basis of trial and error, and not all mines were to strike seams containing metals in commercial quantities. Nevertheless, the rewards for the prospectors and miners who did strike lucky was immense. Speculators from the East would finance the sinking of a new mine, encouraged to invest by scant assay information; often, the information was based on wishful thinking, rather than investigation and hard science. Even so, the richness and abundance of the gold and silver-bearing rocks beneath the city rewarded some of the foolhardy investors, and they would be saved from the derision reserved for those duped by a fanciful report. For the lucky few, ridicule would be replaced by the acclaim normally afforded to those who were blessed with good judgement.

From Virginia City, the mountains of the Sierra Nevada could be seen to arc into the far horizon; for 'a hundred miles' it was said. Snow-capped from mid-October, the successive peaks were a pink-white in the afternoon sun, but in late summer, they became an ochre scimitar that sliced through the blue of the sky.

For his own security, John chose to camp with a group of prospectors; 'The West' was a dangerous place to be. Its climate could be extreme at such an altitude, and the hostility of the Washoe tribe of Native American Indians kept them on their guard. For four months, he took work as he found it, cleaning stables, laying rail for a new railroad and labouring amongst the spoil of the mines. As the Welshman said he should, he became known as a young Cornishman; a 'Cousin Jack', waiting for a chance to use his skills, all the while becoming fitter and stronger. His beard had taken on the vigour of a man much older, and he was sure it wouldn't be long before he'd find well-paying work at a mine.

The settlement was barely big enough to be called a town, let alone a city. It had been built on an east-facing slope and sat directly over the ore-bearing seams. From early afternoon, it had been in shade; the sun had slipped behind the mountainside to which the town clung. The rocks above were weathered a yellow-brown and fashioned into uneven crags and crevices by the blaze of the desert sun and the frostbite that accompanied the shining of the moon. Virginia City had become full of industry. The people lived alongside the mines, a surprisingly ordered community, and a host of different businesses provided services to those who lived there. The streets ran horizontally across the mountainside, parallel to one another. They were named alphabetically from 'A', the highest on the hillside, to 'Q', at the hillside's foot. The connecting streets ran downhill at right angles, like posts in a wire fence. They were given proper names such as Washington, Union, Carson and Taylor St. Some streets had pretentious epithets, such as 'Avenue', but they were few.

Most of the supply stores, residential and administration buildings were to be found in streets A to G. The city map of the time listed the buildings in what must have been thought to be their order of importance. High on the list was the Court House, followed by public schools, Churches, of which there was four, and, men's clubhouses (for the use of those belonging to the professions). Also high on the list was an opera house. The twelve mining companies, who were the reason for the City's existence, were bottom of the list. There were glaring omissions, as there was no mention of the saloons where the base needs of the miners were catered for. They were not to be spoken about in polite circles, or advertised for all to see in the 'City Map'.

In the saloons, the miners could spend their money on extras that made their hard work worthwhile... alcohol, gambling and women. The bordellos were to be found within, and the ladies to be found there would command a high price for their services; the laws of supply and demand ensured they could. Only the wealthiest miners would be able to afford the prices the Madams asked.

***

Autumn turned to winter, and John stood on the platform of the Virginia City railway depot. It was a special day for the Virginia and Truckee Railroad as it marked the first running of a passenger train to Virginia City, and the townsfolk had turned out to see its arrival. Many of the passengers on the train had travelled up from Carson City and beyond, and most were to attend a stage performance at Piper's Opera House on D Street.

John had boarded the train at Gold Hill, another mining town, just four miles down the track, where he was temporarily trying his luck.

He had stood at the door of the carriage as the train came to a halt. The locomotive was lost for a moment in the rush of exhausted steam, but when it cleared, the townsfolk could see its nameplate on the front of the engine. It was called 'Lyon', its French-sounding name hiding the truth that it had been manufactured at the Union Iron Works in San Francisco. The excitement had built in anticipation of its arrival, and when the noise of the released steam and clatter of carriages had subsided, a loud cheer rang out from those waiting. John cheered from the carriage window as loud as any. Then, from nowhere, the thought came to his mind of an all but forgotten family story of when Almond, his forefather, had travelled on the first steam-driven machine. John had a sense this short train journey to Virginia City was about to change his fortune as it had his great-grandfather's.

John stood in Virginia City's main street. He had most of the day to enjoy what the town had to offer, and an evening to savour its seedier delights. He had not starved, at least not for food, but his meagre earnings meant he was left wanting the company of women and the chance to confirm his newfound virility... and now the sun had set?

The swing saloon doors were difficult to push through, although it wasn't the doors resisting. He knew he'd very little money in his pocket, a few dollars and some cents, plenty enough to cover his needs back in Gold Hill, but in Virginia City, it was only enough to keep him in basic 'vittles'. Light from inside the saloon flooded onto the boardwalk, and the room's brightness convinced John he would be welcome. After all, he'd washed his clothes and trimmed his beard and bathed for the first time in weeks, enduring the shock of ice-cold water that gathered in pools as it tumbled down the hillside. His boots were almost new and took a dull shine. He'd enough to buy a beer or two.

Time enough for his face to become known by the gaffers from the mine, he thought.

In truth, and most urgently, it was a chance for him to be closer to the women who plied their trade. He'd moderated his expectations; to see a woman dressed in such a way, inviting male attention, would be enough for now. He imagined their long, soft hair, gathered to expose a white neck which would take the eye to partly exposed breasts (oh, how he yearned they would be released). And there was more to delight: the sight of a raised leg on a chair, an exposed ankle, the feel of a soft arm rested easily on his, or, if he was lucky, lips that whispered in his ear an invitation of what was to come for *'such a handsome young man'*.

He had no knowledge of women; the images he had formed in his head were sculpted from the fireside banter of 'experienced' miners. Even so, he was wise enough to know such delights needed to be encountered piecemeal so he wouldn't be overwhelmed at their discovery. A beer or two in the saloon would be a start. He could later get to know the women who would satisfy his needs. He pushed through the swing doors.

The bathe of light in the saloon was even greater than he expected. Hanging from the ceiling were chandeliers that reflected the glow from their candles to all corners of the room. A mirror of outlandish proportions hung behind the saloon bar. Against it were displayed row upon row of bottles of strong liquor sourced from all parts of the world. The spirits were coloured in bright shades of lurid red, green and amber. A log fire flamed and gave a warmer glow to the room; it tempered the pale yellow of the candle flame. In the far corner, a piano played a familiar, jaunty melody, and it emphasised the welcome to be had. But did it play for him? John was to put it to the test.

No one seemed interested in the newcomer, even though his walk to the bar was through tables set for drinking and gambling. To his relief, he went unchallenged, other than a sideways glance from a young lady not yet spoken for. At the bar, men sat alone with their own thoughts: a loss of money at the table, the continuing refusal of a seam they worked to give up its gold in the quantities it once did, or, most melancholy of all, thoughts of the homeland and family they once knew. Even so, there was space enough for John.

The barman wasn't already engaged in Virginia City banter or the pouring of alcohol. John sat at the bar and asked with uncommon politeness,

'I'll have a beer, sir, if you wouldn't mind.

Politeness was in short supply in Virginia City, except on Sundays at church service. In a frontier's town, politeness was not appreciated. John's attempt to be unobtrusive failed miserably.

'Mind! Why would I mind? If you've got the money, I'll serve you a beer. That's why I'm standing this side of the bar and you're on the other.'

The men either side of John half-turned to see how the encounter would play out. They looked into John's eyes to see if he had the 'steel' necessary to survive in this western 'armpit' of a town. John knew he was being tested and gave his reply. Leaning across the bar and staring the barman in the face, he responded to the challenge.

'In that case, I'll have a beer... and I'll have it *now!*'

They barman backed off... a small adjustment in his stance, but it was enough to show that John had established the right to ask for what he wanted in the way he wanted. Even so, the barman's job of collecting payment allowed him one more try at denying this stranger.

'Before I do, I still need to know if you have two dollars to pay for it.'

John slapped the coins on the bar but held his hand an inch or two above the silver dollars. As the barman motioned to take the payment, John pulled the coins back.

'Well, Mister, do you want a beer or not?'

'Thank you, my good man, a beer would be fine.' He slid the coins over the bar.

Well, at two dollars it will only be the one beer, thought John.

Space was made next to him as a miner moved on home and it was filled almost immediately. John took no notice, but a fragrance drew his attention. It was a sweet smell, reminiscent, in equal parts, of a New England spring and freshly washed linen. He turned to inquire where it came from. His curiosity didn't disappoint him. It was the young lady he'd seen when he came in.

She was small in frame, with bobbed, jet black hair. Her unblemished pale-white skin seemed to radiate its own light, her features childlike; for she wasn't any older than John. Her comeliness spoke to him of the pleasures he had dreamed of; as did her first words, lilted on the air, soft, with a European accent.

'My, you *are* a handsome young man... Have you come looking for some warmth on such a cold night?' She moved closer. The soft down of hair on her forearm touched his hand, and her intimacy had its intended effect on him. He was speechless, and was slow to respond. What conversation there'd been in his dreams of women now seemed inappropriate. In 'real-life', there could be no headlong rush into the physical pleasures this lady offered; at least, not until the price had been negotiated, and he had been led upstairs to the bordello with its vacant stall. He hoped his lack of an immediate reply would suggest he was a man of experience and someone who wouldn't be 'taken in'. When he spoke, his garbled response gave the lie to that.

'Yes... err... I mean no... Err... I've only come in for a beer,' he lied.

The young lady smiled at him. She knew what he needed, and she'd take her own pleasure in providing it; the pleasure of having his dollars in her purse. What those dollars could buy far outweighed any thrill she might gain from this young man's deflowering.

'My name is Chloe. It's French you know...?' Then continued,

'My, you look so strong, my lovely American friend.'

'That's where you're wrong. I'm from England, from Cornwall.' It was less than a half-truth, but it was in keeping with the new identity he had adopted.

'You do speak American in a funny way. So, what's your name, Mister English?'

What was John to do? How was he to answer? Even a thousand miles away from Boston and his family, the moral constraints instilled in him from the pulpit of his chapel weighed on his conscience; what if his family could see him now? He didn't want to give his name, as that linked him to them and to their beliefs. He sought refuge in what was more than a half-truth.

'My name is Almond.'

'Almaund? What a strange name?'

'Well, it's my name... but it sounds better when you say it.'

John was surprised at the familiarity of his reply. After all his self-doubt, it was, after all, not so difficult to talk to an attractive young woman; forgetting she was a lady who earned her living by having to listen. Back home, because of his youthful shyness, he would have avoided a young lady's glance and be teased for doing so. Chloe knew how to tease a man in ways crafted to bring him back time and again, not drive him away.

'Yes, I say your name in French and it sounds more, how would I say... *romantique*... yes, *romantique*.' Pursing her lips and emphasising the vowels she whispered.

'Almaund, do *you* feel ... romantique?'

She had moved close to him. Her lips were an inch away from a kiss. John wanted more, and said,

'*Almaund*, I shall be,'... trying all he could to affect his best French accent, whilst at the same time pursing his lips yet closer to hers.

Chloe waited for his response but Almond left the question open. Chloe sought a reply. In her trade, small talk was at a premium.

'And, *are* you romantique this evening, my sweet English boy?' She placed her free hand on his thigh, a choreographed manoeuvre she had employed many times before and was sure to move the transaction along. He swayed forward, wanting to know how a kiss joined in passion might taste. Artfully, she swayed away but kept her gaze firmly fixed to his, her smile unchanged, enticing him to close the deal.

'You have money to pay, my dearest Almaund?'

John remained silent. The negotiations were over... she could not be his. Chloe sighed with regret, and slowly turned and slipped away.

The game was on, and, for now, she held all the cards. He would return to her as Almond, the man he had grown to be. The next time he met her he wanted it to be on his terms. He knew they would meet again. Her proffered charms and his hard-earned wages would surely be consummated.

***

Almond, as he was now known, continued to take whatever work came his way, but none of it was at the rock face where the real money could be earned. Soon enough, his reputation as an honest and reliable workman became established. He would turn up each day in the hope he would be employed in the mines, having only to be content with a lesser task. He would be glad to take it. It kept him fit and strong, and he was in sight of a 'Gaffer'. It had been more than a month since Almond had gazed into Chloe's eyes. It was then that Joseph Tonkin, a mine foreman and a Cornishman, considered Almond for work in the least productive mine in Virginia City. There was little competition to go work down what was thought to be a worked-out shaft. Almond stood out, as he was amongst mine-damaged men plying for the job. It offered a low rate of pay; able-bodied miners would turn their nose up at it. Even so, Joseph was not sure he would employ the young lad.

'You keep telling me you're a Cornish miner, is that true, son?

'As true as I stand here, I worked in the mines in Camborne from age twelve.'

He lied, but now, as the man named Almond, he could tell his great-grandfather's tales as if they were his own. He hoped Joseph wouldn't probe too deep. Joseph chose not to, although his suspicious mind told him something didn't add up. The accent for one; it was as much American as Cornish, and this lad seemed 'too cocky' for someone subjected to the horrors of a Cornish mine? Joseph put his doubts to one side. Almond was a likeable lad and he looked as strong as an ox. Joseph decided to believe him.

'Right, son, I want you to go in with Walter and Manny. Walter will tell you what to do. You have your tools with you I see. If there is anything else you need, Walter will kit you out.'

Almond had purchased clothing designed to resist the elements found in a mine: strong boots, a woollen undershirt, 'long johns', canvas trousers, a sleeveless oil-cloth coat and a leather hat. They would be put to their first real test. Slung over his back were the tools of his newly acquired trade, a pick, a shovel and a mandrill. His hammer was slung from his belt, as was his lantern.

The mine shaft had been sunk directly into the hillside; its mouth surrounded by spoil heaps not taken away, as the shaft was exploratory. In profitable mines, there would be found vast excavated caverns filled with a wooden framework of floors, roadways and connecting stairwells. Instead, this unprofitable shaft had been continually dug deeper, in the hope it might find deposits on a larger scale, but the mine owners were losing hope. The once-promising seam was tapering away.

Walter and his son Emanuel were English, but not Cornish. From their accent, Almond couldn't tell exactly where in the 'Old Country' that might be, and he didn't ask. Almond was last to enter the mine. He needed to watch what his companions did and learn as he went along. They were to descend to the workface using ropes and ladders. There was not the luxury to be found of a steam-driven lift. Lifts were reserved for profitable mines.

Almond's lantern illuminated the shaft immediately below him but very little else, and the light from above soon dimmed to extinction. The fear of the unknown gripped him.

He had harboured a notion of what being in a mine was like, but the reality of the darkness and the claustrophobic nearness of the surrounding rock overwhelmed him. His pace of descent slowed. His companions went about their task and they were soon lost from sight. The reflected light from their lanterns dimmed in each turn of the shaft, and the sound of the metallic clatter of their tools on the rock became distant. All of which added to Almond's sense of isolation. His breath quickened and shortened. A sense of panic held his chest in a vice.

'I must get control,' he mumbled to himself.

He closed his eyes and clung to the wooden log that formed the central pillar of the ladder on which he stood. He remained still. He needed to slow his breathing and gain composure. When he opened his eyes, the rock was the same, but perhaps not as close as he had thought.

He was starting to cope. He knew he would cope. A shout came from below.

'Almond! Are you there, lad?'

'Yes, coming. My pick got jammed in the shaft. I'm on my way now.'

'Get yourself organised and hurry up; we've got work to do.'

'Yes, coming.'

He continued down to the end of the ladder. At the next level, he saw the continuing shaft and a knotted rope would take him down another twenty feet. His panic had eased; if his great-grandfather could work mines like this, so could he. It was after two further flights of rope he met with the others. They were in a 12-foot, square chamber. It was the level they were to work. Loose spoil had been stacked against its back wall, reducing the available space.

'You took your time, lad. We can't afford to be standing around.'

'Sorry, I was getting used to the shaft and making sure of my footing.'

From this level, tunnels had been dug at 90 degrees to each another. One continued downwards following the original seam. To its right, and at a shallow angle, a wider tunnel disappeared into the mountain rock. Walter spoke up.

'Now then my young lad, it's the tunnel off to the right is where you'll work. We'll work the other. It's almost been worked out, but we are to give it one more try to get all we can from it. You've to go to what is a trial shaft that followed another vein. It's ten yards to the face, and the shaft is wide enough for you to work it alone. Back clear the spoil as you go.'

Almond felt uneasy about the suggestion.

'I have to do that on my own? I don't think I'll get much ore out without there being someone working behind me to take the spoil away.'

Almond had known from conversations with other miners how they always worked in pairs. Without someone at his back, he would continually have to stop and clamber over the mined rock to clear it back to the level. And there was also the issue of safety. Miners would not agree to work alone, if they could help it, and would ask to work with a 'buddy'. It was clear to Almond, that the owner was cutting corners to keep down the costs.

'You'll be alright. Manny will work for us both. He'll take turns hauling the stuff back to here. We'll not move a great deal between us, tis true, but it'll give the assayers chance to see if the ore in your tunnel has enough in it to carry on digging.'

'And if not?'

'If not, you'll have work enough, at least for tomorrow, retrieving as many props as you can. We can use them elsewhere ... in some other mine.

'There are props?

'You've not done this too often have you lad? In this 'ere mountain, God has seen fit to shuffle the rock with his bare hands. We dug that gold vein because it was there, then, all of a sudden, it wasn't. Just fractured rock either side of a fault line. It's them shuffles that's the bugger, and there's one of those at the face you'll be digging.

'Why am I to go back then?'

'The vein we're working is all but petered out. I may dig the last of it today. Tonkin's got interested again in yours. For the last couple of days, Manny and me dug through that shit rock.'

'Why would you do that?'

'Old man Tonkin had in mind the seam on the other side might not be too far shifted... one way or the other, up or down. He said, all pompous like,'

'*Looking at the rock, it might be still there on the far side of the fault,'*... and it was... smug bastard... but it had shifted up a yard.'

'You were lucky to find it!'

'Luck's what it's all about, though we hadn't figured on how much of the fractured stuff there was. At the end of the day we'd nearly given up digging. Then we got through and struck the base of the vein at head height. We left it until today.

'Is it safe in there, what with the loose rock?'

'That's where the props come in. We propped it up as we went. We got some of the ore out and sent up a bit of it, but they still want more. They'll see how much gold a ton of it will give back. It may not even be the same seam. You're here to find out.'

Almond turned and stooped at the shaft's entrance. He looked into the darkness that stretched ahead. He needed reassurance and turned to Walter, and asked,

'What will I find at the face?'

Walter sighed in exasperation and replied,

'You could just go look see... but as it's your first day I'll tell you.' He sighed again before continuing.

'You've got a bit more headroom than you'd think.'

'And how much would that be?'

'More than you need. As I said, we'd to dig upwards to find the seam, so if you drop on one knee, you'll be able to swing your pick above your head and to the side. The ore's in a vein about a foot deep. You'll need to undercut it to get it out.'

'How much am I expected to shift?'

'Manny's first few trips back here will be with the spoil, about half a ton between us, and we'll not get paid for that. Once you've done digging spoil, you'll need to dig at least a couple of hundredweight of the ore for them to assay. You know what a hundred weight looks like?'

'I do.'

'Well anyway, I'll tell you when you've enough. We'll join forces to get what we dig out to the surface. The ore goes first, the spoil will wait and as things stand, it may never see the light of day. Now enough of your questions, it's off you go.'

Walter was about to disappear into his tunnel when he stopped and looked back at Almond.

Their eyes met in the glimmer of the lamps. Almond could tell Walter was not sure he was up to the task. He was right. Walter challenged his young workmate to come clean by asking in his round-about way,

'I suppose it'll be nowt that you've not done before, lad?'

Almond didn't answer. He stepped into the darkness.

***

The shaft had a downwards incline, and his lamp illuminated his way. But the rock face was not to be seen, as it was hidden as the tunnel levelled out. He braced himself with his hands flat against the sides of the tunnel, and trod carefully so as not to lose his footing.

Removing the rock would be a challenge in itself, never mind the mining of it. He thought.

He bent forward, and half walked, half scrambled ten yards, to where he broke into a six-foot by four-foot chamber. The chamber had been increased in height as he'd been told. Evidence of the fault-fractured rock was plain to see. Loose pieces of shattered rock were scattered across the floor. On either side, upright props were spaced every three feet, and they, in turn, supported cross beams holding the roof timbers stopping loose rock from falling. The chamber ran twelve feet to the face. As Walter had suggested, he would be able to rest on one knee and swing his pick. He would work bare-chested. The heat within the mine, and the heat he would generate digging the rock, saw to that.

He could see what he was looking for. Quartz crystals within the ore deposit shone in the light of his lamp. Vague discolourations amongst the quartz hinted at the riches to be found within it. He arranged his tools and took up his position to undercut the deposit. He swung his first blows to very little effect.

This is not going to work, he thought.

He looked back to his mandrill and hammer. He would need to bore holes beneath the vein, to weaken the rock enclosing it. Once a shelf had been cut, the ore would be easy to remove. Its own weight would aid its recovery. Laying his pick to one side, he lifted himself off his haunches. As he did so, his trailing foot slipped on loose gravel. In order to gain purchase, he pushed his foot back against the nearest upright prop. There had been some movement of the prop, it was no longer vertical, and Almond's push at its base was all that was needed for the prop to fail. The unsupported roof fell in an instant.

Almond's light was extinguished.

He was not left there. Two days later, Walter and Manny were able to dig through to him.

***

Word of the miner's death got back to the saloon, and to Chloe.

'Almaund, did you say? I remember an Almaund. Yes, I spoke to him once... Almaund...? I remember his name. It was a nice name... but I can't remember his face...' She had looked into too many men's faces for her to be sure. But a picture of Almond swum into her imagination... she spoke,

'Almaund, yes, Almaund... A Cornishman, you say? He said he was from England?'

Manny tried not to laugh... It would have been disrespectful.

Chloe was sadder than she thought she would have been at the news of the death of a prospective client.

'He was a sweet boy.'

***

His body was taken to the cemetery at the edge of town. Over the ages, a stream had deposited water borne mud and gravel in sufficient depth to allow the City's dead to be given a Christian burial. Three sections of the cemetery were set aside, one for 'Freemasons' and another for 'Odd

Fellows'. Important and respectable places, for sure, as they were shown and listed on the town map. In these enclosures, stone monuments were chiselled with words of fond memory and commiseration.

John's was a pauper's grave in the third part of the cemetery where the topsoil was least deep. It was reserved for persons of no account or influence.

The priest attended and spoke from the Holy Book. The only others in attendance were the men who had dug him out. It was the last respect they could pay a fellow miner; even if it was someone they hardly knew.

Standing a discrete distance away from the burial ceremony, Chloe wiped a tear from her eye.

Later, someone fashioned a wooden cross, upon which was written in unusually neat script,

'Almond Rowe, a Cornishman'.

***

Across the globe, other members of the Rowe family were unaware of their American family's existence. They, too, were engaged in dangerous occupations, but with no chance of striking it lucky.

23

The Cost of Coal

Cilfynydd, South Wales, 1894

The terraced house was set low in the river worn, and weary worn, valley. Even in the month of June, a South Wales morning would often be cool, with the sun reluctant to rise above the hilltop.

It was a Saturday, and Patricia Rowe, the grandmother, was first up, laying the fire; she stacked pit-pilfered 'stick', and set upon it coal and remnants of coke from the previous day. When lit, it would chase the early morning chill from the room.

The fire would catch in fits and starts, having to be cajoled into flame. It sat in a cast iron 'range' upon which breakfast would be cooked. Sarah cooked for James, the grandfather, and Almond, his son, her husband. So as not to disturb the children, she spoke quietly as she fried egg and bacon... special for Saturday.

'Make sure you eat it all, Al. You'll need something hot inside you. Your jam sandwiches are already in your snap can.'

'Ta, Love.'

'Yes, thank you, Sarah,' said Dad, absent-mindedly.

'That's the last of Gran's wimberry jam. You'll not go hungry.'

'Great!' said Al, paying slightly more attention than his father, Jim.

'It'll be a couple of months before you get some more of that.'

'Doesn't seem five minutes ago you both were picking for it.'

'Gran'll have us up on the Common first chance. The children, too.'

'You all go mad picking those little berries, but I suppose it's worth it.' He winked and gave her a kiss on the cheek. It made up for his making fun of her... and it worked. She cooed,

'Oh, thank you, love.' Then she changed the subject to the coming day.

'I hope you come home straight away. We're to go to my mother's for tea, remember?' Dad replied in a mild grump, not wanting to be tied down by vague promises of tea from Gwen Thomas.

'We'll come home when we're finished. I'm not sure when that'll be. We've agreed to carry over from the day shift. It's only for a couple of hours, doing maintenance. We should be back in good time.

'What is it you do on *'maintenance'*, anyway?'

'Not too much, I hope. Tidying and things like that.'

Sarah seemed content with the answer and returned to her chores.

Almond hadn't worked on Maintenance before and didn't know what to expect. He asked,

'What *will* we do on Maintenance, Dad?'

'Overman Evans is the gaffer tonight, and he'll tell us when he comes down at the end of the day shift. It could be anything. He seems to make it up as he goes along.'

'I hope it's not on the coal dust, Dad. It's a real mess down there now, as most times it's left where it lays.'

'Aye, it's been weeks since it was done properly.'

'Someone should report it to the Inspector. It can't be safe.'

'But who'd be brave enough to be the tell-tale, Al? Remember what happened to John Kemp?'

'Aye, poor bugger... so it might be we'll have to shift the dust today and it'll be a shit-job if we do.'

'We'll see what happens. Anyway, we should be away by five at the latest and scrubbed down nice for our tea at Gwen's.'

As usual, Sarah was able to filter out the bits of conversation concerning the way she ran the house, and called from the oven range where she was making a pot of tea.

'You'd better be! I'll heat the water for your baths by quarter past five. Don't let me see it boil away on the fire.'

For the men assigned to maintenance work, it would still be another hard shift: mending roadways, installing support props, closing down exhausted galleries and back-filling them with the rubbish left from the mining. James had agreed with John Evans that he and A would join with some other men from the Saturday shift who had agreed to stay down.

There had been some talk of removing pit-props on the 'Grover's' side of the mine; the night shift would be delayed coming down for half an hour should there be any shot firing. If the props were blown, then the bringing of 'stick' to the Rowe household would be ensured; the continuing supply of stick was important to the women of mining families.

Experience gained over the years had shown small explosives charges would do the trick. Once the props were blown out, the tunnel they supported would collapse. On most occasions, the roof would remain in place, but, in time, the weight of the rock above would squeeze the workings shut.

The men left the house a little after seven. They were most likely to be home after putting in a ten-hour shift; the usual seven-hour shift on a Saturday and whatever else was asked of them.

'Quiet now, the children are asleep.' Sarah cautioned. Then she kissed Almond's cheek.

'Bye love, bye Dad. Take care... Don't forget to get some stick.'

Alongside the clatter of the closing of the door of their sleep-filled home, the hush in the street was broken by random opening and closing of other doors, with their own associated melody of a click of a latch, or the clack of a once slumbering door knocker. Up and down the street there were of whispered farewells.

In mid-summer, the street should have already been bathed in sunlight, but low cloud had settled overnight and it held the village in a stubborn embrace, and it imposed a mist-damped calm. As the miners made their way, they were accompanied by the rhythmic clatter of snap-cans against hip and the scrape of boots on pavement.

On a winter's morning, there would be light from the street's gas lamps to blush the road and warm the cardinal-red doorsteps of the houses. This time of day, in mid-summer, the lamplighter had come and gone, leaving an unseasonal gloom in the street. Not a dog-barked, nor did a cock crow. There was but the optimistic blackbird's call, chirped from the top of a tree that fringed the river. It gave hope the sun might shine.

The men spoke when they cleared the end of the street.

'What time did you get back from the pub last night, Al?'

'Late, I got 'shut-in', Dad.'

'These days you seem often to be shut-in. The door of the pub still has a key you know. You can get up off your arse and unlock it.'

'I'm not always there for the shut-ins, Dad. You can't say that.' They walked in silence for a few more steps, and then Jim asked of his son.

'What is it with you and Sarah? Why are you both still at each other? I hear the rows you know.'

'It's better than it used to be, Dad... Our rows and my drinking... Leave it to me, I can handle both. Anyway, she was fine with me this morning.'

'Still, I'm worried about the two of you... and the kids... and me if it comes to that. I hope you can see straight enough to shoulder a sledgehammer if we need it?

'I'm alright, Dad.'

Not content, Jim continued,

'You know, I worked hard to get us this overtime. We need the extra money it will bring in. So, what do you do? You stay out late the night before and get a skinful.'

'I said, I'll be alright... and I'll not be out tonight. I'll spend time with Sarah and the kids.'

'Come on, I'm not daft, "butt". It's only because it's Sunday and the pubs are shut. It's the rest of the week that I worry about.'

'You're making too much of this. I don't drink as much as some of my "buttys" do.'

'That shouldn't be difficult knowing some of the buttys you've got. They're a bad influence on you.'

'Come on Dad, you don't mind a drink yourself. It's often you do stop for a drink after work.'

There was nothing more Jim could say about the matter he had not said before; and it was true, Jim also drank too much. The thought of a beer or two in the Cilfynydd Arms after a shift was a cheer to them both. And it wasn't only the beer. As always, music was to be found there. A makeshift choir would come in, by dribs and drabs. They would be black with coal dust, so there was a special area for them to drink, set away from other pub users. More often than not, there would be more than enough basses to balance the tenors with their shrill, too loud, and too enthusiastic renditions of pious chapel hymns. Tenors would always sing, not taking any notice of whether they should, or if anyone might care if they did. Inevitably, the drink would wash away all their pretentious piety. Songs of Jehovah would soon be sent back to the 'Gospel Hall' in time for evening worship. For it was in the chapels the hymns would find God-fearing village folk who were content to sing up only for their Lord. They wouldn't have need of the 'demon drink. For the 'gospellers', faith was enough to soothe the hurt of having to live in a village that only existed because of the pit.

The songs the miners held dear, songs of love and loss would start quietly. One would begin and then catch the ear of another. It would spread as if it were an infection. The men who worked in the pit needed a quick release from the terror of the pit. Terror exited the mine with them and trod behind whispering, to remind the miner he needed to return the next day, the next week, on and on until...? The remedy for such thoughts was to be found in song. The nag of Terror was left at the pub door.

Back in the Rowe family home, life continued.

'How many times do I have to call you children before you get up?'

Once awakened, and after several calls, the children would run from their cold bedroom and find their clothes for the day laid out by the fire. Ethel, the youngest, would daydream, as she always did, with one sock hanging loosely from her hand. Socks were always difficult for one so young. As for vests? Well! They would be inside out, back to front and then inside out again. Socks and vests did battle with the children each day of the week, and sometimes they would win, socks and vests being dispensed with for the day. But not on a day as cool as this.

'Mam! There's no school today Mam, and I was so warm.' John, the eldest boy always had something to say.

Ethel yawned and looked up, sleepy-eyed, still trying to put on her sock. She lifted her head to say something but was too tired. Her head dropped, as did her sock.

'Ethel, come on love, your breakfast is on the table. Some lovely porridge and a bit of wimberry jam for it. Don't tell your Dad you've had jam, mind. He thinks it is all gone, but I kept some especially for you.'

The thought of wimberry jam was enough for Ethel, to be the first at the breakfast table. The day was making progress.

The domestic mayhem was far from the thoughts of the men underground. Their workday had long started.

**

They worked the Cilfynydd side of the pit. A five-foot seam of coal was dug from an eight-foot rip, so there was plenty of headroom. The mine worked using the 'Long Wall' system, where the road ran parallel to the seam. Double timbers held up the solid rock roof. Both Jim and Al worked as hauliers alongside a coal hewing stall. They loaded coal into trams that transported it away to be drawn to the surface. There were 12 stalls on the level they worked, and the men stowed rubbish wherever they could. Other levels in the mine were worked simultaneously, and there would be a total of up to seventy hewing stalls working on any given day. Over two shifts, 16 hundred tons of coal could be extracted.

An hour before the end of the day shift, the night overman, John Evans pulled the father and son from their stall.

'I want you to go over to the Grover's side. I've others to take over here. Go down Dudson's to the horse pump. You'll find Morris Ashton's already there. He'll tell you what to do. I'll follow soon enough.'

It took twenty minutes to reach the horse pump, and Morris was anxious to see them arrive.

'I expected men down here sooner. Have you pair been malingering?'

Jim was man enough to speak up against this fireman.

'We've only just been told by Evans. We came straight away. Evans is following on behind, and he'll tell you the same.'

'Best get to it if we're going to be ready for to blast away the timbers at the Askett heading. It's a couple of hundred yards along. When we get there, you'll stow the rubbish as far back in the worked-out seam as you can. I'll set the charges.'

A day labourer was making his way to the lamp station before ending his shift.

'Emrys, we need some help stowing up at Askett's, will you stay down with us?'

'I wasn't supposed to stay on this afternoon, Morris. Will I get paid?'

'I'll see to that Emrys. We are behind time and I need your help. Is that alright with you?'

Emrys groaned, but nodded in agreement and responded with a weary,

'Alright, Morris,' and turned on his heels and walked in step with the other three.

The small group spoke along the way. Almond said,

'I saw that Evans had set charges in the Cilfynydd level today, Morris, so it's likely there'll be tidying up to do all round.'

'I expect we've got an Inspector's visit, though I've not been told of it, and I'd be the last to know, what with the way Evans keeps everything to his chest. If they blow the props at Cilfynydd, we are to set our charges off around the same time. It'll be between the shifts, if we can do it, but I suspect we are running late.'

'How will we know?' asked Emrys.'

Evans is coming to set off the charges down here, what with Garnett off with a busted wrist. Dai Griffiths is to blast the Cilfynydd side.'

'He'll not leave it to you?' asked Jim.

'No doubt Evans will want to check what I've done. He's used to Garnett setting the charges. Even then, more often than not, he comes to look himself.'

'Two blasts set off at the same time? We've not done that before.'

'We've noticed the state of the timbers up here. The roof has come low and we need a controlled fall before it comes in on our heads whilst we're working.'

'Still, two blasts at the same time is unusual.'

I'm told Askett's has to be done today along with any other scheduled blasting. If an inspector did come and he sees this mess someone would be in for it.'

When they reached the heading, it was clear that there was much to do. The rubbish had accumulated and there was an excess of coal dust. Thirty horse-drawn carts a day were moved from this level, and they would be full to the brim with coal, and always against the draught of the ventilation fans. The dust accumulated. Dealing with the rubbish from the lower levels of the mine was always difficult.

'So, these are the workings we are to close down, lads.'

Emrys spoke up.

'This roadway is a mess, Morris. Aren't the night shift meant to clear most of this rubbish away and get it to the tip.'

'Yes of course they are. But you know as well as I do that the management has dallied in putting enough men to it, especially down here,' he gestured around him, 'out of the way, like. Now with inspectors on their way, you'll see lots of hiding away of rubbish, and the doing of maintenance jobs. Jobs that should have been done weeks ago.'

'This is a disgrace, and dangerous, too,' spoke Almond.

'I expect there's those on the Cilfynydd side are complaining as we speak, just like you.'

'Not too loud, though, not with Evans about.'

'Just get on with it, Al. The sooner we start the sooner it'll be done.'

'Where do you want us to start, Morris?' asked Emrys

'You'll come with me, Em'. I'll need some help with drilling. You two, shift the rubbish as far back as you can. I'll shout when you are to get out from under there.'

Jim and his son set to the task, and it was to his dad that Almond looked for reassurance. When down the mine, Almond was his father's 'Butty'. They worked well together, but Jim's experience always held sway.

They looked at the task before them. Behind the workface, the worked-out seam was lost in the darkness. Almond was prone to state the obvious.

'We'll push it as far back as we can, Dad?'

'Unless you think it's a better idea to pile it up here at the front?'

Jim waited for the penny to drop. It took a second or two... They both laughed. Then, Almond replied,

'You could shovel your stuff to the far end and I'll shovel to here. We could meet in the middle.'

'Yes, just in time to eat our sandwiches and stop for a beer whilst the charges go off.' They laughed again.

'We'd be in a bit of a jam.'

'So would our sandwiches.'

'Nah, let's not do that. It would be a waste of good wimberries.'

They were soon put to task by Morris.

'Will you two stop fooling around and get on with it.'

Whilst working, Jim thought about what was likely to happen when they finished moving the rubbish. He spoke up,

'Blasting is going to raise a lot of shit, Morris, even when we've done here. We'd better water the roadway, walls and roof for at least twenty yards each way.'

'Yes, you do that, or we'll be spitting up dust from our lungs for days.'

'We will anyway. A bit of dust up our nose is worth the 'time and a half' they'll pay us for the pleasure,' said Emrys

They continued to move the waste into the tunnel. Their way was lit by their 'Clanny Lamps'; safety lamps that safeguarded its flame from the methane gas that could seep from the bituminous, carbon-rich rock that surrounded them.

Evans could be heard arriving on the scene. He had been delayed beyond the interval between the shifts, and as a result, along with him came the first few men on the night shift. His voice carried above the gathering clamour that rang throughout the workings.

'You men stay back fifty yards or more whilst I deal with the blasting. One of you had better go back and stop any more men coming down to this level until I give the all-clear.'

Evans' lamplight grew larger as he approached, and soon he was alongside Morris.

'You've set the charges?'

'I have Mr. Evans. Do you wish to inspect them?'

'I do.' They moved to the first of the props.

'Good! Drilled and packed at the collar, and with the correct fuse length.'

'The road has been cleared as best we could in the time we've had. Shall we wait until Mr. Griffiths is ready to fire on the Cilfynydd side?'

'No, we've been dealing with other issue, that's why I am behind. That firing won't take place today. Dai Griffiths prefers to wait for Monday, between shifts. It's his call, but we agreed this firing should go ahead.' He pointed at the props and the weight of rock bearing down.

'This bowing of timbers has gone too far for it to be left till then.'

'I'll get the lads to water down the road.'

'We've no time for that. We've got men wanting to get to their stalls. Send your lads back with the rest of them waiting down the roadway.'

John Evans lit the fuse of the first charge from the red-hot gauze that surrounded his lamp's flame and moved on to light each charge in succession. It was a practiced technique that worked every time, and the fuse length gave enough time for all the men to be well clear. Fifty yards back, men were sheltering behind trams and pit props alongside the wall. John Evans, Morris and Emrys came to join them, finding a prop to take shelter further forward from Jim and Almond. Evans was keen to get back to see the results of the blast and to make a decision if it was safe for the miners to return.

'They'll go off with one hell of a bang, Dad.' said Almond

'Keep your ears covered. We're well back and out of harm's way. It should be alright. The way Morris has set the charges, the props will be blown into the old workings. It'll save wood splinters flying up the tunnel

'It' would make good 'stick' for taking home.'

'It's best blown away from us, otherwise we'll be carrying it home with it stuck up our arse. And no, we won't be going in there to pick some up. I don't like the look of that roof. No doubt, some stick will come our way. We'll make do with that.'

'I suppose there'll be enough if we get there first.'

'There'll have to be.'

227

'I'll bet the first will go off at a count of three.'

'I knew all that schooling would come in useful.' They laughed again. Laughter was how men in the mines dealt with the stress.

Almond poked his head around the prop and counted:

'One, two... err, what's next.'

'Stop fooling around and get your head in.'

Even fifty yards back, the blast was deafening. The first prop splintered, and the pieces of wood were thrown, like javelins, into the darkness of the worked-out seam. The percussion of the blast lifted the coal dust in the roadway into a cloud of suspended particles. Then came the second blast; followed closely by the four remaining charges. It was a moment or two later a portion of the unsupported roof collapsed. It shouldn't have been a problem, but a hidden pocket of Methane gas was released above the embers of smouldering timber. The gas exploded in a flame that roared its way along the roadway gathering ferocity as it did so; the flame had allied itself with the coal dust. The energy within both became an explosive alloy. The rush of the explosion continued into adjoining roadways and up through the levels, then onwards to the pithead shafts and out into the warm afternoon air of the quiet village.

The sound of the explosion alerted the villagers. They ran to the pithead knowing that an incident had occurred. Those women with men working on that day were the most anxious to know what had happened. The size of the explosion meant it was likely that men would have died.

Sarah, and her mother, Gwen, stood waiting for word; someone must soon emerge from the pit with news. They waited hour upon hour. Time and again, the same questions were asked,

'Has anyone come up yet?'

'Do we know what's happened?'

'Has anyone been down to see?'

The questions kept coming. Since the time of the explosion, the lifting wheels had not moved. The wheels' stillness already gave the answer to the questions. Even so, they were asked.

It was late in the evening, when the wheels started to move. A cheer raised in the crowd. There was hope that miners would soon be coming to the surface.

'Mam! They've started to move the cage! Men will be coming up soon. They'll be alright, I'm sure of it.'

'Yes. They'll be alright.' said Gwen praying to God that she was right. Fearing the worst, Sarah chose to shield the mothers from any bad news, any reading out of names.

'Mam, you go back now, I'll wait. The children will need to be fed and put to bed. Granny Pat will be at her wit's end, and I don't want them all coming down here.'

'Yes, I'll go back, but as soon as you know, Sarah, come and tell me.'

The explosion would not have been fatal for the men fifty yards back in the tunnel if it weren't for the suspended coal dust. Each microparticle burst into a flame. It, in turn, ignited other particles of coal, igniting yet more as the dust was disturbed by the rolling explosion. The men deep underground were killed by the blast and its debris, or burned to death in the resultant fire. If there were survivors at the lower levels they would have been suffocated for lack of oxygen.

A rescue force was lowered, but only when the temperature in the shaft was such that men could endure it, and when it was assessed by the Mine Engineer that the roadways had been properly ventilated and cleared of the explosion's exhaust gas.

There were several men near the winding shaft that survived the initial blast. When withdrawn to the surface, the men within the cage staggered into the light. They were attended to directly by the company medical staff and by volunteers from the village with the appropriate skills. There was not much they could do for them. They were badly burned and injured from the blast. The cage was lowered several times in the hope any able-bodied miner would take the journey to the surface; none did.

It was a slow process and all the while, the villagers waited and hoped against hope. It was mid-afternoon before exploration of the lower parts of mine was undertaken.

***

Word reached those waiting above ground. There seemed to be no survivors. Not all the levels of the mine had been explored but there was little hope that any men in the mine at the time would have survived. And so it proved to be. The last victims were found two days after the explosion.

The miners were laid out in the loft of the horse stables; stables that were used occasionally, when horses were kept waiting to be lowered down to work the pits for the rest of their days. The pit ponies, like the men, had perished in the flames; their journey back to the surface took place if the need arose.

Identification of the corpses proved to be difficult. Recognition of a repair to a boot, a distinctive fob watch, a pendant, a scrap of clothing that seemed familiar, or a shock of red hair that for some reason remained when the rest of the face had gone, a wedding ring with an inscription of love. Dismembered parts of bodies were a common, and macabre, sight.

Jim and his son were amongst the last to be brought out that night. Sarah had waited, not knowing their fate.

An attached snap can, with its tell-tale dents, the remnants of half-consumed wimberry sandwiches and a scrap of paper upon which was drawn a charcoal 'Mam and Dad' confirmed who owned it. Sarah was sure it was her husband, and, alongside him, was his father, James.

No record had been kept of exactly how many men were in the pit that morning. There was no obligation for the management to keep such a record; the informed guess was that 182 men and boys did not return to their homes that day.

***

An investigation of the disaster was undertaken, and a Public Inquiry was held into its causes of the disaster. The mine owners were excused of blame, although the mine foreman, the person who gave the instruction to blast the pit props, was fined for employing poor working practices, and two workmen were fined £10 each for the improper storage of explosives.

Professor Dixon, of the Mines Inspectorate, was clear in its opinion. The catastrophic explosion was due to the ignition of suspended coal dust. The mining company disagreed and laid the blame entirely on the release of gas ignited by an unprotected flame.

The final hearing report contained damning recommendations:

a) The use of explosives to remove pit props was to be discontinued.

b) Old roadways were to be closed in a proper fashion.

c) Records were to be kept of the number of workers at the mine at any given time.

d) In future, 'more thorough inspections' were to be made by the Government Inspectors.

As no blame was placed on the mine owners, no compensation was given to the family of miners who had lost their lives. Those men who had not completed their shift on the day of the explosion were paid only for the hours they had worked. The villagers were left to support each other as best they could.

There was scarcely a family in the village left untouched by the mine explosion.

**

The sight of a horse-drawn hearse halting at yet another house in yet another terrace, played out time and time again: William Street, Ann Street, Market Street, Pontypridd Road. They were houses of identical structure in which identical tragedies were enacted. As custom demanded, the coffin lay in the front room, the curtain drawn shut to the road outside.

'Family' would visit, as would friends of the house. At the open coffins, they would pay their respects to the dead; but only if the body inside was recognizable, not mutilated. Then, retiring to the kitchen, the visitors would find the living and give promises of support. In response, there would often be an acknowledgement of their mutual loss;

'They were lovely boys, Cissie. Our Idwal always said how they worked hard and were a joy to be with, always a smile.'

'Thank you, love. Your Idwal is to be buried tomorrow, Mary?'

'Yes love, tomorrow, back in Abercynon. There's a family plot at the church.'

'Oh, Mary... and you came here today?'

'Yes, Cissie. Time enough for me to grieve after tomorrow.'

'He was a kind man, your Idwal.'

'He was.'

'And Sarah and the children?'

'The little ones are inconsolable today, what with the funeral. Sarah is upstairs with them now. She doesn't want them to see the coffins leave.' Changing the direction the conversation had taken, Cecelia continued,

'We aren't going to have a wake for them... there's no point.'

'We'll pray for their souls, no matter, Cissie.'

Few families were spared a similar scene within their own front room.

Front rooms were, for a long time after, sombre, unwelcoming places. They were not used to celebrate the joy of life, only its rituals.

The hearses assembled in Cilfynydd Road. The people of the village, and the villages beyond, lined the road to pay their respect to those who had died.

Only men attended funerals, as was the custom. The massed cortege moved off towards Pontypridd. Along the way, individual hearses would break away from the procession to allow a miner to be laid to rest at the church where he and his family had worshipped. Most carried on to the municipal cemetery at, Treforest, two miles down the road.

A small group of hearses would have taken the steep road up to the Cilfynydd Common and on to Llanfabon with its tiny church.

***

The day after the funeral, Ethel, Sarah's youngest, a frail child of five years of age, had taken her mother's hand. Ethel knew something was wrong. A mantle of grief had wrapped her mother so tight she could not speak, and her daughter wanted her to be 'Mam' again, to help her understand why Dad and Granddad had been taken away. Sarah became aware of the child at her feet.

'Come with me my love,' she said.

They left the house and the mournful people of the terrace.

Since daybreak, Cilfynydd had been cloaked in valley-sunk mist, as on the day of the disaster. Sarah and Ethel climbed the hillside behind the village. Their destination was the church at Llanfabon. They followed the winding, oft-trod path of the faithful, until impatient with her progress, Sarah cut corners, and walked across the dew-watered wimberry and waded through the knee-high fern; Ethel trailed behind her, for shelter from their watered fronds. There was no need to hurry, the path meandered its way up the common and was pleasant enough, but Sarah had an urgency of purpose, a grievance she needed to settle.

Ethel stood with her mother on the church path, close to her father's freshly dug grave. She wheezed a whistling breath. The exertion of the climb and her frailty of health worked in concert to girdle her chest, allowing only small, melodic gasps of relief.

High on the hill, the sunlight had washed away the remnant wisp of grey mist from the church's slate-hung roof, but it still draped over the fresh mounds of earth. The cemetery was quiet now, and they, too, mother and daughter, stood in silence.

Sarah raised her arm and shook a fist at the heavens above. She spoke with a voice clear and strong...

'Where's your compassion, Lord? Where are your miracles? Where were *you,* when you were needed?'

She had begun to doubt the Holy Book.

24

Cedric Popkin. The Hero?

Cedric Popkin was a sergeant. Who would have thought it? He'd been in trouble with authority for most of his life, falling foul of the Australian police force, having stolen from his school; it was a cadet cap, but it was sufficient for him to be recorded as, 'Of bad character'. His mother, Lillian, had died when he was aged twelve, and his father was often not present in the household, as he travelled with his work as an insurance agent. Both he and his younger brother Roland were left under the control of his elder sisters, Edna and Marjory. The boys reinforced each other's argumentative nature; and to control their deteriorating behaviour, Rowland was sent back to live with relatives in South Wales.

Cedric eventually settled down when he entered the workplace as a carpenter and builder. Upon marriage to Nellie, he was moulded into an upright citizen. It was as such that on the 6th May 1916 he enlisted into the Australian Army. In March of that year, on the other side of the World, his brother Rowland had enlisted in the British Army.

Cedric travelled by ship from Melbourne, first to Sierra Leone, and then on to England where he was trained in a camp on Salisbury Plain. It was here his rebellious nature resurfaced. The rigours of the training camp had rubbed away the veneer keeping a lid on his temper.

After a 12-mile march over Salisbury Plain, in teeming rain and unseasonably cold, Cedric was met back at the camp with abuse from his Sergeant Major.

'Fall into line, you sad excuse for Aussie soldiers. My grandmother in Adelaide could have run faster than you pathetic examples of fighting men.'

Cedric, in his effort to get into line, dropped his rifle. The metallic clang as it hit the hard parade ground drew the attention of Sergeant

Turner, who marched up to the soldier, and with his face an inch away from Cedric's, he shouted at the top of his voice,

'Popkin, you stupid bastard-son of a Sydney prick. If you'd dropped that there gun in the mud of Flanders, your aforementioned gun would now be useless!'

'Sorry sergeant, it slipped.'

'Slipped? A pretty-boy called Popkin is easy meat for a German gunner, especially if that pretty-boy called Popkin 'as dropped 'is gun and can't fire back... Pick it up!'

'Yes, sergeant.'

As Sergeant Turner moved away, Cedric bent to retrieve his rifle, thinking the sergeant was off to torment the rest of the squad. Standing back to attention, Cedric was confronted with the sergeant who had returned for a second go, thinking there was more fun to be had with this hapless lad.

'Anyways, Popkin, where did you get such a stupid name as Popkin, Popkin? Have you made that name up, lad?'

Cedric paused, not knowing if he should answer, or was the sergeant making a jibe as part of his attempt to ridicule him? Cedric decided to speak.

'No Sir, it came from my great-grandfather.'

'So, it was your Granddaddy who done it?'

'He was Welsh, and his name was ap'Hopkin'. It got shortened to...'

'Shut up, we don't need your life's 'istory. I just wanted you to know that I think it's stupid... just like you.'

Cedric had enough of this abuse. He broke...

'Well, fuck you, Sergeant! If it was good enough for my father, it's good enough for me.'

That was more than enough for Cedric to be on a charge for insulting a Non-Commissioned Officer. He paid a price. His 'jankers' was the usual repetition of mindless tasks and pointless parade-ground marches, with Sergeant Turner as his tormentor.

His time in the army was punctuated with relatively minor outburst of insubordination. Under normal circumstances, it would have ensured he remained a Private, but his specialist training, on the Vickers machine gun, meant he was an important soldier on the field of battle. He remained in his post.

As the war progressed, his superiors were, one by one, lost in battle, including Sergeant Turner. Cedric stepped up into their roles, as his continued experience in the field became an asset.

On the 21st April 1918, he manned his machine gun as 'Sergeant' Popkin. He was positioned near Morlancourt Ridge, the Somme. Above the nearby woodland, there appeared an RAF Sopwith Camel pursued by a German Tri-winged, Fokker DR-1. The German plane was red in colour and Sergeant Popkin and his men recognised it as that of the German Ace, 'The Red Baron', Manfred von Richthofen.

Riflemen around Cedric fired their Royal Enfield single shot, bolt action, guns at the pursuing tri-plane; they had shot at enemy aircraft many times before, to little effect. Cedric swung his Vickers machine gun in the plane's direction and motioned members of his squad to reposition the ammunition box to ensure a smooth transfer of bullets from its belt. His squad didn't need instructions, they knew what to do. Cedric pressed the trigger for a short burst of fire. As the aircraft flew closer, he set off a longer burst. The plane swerved and banked to the left. Cedric had hit his target. In an attempt to land, the aircraft flew closer to the ground, just over the tops of the trees of the nearby wood.

'I got the bastard!' shouted Cedric and he and his men ran to the fields beyond, expecting to see the crashed plane and the Red Baron, dead or alive.

When Cedric reached the plane, it wasn't in a crumpled heap as expected, it had landed successfully and was not badly damaged. The pilot sat motionless in the cockpit. Surrounding the plane, other soldiers had already arrived on the scene.

'Is that the Baron?' someone shouted.

'If it is, he's a dead Baron now.'

'How did he manage to land the plane?' An Aussie, who had been first on the scene, knew the answer.

'Oh, he was alive when we first got here. He looked up and said, as clear as you like, "Kaput". Then he shuffled off, taking his mortal coil with him.' He laughed at his attempt at a joke, though few understood, and no one joined in the laugh

Cedric took his turn to look at the body, still certain his gun had brought the Baron down. There were three open wounds. They had bled profusely and still seeped: one in his side and two in his chest. They were arranged in a pattern consistent with those inflicted by a machine gun. To those around him, he said,

'It was my gun that brought him down,'

'Give over. We all 'ad a pop at him with our rifles. Could have been any one of us,' said a Cockney lad, whose crossed eyes suggested he would need to fire at two barns in order to hit a third.

'It was me I tell you.'

The Baron's body was removed from the plane and his identity established from the documents he carried. He was treated with respect and would be given an honourable funeral. His plane, however, was hacked at by souvenir hunters, each wanting to retain a piece of the famous plane, and it was almost completely lost within days. Eventually, from a British unit nearby, guards were placed around the remnants.

A few days later, Cedric revisited the site of the crash, where little of the aircraft remained: its engine and cowling, the wheels and some of the wing supports with its wiring. Two British guards stood in the rain with their heads bowed, as if praying for their duty to end. They took no notice of a single 'Aussie' soldier wrapped in his rain cape. They must have thought,

Not another who's come to gawk?

Cedric stood alongside the wreck for a minute or two, and then realised the insignificance of what remained. He left the scattered remnants in the care of the two bedraggled soldiers, whose duty it was to see out their task.

An hour later, the guards were relieved of their duty. A corporal came with orders what to do next.

'Popkin and Thomas, you are both to report back to your unit where you will receive further instructions.'

'Is no one going to take over from us, corporal?' asked Rowland Popkin

'Not much point is there, lad? The British army's got better things to do.'

'You're right there 'Corp'.'

'I'm always right. Now off you trot, there's good lads.'

Rowland Popkin was glad to be back with his unit where he could dry himself and get some food in his stomach.

Rowland sat in his trench eating his ration. He spoke to a 'Tommy' alongside,

'What a God-forsaken place for such a flyer to die.'

'Where else was it likely to be?' replied his companion.

'True enough. But what was the point of me standing guard over bits of his plane?

'There were worse places for you to be.'

Soon after, Rowland was reported as 'Killed in Action'. Cedric fared better; but not by much, some would say. He was wounded by gunshot, and at a field hospital, his leg was amputated. Before leaving France, he, and thousands of other soldiers, contracted Spanish Flu. He survived both, and was invalided out of the Army and lived to old age.

As far as Cedric was concerned, he and Rowland never met in France, in the rain, at the site where the Red Baron met his end.

Selwyn Berryman-Morgan

25

The Safe House

Merthyr Tydfil, 1923

The McCarthy family had fled the potato famine in Ireland, and had settled in Merthyr Tydfil. The work was hard, but at least there was lots of it, and it meant there was food on the table and a worker's cottage to live in.

The intervening generations had become Welsh by birth, but if they were to be judged by their religious beliefs and heritage, they remained Irish. Their Roman Catholic faith set them apart, as did their names, which were often adorned with the prefix, 'O', the Irish equivalent of the now-forgotten Welsh, 'ap', (son of). There was O'Donnell, O'Donovan, O'Leary and sometimes the alternate Gaelic prefix, 'Mc', as was used by the once-powerful Munster clan, of McCarthy.

The McCarthy home was dominated by the mother in the household, Dolores. She was loud, larger than life, and a person who was alternately feared and loved. She was 'chopsy' and opinionated, and she *knew* what was right and what was wrong. It was Dolores who would dispense justice to her six children; who, if truth be known, were due a 'hiding'. But no matter, at the end of the day, there was food on the table, their clothes were washed, and at bedtime, there was the comfort of one of their mum's lilting lullabies. In addition, there was always a goodnight kiss for the children young enough to want one.

Colm, the father, did what all fathers seemed to do. He worked and played hard. He had been employed in the ironworks, then, as the industry declined, he started work in the colliery. Workers were now paid in cash, not in tokens to be spent in the company shop, and what he earned was enough to support the family. Sometimes, the little money left over bought him too much beer, but he was never violent 'in drink'. His anger about his working conditions never spilled over into his family life. To justify his drinking he would say,

'Who wouldn't drink having to work in the pit, Dolly?'

That never washed with Dolores, who hadn't the time for self-pity.

'It's hard for us all, Colm. I need you back here. The three youngest need their dad around, it settles them down. The mischief they get up to in the town is getting us a bad name. You get back home, worse for drink, and are of no use to me in trying to discipline them.'

'It's high spirits. They do no harm, Doll.'

'They do enough...'

Dolores still carried the resentment felt for the Irish Famine with her. She had heard the tales from her mother, of how, with their last strength, her grandparents had fled Ireland. As she saw it, the population could have easily been fed, but they were left to fend as best they could by the British Government. The hatred of that injustice weighed heavily upon her, and the recent Civil War in Ireland had reopened old wounds. The English, with the connivance of a 'Puppet' Irish government, looked to keep her people impoverished and worse, divide, North and South. That conflict would see Dolores and Colm provide a 'safe house' for the men of the IRA.

***

Colm rolled in from the pub, happy enough, but Dolores had that look about her. It said she had something to say, and he knew it wouldn't take her long to say it.

'Colm, you must stop drinking on the way home'. Then, moving close enough to Colm that he feared a tongue lashing was not going to be good enough, she instead whispered,

'Listen, we have a job to do for *our boys.'*

The way Dolores spoke, Colm knew she didn't mean *his* boys. The boys she referred to were the young men across the water. Boys who were faithful to the Irish cause.

'I've word from Cork. Some of our lads are on the run and, more than that, someone from our family will be amongst them. I'm told they'll probably be dropped off along the south coast and come up from Newport or Cardiff.'

'So, why does that concern us?'

'We've been asked if they can stay low with us for a couple of weeks until a passage out is found for them.'

Colm had agreed with Dolly to let it be known to her family in Ireland, their house was safe for those that needed refuge; it had a large, dry cellar, only accessible from within. He made no objection to the prospect of them being outside the law. In any case, on this subject, Dolly had a will of steel, and if he'd objected, he would have been overruled. Nevertheless, he felt compelled to speak of the difficulties they would face in trying to help. His arguments weren't convincing, at least not to Dolores

'We could be at work when they arrive. We're often at work at the same time. How will we know where and when to meet up with them, and we'd look suspicious with strangers in tow... especially if they arrive in the daytime? And what if they are being...'

Dolores brought his rambling to a close.

'Enough! We'll have to do it. Let's think.' She began to imagine the sequence of event. 'They won't come on a Sunday as they would be too easy to see... strangers travelling who knows where? No, it will be in the week, I'm sure of it. In that way, they'll be lost in amongst the changes of shift... night shift would be the most likely, when the roads and trains are full of men on their way to and from work. The days are drawing in and they'll have better cover in the dark.'

'Yes... and I suppose someone will get us word. They'll not turn up without us being told they were coming.'

243

'I've thought about it. We'll have to involve Cornelius. He works regular hours and is around every evening when shifts change.'

'Is it fair to involve him, Doll? He got a young family now, and we need to think about them, too.'

'All of us who care about Ireland will need to sacrifice, Colm.'

'Sacrifices for Ireland are easy to make... if you don't get caught making them.'

'It's the cross we bear.'

Colm said no more. He knew Cornelius was an Irish Republican at heart. His mother had told him of the Irish famine and the treatment of his family at the hands of the British. But would Cornelius want to take the risk? Colm was worried he already knew the answer. Cornelius would not go against his mother's wishes.

***

At the time of her marriage to Cornelius, Ethel Rowe and her mother, Sarah, had moved to Merthyr Tydfil from their family home in Cilfynydd. They had two children, Evelyn aged six, and William aged three. The family lived in their own home. It was one of the hundreds found in parallel rows alongside the industrial sprawl. They ran in neat lines, the frontage of each row looking across the street to the opposing terrace. There were two rooms up and two rooms down, a scullery out the back, and beyond was a garden put to vegetables. Set against the garden wall was an outhouse, toilet and coal shed. Beyond the wall was an alleyway separating the backs of the rows.

Grandmother Rowe looked after the home whilst Cornelius and Ethel worked day shifts, he in the chain works down the valley, and she at the mine. Ethel remained frail in health and was fearful of a third pregnancy; Cornelius was an understanding husband who took what precautions he could to safeguard his wife, but there was always the risk of an unwanted pregnancy. As it turned out, William was to be the last of Ethel's children.

***

The clean air of the hilltops above the town was in stark contrast to the industrial pollution of the valley below. It was here Cornelius would escape when he needed to think. It wasn't possible to think when you were smothered under the blanket of despair in the town. The hill was tough to climb, as the sides of the valley were steep, having been gouged by glaciers thousands of years before. From the top, the views were panoramic; there being little left of the once extensive oak woodlands that might have blocked the view. To the north, sat the market town of Brecon, with its surrounding hills known as 'The Beacons', and to the south, some 25 miles away, could be seen the coastline of the Bristol Channel, with its ever-expanding ports. The valley itself was narrow and oppressive, and day trips for the family out to the local town of Pontypridd did little to lift the gloom. The canal remained, and barges continued to transport coal and pig iron to Cardiff, but the tramway that Trevithick had travelled had long since fallen into disuse. Both the canal and tramway lost out to the new railways that now took out the bulk of the freight. The railways had started to provide some freedom of movement to work outside the town, and Cornelius hoped the railway would one day be his family's means of escape altogether from the confines of 'the valley'.

He hated living where he did. There was work enough, but the ironworks were in decline. Fortunately, there was still plenty of coal to export, and it was the mine owners who kept the bulk of the people of the town employed; but few were 'well off'.

Cornelius regarded the mine owners as an extension of the ruling classes, and he knew his Irish relatives in Cork were subjected to the same oppression, if not worse; not that he knew them personally, but they were family nonetheless. They, too, wanted to cast off the centuries of exploitation and forge a new nation in doing so. The 'struggle' facing the Irish and their cause, was faced wherever men and women sold their labour in support of the industries that employed them.

The troubles in Ireland focused Cornelius' attention. Men were on the move, escaping the retribution of both the Irish and British governments, and his mother had asked him to help. Standing on the hilltop gazing down the valley to where his own freedom lay, he knew he would be glad to do it, never mind the dangers of doing so.

26

On the Run

Terence and Peter had hardly said a word to each other since getting off the 'tramp steamer' which had recently arrived in Cardiff Docks; their Irish Brogue spoken at any port on the British mainland would have aroused interest, if not suspicion. Avoiding the security surrounding the docks was easy enough, as there were accomplices, aware of their arrival, who would smooth their way.

'Take hold of this crate... one either end... Take it through into the warehouse and someone will tell where to go next... Come on now, look lively.'

They kept their heads down in a dockland pub sympathetic to the IRA and its cause. It was the rendezvous where they would meet their final contact; a young lady called Millicent. It was early afternoon, and they were glad to hide from suspicious glances and the threat of being asked difficult questions. Millicent's question was much more palatable.

'And what can I get you two fine lads?' Terence McCarthy pulled up his collar; unsure if this was the lady they should meet. He pointed at the first pump, and read out its label.

'Would the 'Brains' be a bitter ale?'

'Yes, it's a 'bitter', but none the worse for that. You'll have two pints?' Terence nodded in agreement. The contact had been made and it was safe to stay.

'That will be one shilling and sixpence... You both look frozen. Go sit by the fire, I'll bring them over to you.'

To sit at the fire, in the knowledge the first part of their escape from Cork had been successful, was the first comfort they'd had on their journey; the beer was to be the second. They hoped to eventually travel to the Continent and then on to the United States. A direct ship from an Irish port would have been too dangerous. The longer escape route to New York, via France, was less dangerous but it would take time to get them on a channel ferry disguised as part of the crew. In the meantime, they would lay low.

'So here we have them boys, two pints of bitter' Millicent laid the tray on the table. Terence passed a pint to Peter and took the other himself. He spoke quietly to the barmaid.

'Thank you, and what would be your name?

'Best you know me as Mary… for now, at least,' she flirted.

'Ah, tis a fine name, Mary.'

'You boys, enjoy your pint.'

'I'm sure we will, especially sat here by the fire.'

'You stay there as long as you want, and if you need another beer just catch my eye. There's no need to come to the bar.'

She picked up the tray and Terence pocketed the rail tickets he had expected to find beneath.

***

A smoke-laden fog cloaked and choked the Taff valley. The bituminous smell of coal fires invaded the nostrils and caught on the chest of the two men in the carriage of the train. Even so, they were pleased for the gloom, as it obscured the view to be seen of them from outside. They both sat with their flat cap pulled down over their face and their collar turned up. Above them, a carriage light had broken, which further hid them from view. They sat as if in sleep.

The journey had taken them through the villages of Taff's Well, Treforest, the market town of Pontypridd, then onwards to Abercynon. The towns and villages appeared from the darkness of the night. The villages' herald would often be diffuse street lights from occasional gas lamps, before the train pulled into the brightly lit stations. On arrival, the windows of the carriage doors would slide open with an accompanying 'slap' of the retaining leather strap that had secured the window shut against the cold outside. The handle on the outside of the door could now be reached and turned, releasing the door from its frame. The clack of its opening would be accompanied by the clang of the carriages careering one into the other as the train incrementally adjusted to its designated stop along the platform.

At each stop along the way, passengers would leave the train in greater numbers than those who wanted to board. By the time the two men hidden in the shadow of the unlit carriage had reached their destination, there were a score of passengers remaining. The station sign, 'Merthyr Tydfil', alerted the men; it was the last stop for this train. Doors began to swing open and passengers spilled out. The last person through each of the doors swung it shut. Each door sounded a satisfying clunk; and rang a musical percussion above the drone of the engine's steam exhaust; the final coda an assurance the journey was complete. But the sound of one of the closing doors was muted; a tired, miss-timed kick from a booted foot had ruined the satisfaction to be had at the end of a working day. The man's intention was to leave it as it was, but the train's Conductor would not let it be. He mumbled oaths, before shouting down the platform,

'Hey, Butty! Shut your door properly.'

The two culprits would have preferred not to have drawn attention to themselves, and they quickly obeyed. The door was reopened and given a determined shove back into place.

No one else spoke; after a day's labour, to speak was an effort and they had homes to get to. The two men had joined the last to get off the train and followed along, a few steps behind. They swirled their way down the platform through the remnants of exhaust steam and persistent fog, and into the night. They lingered at the station's exit and awaited their contact. It was March 1923.

Two months earlier, in Ireland, the weather had been the same.

***

A few miles outside Cork, on the train line connecting the city to Dublin, two men of the Irish Republican Army (the IRA) were attempting to sever the rail link.

Even in the Republican movement, there were men who had heeded the call to serve in the British Army during the First World War. These men had the necessary skills to handle explosives.

The 'soft' weather was a blessing; it hid their purpose. Their enemies were fellow Irishmen; men of the 'Free Army Railway Corp' (a division of the 'Free State Army'). Its members were often former IRA, but they were men who had agreed with the signing of the Anglo-Irish Treaty of 1921. The IRA had once been united, but now the men on both sides of the conflict would be willing to kill their former comrades. Ireland was in the grip of a civil war.

The previous August, Cork City had been retaken from the IRA by the 'Free State Army', and after, Terence McCarthy had fought with Brigade Commander, Tom Barry, at the 'Crossbarry Ambush', where a hundred IRA men escaped encirclement by over a thousand strong, British force. Military reversals had meant Barry's men were on the run, but they were continuing to strike back wherever possible. Sweeps of the countryside by the local constabulary and the Army had chased them from a series of 'safe houses' limiting their freedom of movement and freedom to act. Tonight, Terence and Peter would hit back. Terence brought with him his experience from the First World War in the use of explosives.

'Watch now, this is what we do. You may have to do it yourself one day... Place the charge beneath the joint of the two rails. That's where it's weakest. Even if we don't derail the train both lengths of rail will need to be replaced before a train runs again.'

Peter was on his first mission. He didn't speak but nodded his head to confirm he understood. They were both young men, Terence was twenty-four and Peter was a year older. They had met in a pub in Blarney, one of several fronting onto the village square. Late in the night, the doors of the pubs were shut to the casual drinker, and the remaining 'regulars' would be 'locked-in'. They were the hardened boozers and those who needed a place to talk. Terence had earlier moved between the pubs on the green, gauging the sentiment of the men who talked at the bars. He would fit in with the mood of the drinkers, not speaking much, but enough to agree with whatever was being said, so he might win trust and identify men he could recruit to the cause. He sat amongst those of a rebellious nature who knew it was wise to speak in whispers.

'If we had cooperated amongst ourselves and stood firm, we could have stopped the Army in its tracks. But no, what did we do, we fought our own little wars with too few weapons and too few men,' spoke Peter O'Mahoney. Dermott was quick to reply.

'Aye, the Army was always going to outgun us, Peter.'

'We bloodied their nose in Cork, though.'

'But not enough... we lost the day!'

Terence judged it was time to speak and add fuel to the dangerous conversation. His face was known well enough, and even if he wasn't from Blarney, those in the pub seemed to think of him as one of 'the boys'. He said,

'There'll be other days we can fight. We'll get more guns, more explosives and more men.'

Peter spoke up.

'Aye, you may be right, mister! There's chance yet as De Valera is gaining support amongst Irish Americans and other Americans who have suffered under the British heal... They hate the British as much as we do.' It was Terence's chance to take things further.

'We can't wait for De Valera to sweet talk the Americans. We have to begin the fightback now, or otherwise the movement will burn itself out.'

'And how, exactly, are you going to do that? Do you have so much as a hurling stick with which to beat them?'

Terence pressed his point.

'Some men are doing it already. We can't defeat them in a pitched battle, but we can harass them, sap their strength... and their commitment. There are many who are willing to support another uprising, and more will come over to us...' His fist hit the table. 'Our cause is right.'

The conversation went round in circles as they drank more pints of Beamish, the local porter. The conversation ebbed away, there being no new ideas to break through the alcoholic haze, and the night drew to a dissatisfying conclusion. The voices that spoke of resigned acceptance of the new order outweighed those wanting to continue the struggle. It was time to leave.

The back door of the pub was unlocked. The men left in twos and threes, and made their way home in silence in order that their late-night meeting would go unnoticed. In any case, most of the villagers would have turned a blind eye, but it was best not to stir from their beds those whose allegiance might be wavering and who would be suspicious enough of such a late gathering to report it.

Terence fell behind Peter as they were the last to leave and they walked in line up the hill from the Square. Terence tugged Peter's sleeve to get his attention and nodded to the gated entrance of the church. He said,

'Come talk for a moment before you get on your way.' Peter was guarded.

'And who, exactly, might you be...? I see you around of an evening, but you're not a Blarney man.'

'As good as... I'm Terence, from Cork. I was there in August when I was forced out of the city along with others who came from these parts. I have Irish blood on my hands from the battle that day. Some of it from the Army men I shot, some from comrades who I carried out.'

Peter didn't speak. He waited for the 'Johnnie come lately' to come to the point. Terence continued.

'Peter, can I ask? Would you shed a fellow Irishman's blood for the cause?' Peter stood his ground, and nodded, signalling his willingness.

'Let's speak in the shadow of the lychgate.'

Behind them, on the hill, stood the Church of the Immaculate Conception, where some of the congregation spoke of a war against their own countrymen, even though the Church, with its neat brick fringed windows and doors, was a symbol of unity of purpose; it having been reconstructed and maintained by the workers of Blarney's woollen mill. But the unity of purpose had been compromised. It was well known some parishioners thought of revenge on the government in Dublin; a government that threatened their hope of an independent Ireland. They would have endorsed and encouraged the conversation that was taking place at the gate that opened onto the path that led up to their house of God.

'We know we have the support of the people here in the south, and our actions will encourage them. Soon the uprising will overwhelm the puppets of the British and drive them out of Dublin Castle. Are you with me Peter?'

'I am... Tell me, Terence, are you in peril? Do you have a place of safety?'

'Not permanent... Not here in Blarney. I need to find a place nearby to be close to other comrades operating from hereabouts. Do you know where I can stay for a while?'

'You can come with me, and I can help you to recruit more men so we can begin to strike back. The boys I know have spoken about it but we've lacked someone to lead us.... you may be our man?'

***

The rail line curved gently north as it ran out from Cork City. It then straightened, to run up the coast to Dublin, and passed over a bridge that spanned a country road. Close by, men were at work on the rail. Their activities were obscured by the dark night and a 'soft' mist typical for the time of year.

Terence primed the fuse of the explosives, and he and Peter retired into the safety of the copse of trees alongside the rail embankment. They worked alone; a spectacular explosion with its resultant destructive effect would help in their recruitment of other men from the area.

The flash of the explosion was followed by its roar. A rain of gravel passed through the branches above their heads and peppered them as they sat on their haunches.

Perhaps a little too much explosive, thought Terence.

The excitement of once again being on active service came as a surprise. He'd thought he had seen enough destruction to last him a lifetime, but here he was, once again, using weapons of war to disrupt, destroy and kill his enemies. During, and after, the First World War, he was disgusted with the pointless carnage. Even so, in his own country, he was employing his skills, and he was sure his actions were justified, not just for the nation but for his right to practice his religion without persecution.

Although Peter was enthusiastic for 'the cause', he was less sure of his motives. The consequences of their mission did not sit well with him. All this was new to him, the rebellion against authority and the savagery of the intended outcome; the derailment of a train. How would he feel if they succeeded? He was not sure. If the oncoming train was derailed and people were killed, how would he live with it on his conscience? He hoped he could.

His misgivings were soon forgotten, as Terence pulled him up and out to the track to survey the damage they had done. By the light of their dimmed lanterns, it could be seen the rails were blown apart and a two-foot crater had been blown in the bed of the track. The rails either side of the joint were bent back upon themselves. If the damage to the track was not discovered then the early morning freight train would be destroyed as it hurtled at speed around the curved track, the damaged rail would be unseen through the dawn's half-light.

Terence knew the small charge would create havoc and disrupt the provisioning of the Army's forces in Cork. He hoped further guerrilla actions would bring the garrison to its knees.

Terence looked at Peter. He saw in his face not a look of triumph, but a look of anguish and fear. Terence placed a hand on his shoulder so he might convey to his comrade some of his own strength and determination, and spoke,

'We will succeed. This is our first step.'

From the bridge, fifty yards up the line, opaque auroras of light appeared, and they danced and flashed low in the sky. There were shouted instructions as to the direction from which the sound of the explosion had come.

'I heard it back along the line to Dublin. Are they lights I see?'

Those at the bridge would not be supporters of the IRA. Not out at this time, innocently inquiring the reason for the sound of destruction. Terence reacted immediately,

'An Army patrol, Peter... Quick, back through the woods.'

Rather than run immediately, Peter turned to the sound of the voices on the bridge, and his face was briefly illuminated by the torchlight focused upon him.

'I know that face!' someone exclaimed.

Peter turned and ran, following Terence back into the woods. Terence spoke loud enough for Peter to hear.

'We know our way. Keep your lantern low in front of you. It'll mask the light from those behind us. With luck, they'll not hear or see us.'

In the safety of the woods, the commotion on the line and the noise of the shouted orders hid the sound of their hurried, footfall.

'The bastards, they have blown the line.'...

'Get word back to the signal box.'...

'You run south and try to stop any train that might come, and I'll go up the line and do the same.'

Terence and Peter were soon through the woods and away across the fields, heading for Blarney and the safety of Peter's home. It was several miles away, across countryside they knew well. They made progress using an indirect route through fields farmed by men and women who were true to the cause. Even if they had been seen by such patriots, no one would speak of it.

They approached Blarney from the north, stooping low in fields alongside the Dublin Road.

Peter's family home was modest, as were most houses in Blarney. It was in such houses that the guerrilla forces of the IRA would hide out. Questions weren't asked, for fear of being told an answer that could be extracted under interrogation.

The men on the run heard shouts carried on the morning breeze. They took cover behind a hedgerow and listened.

It was clear Peter had been recognised at the scene of the explosion, and the loud voices were from local constabulary shouting out orders.

'Open the door.'

'Open the door, or we'll knock it down....'

'Where is your son?'

The cry of innocence was from Peter's father.

'We don't know where he is... We've not seen him for days!'... 'It's no use looking, he's not here...Take care... She's no more than a child... Careful I said.'

A sharp cry of pain carried on the morning air like the crack of a whip... and it lashed Peter's heart. He was responsible for what was happening.

'What have I done?' he asked of Terence, and held his head in his hands, covering his ears to block out the sound.

Terence's mind was elsewhere. He looked to see an alternative escape route across the open fields.

***

The fugitives were amongst a dozen or so passengers to leave the Merthyr station. The 'contact' would be waiting outside to take them to their temporary place of refuge. The police knew there were Irish Republicans, on the run, and the ethnic melting pot of industrial South Wales, with its immigrant Irish community, was somewhere the police would be asked to keep watch. But would they bother? In the opinion of those who knew the local constabulary, it seemed unlikely they would put themselves out.

Wearing flat caps, workmen's clothes and self-applied workaday grime, the two men looked the same as any other man, and their disguise helped to hide any trace of fear.

They had waited a moment in the shadows until the footsteps of the stragglers off home were lost in the constant rumble of a Welsh industrial town. They moved to the street. Across the road and one lamppost down stood a figure sheathed in the gaslights glow, the collar of his greatcoat turned up, wearing a Trilby hat, less common amongst the flat 'Dai-caps' worn by the miners. He held a parcel under his left arm... The contact was made.

Crossing the road, Terence and Peter walked past the man under the light and then Terence turned back and spoke, not attempting to hide his Irish brogue,

'Would this the way to the town square, Sir?'

'Just a quarter of a mile down the road...There you'll find a welcome.' The two men shook hands.

'You'll be Terence McCarthy, then?'

'It is, and you'll be Cornelius McCarthy?'

'That I am.'

'My family have often talked about our Welsh cousins, you'll not know what a pleasure it is to meet up with you. This is Peter. We'll not use his last name.'

'Hello, Peter. We'll soon have you both safe. It's not far to...'

'Stop there, lads!'

The voice came from the direction of the entrance to the station, and out of the gloom walked police sergeant Rhys Morgan with Constable Bryn Meredith at his side. Seeing the policemen, Peter, knowing he had no papers, lost his nerve and ran into an adjacent row of houses. As Peter had bolted, Terence then had no choice but to run; there would be no getting away with the pretence of being a local or an Irishmen in search of work. To divide the attention of the constabulary, he chose to run towards the centre of town.

'Constable Meredith, follow the man into the terrace. He'll find it a dead end. I'll stay here with this gentleman.'

Sergeant Morgan took Cornelius by the arm. 'One of your friends seems not to know the streets of Merthyr and is in a hurry to avoid our questioning.'

As Cornelius lifted his head, his face caught the available street light...

'Cornelius? Good God man! What are you up to?'

Cornelius knew Sergeant Morgan well enough. There had been drunken occasions in the pub, when his Irish ancestry was brought up in derogatory terms and the evening would end in a brawl. He would spend the night in a cell followed by a lecture from Rhys Morgan on keeping the peace, 'or else.'

Cornelius attempted to make excuses for his escaped companions.

'They're family arriving from Ireland looking for work, Sergeant.' He immediately regretted suggesting they were family, as it would implicate him yet further. Sergeant Morgan latched on to the connotation.

'And your family is worried about an ever-so-polite Merthyr 'Bobby' asking the time of day?'

'They've not been made most welcome here, Sergeant. You know what it is with the Irish?'

'They were quick to take offence, seeing they've just got off the train.'

Peter burst back into the street. He had avoided Constable Meredith, who was hot on his heels. They both ran towards the town centre

'Well, it looks like your Irish cousin has avoided the acquaintance of my constable. It seems they'll not make good friends, at least not the way he is scampering as if his life depended on it. I'll be round to see you when those two lads are in our cells.' The sergeant ran to assist the constable, and shouted over his shoulder,

'You stay put now. You know I'll be able to find you if I want.'

Cornelius ran in the opposite direction. Never to return to his Merthyr home again.

Neither, Terence nor Cornelius McCarthy was brought before a British magistrate to be tried in accordance with the laws of the land. Terence and Peter made their escape, moving at night, to the relative safety of Cardiff, and their first contact, Mary. Their final refuge was found in New York, USA. Cornelius lost himself in London and assumed a new identity, taking a new name. A name that hinted at a different ethnicity… John Josephs.

Although Dolores and Colm were suspected of involvement, it was not possible to prove any connection; after all, no suspects were ever found, and no other links could be established. Nevertheless, Cornelius received word from the IRA,

'It would be 'best' if you did not return home.'

***

The consequences for Cornelius' wife and children were severe. Without her husband's salary and day-to-day support, life for Ethel was difficult. She took employment wherever she could find it, and Evelyn grew up quickly, as she needed to take care of her young brother. Evelyn had to be a mother to William throughout his childhood, but at a cost to her own. She earned some pocket money, running errands and taking on chores for women who were out at work during the day; all of which paid very little, but was of help in keeping the family together.

At the age of fourteen, William found work at the engineering workshop of the Chain Works. The men there remembered Cornelius and often spoke of him. It was hard for William to talk about his father, but he would listen to what they had to say.

'He was a good bloke, your dad. I'd go for a beer with him after work more often than not. He always had a story to tell.' Another chipped in.

'He was good with his fists, too. He boxed at the Town Hall. Not a big man, but tough.

'Aye, he took on blokes twice his size.' The conversation paused, as the exaggeration was noted and the statement amended.

'Well, anyway he used to take on big-uns.'

Another said,

'I can't think why he would have had anything to do with those Irish on the run... but then why did he go missing?'

It was if his workmates were still trying to get their head around the whole affair, expecting William to provide some answers. He never gave any.

From what they told him, he was able to piece together the events leading up to his father's disappearance, but that was almost ten years before. For all he knew, his father was dead, as he still hadn't tried to make contact with his family, and William had long since decided not to forgive him. The hardships the family faced were down to his father leaving, and as far as he knew, there was no reason for him to do so. Talk about the IRA was just that... talk. His mother had sworn it was not true.

Over the years, the family prospered well enough, only for their good fortune to be reversed as the World around them descended into war.

27

William Rides Out

William's enthusiasm for the Boy's Brigade had given him his interest in engineering. He excelled in the maintenance of old Army vehicles given to them for use in their training exercises. On the parade ground in the village, he was allowed to drive the old staff cars and army trucks to test the repairs he had made to them; but mostly he drove them for the fun of it. Vehicle maintenance and repair was easy for William... machines made sense to him.

He was fortunate enough to have been given a 1922 Wolseley seven, as the owner had despaired of ever getting it to run again. William had begged and borrowed parts to restore it, and by the age of fourteen, he was often seen driving through the village and along the Broadway into the town of Pontypridd. Having his own car made him quite the celebrity amongst the girls. Of those young women, it was Joyce caught his eye. Soon they were courting, but William had ambition to leave the valley, and the Wolseley provided him with the means by which to do so. He applied for a vacant position as Chauffeur to a well-to-do family in Henley-on-Thames. He drove to the interview, and after giving examples of his understanding of, and enthusiasm for, motor vehicles, he was given the job.

He settled in well to his new role, sending money home on a regular basis. He was to occasionally write to his mother and Evelyn

Dear Mam and Evelyn

Its very nice here. I have lots to do. I'm not only the chauffeur, but I have become the handyman as well. I fix anything that brakes around the house. I feel like part of the family and eat in the kitchen with the rest of the staff. Mr. Johnson, the landowner, has two cars, a big one for the hole of the family and a small one for running into the village or picking people up from the station.
Well, that's all the news for now, missing you both.

Lots of love, Bill. xxx

There was only so much an eighteen-year-old could write before finding something else more important to do. In fact, anything, other than the drudge of putting words together that vaguely amounted to something of interest. Of course, his mother and Eve poured over every word, looking for any hidden meaning that might hint at his unhappiness at being away from home. No matter how they read the letter, it remained just a short note from a lad with better things to do than write home to his mum. In contrast, his letters to Joyce were frequent and full of a young man's passion; with the words and spelling checked by Maisie, the children's governess.

My dearest Joyce,

I know it was hard for us both to part, and for you to see me on the train in Cardiff. It broke my heart too. But we know it's the best thing for us to do so that we can start up somewhere new together, away from the Valleys. As we thought, it's taking time for them to get to know me and what I can do, but I've made a good start and I've been given more jobs to do with more responsibility.

Oh, how I miss you. I will have to find a way to get you here with me. You are always on my mind, no matter what I'm up to. Drive his Lordship to town, I think of you, eat dinner with Mrs. Flynn, the chef, and I think of you, fix her tap and I think of you, (a joke, but true. I hope you laughed). I remember your laugh, your silly jokes, which are worse than mine, your funny Abercynon accent, the way you skip, rather than walk like a proper lady, the Al Johnson song you sang to me in Ponty Park, to the wrong bit of the tune, and only half the words in the right place (nice though).

Having thanked Maisie, he added a sentence or two without her help with the spelling.

*I think of you at night to, especially at night.
I long for you. How can any girl have hair as beautiful as yours? Red as a penny stamp.
Skin like the cream on the top of the milk, eyes so blue that I think you stole them from the sky of a summers day. I think of the way you touch me and the way you let me touch you.
I must see you soon.
I love you with all my heart,*

Bill xxxx

William was going to add, S.W.A.L.K. at the bottom of the letter, but thought better of it.

Maisie had not read the concluding sentences. Even so, she had wished someone would write such nice love letters to her.

***

But this new life was soon to come to an end. After six months in the job, he received his call up papers. They were delivered to his mother's home, and he was to report to the Town Hall back in Pontypridd where he would be enlisted into the Army.

The news in the first two years of the war had been relentlessly bad. It started with the defeat and desperate evacuation of the British Expeditionary Force sent to support France against the German invasion.

Then came the loss of Singapore to the advancing Japanese, followed by military reversals in North Africa. On the sea, the sinking of HMS Hood by the pocket battleship, Bismarck did much to destroy any lingering belief in Britain's invincibility.

***

The defence of Britain's airspace was the one outstanding display of the country's resistance and resolve to meet the challenge of the German Third Reich.

In the skies above the South of England, young men threw their aircraft time and time again against German aircraft intent on bombing Britain into submission. The British won a victory, of sorts. For both forces, the toll in men and machines was immense, but in the face of continuing heavy losses, Hitler decided that an invasion of Britain should be postponed. He decided on a new strategy, and would turn his forces towards Russia in the east. Britain could wait.

Confidence soared amongst the British public. The air battle had shown that the war against Hitler could be won, and the airmen involved in the battle were heroes.

***

After the refinement of the 'Manor House', life in the Army was a shock. The war had taken William even further from the Valleys than had his employment as chauffeur. His basic training had been in Newry, Northern Ireland. There, he showed his willingness to both conform and contribute. He began to progress through the ranks, and he soon became a 'full corporal'. He had learned not to play the fool, and impressed his superiors with the diligence he applied to any given task. What was also noted was his ability to give, and to take, orders. William was aware of the need at all times for clear and precise communication. Soon, his easy-going 'Valley's Boy' sing-song voice was replaced by the clipped, direct address adopted by those who required others to obey without question. However, his ambition lay in another direction, and William asked to see his commanding officer.

'With your permission, Sir, I would like to volunteer for the Air Force to train as part of a flying crew.'

'And what makes you think they will accept you McCarthy?'

'I think you know of my technical ability maintaining vehicles at the barracks. I believe my promotion, which you endorsed, was based on those skills, Sir.'

'I still don't see what bearing this on your request?'

'There is an urgent need for aircrew, Sir.'

'That is well known McCarthy, but why you?

'Flying an aircraft requires a technical understanding of what makes it take to the air, and to have the physical coordination to ensure it does so. I think I have the ability to do that, Sir.'

'I can't disagree that you have the ability to learn how to fly, McCarthy, but we need your skills here, in the Welsh Regiment.'

'I have enjoyed being in the regiment, Sir, but I feel I want to be doing my stuff directly for the war effort.'

'Perhaps you might want time to reconsider? I can't promise further promotion, but I am willing to press your cause. What do you think?'

'I have been thinking about it for quite some time now, Sir. I think the Air force is the right place for me, and they are looking for volunteers.'

'I understand. Put in your application. I will consider whether I will endorse it or not. That will be all, McCarthy.'

Later, by way of commendation, his platoon commander wrote to William's mother.

Newry
28.1.41

'Dear Mrs. McCarthy,

Your son applied a short while ago, to go into the R.A.F, passed his medical and is now just waiting to be called. I am sure he will be pleased when that day comes; it will realise a great ambition.

I, his platoon commander, will be very sorry indeed to lose him but of course, I do not want to stand in his way at all. He has done a grand job of work for me here in keeping my carriers in first-class condition, and it will be hard for me to replace him.

In his new work, he will advance with great strides and I take this opportunity again of wishing him every success.

You have a son, Mrs. McCarthy to be proud of.

Yours sincerely,

Gordon E. Collett

Selwyn Berryman-Morgan

28

Cranwell College. The Stuff of Dreams.

Lincolnshire, March 1942

William was about to complete his initial training as a pilot in the Royal Air Force and his time at the prestigious Air Training College of Cranwell was coming to a close. He had no illusion he'd been chosen to be there on merit, it was because all air training establishments were thrown open to volunteers, and the chance had fallen to him. Be that as it may, as he flew his plane on his final flight assessment, he knew his competent handling of the aircraft, coupled with a proven knowledge of aeronautics, would ensure there'd be a role for him to play in the Royal Air Force.

The twin engine Oxford Airspeed turned slowly to the left, to line up its approach to the airfield from which it had left an hour before. William flew unaided, his instructor sitting beside him acting as an observer and adjudicator. As he had done on previous training flights, William had successfully taken to the air and navigated his course over the English countryside.

The flight examination was almost complete and William made his final approach to landing. The weather had been set fair, but the winds had turned blustery, the darkening clouds to the east scampered in the wake of a February cold-front from off the North Sea. It cut its way across the Lincolnshire flatlands, chasing away the damp calm of the previous two days. The clouds were outriders of the menacing storm on the horizon.

William was determined to concentrate on the job at hand. Despite his resolve, his concentration waned and he thought of home and of Joyce. She would have loved to see him flying his plane and had no idea how far he had progressed in his ambition. A sudden swell of pride at his achievement let his mind wander. He thought back on the journey that had brought him to the verge of earning his 'wings', and of when he first spoke to Joyce of his intentions.

They lay together in the back bedroom of his Treforest home... his old bedroom. The rain outside fell as a soft mist, penetrating the absorbent fabric of the physical world and the souls of those who were unlucky enough to live in it. It dampened his spirit, but he was determined to speak to Joyce of his new challenge.

'Joyce, what would you say if I...'

William was alerted by a sharp tug on the control stick. The plane was caught in a downdraft and he needed to take charge of the situation; if he didn't, his instructor would take over.

'I've got her.'

William had reacted in time

He righted the tilt of the wings and returned the aircraft to a level flightpath.

***

The final decision as to whether William became a pilot, or be recommended as a navigator, would not take long. The huge loss of British pilots in the 'Battle of Britain,' meant aircrew needed to be replaced quickly, and if William was to be made a pilot, there would still be the question of what type of aircraft he would fly, fighters or bombers?

The hope of most trainee pilots was to fly fighter planes, the Spitfire by choice, if not, then the Hurricane. The men who flew those machines had covered themselves in glory, fighting back the massed formations of German bombers during the 'Battle of Britain'. They were special characters, who, by nature, lived life on the edge: fast planes, fast cars and the occasional fast women. They flew instinctively, by touch, and with great skill and bravery. They were the inspiration for many of the volunteers who came forward to train as pilots; William included. The bomber pilot, on the other hand, needed dogged belligerence and determination to win through; perseverance was their watchword, no less brave, but less flamboyant. The responsibility of flying a plane for up to eight hours over enemy territory, reaching the target to dispense their bombs and ensuring the safe return of the aircraft and crew, would weigh heavily in the decisions the bomber pilot would make. Unlike the flamboyance of the fighter pilot, they needed to be steady and dependable.

Late the next day, William was called into the office of the senior officer in charge of training.

'Sit down McCarthy... I am pleased to tell you that you have successfully completed your training. Your commission will follow in due course.'

William felt a surge of relief. His anxiety that had built up since ending his test flight the previous day eased in an instant. He relaxed and waited for his officer to continue; for he clearly had more to say

Wing Commander, Davies, leafed through the pages of the handwritten document. Then, referring to the conclusions of the document that would determine the way the war would proceed for this young airman, he announced,

'You are to leave at the next available opportunity to the Operational Training Unit at Cranwell... Yes, Cranwell, no less. There, you are to be trained to fly the new heavy bomber that is soon to be introduced. It will be, as you may well know, the Short Stirling.'

So, I am to be a bomber pilot, thought William. He felt some disappointment at the news he was not going to be a fighter pilot, someone who would directly confront the enemy, jousting above the cities and farmland of Southern England, striking back immediately.

Wing Commander Davis sensed William's disappointment, he had expected to see it, and wanted to reassure William this was not a second-rate commission. He deviated from the formal script of the briefing.

'Bill, this is an important role. The Stirling is a formidable four-engine bomber... It'll be powerful enough to take the battle to the very heart of Germany, and you will be one of the first to be able to do it. We think you're up to it.'

29

The RAF, 218 Squadron

The Short Stirling bomber was huge when compared to other aircraft flying at the time. Its nose stood over twenty-two feet above the ground (in comparison a London double-decker bus from that time was 14 ft in height and 87 ft in length; three of the same red buses could have stood alongside the aircraft). The fuselage bristled with defensive armament, with its frame punctured by Browning machine guns. The glazed nose turret housed twin guns, as did a dorsal turret whilst the rear gunner sat in isolation manning a four-gun array. The bomb bay was huge, and as the aircraft had four powerful Bristol Hercules engines, it could carry up to 14000 lbs. of bombs. With such a bomb load, the British airmen could begin to inflict significant damage to the fabric and morale of the enemy.

Because of the shortage of planes, William never got to fly the Short Stirling during his training. Stirling training had been theoretical, whilst his flying training was in a variety of bomber aircraft, including the Vickers Wellington 1C; an older aircraft withdrawn from frontline service. This was thought to be acceptable, as the principles and practicalities of flying a World War II aircraft were similar across the available aeroplanes. Each type of aircraft had its own personality and idiosyncrasies, but the differences didn't mean there was a need to take frontline machines from operational duties to demonstrate what those differences were. Nevertheless, William would fly the leviathan that was the Short Stirling, soon enough, as his 'Operational Training' course at Cranwell would only last three months. During that time, he would learn about the aircraft from training manuals and cockpit mock-ups built to contain all of the important components found on the real thing. His final 'Conversion Training', flying the Mark 1 Stirling, would take place at Downham Market, Norfolk... an operational RAF airfield. Bomber

Command thought it expedient for its Operational Training be carried over for completion within an operational squadron.

William would perform six operational flights alongside an experienced pilot and crew, before taking command of his own crew. That arrangement was to ensure new pilots became totally familiar with the aircraft they were to fly, whilst at the same time helping to take the war to the enemy.

***

RAF Downham Market. April 1942

William stood with his 'Skipper' at the door in the fuselage of the Mark 1 Stirling parked at the perimeter fence of RAF Downham Market. It was the airfield from which 218 Squadron operated.

'Are you satisfied the aircraft is as you would expect to find it, Bill?'

'It would seem to be in top condition, Skipper. There's nothing to be seen on her exterior that would stop me taking her into the sky.'

'I agree. Shall we join the crew?'

Pre-flight checks were to be commenced in order, as per the instruction manual. The crew was at its station when Captain Jefferies spoke to his co-pilot.

'As we previously agreed, Bill, that although you are here playing 'Second Dickey', it will be you who'll pilot this afternoon's flight trial and, if all goes well, tonight's mission. I take it for granted that you are up to the task.'

'Yes, I am, Sir'.

'You're in the pilot's seat for a reason, Bill. Your responsibility has to start somewhere, so why not now? The aircraft will be yours to control.'

'Thank you Skipper.'

'My crew and I are taking a necessary risk, so don't let us down.'

'I understand, Skipper, and I am up to the task.'

'Good. The crew will still be under my command, but I will take charge only if I think it necessary, either for clarification or as a countermand of your order. I hope not to do that. The weather is good this afternoon, and we have been blessed with an easy mission tonight. An all-expenses trip to Paris should not be sniffed at.'

It was the Captain's attempt at a light-hearted joke, and William forced a smile.

'When you are ready, Bill, you will take her up.'

William was to speak out loud the actions he would take so that his Skipper could assess the accuracy and timeliness of his pre-flight procedures.

'I will fire each engine in turn.'

Starting with the outer engine on the starboard wing, he powered the engines in succession, balancing them at each step, until all had roared into life. The plane throbbed with the pent-up energy the feathered engines promised to give. They had breathed life into the bomber.

He spoke to the crew on the intercom.

'Flight-engineer, confirm the Status of the engines, the hydraulic pressures and electrical systems.'

'The engines are running smoothly and synchronously. The hydraulic pressures are correct. There's no indication of any electrical problem. All systems are functioning, Bill.'

The crew were instructed to acknowledge the pilot who was addressing them, remembering the overall control of the aircraft was ultimately that of Captain Jefferies. William continued,

'In order, please confirm you are in position and your systems are working correctly. Tail gunner?'

'Yes, Bill. Bullets up the spout and I have full and free movement of my turret.'

'Mid?'

'At station, and my gun is fully functional' ... and so it went on.

The Navigator/bomb aimer, sat directly behind the pilots, and gave a 'thumbs up'. He was ready to go.

'Well, if you are all sitting comfortably, we'll be on our way.' A chorus of encouragement from the crew flooded the intercom.

'Good luck Bill.'

'You'll soon have her flying,' said another, his words almost lost over other garbled messages of support.

Captain Jefferies turned to his co-pilot.

'Well, Pilot Officer McCarthy, it seems we are ready to go.' He continued with his final words of caution.

'Remember your training and particularly your need to balance your throttles at takeoff. I will take over if I think it necessary.'

William turned and smiled in gratitude for his Captain's support and reassurance. He gave his final ground level command.

'Keep alert, chaps, your eyes open for enemy fighters. We know that Goebbels has promised to attack us in our nest.'

He didn't want his first flight to be his last.

***

William completed six missions flying 'Dickie' to Captain Jefferies. His luck had held out, and he'd learned what it took to command an efficient and effective bomber crew.

It was thought by Bomber Command that three successful missions were the minimum for bomb crews to repay the time and expense it took to train them. Unlucky' crews never had the chance to perfect their skills and repay the debt.

The lessons William learnt would be put to the test. He would now fly his own aircraft and crew on their first mission together.

30

Bill's Crew

The men who agreed to be members of William's crew were a mixed bunch. They had volunteered from all parts of the world, and were now assigned to an operational squadron. It was there, after a few days of acclimatisation, they would be assembled in a hanger on the airfield. They would mill around and start up conversations, with the intention of establishing an aircrew. Having flown Dickie, the captains were there to look for that crew. The purpose of the gathering was clear. If an aircrew was to succeed on their missions and survive the war, they would need to be able to work together.

Prior to the meeting in the hanger, William had taken steps to build his crew. One crew member was already in place. During his fight training with Captain Jefferies, William had met Alex, and he was already recruited to his cause.

Alex was an air-gunner and had already completed one tour of duty, flying in the Handley Page 'Halifax' bomber. Up to that point, the Halifax had been the workhorse of the Air Force's response to the German aggression. Having completed his allotted 30 missions, he had been posted to Harwell for six months. He was to instruct trainee air gunners, before converting to the Stirling bomber himself and was soon to return to active duty; a further tour of 30 missions.

The Halifax had done its job well enough but it didn't have a big payload; typically, the aircraft would fly with 16 x 500lb bombs. In the meantime, the Stirling was beginning to enter service with a number of squadrons, and it was touted to carry up to 50% more bomb load than the Halifax and it had an extended range. The Stirling also had better defensive armaments, having a total of three gun-turrets; in particular, the tail gun was equipped with four 0.303mm Browning machine guns.

It was towards the end of William's Operational Training at Cranwell College when he met Alex in the 'Mess'. Alex was already at the bar when William came to sit next to him. The Mess provided William with the chance to get some respite from the intense training sessions; he had that afternoon begun his first practical training in a mock-up of the Stirling's cockpit. It had lifted his spirits as he was able to get his hands on something tangible, rather than just plough through theoretical aspects of the aircraft. Now he needed an hour or two to relax and take his mind off the machine that would take him to war.

He recognised the face of the sergeant sitting at the bar but couldn't put a name to him.

'Hello! I'm alright to sit here and join you?' asked William.

'You are. At least for a while until my girlfriend arrives in the village.'

'You're lucky to have a local lass for a friend.'

'Having completed a tour of duty I'm lucky to still be in one piece.'

'Yes, I know what you mean.' William was knocked from his stride, and wasn't sure if the man was best left to his beer. But he tried again

'I suppose one of the benefits of this war is that we leave home and meet new people. I had a girlfriend in Belfast, nothing serious, as I've a steady girl back home I'm sweet on, but it's nice to have company, especially that of a young lady.'

Alex responded, but with a jibe meant to keep William on his toes.

'You've not got the 'proper' English accent I'm used to hearing around here.'

Bill laughed, and replied,

'I'm working on it, but sitting in a pub... well, it's as if I'm back home... In the '*Royal*' Air Force, I find it pays to sound more like a Toff than a 'Taff', but put a pint in front of me I forget where I am.'

'Ah, so you're Welsh.'

'Yes, and part Irish. Neither of those accents gets you very far under normal circumstances... I guess you're Australian? Standard issue

battledress doesn't help me decide but your accent gives me a clue.'
William was placed at a disadvantage, again, by Alex's reply.

'Ah, that's where you're wrong, young Taff. I'm from New
Zealand. I keep telling everyone I sound nothing like an Australian.
How you Brits can't tell the difference is beyond me.'

William was able to see the humour in it, because most people
found it difficult to tell the accents apart, and the half-smile on Alex's
face seemed to reveal his nature. Alex continued the banter,

'Anyhow, I hear we'll get our own Standard Dress soon. It'll be
better than this scratchy British stuff and tailored in Savile Row by chaps
you would rather not let measure your inside leg.' They laughed at the
absurdity of the suggestion. The ice was broken and William decided to
join in the fun.

'We Brits insist on only the best for our Colonial chums.'

A reference to rank and privilege was to be expected, and it came
immediately.

'As a Pilot Officer, you won't need to wear this rough stuff. You'll
have your uniform made out of soft mohair that's been chewed by
Tibetan monks.'

'I'm not sure I can afford that, even on my officer's pay?'

Alex gave William a sideways look, but William continued,

'Don't get me wrong, I know I'll earn a fair bit more than you non-
commissioned lads, but it doesn't stretch far when we have to buy our
own uniform. We're not even sure if we'll continue in the job past a few
missions. I hear you can find second-hand Officer's uniforms that I'll
chew myself.'

'I'll keep ear out for you.'

'Thanks... So, you're a New Zealander through and through?'

'Some Scots... Oh, and going back a fair bit, Cornish.'

William introduced himself.

'I'm Bill McCarthy. That's thanks to my Irish father, wherever he
is.'

'I'm Alexander Rowe... My surname is from my Cornish ancestors, whoever they were.'

'Rowe! Well, what do you know? That's a name found in my family, as well. My Grandmother was a Rowe. She always claimed her family from way back came to Wales to escape from the Cornish tin mines. They ended up as coal miners instead. If my build is anything to go by, they were well suited to it.'

'We're not far off the same build, alright. It helps me to fit into the piddling space they allow for air-gunners on these bombers of ours. I'm pleased to say I leave more room for bombs.'

'I'll have to have my pilot's seat adjusted forwards as far as it'll go, so I'll do my extra little bit for the war effort, too.' They chuckled at the thought.

Neither William nor Alex would have been described as 'short', but they were not bothered by the low door frames in the village pub, and it was not long after that they met there, along with Alex's girlfriend, Cecilia. She was bright and chatty, and couldn't help herself telling William about her relationship with Alex.

'It was in the blitz, in London. Alex was passing through on his way to his previous posting. We met by chance in Hyde Park., didn't we love?'

'Yes, we did.'

'Him being an airman, it was hard to get his attention for all the other girls wanting to chat with him, so I didn't bother. But he spotted me and came right up to where I sat with a friend, eating our sandwiches, and asked who I was.'

'I thought you came over to me?'

'No, you came over to us as bold as brass.'

'That'll be me, then.'

William brought the banter to a stop by asking,

'So how did you get here?'

'We kept in touch by letter. He invited me up, knowing I've family around here, and I'm staying with them for a while. I get over by train. It's not far, really.'

Later in the evening, when Cecilia had left to 'powder her nose', William took the opportunity to ask Alex what he intended to do, knowing his training was soon to come to an end. He first asked about his girlfriend.

'She's a very lovely girl, Alex. Have you an idea of how you'll keep in touch when you finish here and have to move away?'

'I don't suppose I'll move that far, and if I get through this war, I'll ask her to come back to New Zealand with me... if that's what you mean.'

'Not really, but a new life in a country that's not had its cities flattened by Hitler's bombs... how could she say no?'

'I live in hope, and you never know, you might be right, and she might say yes.'

'You'd also hope to be stationed around these parts, close enough to her, I expect'

'Well, that would be a help.'

'I'll soon be allocated to a squadron. It can't be too far from here. Are your plans in place yet?'

'No, I haven't been allocated a posting. I just know that when I've finished here, I'm back into active duty.'

'Still, it's been a good break from the war for you, what with your tour as an instructor.'

'Instructing is meant to be 'R and R', but getting you guys ready to fly, whilst, at the same time, saving my arse, is as difficult as flying to Berlin and back. Sometimes our training flights were lucky to get off the ground.'

It was an exaggeration, but they both laughed as nothing was quite like flying into German airspace, as Alex knew only too well, and William was soon to find out. William said,

'We couldn't have been that bad as we are both here to tell the tale.'

William remembered his train of thought and the purpose of his original question.

'Alex, I could do with someone with your experience onboard with me. Would you be interested, and are you available to volunteer your services at this time...? How does it work with the New Zealand Air Force?' Alex didn't reply.

William added,

'It's a long shot, I know, but I thought I'd ask.'

'I'm not sure. But I will have to decide on a crew soon enough. It'll depend on where I'm based, I suppose, Bill. You'll not be surprised that so far, you're the only one to ask. Let's wait and see where you'll be stationed.'

As it turned out, Alexander Rowe found his way to Downham Market. He flew missions as temporary crew, before committing to William.

***

In the week before the scheduled gathering of men in the hanger, William was to make the acquaintance of his second crew member; a person who would sit next to him as he flew over Germany

William had taken up with Sergeant Henry Russel, who was from the small town of Regina, Saskatchewan. He was a tall man with blonde hair. He also sported a fashionable, well-groomed, moustache; it would have been a hit with the young ladies in the village, had he been inclined to take advantage of the fact.

Being less outgoing than many of the men, he found the over-the-top banter that flowed in the Mess too much. He enjoyed a pint of beer and a joke, but the excesses at the bar were not to his liking. He would take an opportunity to leave.

'I'll see you guys. I'm off to get my head around the workings of the Browning tail guns.'

The men at the bar let him go lightly, and one said,

'This early, Henry? Have you a village lass waiting, and wanting your attention.'

'He probably has, because we know Pilots only need to shoot straight when they're up close and personal.'

Henry would rely on his good sense of humour to see him sail clear of the barrack room innuendo. He replied,

'I hope it's not put to the test. But just in case I've got a Jerry up my arse and my gunner's gone outside for a piss, I thought I would find out how to point the thing for myself.'

'Aye, it's best to be first in the queue.'

William had watched the exchange. Henry could handle himself and be on equal terms with anyone without getting people's back up. A good chap, thought William, and he fell in line with Henry as he made his way to the door, fending off the last appeal for him to stay.

William had already established Henry was expecting to co-pilot and he looked like a man he could fly with. William introduced himself,

'Hi, I'm Bill.'

Henry gave William a sideways glance of appraisal and replied cautiously.

'Hi there, 'I'm Henry.' They shook hands but continued to walk out into the evening sun.

'Henry... Can we talk?'

'Sure Bill... Can we walk and talk at the same time?'

'I'm not sure? We haven't had the ''walking and talking' module of training yet, but we can try.' They both laughed.

A good start, thought William, and continued,

'I guess you haven't hooked up with a crew yet, Henry?'

'I've been fighting off would-be pilots for weeks now Bill.' They both laughed, knowing there had, as yet, been little opportunity to form crews.

Henry was pleased Bill had seen the humour in his response, and continued,

'It's not that I've any right to be been choosy.' They laughed again, as the joke had not yet run out of steam.

'There's a couple of aircrews that have been formed as soon as men set foot in here, and I want to get my co-pilot in place before there's no aircrew to be had, other than the squadron's pet cat.'

'I wouldn't want you to deprive the airfield of its ginger Tom.' Said Henry, pretending to be affronted. He continued,

'And you are wondering if I would join with you on behalf of the cat lovers amongst us?'

William laughed, in the hope they were still telling jokes, but then changed his tone to indicate he was coming to the point.

'To tell you the truth, Henry, it's hard not to respect the airmen from overseas. It seems to me there's something more to men who come all this way here to fight on our behalf. So yes, would you consider co-piloting with me as Captain?'

Henry didn't reply straight away. The decision to join a crew committed an airman to the good, or bad, fortune they would make for themselves. Their future could well depend on the discipline and ability of the weakest in the link. A careless crew member affected the safety and performance of everyone on board. It was particularly true if the weak link was the pilot.

William understood the importance of the decision he was asking this airman to make. On what basis could he make it? It was one thing to be pleasant and comradely in the Mess or down the local pub, or even when planning the next operation, but what of the reality of flying an aeroplane in the skies above Germany? There was no possible way they could know. William addressed the issue and spoke with a confidence he was not altogether certain of.

'I know I can make this aircraft fly. I'm not gung-ho. But we have a job to do, and I can promise I will do it to the best of my ability, taking risks my crew members would take, if our roles were reversed.'

William paused to allow Henry to speak, but Henry waited to hear more. He knew there was always the matter of the small print of any agreement, written or not, especially when being flown into a war that had already taken millions of lives. William knew it, too, and continued.

'Having said that, we volunteered in the full knowledge of the dangers and risks involved, and so I expect my crew to support my decisions during operational flights. Questions about the ethics of what I ask you to do, or how I ask you to do it, will only be taken after we get back from a mission. I expect my crew to be upfront in any criticism and not to talk in groups behind my back. It's a reasonable request, wouldn't you agree?'

Henry didn't immediately reply, and William worried he had said too much, but Henry wanted more.

'So, is this to be a business relationship?'

'When we're on a mission, it has to be. I wouldn't let any friendship I may develop get in the way of a mission's objective. On the ground, we can be friends, it would be a bonus, but it shouldn't have any bearing on the tasks we are asked to carry out.'

'That's a position I can agree with. There could well be a situation where I would need to take control. It works both ways.'

'It does, of course. I would prefer us all to be friends, but that remains to be seen. Above all, we need to be a close-knit aircrew that remains focused and disciplined.'

William had said what he needed to, but was again anxious he might have said too much. Henry's answer seemed to confirm that might be the case.

'You'll need to give me time to think about it?'

'Of course, I would expect no more of you. It is an important decision for us both. Let's think on it. I won't lose you in the crowd. Not with that moustache.'

They parted, and William wondered if his direct approach was right for this man. He had judged it to be the case, but it would not be the right approach for all the men he invited to fly with him. He continued in his task to try and forge his crew.

***

Flight Sgt Ronald Bird was fresh from appearing in the propaganda, come documentary film, *'Target for Tonight'*. He was young and fresh-faced, as required by the film unit; the unit wanted to promote the work carried out for the nation by its enthusiastic bomber force. He was posted to Downham Market for the completion of his conversion to flying as gunner in the Stirling.

The film followed the plane's crew, before, during and after a bombing raid into Germany. For obvious reasons, care was taken not to reveal anything not already known about wartime bomber operations, but in an effort to improve the film's authenticity, serving airmen were recruited to act the roles they played. In1941, having just finished a tour of duty on a Wellington bomber, Ronald was cast in his role (his 'Rest and Recuperation' duty was to be most unusual). His was a minor part, but he got to speak and seemed natural enough, even if his affected 'Air Force accent' failed to completely convince. Ronald's 'cheeky chappie' Cockney personality was appreciated by everyone at Downham, but he was careful to hide his real accent on screen.

He was known as 'Errol' when in the Mess, in reference to the screen idol Errol Flynn. He would make his usual bustling, jovial entrance. As always, someone would announce him.

'Here he is, our very own Hollywood idol.'

'Well! If it isn't our Errol', shouted someone else, who continued,

'Fresh from deflowering a village virgin, no doubt,' the announcement was followed by a lewd cheer in recognition of the fact, for most of them, chance would be a fine thing.

Gathered in the hanger, he, too, was trying to attach himself to a crew. William came over to where Ronald stood, and struck up a conversation. William had not been let in on Ronald's claim to fame.

'Hello, I'm Bill. I'm told you are Errol. Lads in the hanger pointed you out to me as being an air gunner. Can I call you Errol?'

'If you like, I don't mind, but I'm Ron... Ronald.'

'Oh! Well, I'll call you Ron. That's easy to remember, because Ronald's my middle name, too.'

It was a good, if faltering, start, and after a few beers, Joseph Ronald Bird agreed to become William's air-gunner and his third crew member.

Not all Pilot Officers got to fly their planes. Their rank didn't give them a right to be the officer in control of the aircraft. At the Operational Training Units, men were trained in the skills they were best suited. Rank in Bomber Command was of less significance than in other forces and the ranks freely associated with each other. A case in point was another Canadian, Pilot Officer Vincent Trowbridge. He trained as a wireless operator and front-gunner.

William and Vincent spoke at a table where tea was provided. It was always strong or, if not, over-brewed. Theirs was a chance encounter. They both reached for the sugar; it was under strict war time ration, but it was readily available for such occasions. They introduced themselves, and, as oft times happened when men were far from home, the conversation turned to those left behind.

At the age of 28, Vincent was older than most of the airmen that congregated that day. His thoughts of home reflected that.

'I have a wife at home, Bill. It was difficult to leave her but I felt I had to get involved.'

'I've haven't taken the plunge yet, Vince, but I have someone special back in my home town, in Wales. Maybe, after the war...'

William's voice tapered away. They both understood the dilemma, and Vincent slowly nodded his head in acknowledgement. William gathered his thoughts and continued,

'I look around, Vince, and I am amazed at how many Commonwealth airmen have volunteered to join in our fight.'

'I guess it's our fight, too. We saw what happened in Europe and the bomber attacks on London. Film of the Blitz was on all our movie screens back home. It's not just you British who want revenge.'

In Vincent, William had found a kindred spirit, and, as a Canadian, it was obvious he had committed himself to the fight over and above what was expected of him. William continued,

'I am going to make my crew a Commonwealth crew. I already have some men from other parts agreeing to fly with me. Already one other is a Canadian'

'I like that idea, Bill. Perhaps I can be considered... if you've not got yourself a Wireless Operator, that is.'

'I haven't Vince. You'd be welcome on board, if you'd have us,'

and continued,

'Although, I seem to be finding men who have been given names the same or similar to mine. Having two middle names doesn't help.

'Well, Bill, you may have just added to the confusion... My middle name is William.' They laughed out loud and drew attention to themselves.

There was yet another Pilot Officer to join with William. Thomas Scanlon was from the north of England, a Geordie. He was a navigator, a role on the aircraft that was often filled by officers, who decided not to pilot, or who were judged not to possess the necessary skills to do so. The navigator's task was the most technically demanding, and only second in importance to that of the pilot. Ranks were not as important in bomber Command, and a pilot could hold a non-commissioned rank, and often were Flight Sergeants. Never the less, the Captain was the senior airman aboard.

William needed two more crew, a 'Bomb Aimer' and a 'Flight Engineer'; both vital components of the aircrew. It was Alex who introduced Lawrence Jones to him.

'This is Larry Jones, Bill. He's a New Zealander, too, and could be the bomb aimer you're looking for. I've told him about me joining in with your crew and he's interested to join us as well.'

'Hello, Larry. I'm pleased to meet you and I'm glad you'd like to join us. I guess Alex has told you how I would want to run the crew, relaxed on the ground but disciplined in the air. If that suits you, you're more than welcome?'

'It's the way I'd want it to be.'

'Good! By the way, you're not by any chance also called Bill or Ronald?'

Lawrence was unsure of the question...

'Err... well no, just Larry.'

William explained why he had asked, and the three of them laughed, as they often would do during their time together.

The Flight Engineer who eventually joined the crew was put forward from a pool of newly trained airmen. He was RAF, and his name, Harold (Harry) Forshaw, also had the possibility of causing confusion onboard. Having a Harry, a Henry and a Larry, whilst communicating instructions on the intercom, was sure to cause trouble. William would have to deal with it.

Selwyn Berryman-Morgan

31

'Bomber Harris' Takes Control

In the early years of the war, after a night's bombing, photo-reconnaissance photographs would often show primary targets left undamaged. The 'dead-reckoning' techniques used by the navigators proved to be inadequate to the task: adverse weather, cloud cover, dazzling searchlights, ground lights used as decoys, all would play a part to blunt the attack. Additionally, identifying specific targets amongst the mass of factories, townships and residential areas proved to be almost impossible. Consequently, early raids would only deliver a pin-prick of damage to the vast area of industrial and civilian complexes strung along the Ruhr valley.

***

In the spring of 1942, raids were carried out using only radio beams (known as 'GEE') as a guide, dispensing with dead-reckoning altogether. In doing so, it was found better accuracy and precision was achieved. In addition to the improvements in navigation, a new technique of path-finding was introduced, the 'Shaker' technique'.

Aircraft would be flown in three separate waves onto the target. The first wave of bombers would be fitted with GEE receivers and they would drop marker flares onto the target as a guide for the main force. The second wave of aircraft, not yet fitted with GEE, would drop bombs and incendiary canisters into the area marked by the flares. This would further light up the target. The third and final wave would drop high explosive bombs into the flames.

***

In February 1942, Arthur Harris became the Commander in Chief of British bomber forces, and he needed to impress upon Winston Churchill the effectiveness of the bombing campaign. It was his contention, that intense bombing of specific targets in Germany would hasten the end of the war, if not win it for the Allies. The extensive damage caused to the ancient city of Lubeck on night of the 28/29th of March, using the Shaker technique and a large force of 234 bombers, was encouragement enough for Air Marshal Arthur Harris to propose a larger raid on Cologne. He was determined the Cologne raid would not be another big raid, soon lost in the avalanche of news coming out of the war. He wanted to strike a blow remembered by the British public, the Commanders of the various UK and American forces, members of the British War Cabinet, and, most importantly, Winston Churchill.

The destruction wrought needed to be a major blow to the German war effort, and a blow to the morale of the German people. If the raid was successful, the continuation of Harris's bombing strategy would be assured.

32

'By the Light of a Silvery Moon'

RAF Downham Market, May 30th 1942.

On their 7th mission, William and his crew, in their aircraft flight code HA-G, were to take part in a 1000 bomber raid on Cologne. This raid was to go down in history for both the scale of the attack and the scale of the destruction.

At the briefing for the night's raid, the aircrews were addressed by the Station Commander, Paul Holder, and Acting Group-Captain Herbert Fitzpatrick stood at his side.

Curtains hid the operations map hung along the length of the wall behind the senior officers. When they were drawn back, it revealed the target for the night. It was yet again, Cologne. There was an audible intake of breath from the crews. There was to be no let-up of the pressure being placed on the men of the squadron, or the inhabitants of the city.

Holder stated the obvious. He was an officer of long-standing, having become a Pilot Officer in 1936, and never minced his words.

'Yes, once again we are hitting at the guts of the German industrial might, and as you would expect we are again to deliver the full force of the Squadron's weaponry against the factories of Cologne.' He waited for the information to sink in and for the chatter to subside a little. Then, to bring the airmen to order, Commander Holder continued.

'Right, quiet down... Thank you... Thank you!' The airmen focused their attention.

'Our previous efforts, although successfully carried out, have left large parts of Germany's manufacturing capabilities intact. Tonight, we intend to put that to right.'

William with his crew sat on their 'lucky bench' halfway back in the briefing room; to sit elsewhere would have been a change to the routine that had served them well.

As tough as the mission was, they knew what to expect. But why this raid should be any more decisive than the others they had flown had yet to be revealed?

Commander Holder pointed to the board at a line drawn across a map of Europe,

'As you see, as is normal on these forays into enemy territory, your flightpath to Cologne is a slight dog-leg, which is, of course, a version of our usual feint.'

The groans from the audience were loud enough to show the airmen's displeasure at the thought. Undeterred, Holder continued,

'I know, by now the German air defences are well aware of it.

'What they will not be expecting is the size of the force flown against them. For, gentleman, we intend to send a flight of over one thousand bombers onto the target.' There was a gasp from his audience, followed by a spontaneous cheer.

When the noise subsided, Holder paused for effect. He then concluded his participation in the briefing by giving encouragement to his men.

'Yes, Air Marshal Harris has given the go-ahead for the first '1000 bomber' air-raid. We, gentlemen, have the privilege to put his plan into action.' He continued,

'You have the capability to strike a blow that will send a message directly to Hitler. It will tell him that his continuation of this war will result in the destruction of his country.'

A cheer rang out. The airmen wanted to make the difference in the war, and this raid had the potential to do that. Holder continued, shouting above the noise,

'I see you are ready for tonight's task!'

The men cheered once again. He called them to order.

'I will now pass you over to your Squadron Leaders, in the full expectation you will successfully carry out your mission. They will continue your briefing. Thank you, and good luck to you all.'

William was part of the third Flight of the three, from Squadron 218. Flight 'C'.

Each flight consisted of up to nine bombers, depending on the number of serviceable aircraft. There had been a short lull in operations flown over the previous few days, probably in readiness for this big raid, and all the Squadron's aircraft had been maintained and flight tested. William's Squadron Leader confirmed as much. He spoke, uninterrupted.

'Your ground crews have ensured your aircraft is in tip-top condition, as your flight tests will have surely confirmed. We will set off in three waves to our assembly point off the Cambridge coast, where we will meet up with the other squadrons involved. The navigators will be briefed in full, but you will be familiar with this part of the operation. Our Stirlings will form up as part of the third wave into the target. A diversionary attack will not be made. A flight of one thousand bombers is sure to be noticed and we would expect Jerry to guess our Target will be the Ruhr, and probably the area in and around Cologne.'

A rumble of discontent came up from the audience but no one stopped the Squadron Leader Phillips with questions when he was in full flow.

'Bomb aimers will have their own briefing. It is sufficient to say, our Mosquitoes, now equipped with GEE, will pinpoint the target, and they will drop a combination of red flares and incendiaries. Twenty minutes later, the second wave, comprised mainly of our Halifax squadrons, will drop incendiaries onto the target, by then it should be plain for all to see. Twenty minutes after they have left, we, the main force, will arrive, dropping a combination of incendiaries and high explosives into what should already be an inferno. You can expect the usual levels of flak on the approach to the target. However, as a result of the heavy bombardment of incendiaries already laid down, anti-aircraft batteries should be firing blindly into palls of smoke. And, for the same reason, the searchlights are likely to be ineffective. Be sure to hit your target, and then get the hell out of there. From the map, navigators will have seen our proposed way home. German night fighters will be up in their dozens and are expected to harry you from the moment you enter enemy airspace. We have them at a disadvantage, in that we have a 'bomber's moon' and clear skies. You will be able to see them long before they can make contact, and as you are in large formations our defensive fire will be concentrated. They should not be in our portion of the sky for long.'

There was a murmur of muted conversations, and Alex took the opportunity to pass comment. He leaned into William and whispered,

'He always forgets to mention that a bombers moon is just as bright for the night fighters. Advantage all square by my reckoning.'

William whispered back,

'And you wouldn't want to be flying on three engines, spooning by the light of that silvery bastard.' Alex suppressed his urge to break into a well-known song.

***

The fully loaded Stirling bomber HA-G lifted off the ground displaying its usual ponderous transformation into an effective flying machine. William was always amazed at how the aircraft changed from a cumbersome assemblage of riveted metal, bolt-on engine and whirling propeller, into a compliant flying machine, as close to being a bird as William would ever know.

The flight of aircraft from Downham Market assembled in the sky over the English Channel. In the air around them, hundreds of other bombers from aerodromes along the east coast of England joined them in the sky. In the light cast by the full moon, aircraft could be seen, funnelling towards the Dutch coast. Ahead of them, the flight of Halifax bombers had reached the far coast, and beyond them, the Mosquitoes were well into enemy territory. Hurricane and Spitfire fighter aircraft flew alongside, providing vital air defence. They would stay with the bombers as long as they were able. When the fighters turned back, the bombers had to fend for themselves. Several thousand pair of eyes looked out in armada's defence.

***

Air raids were a test of the crew's endurance. Bomber aircraft were freezing, and the airmen's flying suits were hardly up to the task. The crew would need to endure these conditions for up to eight hours, and always fearful of an enemy attack.

Usually, at the first sight of an enemy plane, a bomber would take evasive action, flying into cloud or swerving and diving away if there was none. But with so many aircraft in the sky, evasive action would be dangerous, and although there was some cloud cover, another bomber might be making use of it.

Unless he found it necessary to deviate from his course, William had decided to fly straight and true. He announced to his crew,

'Keep your eyes peeled. Not just for Jerry, but for our own bombers, too. Alex, take time to check above and below. I don't want some fool landing on top of us because he fancies a new bit of sky. I will try to repay the compliment.'

'Will do, Skipper', replied Alex, knowing, as tail gunner, he had the best view of the surrounding sky, and would also be relied upon to cover the enemy's most likely point of attack. William continued,

'If we get our way, we will be flying a direct path onto our target, but we will soon be over Happy Valley where anything might happen. Make sure you're strapped in.'

The flight had been uneventful. There had been attacks by night fighters on both flanks of the armada of aircraft, but none had penetrated as far as the flight from Downham Market. The mass of aircraft was proving to be an effective defence, but as they approached the Ruhr, the batteries of ant-aircraft defences were throwing up walls of exploding shells. The bright orange flashes ahead, and in amongst the bombers, increased in intensity. Searchlights picked out the occasional aircraft from the massed formation. As for the rest of the aircraft, German artillery gunners had to make their best guess as to their position and altitude; approximate Information was being fed to them from radar and sonar positions along the flightpath, but still, their fire lacked accuracy and was ineffective.

William's aircraft was filled with bright light; the comfort of the moonlight's gleam, with its soft, silver shadows, was rudely washed away. They had been detected by a searchlight, and had been pinpointed in the sky. The aircraft became 'coned', as other lights on the ground focused their light on the single point in the sky occupied by William's plane. HA-G was clearly visible to the artillery defences and the night fighters scouring the sky for prey.

William and his co-pilot, Henry, assessed the dangers around them. When was the best time to take evasive action, and in which direction: when a searchlight lost its fix, the sighting of an approaching night fighter, the glimpse of a nearby bomber that obstructed an intended manoeuvre? All the alternatives were to be weighed as concentrated flak burst around them, and tracer bullet trails revealed the presence of a Dornier or Messerschmitt searching out its prey. It was as if the whole of the German defences had focused their rage against them. William needed to fly by instinct, and he reacted as soon as his senses allowed. He threw his aircraft into a corkscrew to the right. It was his only defence, as there was no cloud cover to help him. Further back in the plane, the crew knew what to expect, but even so, the ferocity of the centrifugal forces took their breath away. Those in the body of the aircraft had no reference to the sky, the horizon, or the ground beneath. They were in a tumbling metal box. It felt as if an unseen opponent had grabbed their harness and was trying to tear them away from the metal frame to which they were secured. A scream of terror would not have been out of place; if only their lungs weren't close to collapse. As quickly as they were thrown away from the airframe, they were thrust in the other direction, hard against the fuselage. The sides of the plane, its instruments, its chairs, navigator's table, although tied down, took on minds of their own and maliciously attacked those strapped adjacent to them. One moment, the airmen's body weight was intolerable, only for the sensation to change to that of weightlessness.

At the apex of the corkscrew, the plane righted itself. Gravity aligned in a familiar way. The usual 'up' was up, and down was where they placed their feet, and the befuddled airmen were relieved of the urgent need for the contents of their stomach to be evacuated. But it would be a momentary respite. It happened again, only in the opposite direction. The first attempt to loosen the grip of the searchlights had failed. William corkscrewed down and to the left. The forces on the aircraft came in all directions as the manoeuvre was carried out. The turn was accompanied by a steep dive, followed by a sharp climb and a turn in the opposite direction. The airmen placed their faith in their pilot to get them out of the 'cone'. They hung on for their lives.

William could not loosen the grip of the searchlights. He corkscrewed twice more. On one occasion, he thought he had found a haven of a dark sky only to be coned again. There had been no option but to throw his aircraft around the best he could. And still the searchlights followed him, as did the guns rained against him. His arms ached and he wasn't sure where in the sky they might be.

The physical effort required to make the course changes needed both the pilots to coordinate their control of the aircraft. Each pilot's stations had a control column, 'the stick', surmounted with a control wheel. The 'corkscrew' manoeuvre had been rehearsed many times in training. Their actions when using the stick were choreographed to ensure the pilots acted in unison and there wasn't the need for complex instruction from the pilot. William would look across to Henry, who was prepared for the command, and William would shout 'Now'. They would push the stick forward, pitching the aircraft downwards and at the same time turn the wheel to roll the aircraft, right or left. At the bottom of the descent, they'd pull back the stick and level off. This they did, at the bottom of their fourth corkscrew,

They had lost the night fighters, but they remained illuminated as if the sun had risen on them.

'What shall we do now, Bill?' asked Henry.

'We've no choice but to carry on doing what we're doing.'

'But will the kite take more of this?'

'We'll soon find out.'

'An enemy fighter!' shouted Alex over the intercom

'He's below and to our left.' Alex let off a burst of fire, as did the fighter.

The fighter's cannon shells traced a slanted path ahead of them before puncturing the fuselage. It had been an opportunistic burst of fire, as the pilot hadn't correctly aligned his aircraft for the kill.

Bill and Henry both pushed on the yolk without the need to communicate. The decision to corkscrew again was made for them by the pilot of a Dornier 128.

The dark of night washed upon them as if someone had doused the light on a wild party that had got out of control. The searchlights had lost them. Perhaps the night fighters had found easier prey?

After several minutes of weaving left and right and adjustments to gain height, William felt confident enough to speak to the crew on his intercom. He tried hard to sound controlled, and he made light of the deadly circumstances they had found themselves.

'We seem to have finished our helter-skelter ride. From here on in it should be a cakewalk. Confirm you are unhurt and the aircraft is sound.'

The crew, in turn, acknowledged they were safe and that the equipment they were responsible for remained functional.

'Shame, I was enjoying the ride, Skipper,' said Tom, whilst at the same time rubbing a bash he'd taken to the head. 'There's some shell damage here but nothing serious, and I'm happy to report both navigator and flight engineer are safe and sound.'

'I'm okay, and there's no damage,' said Alex

Larry groaned and then came on the intercom.

'As usual, there's no one happier than Larry. I'm at the bomb aimer, all seems to work. No sign of damage. Although I've a hole beneath my feet, and there's a new view of the ground for anyone who cares to look.'

'I can confirm that I have a view of the night sky above my head and I'm pleased to say I still have one. The gun's fine, by the way.' said Ron.

Vince spoke, but for some reason his intercom didn't work. He put his thumb up to show otherwise he was okay.

They had been lucky. The aircraft had been coned in light for a full ten minutes. Their destruction would normally have been assured, but the mass of targets available to the defending fighters had meant only one had been patrolling their area of sky, and it had only been able to fire a single salvo at its skittering prey; it would be successful elsewhere.

The scene below them was of a destructive intensity no one aboard had seen before. Fires raged over huge areas of the ground. It was as if molten lava ran beneath. Flashes of gold and silver erupted from within it, as bombs from the attacking aircraft were swallowed into its flow and were belched up as indigestible. The sight was as fascinating as it was terrifying.

HA-G was there to do a job. It was the crew's responsibility to carry out the given task. There was a good reason for their mission; they had been told so by their superiors, and how they had longed to strike a massive blow against the enemy. From what William could see, little of the city would remain of use, after the thousand bombers had sown their deadly seed. And as for those who lived within the buildings already in flames...? Now was not the time to think of that... even so, William found it hard to keep at bay the thought of those souls who would perish within the inferno.

Larry had taken control of the flightpath of the plane and directed his Skipper; though the target was plain to see,

'Left, left... now straighten... left again... straighten, maintain height and flightpath... ten seconds or so... Bombs away!'

They turned and headed for home knowing the night's terrors were not yet over, as they were again to run the gauntlet of the fighters.

And yet... they knew the terrors they now faced were nothing compared to the terror of those they were leaving behind, in the flames.

***

Back in Downham Market, the success of the raid was played up, and the hardships, injuries and losses to the squadron were left to speak of at another time. For all those on-board HA-G that night, the experience had been terrifying. Being coned for even the shortest of time meant the chances of survival were slim. But it was by chance they had survived. Perhaps it was poor visibility at the ground level where the ack-ack batteries were stationed, or the disengagement of the attacking fighter due to a lack of fuel, or its destruction from accurate fire from an adjacent bomber's tail gunner, or maybe it was the confusion created by the massed bomber formation? For all, or none of those reasons, they had survived. Some might say it was fate; it was not the airmen's time to die... In any case, on their return, and for the rest of their war, William and his crew were known to be calm and competent under fire. Over and above, they benefitted from more than their fair share of luck; a prized possession.

Selwyn Berryman-Morgan

33

One More Time

'You know my orders Bill. Having done thirty operational flights, my New Zealand Command has ordered an end to my tour of duty. I'm sorry to say, I'll not be on your next mission.'

'They're sticking by the rules, Alex... We'll miss you, but thirty missions are enough for any airman. Adding a further mission, as the RAF has done to us, is 'taking the piss', as you Colonials would say.'

They laughed, knowing that during their time together, unusual phrases from the vocabulary of the allied nations had been adopted by them all, as and when it better explained their joint predicament.

Alex had other ideas about it.

'My lot likes to take the piss as much as yours and I'm sure they don't give a damn for the rules? They've just found a better way to torment me.' William was forced to concede the point.

'Who knows what they'll get us to do next? I hope they'll not extend our tour of duty too far.' Then he brightened and returned to Alex's news.

'I hear you've gained your commission, Alex?' Alex nodded, and replied,

'It's about bloody time! Two tours of active duty, and what is soon to be a second tour as 'Air Gunnery Trainer', seems to have twisted their arm. But I'll not complain. A bit more cash in the bank for when this nonsense is over won't go amiss. This way, I'll get three months of it, no matter what.'

'Before you leave, we'll have a photograph done with Frank. He's to take your place on board. It will be the rear gunners of HA-G. We'll be the three musketeers.'

'Well, two musketeers, and one d'Artagnan.'

William wasn't sure what was meant by that? But anyway, they all laughed; it must have been the thought of themselves in wide-brimmed hats sporting a feather.

Francis Medhurst (?)   William McCarthy   Alexander Rowe

34

The 31st Mission.

'We've to welcome aboard Francis Medhurst. He tells me he's from 'Sussex by the Sea'. You've all had a chance to meet him and I am sure he'll fit in well.' The rest of the crew of HA-G joined in over the intercom, the welcomes piling on top of one another.

'Nice to have you onboard,'

'You'll have fun, Frank'

'This mission's a breeze, Frank.

'It beats a trip on Brighton's electric railway, hands down.'

The welcoming responses were reduced to an indistinct wall of sound, but there was agreement, Francis, was to be known as Frank.

***

Kassel, in the heart of Germany, was no easy ride.

The take-off was routine. 10:30 at night into a darkened sky.

Early in the flight, William was faced with a problem. An engine wasn't running smoothly. He could feel the vibrations it set up and couldn't balance it out by adjusting the throttles on the other three engines. The aircraft wasn't on-song.

William had to make a decision. The crew wasn't aware of the problem, and if he decided to carry on, in the hope the engine would right itself, they would be none the wiser; unless, of course, it finally gave out. Alternatively, he could tell them his concern, and that would cause them to worry for the rest of the flight, probably for no good reason. His third option was to abort the flight.

To abort wouldn't look good. His reason to abort, although justified, wasn't obvious enough to avoid doubt being cast in the minds of his superiors. The engines ran and provided enough power for the flight, and there were no other tell-tale signs: no loss of oil or black exhaust fumes that would indicate engine trouble. The engine just felt wrong, and given the circumstances, his commanding officers would assume that the easy option had been taken, rather than press on and complete the mission; the 31st mission they had imposed, one more than the usual tour of duty. William decided to press on and not tell the crew of his concerns.

The run into Kassel went as expected, with increasing flak, and an occasional sighting of a night fighter briefly picked out by the defenders' searchlights. The level of fear was nothing new for all but one of the crew. Over the intercom, Ron took the time to reassure Frank.

'This flak is nothing unusual, Frank, and Bill's weaving about is keeping the ground batteries guessing where we are in the sky.'

Just as he spoke, above and behind them, a bomber pitched out of the sky ablaze, and fatally damaged, having either been hit by flak or strafed by a 109. Then, a nearby shell explosion filled William's aircraft with a thunderous noise and a flash of light. Ron was again there to reassure Frank.

'Worry not, Frank, that one was nowhere near. They've not a clue where we are and are firing blind.' William came on the intercom,

'Keep the chatter down lads.'

Frank would need to learn from experience.

In order that the bomb load would fall as accurately as possible, the bomb run into the target was straight and true. Larry was in control of their flightpath, and would only be ignored by the pilot should the Sterling be attacked by a night fighter. Larry was glad to announce,

'Bombs away, Skipper!'

The ordinance on board, incendiaries and 500-pound bombs, were delivered into the flames that covered the ground below.

William breathed a sigh of relief. On a previous mission, he had to repeatedly fly over their target to ensure the bombs hit home. Each of the return runs attracting yet more attention from the ground defences and the predatory fighters. They had survived, but it was another occasion when, on landing, it was found the fuselage of the plane was riddled with flak and cannon shell holes. The 'Lucky Crew' had ridden their luck again, and, apart from minor injuries, had returned unharmed. Tonight, there wouldn't be the need for such heroics. They would turn straight back.

Down the intercom, William shouted,

'Let's get the hell out!'

No one answered back to suggest they should stay a while longer to admire their handiwork. They had long since had enough of playing 'merry-go-round' over cities in the Ruhr.

William pulled his aircraft up and turned away towards the proscribed route home, finally settling on a course given to him by his navigator, Thomas.

Ten minutes into the return flight, William spoke to his co-pilot.

'Usual drill, Henry, we'll maintain maximum height and zigzag along our flightpath. Make course corrections every five minutes. Inform Tom of our intention and have him update us on our course corrections.'

Henry would have a lot on his plate keeping them on a true path. On every mission, there was hardly a time when he had a moment for his own thoughts, and this mission was no different.

Now they were on their way home there was a light relief in the voices of those on board. Ron Bird was the first to speak up.

'Half a pint of beer would hit the spot right now.'

'What's wrong with a pint', replied Vince, the wireless operator who was now at his alternate position of front gunner.

'I'd spill too much because of my shakes. My life has been too exciting of late.'

William stepped in to quieten them both.

'Enough chatter, lads. I've a plane to worry about flying.'

There was no apology needed, their silence was sufficient, and there was enough for William to worry about.

Harry Foreshore had been monitoring the labouring engine. William had asked he keep an eye on it. At first, he wasn't able to confirm any obvious problem, but now, on the return journey, he was sure it was in trouble.

Harry spoke to William.

'Skipper, the left outer is slowly losing power.'

'I was afraid of that. If I keep its current speed, do you think it will give out on us?'

'It shows signs that it might. It's clearly overheating, so there's something up with it. I suggest you throttle back on it and I'll report back to you how it behaves.'

William confirmed his intention to preserve the engine.

'Throttling back engine one.' He then spoke to the crew.

'Listen up, chaps. We no longer have the ability to maintain our maximum altitude and our airspeed is somewhat reduced. It's nothing that hasn't happened to us before but we must keep our eyes peeled. There'll be no more talk other than that required to complete this mission.'

The new crew member, Frank had said nothing for the entire flight and he certainly wasn't going to start now.

The accompanying bombers drifted by and were away into the distance. It was only the clear night sky and its bright moon kept HA-G company.

They flew on, William nursing one engine so it would continue to play a part in the safe return of the plane. His efforts were paying off.

Ahead, in the middle distance, was the shimmer of the English Channel, and beyond, in darkness, the promise of safety.

William couldn't help but focus on the ribbon of reflected light from the breaking of the waves on the shore of the Dutch coastline. It was the last in a series of imagined hurdles. Once it was vaulted, it would end in another successful mission. He let his mind wander. It was a familiar memory...

William gazed through the small sash window down into the backyard, with its wash-room, coal store and outside toilet; all of which was shared with their neighbour, 'Gran Evans'. His life had once been centred on this terraced house; one of a dozen identical houses that stepped up the hill from the river Taff to Treforest station, and on arriving home on leave, the houses had looked grim, set in a grey, misty drizzle. It was hard for 'Bill' to come back again, even with Joyce at his side, in bed, warm and willing.

From out of nowhere, and with no apparent forethought, William said,

'Joyce. What would you think if I volunteered to join the Air Force and trained to be a pilot?'

Joyce had nestled in the crook of William's arm, close to sleep, lost in that joyous halfway place between climaxed passion and quiet contentment, but being called 'Joyce' had jarred her back to the reality of war-weary Wales. The 'make-believe' spell had been broken. To be called 'Joyce', not 'Joy', was time to be serious. In an attempt to retain the warmth of the afternoon spent in his embrace, she replied, but with a pretence of sleepiness.

'What's that, my love?'

'Should I train to be a pilot?'

'Hmm... Can't think... My brain is not connected to what's happening in the real world... What are you saying, Bill?'

'Oh... I don't know... It's just I am bored with the waiting to get stuck in...and at the same time, scared of what it might mean. You know I don't want to be too far from you and what we have together, but I must be posted soon. North Africa, or the Dominions, perhaps... I know I don't want to go to the Far East... we have to guard against the Japanese, too, and by all accounts, they are evil bastards. Even if we invade France, I don't want to be in a trench, up to my neck in mud, like our dads were.'

'Don't worry about the future, Bill. It's not ours to control. Just stay here, with me. Let's pretend we are in our own home, there's no war, no end to your leave, just our time to spend as we want 'She rolled closer to him, pressing her body to his so he could feel again her need for him, her submission to him. She wanted him back under her spell and knew how to make it happen.

'Come, make love to me again.

Flying above the Dutch countryside, he imagined Joy's warm breath on his face, her urgent kiss, wet with intimate intent, her soft hand enfolding his willingness to submit to her. There, in the confines of the cockpit of his aircraft, it was as if she was in touching distance.

500 feet below HA-G and to its left, a German night fighter positioned itself in readiness to attack. The pilot was Oberleutnant, Ludwig Becker.

Becker had been a Luftwaffe pilot in the Spanish Civil war, where he flew a Junker 88, the 'Stuka', in support of General Franco. Later he became a test pilot, flying the Messerschmitt BF110 during its initial trials; very nearly losing his life in the process, having crash-landed. But it was as a night fighter pilot he was to achieve his fame.

Above him, set in the clear aspic of a moon-beamed sky, was his prey. Ludwig had already seventeen 'kills' to his name. He was intent on adding another.

He was flying a version of the same plane, the BF110, as he flew in his days as a test pilot, but this plane bristled with upgraded nose cannon, onboard radar and a forward looking, infrared sensor. Josef Straub, his navigator, flew with him to direct Ludwig's approach onto their prey. The ground radar communications had brought them within striking distance, but on such a clear night, the infrared sensor was not needed, the target could easily be seen.

How the game of cat and mouse ended, would depend on whether or not the bomber's tail gunner saw them as they approached.

35

'Joy Ride This Ain't'

Molesworth Airbase Cambridgeshire, England. 26th February 1943

Walter Cronkite struggled to put on his flying gear. Alongside him were other war correspondents, tugging at their thermal boots or grappling with flying suits. They had all been a given crash course in the minimum skills required of an airman in the US Air Force. The group had been familiarised with the Aircraft in which they were to be flown. It was just enough to ensure they'd be no hindrance to those who had to carry out today's bombing raid. For the first time, American journalists were to be allowed on active flying missions.

The correspondents were assigned to various squadrons flying from Molesworth that morning. Cronkite, of United Press, was to fly with the 427th Squadron of B-17 Flying Fortresses, as was Homer Bigart of the New York Herald Tribune. Other journalists were to fly in B-24 Liberators. They had trained with the American Air Force for a week, learning relevant safety skills, such as the use of oxygen masks for high-altitude flying, the use of the parachute, should they need it, and survival procedures and techniques should they find themselves ditched in the sea.

The Allies had decided on a coordinated Air Offensive against Germany. The RAF was to continue night raids, using the skills they'd honed over the preceding years; that of accurately finding and hitting targets in minimal light conditions. The US would take over by day, doing the same; both air forces would find and destroy the military and industrial infrastructure supporting the Nazi regime.

The RAF had used a variety of aircraft to do the job, but by the beginning of 1943, the older heavy bombers, such as the Wellington,

Halifax and Stirling had been reassigned to less demanding roles, their job done. They had been the first of the 'heavies' to take the war to the enemy, but now, the new Lancaster bombers were the main British strike force. The Lancaster was durable in operation when under attack, and it was also able to carry a large bomb load the distance required to reach all parts of Germany.

The Americans used the Flying Fortresses and Liberators. These aircraft also had the ability to carry a large bomb payload, but, additionally, they had formidable defensive capabilities better suited their role in daytime operations. The B-17 and B-24 bristled with machine guns spaced along their fuselage: at the nose and tail, a dorsal turret, a ventral ball turret and two' waist' guns, placed centrally, either side of the fuselage. Flying on their own they would be difficult to attack even by the most capable German fighter, but when flown in formation the defensive shield was formidable. Each aircraft covered the other. With strong defences, being able to see your enemy coming was a distinct advantage. At any moment, a thousand pair of eyes would scan the daytime skies for sight of an enemy attack. And if a single bomber was attacked, machine-gun fire would pour down in defence from aircraft nearby. Luftwaffe pilots likened this defence to a 'flying porcupine', '*fliegendes stachelschwein*'.

Even when damaged, the Fortresses kept flying. Stories would abound of aircrew getting back home on one engine or with most of the tailfin missing. It had been estimated, the B-17, for example, would have to take on average, more than 20 hits from cannon shell before being mortally damaged. That hit rate was rarely achieved, given the hectic speed the Luftwaffe fighter pilot was forced to employ when attacking a US bomber formation. The B-17 and B-24s were hard to bring down.

***

The estimated total flight time was to be around 5 hours to the Focke-Wulf aircraft factory in Bremen, when Walter Cronkite, boarded the aircraft named *'S for Sugar'*.

The rest of the crew was already aboard. Sergeant Edward Harmon, the tail gunner, had already climbed into his turret, where he would remain isolated for the rest of the trip. The waist gunners Staff Sergeant Durward Hines and Sergeant James Pennington were harnessing themselves to the fuselage, adjacent to the guns they would man for the duration of the trip. Ahead of them were: the flight engineer, Charles Zipfel, who was surrounded by his instruments and telemetry, the Navigator, Walter Soha, at his desk of maps and compasses, the Radio Operator, Clarence Coomes, and dangling from the top machine gun turret were the protruding legs of Sergeant George Henderson. The bottom ventral ball turret was manned by Howard (Howie) Belk. He stood ready to squeeze himself into the lower ball turret. Forward of the group were the Pilot, Captain Glen Haugenbach and his Co-pilot Lieutenant John Barker. Yet further forward and below the pilots was the Bombardier/nose gunner, Albert Dieffenbach. Eleven crew in all, plus Walter.

'Hey Walt, welcome aboard. Have you come to see what *real* war is about?' said George, always the joker. And then with a meaningful jibe. Durward chipped in.

'Be sure to keep your head low and your ass firmly in your seat.' He was good-natured enough, but he really didn't want this intrusion;

'*Some Tom Fool of a reporter careering through the cabin when things are getting hot,*' was a sentiment he had expressed on hearing who it was flying with them.

Walter replied in a relaxed and easy way.

'Don't Worry. My ass will be stuck to that seat with US Air Force issue Araldite.' Although there was probably no such adhesive issued from air force supplies, the urge Walter had to cooperate was understood, and there was a roar of laughter from the crew. Even so, they hadn't finished pressing the point...

'Make sure it's double strength, Walt... Fritz is no Prince Charming.'

Walter was used to passing references to his Disney namesake, unintended or not. He waited for someone to pick up on it. This time, a laugh at the first of the jokes was sufficient, as everyone was too busy readying themselves. Mercifully, they decided to let him be. There would be time enough to make him squirm, even before the shit hit the fan.

Moving forward in the plane, Walter took his position in the jump seat and donned his headphones, as he had been trained to do.

'Nice you could make it Walter,' said Captain Haugenbach over the intercom, having picked up on the banter.

'Wild horses, and all that...' replied Walter, who continued,

'But seriously, this means a great deal to me, a chance to support you guys and perhaps make a difference back home.'

'They've no idea, Walt.'

'That's where I come in. I want to tell the whole story of what you do, day in day out. No 'Newsreel' crap.

There was a moment's silence. Walter knew he had already said too much. He admonished himself. *Keep it simple you fool!*

'Nice speech,' came a reply, and Walter knew he was right.

His actions would have to speak for him. In a war situation, it was what you did that mattered. Words came cheap.

Captain Haugenbach was to break the tension.

'Even so, you're welcome... You met Jacob who sits up beside me at the briefing yesterday. Up and across from you is Otis. It's his job to get us there by the shortest route, and, if he can, get us back quicker'. Walter looked forward, along the fuselage, he and Otis exchanged greetings.

'Hi, Otis.'

Otis touched the tip of his flying cap in a mock salute.

Haugenbach had misgivings about the idea of letting civilians on his war machine and into his war. The crew held Haugenbach in great respect. They had confidence in his leadership and his decision-making when the theory of war became a reality, and they were under fire, cannon raked, and flak infested. Walter was someone new; he wasn't surface hardened, with a core tempered and toughened by battle.

Haugenbach didn't want his crew to feel his attention was not entirely focused on his plane and his crew. Cronkite needed to know who was boss and now was the best time, before the shit started. The polite talk needed to stop.

'OK Walt, strap yourself in, we're on our way. We need you to sit tight and to jump to it when any instruction is given. Above all, be prepared to be scared. Keep any questions you have until we get back, and remember, do nothing that will interfere with the duties of my crew,' and then added, as if to himself, 'Joy ride this ain't.'

Walter was there to observe. His job on his return was to report what he saw and what he experienced. There would be no problem remembering.

Haugenbach prepared for takeoff.

After checking the mechanical controls essential to the aircraft's flying capabilities, Haugenbach coaxed the aircraft's four radial engines into life. Each, in turn, belched and coughed protests of black smoke, as the fuel in the radial-mounted cylinders failed to properly ignite. They would continue to complain until the engine fired. Immediately the stuttering, bellicose rotations of the propellers changed to a blur of unharnessed energy as the idling speed of each engine was maintained. The Flight Engineer checked the performance of each unit in turn. Its oil pressure and its fuel consumption, and he applied his 'engineer's ear' to how it sounded. Turning to his Captain, Charlie gave the 'thumbs up,' and confirmed through his intercom,

'The engines think it's the fourth of July and they are playing a Sousa march you could hum along with. They're ready to go Captain.'

The other aircraft in the flight were throttled up and were ready to taxi to the runway and to take off. If it were not for their ear protection, the noise from the aircraft engines would have been deafening for the ground crews assigned to release the bombers.

Haugenbach's plane moved slowly into line behind the B-17 of Major Romig, *The '8' Ball.'*... There was a moment's pause, before Romig moved from the apron of the runway to the take-off position. On instruction from ground control, he pushed forward the throttles of the engines. Walter Cronkite noted how the decibel level rose even higher as Romig swept by. The plane accelerated towards the end of the runway and up into the wide expanse of an unusually calm, Cambridgeshire, sky. *The '8' Ball* had lifted into the cool mid-morning air. It was not yet a content flying machine, at one with its surroundings, but with increasing height and speed, it would soon be comfortable, flying at a cruising speed of over 200 miles an hour and an altitude of 25,000 feet. The monster would be responsive to small adjustments of height and direction, and compliant to each request the pilot would make of it.

As if in anticipation of the task ahead of it, *S for Sugar* trembled whilst awaiting its take off run. The engines had been set at idle, but were now given full throttle. This transmitted a high amplitude shake throughout the fuselage. Its nose dipped, as its engines strained against the wheel brakes.

Haugenbach released the brakes and their journey had begun. The roar of the engines increased to a scream, as full throttle was maintained, and the plane shook violently from the impact vibrations of the wheels on the uneven runway. Walter wondered if there was enough runway left to get airborne, but soon the nose of the aircraft rose to the sky. The scream of noise soon reduced to a blissful roar, and when cruising altitude was reached, the noise was a whisper of what had come before... The B-17 was in its element.

The Fortress merged into formation with the rest of the force. Howard Belk was now free to install himself in the ventral ball-turret. He had long since been instructed, after some particularly gruesome accidents, that it was too risky for the ball-turret gunner to take up position during take-off. The hydraulically operated 'Perry Ball-Turret' was a closed unit when its operator was inside manning the guns. If the undercarriage was to fail there was no quick way out, and the gunner would be smeared along the belly of the fuselage as it scraped along the ground. To get into position, Howard opened its top hatch, and his feet searched for the stirrups of the internal harness. Howard shouted to everyone, in hearing distance or not,

'See y'all when we're done... and don't start the party without me.'

Howard's invitation to 'party' was given on all of his operational flights, his pronouncement being a verbal talisman, his affirmation they would all get back in one piece and continue living for the day.

He lowered himself into the turret and closed the hatch behind him. The transparent bowl would be home for the next five hours. There he would stay, curled into a foetal position inside a Perspex bubble, gazing out into the surrounding sky, swaying with the motion of the aircraft, with nothing but passing cloud between his suspended existence and the ground below. His job was cold, lonely, and dangerous. Only on the plane's return, and just before landing, would he re-appear as if by caesarean section, his job done. Howard would often say, when down in the village pub and slightly 'over-emotional',

'On our trips to pay Gerry our respects I'm just like a baby in my Mama's belly'. Any listener, who hadn't heard the story before, would find it hard to understand what he was going on about and would decide Howie was more than a bit mad. Howard, no doubt, would have agreed.

Walter gazed out into the surrounding sky; its bright blue was tinged green by the age-yellowed window. Distances were difficult to establish. The sky blended with the North Sea, and from his position on the plane, there was yet no glimpse of occupied Europe.

They had formed up behind their lead plane 'The Eight Ball.' At least, the sky wasn't empty. Then Walter saw the converging of other squadrons at the predetermined assembly point. There were other B-17s but also 'Liberators', Constellation B-24s. The Liberators were an awesome sight in the clear sunlit sky. Their box-shaped fuselage and twin tailfins distinguished them from the B-17s. They were bigger and faster, and carried a greater bomb load, but they were not the favoured aircraft of the majority of US aircrews. They were judged to be more difficult to fly and less durable than the B-17s. A 'belly landing,' not a good idea at any time, was never to be recommended in the Liberator, as the wings were set high in the fuselage. This meant the plane's box-like structure was less rigid than it might otherwise have been. Walter knew little of these problems, he was in awe at the might and muscle of the giant aircraft, the wonders of its construction, and, most of all, its beauty. The aircraft's shortcomings, he'd leave for others to debate.

Walter marvelled at the strength of the attacking force. They were a mass of men and machine, filling the sky and dominating the surrounding airspace with their defensive capabilities. He could make out the painted motifs of many of the adjacent aircraft; most from his own, adopted, squadron. At their cruising height, the bright sunlight reflected off their fuselage and lit the high cloud surrounding them in a halo of spectral colour. It was as if the aircraft were protected by a spiritual presence, and it confirmed, and condoned, their mission. Whatever came from it, the outcome would be for the benefit of everyone, friend or foe. Walter pulled himself together, and fought against this emotion of self-justification for the havoc and destruction they were about to deliver on the German population; military or civilian. He was there to report the processes and procedures of doing so, the bravery of the airmen involved, and the outcome, as best he could judge. The reading public would make their own conclusions as to the 'rightness' of the day's events, applying their own spiritual and political spin. Walter would, however, be sure not to criticise the mission or the brave men involved in it. If there were to be criticism, then it would be best left until after the war was won and the vanquished re-assimilated. To criticise now, would only offer encouragement to the enemy they were pitted against.

Close by, and to the left, was a converging B-24. It had as a passenger, Walter's fellow correspondent, Robert Post of the New York Times. Its pilot glanced across and waved, acknowledging their presence, as if to confirm they had all made it safely thus far. There were 500 aircraft flying against Germany. Walter was reassured.

It was against this formidable force the night fighter ace, Ludwig Becker, and his radar operator, Josef Staub, was ordered to attack.

Selwyn Berryman-Morgan

36

Ludwig's Last Throw

Oberleutnant Ludwig Becker had taken off in his night fighter from the Luftwaffe airbase at Leeuwarden in Holland. He was to attack the massed US bomber formations headed towards his homeland. He flew according to his instincts, honed by adherence to procedures and tactics he had evolved when achieving his forty 'kills'. His instincts were tuned to his night time prey.

Over the years they had flown together, they had perfected their lethal game of pinning a flaming tail on a surprised, plodding donkey: the easy targets of a laggard Halifax, or a crippled Lancaster flying on three engines. Becker was hindered by the blindfold of night, and the first directions given to him would have been from the vectors from the ground radar. They would give an approximate location. Commands transmitted by his ground radar control were translated by Staub into course adjustments to the fighter's height and orientation. Staub would then seek the bombers out in the dark sky, using an infrared scanner, and when within 500 metres, the onboard radar was able to locate the enemy aircraft exactly.

'Four hundred meters ahead, twenty degrees to the right, one hundred meters high, Oberleutnant.'

They would manoeuvre to bring the target closer, Staub providing the fine adjustments needed to provide his pilot with visual contact of the prey. The approach was always from below and behind. The endgame was Becker's to conclude. As long as he kept his prey in sight, he could position himself perfectly for the kill. A bank of cloud could yet save the bomber or perhaps, if the night fighter was spotted by the tail gunner, their captain could perform an abrupt course change and disappear into the night sky. But once Becker had 'locked on' the result was usually the same. He would shadow fifty metres beneath the bomber and would fire his cannon as he raised his aircraft's nose. The bomber's flightpath would take it cross the fighter's line of fire and be raked by shell. If possible, Becker would direct the cannon to where the bomber's wings met the body of the plane; a plane minus a wing was transformed into a mass of metal in free fall. Even if the wings remained attached, the trajectory of the cannon shell would probably sever the fuel supply and the hydraulic pipes used in the control of the aircraft, before travelling on to the cockpit, and to the pilots of the plane. The crew of the stricken bomber would probably never see their enemy. The first they would know was the flash of flaming projectiles accompanied by the explosion of broken airframe. The monotonous drone of the engines would be instantly drowned by a hissing, whizzing, metal ringing cacophony of sound. Any thought of home, of comfort, of safety, the bomber crew may have allowed themselves to imagine, would be replaced by the terror engendered by the enemy's attack. It would be an attack of immense brutality, of ear-splitting, flesh tearing reality. For many aircraftmen, the war would end in an instant. Some would escape the aircraft and parachute to land and almost certain imprisonment, or into the sea where they would probably face their death from exposure and hypothermia. Others would remain with the craft until the ground came to meet it, or the sea engulfed and entombed them.

At night, it was easy to 'kill', but now Becker had been commanded to fly by day against an enemy who could see him as easily as he could see them, and there would be many gunners who would have him in their sights.

Ludwig Becker's Commanding Officer, his friend and fellow Pilot Ace, Helmut Lent, had spoken to him before the attack on the American bombers.

'I know this is not your type of war, Ludwig, but we are commanded by the Führer to throw all our available aircraft at these American Fortresses. They continue to devastate our homeland, and with it our ability to continue the war. You will fly against them today.'

Their eyes met. The likely consequence of this request was clear to both of them... At a time such as this, there was more to be said. Ludwig was first to speak.

'We have flown with each other for many years and we can speak honestly, without fear... We both know the war is lost. The men and machines sacrificed on the Russian Front have ensured we will not be able to end this war on our terms. The Americans will overwhelm us, and our attempts to shoot them out of the sky will come to nothing.' Helmut Lent replied,

'Our duty is clear, Ludwig. Our opinions regarding the conduct of the war are not relevant.' Helmut took one step back and stood erect. He continued,

'Oberleutnant, Ludwig Becker... you have been promoted to the rank of "Hauptmann", and it is further my privilege to inform you that the Führer has seen fit to award you the "Knights Cross, with Oak Leaves". You know it is an award given to very few, and it is in recognition of your valour and your devotion to the Fatherland.'

There was no more to be said. They shook hands, and Helmut then raised an arm in salute. Ludwig returned the salute and as one they proclaimed, 'Heil Hitler'.

Selwyn Berryman-Morgan

37

To Meet Once More

Orders came for the American bomber force to change course onto the secondary target for the mission, the submarine pens at Wilhelmshaven. The weather conditions over their primary target had deteriorated.

The transmitted instructions had been encrypted using a predetermined code, and Walter Soha, calculated the new bearings and relayed them to his captain who responded immediately; as did all the other captains in the task force. They turned towards the new target.

The Captain spoke to his crew.

'Waist gunners, keep your eyes peeled as we change course. I don't want any aircraft within 100 yards of us until we are on course. Top gunner, tail gunner and ball-turret, do the same, and keep your eyes peeled for Jerry. They'll have a go at us if they get the chance.'

'Yes Captain,' the gunners answered, almost in unison. They knew their job, and were already on the case.

Each aircraft in the flight took care to maintain altitude, and to keep close contact with one another. Their best defence was still their massed formation.

The aircraft turned gently to their left, as each pilot established their new north-easterly course to the Baltic coast.

From out of the sun, pounced the Messerschmitt 109s. The top gunner, George Henderson, was first to see him.

'Gerry's above right!'

The waist gunners adjusted their firing positions and strained to fix the target. The ME-109s dove through the massed bombers. The slightly detached planes were the main targets for the fighter pilots.

In the seconds it took for the fighters to pass through the formation, their cannon had scored a kill and severely damaged one other B-24.

The German fighter planes were now most vulnerable.

The American gunners were waiting for the screaming, fire-spitting 109s to pass into their sights, when they would fire a continuous burst from their guns. Every second of time the fighters were in view of the gunners was a precious gift; once a fighter was first seen, it was a few seconds, at most, before they were out of range. The gunners would try to sweep their guns from the 109s cockpit to its tail fin; it was as if they were on a turkey shoot, the prey being driven for the sport of the US Air Force.

Two of the marauding 109s were hit and sped off, fate unknown, both spewing black smoke from crippled engines. Another lost a wing and spun to earth like a fiery maple seed. The others raced away to muster in the clouds and return to battle, the second time from in front and beneath the speeding bombers, like porpoise attacking the belly of a whale. The German planes continued to attack until they had no ammunition, or were short of fuel, or they were shot from the sky.

It was during the second such battle when, once again, the rear gunner, Edward Harmon saw an approaching enemy aircraft. It was a twin-engine plane, coming from beneath; an unexpected angle of attack by an unusual plane.

'What the...' he shouted down his intercom. Then remembering he needed to warn the rest of the crew of an approaching aircraft, he announced its type and its position in the sky.

'Jerry "110" at 7 O'clock... 200 meters below... I've got him skipper; this will be like shooting ducks at the fairground.'

Even before Edward opened up, other gunners in the formation had seen the fighter and had already engaged it with their guns. If the pilot of the enemy aircraft thought there was a possibility of surprise in his choice of manoeuvre, he was mistaken. Tracer shells rained down onto the target from multiple directions. The fighter flew on past Edward, leaving Howard, the ball-turret gunner, to continue the defensive fire. He let go a final burst and Howard was to confirm the kill.

'Got the bastard. He won't be going home for sauerkraut this evening.'

A cheer rang through the Aircraft. The captain spoke over the intercom,

'Let's just agree he's dead. Keep our eyes peeled, there's more out there for you to take pot-shots at.'

Back at the airbase, no one could truly lay claim to the kill, and there were dissenting voices from crew members of adjacent aircraft

'I think that one was mine…'

'No chance, I peppered his ass good…'

'I got him… He was dead before you guys finished your sarsaparilla.'

What they all agreed on, was how they all revelled in the spectacle of the plane exploding in mid-air, and the way its skin peeled away from the fuselage.

At the time, one gunner had said,

'He cooked like a flambéed banana,' as the skeletal fuselage arced towards the coast shrouded in a flame that trailed smoke in its wake.

Becker's Messerschmitt Bf 110, and its cremated contents, was delivered towards the icy waters of the North Sea. There was no graveside gun salute, no eulogy, and no appeal to God to 'accept unto Him'. There was only the hurtling mass of metal and flames that instantly extinguished when plunged into the ice-cold sea. No one was there to observe the spectacle; not even the unseeing eyes of William McCarthy, as he sat with his aircraft HA-G, and the remains of his crew. They rested on the seafloor nearby having been destroyed a year previously by their new companions.

For both crews, their dedication to their comrades, their country and its leaders, had reached the same conclusion. They had sacrificed their own existence in exchange for a better future for their own citizens, and for their country brought to its knees by war.

***

The American bomber force flew on. It was almost unscathed given the ferocity and determination of its adversaries.

In a flight of B-24, adjacent to Haugenbach's squadron, ball gunner Al Haroldson scanned the sky around him; they were never out of the woods on these missions. He, too, had seen the German twin-engine bomber and had witnessed the engagement from start to finish.

Poor bastard, he thought, *he doesn't know what's about to hit him.*

Haroldson was one of the first to engage the German plane. Before he did so, a narrative, half muttered, ran through his head.

'He'll disengage if he's any sense...'

The fool keeps on coming... Well then, he's going to be mine.

'Come to Papa... just keep coming...'

He fired into the fighter's flightpath, and sent a hail of machine-gun bullets at his target, firing continuously as the ME 110 ran under and across his field of vision. The other planes around him joined in the shoot but he was sure it was his final rounds that had hit home. The plane was in flames before it exploded, and he felt a surge of exhilaration knowing he had eliminated his enemy. He also knew that self-doubt and remorse would soon follow... it always did.

As they flew on, temporarily unhindered by screaming 109's, Haroldson's heart sank.

What the fuck am I doing here? he thought. *A boy from Boston... My ancestors are Swedish, for God's sake.* His rage boiled over, and he shouted out loud,

'I'm an American you fuckers! Leave me alone!'

He had always considered fighting the '*Japs*' was his duty, but flying over Germany, beating the crap out of Europeans wouldn't have been his intention when joining the war, and here he was defending the British. He had nothing to do with the British... except... except?

He knew from his grandparent's stories, there was a British sailor who married into the family, '*a great-grandfather, going back a few generations,*' but their daughter had soon enough married a Haroldson again, a case of '*Kissing Cousins*'. He was proud of his heritage, and he knew it was marriage within the immigrant community from the 'Old Country,' that kept the traditions strong.

And now, here he was, a Swedish/American, even if he had inherited a stupid English name from way back, trussed up and suspended in mid-air with the world and his wife trying to burn his ass. Being called Almond wasn't a good enough reason.

'Almond!' He shouted out loud.

'Almond, for fuck's sake.' As testimony, he continued.

'Not even a bastard child of mine will be called fucking Almond'.

Then, to his right, a B-24 blew up in a flash of orange, yellow and putrid, black smoke. The aircraft was a pile of debris in an instant, and it fell away to scatter itself across the landscape beneath. Along with it were the remains of Robert Post of the New York Times.

Selwyn Berryman-Morgan

38

My Memories of the Carnival

Rhydyfelin, South Wales, June 1964.

Evelyn had mourned the loss of her brother in the war, more so, as she and her mother, Ethel, never knew what had happened on his last flight to Germany. The only communication they had from the Air Ministry was the telegram confirming William was missing in action, and a letter confirming his death. Ethel never fully got over the death of her son, but Evelyn had carried on with her life in the way the majority of women did at the time; although she married at 27, relatively late in life. She had five children, the two eldest being girls, Paula and Ann, followed by three boys. I was the middle boy of the three, William (Billy) the eldest and Michael being the youngest of us all.

***

Billy had travelled the world as part of The Royal Air Force Gymnastic Display Team, performing at military and ceremonial events, 'flying the flag' for Britain and its interests. But, on this warm August day in 1964, the location was not far-flung, and the crowd watching the gymnasts vaulting over a raised 'horse' was not 'Royal', or behatted dignitaries. It was a village green 20 miles from the St. Athan airfield, which was the air base where the troupe trained and from where they had travelled at the request of Evelyn and her friend Maureen.

It had been when Billy was back home on leave when Evelyn had cornered him.

'Billy, what time did you get back last night?'

Billy, being the worse for wear after a night out with his Air Force pals in the pubs of Cardiff, some ten miles away, would have preferred not to be cross-examined. He answered evasively,

'Oh, about one o'clock.'

'It was after three,' said Evelyn, knowing full well the time Billy had got in as she stayed awake until he was.

'Oh... right.'

'What were you doing out until that time?'

'Went round to my mate's house in Splott, and then I thumbed my way back. It took an hour or two.'

In truth, he would have talked his way into the late-night clubs, what with him being in his dress uniform and looking older than his seventeen years; he had found the uniform would pull the girls, and it was an advantage not to miss out on. At least thumbing his way home was the truth, but Splott was probably the only district of Cardiff that would have sprung to mind under the terror of our mother's interrogation; how would anyone forget a place named Splott?

Billy was training to be an airframe fitter, but on nights out, he promoted himself to being a full-blown Pilot. He would say,

'Vulcan bombers. You know... the ones with the delta wings, shaped like a dart's flight. You can't miss um.'

Even if the girls were sceptical, his winning nature meant they mostly forgave him. They all admired his bravado, and all through his life, fortune favoured him.

He wasn't a tall man, but he was wiry, with a gymnast's slim, yet muscular physique. His full head of dark hair was cut to a length less severe than would have been seen sported by the 'Army Boys'. That, coupled with his regular, straight features, placed him firmly in the category of 'good looking'. There was a wild side to his nature, and he had a tendency to look for trouble, and it later resulted in his nose acquiring a slight kink. He would boast,

'Got it in a fight with Tom Jones outside the Clarence pub in Ponty I did... before he was famous, like.' No one believed him, but he would persist with the story.

Evelyn took his stories for what they were, stories, and she hoped he hadn't ventured anywhere near Splott; with its hard-drinking dockland pubs, and the squalor that was associated with Cardiff's 1960s red-light district. She was a mum who believed there was a natural progression in the way her children grew up; for her boys, the time when they became men was of their own choosing.

Evelyn changed the subject.

'You know that display team of yours?'

'Yes?'

'Well, we've all been watching you and your team on the telly, from when you were in Australia, and Ceinwen says she could make you out on it. She's got a big fourteen-inch telly has Ceinwen... you all looked the same on your Gran's, no bigger than snowflakes... Still, it was nice to know that one of those snowflakes flying over that horse thing was you...' She rambled a bit,

'All the way from 'down under'... I don't know how they do it?'

'They filmed it.'

'Did they? That's lovely...Well you know we're having our carnival on the field on August the, err... something?' Dates were not Evelyn's strong point.

Billy was loathe to continue with this line of questioning as he knew he was likely to be asked to be involved, but he was sat at breakfast with nowhere to escape. He responded with a caution honed by years of falling into his mother's traps.

'Err...Yes...'

Taking no notice of Bill's suspicion, she continued,

'Well, we thought you might ask your officer if you gymnasts could come and do your somersaults and things for us.'

Billy didn't reply. Evelyn carried on.

'Me and Maureen are organising it this year and we've decided who's doing the sandwiches and who's doing the blancmange, but we're trying to come up with some other ideas of what else we could do, and we thought...' Billy interrupted,

'I don't have any say about where or when we do our displays. We are told what we are doing and where we are going by the Big Wigs.'

'Still, it wouldn't hurt to ask.'

Billy, being Billy, did that.

***

Acacia Field was given to the local authority by a landowner for the building of council houses on the understanding the centre of the field was not to be built on, but, instead, left for the pleasure and amenity of the estate's residents. The street names were to be those of the trees found in the surrounding hillsides; an example tree was planted in each front garden. There were Poplars in Poplar Street, Sycamores in Sycamore Street and Acacias adorned the gardens of the remaining street that fringed the field; Sycamore Street ran along two side of the green. Over time, the impracticality of this idea became apparent. Left to grow unhindered the trees would be too big, in what was a small plot, and so the council would cut back the branches of the trees in order to stunt their growth. The trees would look like giant hat-stands. Between times of pruning, they would produce what looked like a broccoli head of leaves in a determined effort to survive; the pruning had an additional benefit of keeping the estate looking tidy. With the council also having cut the grass on the field, the estate looked at its best on the day of the carnival.

The senior officer accompanying the display team faltered in his announcement over the inadequate public address system.

'Are you sure this thing is on...? It is? Hello... Hello Ah yes...Here we go.' He continued as if his previous words and microphone tapping had not been heard.

'The Royal Air Force Gymnastic Display Team is pleased to be with you today. In between the Royal Tournaments at Earl's Court and displays at Wembley Stadium, we like to support local communities, and we are glad to be in... er...'

'Rhydyfelin,' whispered Maureen. The officer continued,

'Rhydyfelin... sharpening up our vaulting routine and thrilling you all in the process.' The crowd cheered and applauded as loudly as they could.

'A big thank you to Evelyn and Maureen and the Carnival Committee for ensuring we are all well fed and supplied with ample cups of tea... Oh! And my thanks to you all for being here today.'

'Who the bloody hell is the committee?' Whispered Maureen.

He was addressing, perhaps, a couple of hundred people from the houses around and about; to call it a crowd would be an exaggeration. Neither Evelyn nor Maureen (the 'committee') had thought to advertise the event; it was the street's carnival after all. In the ladies' defence, they had invited a reporter from the 'Pontypridd Observer' to come and watch, perhaps take a photo or two. The report, with photographs, would be published the following Saturday.

'Just think how posh the Ponty lot will think we are when they read about us.' said Maureen.

'They'll all have wished they'd been here,' chirped Evelyn, and they laughed gleefully at the cleverness of their one-up-manship. The idea of profiting from the event by placing barriers at the entrances to the field and charging a shilling or two to see the show, had never crossed their minds. After all, the display team was there for free, and the village ladies chipped in to make the sandwiches and drinks for the children and the guests.

As usual with community events in the mining valleys, the men of the village were hardly to be seen. There were some male stalwarts who would participate. One such man was Mr Grenville, who ran the village 'Jazz Marching Band'. The Band was a collection of younger children, mainly girls, dressed in a white blouse, with blue pantaloons, a matching blue dickie-bow and, to top it all, a blue pillbox hat. The costumes gave an impression hinting they were of Middle Eastern origin; pageboys, perhaps, scurrying through the lobby of a Grand Hotel in Cairo, or Istanbul? The band provided its own musical accompaniment, playing tin-plated kazoos as they marched along. The tune would have been any of one of the popular songs of the time. All it needed was for all in the band to recognise it, and it sounded good at the tempo dictated by the stick waving Majorette; an honorary role favoured and sought after, and usually reserved for the longest-serving, or prettiest, girl in the band. But, besides Mr Grenville, who had little fondness for the Working Men's Club, there were few other men who would spend much of their time supporting village events.

***

Saturday was a big day for the Working Men's club. Sport, and the illegal betting associated with it, was the focus of the member's weekend. Over the 'Tannoy', the radio broadcast horse races as they happened. In the club bar, the 'form' of the horses and their riders was mulled over and discussed before making bets. Racing tips, filtered down from the racing fraternity, would be analysed and acted upon, or discounted, based on how the tipster had previously performed. The 'Bookie's Runner' would take bets from the punters and get them placed before the start of the race.

A game of cards was always on the go. But playing cards for money on the club premises was disallowed, by diktat of the club Committee; winnings changed hands when the men left the club.

The carnival was nice for the kids, but the men agreed they weren't needed, and the women could organise without them. But today, Charles left the card table early, so he could be at the field to see his boy perform his gymnastics; he gave instructions about the placing of his horse bets whilst he was away. Charles had little enthusiasm for matters concerning the everyday running of the family. His leaving the club on a Saturday was exceptional in its consideration for others.

'Where are you off, Charlie?'

'Got to go see my boy on the field. He's in the RAF Gymnastics Display team, he is.'

'But you'll lose your place at the table,' said Ted. 'We won't keep it for you. I've lost too much for the game to stop now. Someone else will have to take your place.'

'You go right ahead Ted. I expect by the time I get back you'll have lost your shirt and there will be a space to fill.'

The men at the table laughed good-naturedly, but they, too, thought Ted's luck was out and he would soon have to give up his place. Charles knew that his buttys would get in another pint and wait for him to return.

It wasn't uncommon for the men of the village to gamble their wages away. Ted was down over five pounds, what with the run of the cards and his betting on three-legged nags he had been sure would come up the trumps he was missing from his card hand. If his luck didn't change, it would be a five-pound note less for his 'missus from his pay packet. The inevitable fight over the dinner table had already begun to play in his head.

'How do you expect me to feed the kids on six pounds ten shillings? You and your betting will have us on the streets.'

She had once said, amusing all the family,

'If it wasn't for the horses, Ted, you'd go to the dogs!'

341

Charles would have similar conversations around his own dinner table. There were always winners and losers, but 'winnings' would remain in his back pocket to fund the next opportunity to lay a bet; a bet the bookies would gladly take and almost always keep.

But today, the cards could wait. He made his way to Acacia field.

***

'Oh, you've decided to come then.'

'Evelyn, don't start.'

'You're just in time to see Billy do his routine, but you've missed his Officer making the opening speech.'

'I didn't come to listen to that silly bugger spout on.'

Our mother remained at his side and didn't go back to the conversation being had by the gaggle of dominant women who were orchestrating the proceedings. In doing so, she acknowledged the effort Charles had made; although, I am sure she felt leaving a card game didn't really amount to very much.

Seeing our father turn up, we children gathered around in an uncommon display of family unity. For the moment, at least, he was as much of a star as our Billy; never mind the effort our mother had put into the day, now Dad was our focus. Our pride was clear to see and our unity was on display, and it seemed to announce,

This is our Dad, and he's not such a bad bloke...'

We wanted to believe it, and, in his own way, maybe he wasn't so bad?

To our delight, the airmen performed the last of their tumbles at double speed, their bodies arced through the air in a blur, and thumbed a nose at our certainty that they would crash in mid-flight. The gymnasts had divided into four groups, and, starting at each corner of the field, they managed to successfully crisscross the vaulting horse one after the other. On completion of their routine, they lined up with military precision. The villagers cheered.

Bill's standing with the girls rose to that of hero; *'Biggles' is alive and well, and, for one day only, appearing on Acacia Field.*

He was soon lost in the rush of local girls wanting to know the new 'Billy', all grown up, strong and fit. He was assaulted from all sides.

'Billy, you remember me...? Janet... We danced in the youth club the night before you left for the Air Force. Billy was unsure. Then another voice called out.

'I remember you, Billy. We used to ride our bikes together down the old railway line. What do you do in the Air Force, Billy?'

'Oh, I fly Vulcan bombers; you know the ones shaped like a dart's flight.'

'Wow, Billy!'

Then, quietly, close to his ear, came another voice, a voice Bill did remember.

'I still go to the 'Dickey woods', Bill... and think of you.' Tania moved closer, her nearness could, if questioned, be put down to the crush of the others surrounding them. To help him remember, she pressed on him her intentions. Surrounded by fish aplenty, the poached dish he had tickled to catch was a remnant of a delight from the past. No matter how sweet, it had been a morsel, a starter, and for Billy it was time to move on to a main course.

He turned his attention to another. A girl who had flowered from being a gangly, self-conscious ragamuffin, always tagging along and getting in the way, to a young woman who confidently stood out from the crowd... and she knew it.

'Is that you Alice?'

'It is, Billy. Nice to see you back home again.'

'Would you like to come with me Alice, I've just seen my mum and dad. You know them, don't you?'

Alice didn't need a second bidding. They knew they had each bagged the star prize.

They joined the family group, and our father was first to speak.

'Those gymnastics was great, Bill.'

'Thanks, Dad. We've been practicing that last routine for two weeks and it went perfect. We'll be doing it next month at Earls Court.'

'Yes, it was really good…'

Charles searched for something else to say. The praise he had already given went against the grain. To excel and expect to be given praise was tantamount to 'showing off'. Working down the mine, men had no time for show-offs, the serious danger in which they placed themselves meant 'cooperation' was the watchword; the overconfident 'tomfool', was dangerous to be around.

Charles never had the need for small talk, and he knew he was about to say things that exposed his true feelings of pride, love almost. Love was an emotion he was unfamiliar with, and he felt uneasy. He decided not to give in to his emotions.

'Well, I'm off back to the club now.' and as if it were a reward, he said,

'Do you want to come, Bill?'

Billy had longed for his father to be engaged with him. To teach, to encourage, to advise, but most of all, to hug him in congratulation or, if need be, consolation. Yet again, his father fell short of showing he cared. The best he could offer was an introduction to the world of 'The Club', and although he imagined his father saying, *'Sit there, Bill, and I'll get you a pint,'* it was no longer enough for Bill; it was too little, too late. It was time for Bill to stand on his own feet and leave behind the regrets he felt;

'I might come later, Dad. I have to stay with my friends for a while.'

'Right, later then.'

With that, our dad was off, and we were back to being a family who relied on each other, especially our mum. We got on with our lives without our dad playing a part.

***

The carnival started. The fancy dress contest was to be judged by the Senior Officer. Paula came as Lady Godiva, seated upon a horse, dressed in a skin-toned undergarment and raffia wig, and eating a runner bean picked from Aunty Vi's back garden (no one knew why). The horse had been borrowed from Mr. Thomas, the 'Piggery-Man', who kept his pigs on the other side of the canal bank, and came round the village every week with his horse and cart collecting swill.

'Hello Mr. Thomas, can I borrow your horse?'

'Borrow my bloody horse? What nonsense is this?'

'Well, I'm going to next week's carnival as Lady Godiva and I need a horse.' She pointed at Molly, a light brown mare.

'That's a horse.'

'Lady Godiva... With no clothes on or nothing...? That I've got to see. I'll bring Nelly up on Saturday morning... You look after her mind.'

He had a second thought.

'Have you ridden a horse?'

'Of course I have!' she lied.

I was given the task of holding the horse's reins, as Lady Godiva, sat on the horse, lined up to be judged: along with Pinky and Perky, a Flower Pot Man, Queen Victoria, several cowboys, more than one of which was the Lone Ranger, and two 'Red Indians', Tonto and Hiawatha. Each of the cowboys was given a loaded cap gun that was to be fired as the marching band finished in step to the theme from 'The Dam Busters' (in honour of our guests). The band came to a halt, and that's what the cowboys did.

Bang!

The noise startled Nelly, and the horse broke loose from my grasp. It headed off through the crowd, with Paula hanging on as best she could. It didn't stop until it was back at the piggery.

Paula was declared winner, in absentia, with the rather fetching Hiawatha, second; Hiawatha had the consolation of a hug from the judge, the Group Captain.

The remains of Lady Godiva's runner bean and her raffia wig were eaten by the horse.

Paula was eighteen years old, and such a daring exploit was out of character for her. This was her first attempt to be noticed. The conscientious support she had given to her mother in the control of the household, with its unruly and argumentative children, was soon to come to an end. She would find freedom through marriage, living in Germany as a 'Force's Wife'.

**

The Carnival drew to a close, and the excitement of it all ebbed away. Billy had returned with his gymnastic troupe to RAF St Athan, pleased with how the day had turned out.

Our 'tea' was on the table, and it looked exactly like the sandwiches given out at the carnival; a bit curled at the edges, but still, sandwiches of cheese, cheese and ham or cheese with 'Branston Pickle', were a delight at any time. Our dad would have what was left when he came back from the club.

There was a knock at the door.

'Go get the door, love,' said mum.

I had a sandwich ready to eat in one hand and a half-eaten sandwich in the other. I spluttered.

'Aw mum! Can't somebody else go? I've got my sandwiches.'

'Just go! You're the nearest.'

An elderly gentleman stood at the door.

'Hello,' I said.

'Hello, young man. Are you Bill?'

'No, Bill's just gone back to St Athan with his display team.'

'Who are you, then?' He asked.

'I'm Almond, Billy's brother.'

'Ah, this will be right. Is your mother in?'

I confirmed she was by shouting,

'Mam, it's a man asking for you.'

She came to the door holding a bread knife. Evelyn knew it would be a stranger, as any of our neighbours would have come round to the back door and let themselves in, demanding a cup of tea in the process, or, if there was not a pot already brewed, offering to put the kettle on.

'Oh hello, are you from The South Wales Echo,' she guessed, thinking that Rhydyfelin would be the most famous place in the Valleys on a day such as this.

'No, I'm not from the Echo, Evelyn... I'm your father, Cornelius.'

Evelyn looked at the man before her. He could have been anyone.

Other than surprise, she felt no emotion. There was no feeling of delight at their reunion after 26 years, or any disbelief; although she didn't recognise him. But neither was there any hatred. Here was a man who had knocked on her door for a reason, and she needed to know why?

'You'd better come in and have some tea,' she said, and continued, 'Have you travelled far?'

Selwyn Berryman-Morgan

39

Reflection

To travel east-west on the roads of Sussex is a nightmare, and to travel from Haywards Heath to Battle is probably the grimmest prospect of all. The route is pock-marked with market towns and small villages snarled with the motors of the well-heeled, all wanting their bit of the diminishing road space. But it had to be done. The Eastbourne Air Display added to the congestion, as the free show was advertised as being 'Special' this year.

No one, it seems, drives at the pace the driver of the car following would want them to. The vast numbers of cars on Sussex's 'A' and the 'B' roads ensure that it is not possible to rush. The power to be found under the bonnet of the 4 x 4s that clogged the road was of little use, and that added to the general feeling of frustration. The roads meander across beautiful countryside, but they are blighted by the need of the motorists to get somewhere quickly; somewhere important. And there I was, trying to do the same; although, I let the side down by driving a Citroen Xantia

My good friend, Conrad, was hosting a party in his garden to commemorate the 60th anniversary of the ending of hostilities in Europe, 'VE Day', and as usual I hadn't allowed enough time for the journey; he lived in the same county, for goodness' sake, how could it take so long to get there? The party had already started when I arrived, and I slipped in, giving the impression I had been there all along. Conrad spotted me.

'Almond, there you are, I was just telling Eric here that you had family decorated in the war.'

I wasn't expecting to be drawn into such detailed conversation without having gone through several bouts of small talk.

'I did, Eric. Although he didn't live to see the victory celebrations, nor collect his decoration.'

'Poor bugger,' replied Eric. Conrad became pensive and we sensed he was about to say something. He did.

'Well, that's another reason why we are here today. We'll raise a glass for... err.'

'Bill,' I said.'

'Yes, Bill. We'll raise a glass for him later.' He changed the subject.

'Alison was wanting to talk to you about us meeting up in Rye next month. Something about a curry, or a chinese?'

I spoke for a short while with Jean, Eric's wife, who bemoaned my lot of having to live in Haywards Heath, and, standing in Conrad and Alison's country garden in Battle, I couldn't help but agree. The house was ancient. Not big, but with additions tacked on in fabulously random ways such that it spread out into the garden as if planted along with the hollyhocks. Woodbine invaded the eves and several English rose bushes bloomed in honour of the day. The orchard beyond the country garden bore fruit waiting to ripen before the turn to the autumn's chill.

I continued to mingle and chat. The conversation turned to mundane matters, sometimes self-interested, with more than a hint of a complaint, and other times joyful, for the day that had blossomed bright and clear.

We ate well, as always when guests at Conrad's and Alison's; Alison had a way of making good food extraordinary. We talked about the Curry house she was suggesting we should go (anywhere in Rye would have been good).

Those who didn't have to drive got as merry as I would have liked to have been, but I was content to let the good-humoured silliness spill over me. The sun continued to shine through into late afternoon, and it was then Conrad called us to order. Tapping at his pint glass set before him, he addressed us all. When our host spoke, we listened.

'I think it's time we remembered why we are here. Sixty years ago, we achieved final victory in Europe, the tyranny of Fascist Germany laid to rest. Amongst us today are citizens from across Europe; Holland and France... and Jacob and Anna from Poland. We also welcome Pietro and Maria from Italy who you all know and love. Thank you both for coming and joining us.' The Italian couple were hugged and kissed by those in the group they stood with. They were lovely in the Italian way of being lovely. Conrad continued,

'I think not so much of the victory, because our victory involved so much sorrow, but more the triumph of those who participated in facing the terror. They kept on until the threat was eliminated and Europe was free once more, a Europe for us all to live in. I want us to raise a glass to our parents and grandparents in thanks to them.' He motioned to the glasses of Champagne set out on the table before him and we each took a glass.

'Our parents and grandparents,' we said in unison.

After a short while, when we had talked about our mums and dads in the forces and those who had served in other ways, Conrad called us to order.

'Before you finish your glass,'

'I've finished mine,' said John

'Come and get another one'

'It's the size of these glasses of yours, Conrad. The champagne evaporates.'

'Champagne evaporates out of bottles when you're around, John.

Right, where was I... Yes... I would also like to raise a glass to a decorated airman named Bill who failed to see 'VE day, by way of carrying out his duty...'

Beyond the hedgerows, a low-pitched rumble grew in intensity and our attention was drawn to it. The sound of the Rolls-Royce Merlin engine was unmistakable. The Spitfire flew low, directly above us, and as it passed the edge of the village, it tipped its wings.

We stood watching it speed over the Sussex countryside on its way to London and further celebrations. The sound of the engine lingered, even when the Spitfire had disappeared from view.

The quieter, soothing sounds of an English country garden in mid-July returned: the buzz of insects punctuated by the scuttle of hedge-scurrying Blackbirds. We turned to Conrad, who we knew would have a pertinent comment, only to find him, for once, lost for words. Moments passed. We stood quietly, waiting for Conrad to gather his thoughts. There were tears in his eyes and his voice broke as he said,

'To Bill.'

'To Bill,' we replied.

The End

Printed in Great Britain
by Amazon

57371209R00203